"I HAVE A NEW PROPOSAL FOR YOU."

Immediately, Juliana shook her head. "I have no—"

"Hear me at least, Juliana. What can that harm?"

Reluctance turned her mouth down, hid her wide hazel eyes from his searching gaze. Damn, Ian wanted to touch her, ached to kiss her, possess her. How was it possible that this girl, his lifelong country neighbor, could tie his gut up in knots the way no seasoned London flirt could?

Because he loved her.

"I am listening," Juliana said finally.

"You cannot husband-hunt until next Season. Give me your time until Christmas Day, without thought to your father's feelings in our union. Let us learn about each other, see if the feelings deepen. If you can tell me then that you do not love me, I will never press my suit again."

"Never?" she whispered, questions evident in her eyes.

"Never. But you must give me until Christmas Day and deny me nothing that would not compromise you."

Her eyes narrowed in suspicion. "What do you mean?"

"See me each day. Talk with me about anything— everything." He paused, his hungry gaze unable to stray from her mouth. "Grant me a kiss if you feel so swayed. . . ."

BOOK YOUR PLACE ON OUR WEBSITE AND MAKE THE READING CONNECTION!

We've created a customized website just for our very special readers, where you can get the inside scoop on everything that's going on with Zebra, Pinnacle and Kensington books.

When you come online, you'll have the exciting opportunity to:

- View covers of upcoming books
- Read sample chapters
- Learn about our future publishing schedule (listed by publication month *and author*)
- Find out when your favorite authors will be visiting a city near you
- Search for and order backlist books from our online catalog
- Check out author bios and background information
- Send e-mail to your favorite authors
- Meet the Kensington staff online
- Join us in weekly chats with authors, readers and other guests
- Get writing guidelines
- AND MUCH MORE!

Visit our website at
http://www.zebrabooks.com

A CHRISTMAS PROMISE

SHELLEY BRADLEY

ZEBRA BOOKS
KENSINGTON PUBLISHING CORP.

http://www.zebrabooks.com

ZEBRA BOOKS are published by

Kensington Publishing Corp.
850 Third Avenue
New York, NY 10022

All Kensington titles, imprints and distributed lines are available at special quantity discounts for bulk purchases for sales promotion, premiums, fund-raising, educational or institutional use.

Special book excerpts or customized printings can also be created to fit specific needs. For details, write or phone the office of the Kensington Special Sales Manager: Kensington Publishing Corp., 850 Third Avenue, New York, NY 10022. Attn. Special Sales Department. Phone: 1-800-221-2647.

First Printing: October 2001
10 9 8 7 6 5 4 3 2

Printed in the United States of America

PROLOGUE

Devonshire, England
February 1852

"I have news," Ian Pierce, Viscount Axton, announced to Lord Brownleigh as he entered the fire-warmed drawing room. "Geoffrey Archer is dead."

The portly earl whipped his gaze from London's latest paper and fixed a stunned stare on Ian as he rose from the sofa. "What's that you say, Axton? Archer is *dead*?"

"Quite so." Ian nodded. "I just received word from a school chum who took a commission with the East India Company. The news came with this morning's post." Ian paused. "According to the letter, an animal attacked Archer on the delta somewhere in West Bengal."

"An animal?" The older man's brown brows rose as he set his paper aside. "What manner of animal?"

Ian shrugged. "My friend said nothing except that Archer died most foully last September."

Brownleigh laughed. "A most fitting end for a wastrel."

"You're quite right," Ian agreed. He had never wished death on any man. But if he had, it would have been Geoffrey Archer.

"Too bad news has only now reached us." The earl rose to his feet. Waddling to a nearby table, he asked, "Shall we celebrate with a brandy?"

The old earl did not need more spirits in Ian's estimation. The man looked haggard and weighty, not like the neighbor he had known most of his life.

Frowning, he withdrew his pocket watch. "It's barely noon, my lord. Too early for me."

"Oh, is it?" Brownleigh glanced at his own watch, then made his way toward Ian. "I suppose it is. Well, even discussing such an event is celebration enough for now."

"It is." Ian nodded, hiding a wry smile.

"So," Brownleigh continued, looking pleased, "my daughter is a widow, eh?"

Ian smiled. *That* was the sweetest realization of all. "Indeed."

"And you are still in need of a wife?" The old earl nudged Ian's ribs with his elbow and shot him a sly grin.

"I am, now more than ever."

"That devil of a father giving you difficulty once more?"

Brownleigh knew him well, Ian conceded, as he ought after nearly thirty years as neighbors. "He's grown worse in the last month. I am to stop wasting my time pining for a married woman and procure a suitable bride by the first day of January."

"Or . . . ?"

With a sigh, Ian sat. "Or I lose my inheritance and any hope of obtaining the necessary funds to see my breeding stables finished."

The earl snorted. "The old bugger knows you well. How will you ignore that?"

"I won't ignore it at all. Now that Juliana is widowed, I no longer have to pine for the married woman in question. She will be free to wed me."

"The post says she's returning to Harbrooke, then?" Brownleigh's fleshy face reflected surprise—and hope.

"No, that is the disturbing news. Thus far, she has declined every suggestion by Colonel Archer's superior officers that she should leave India and return home."

With a sigh, the earl dropped onto the sofa beside him and rubbed the girth of his waistcoated belly with a grimace. "Damned sour stomach," he grumbled, then turned back to Ian.

"Well, I confess no surprise at Juliana's stubborn temper. Nor should you." He cursed. "When Juliana began writing her mother of her unhappiness nearly two years past, Lady Brownleigh implored her to leave that fortune-hunting Archer and come home. Juliana refused and insisted she would never return to Harbrooke. I have little reason to believe anything has changed."

"She is a woman of resolution," Ian said. "But she cannot stay there. From what I've been able to determine, she has little money, and Archer's pension will scarce keep her fed."

"The silly girl does not understand the peril she puts herself in, I daresay. That is why she requires the guidance of a firm father ... and an equally strong-minded husband, eh?"

"I will make Juliana a good husband," Ian said solemnly.

"Of course you will," Brownleigh blustered. "Of course. But first we must find a way to get her home. I could travel to India, I suppose." He sighed. "But, gads, I am tired."

"Have you been feeling poorly again, my lord?"

Brownleigh waved his troubles away. "Oh, Dr. Haney, that dolt of a physician Lady Brownleigh persuaded to have a look at me, mentioned something about my heart. But I cannot believe he knows a thing. He's not yet your age and carries a bag of newfangled instruments." The earl rolled his eyes. "Most days I feel fine. Even when I do not feel myself, like today, I am certain the cause is nothing more serious than aging."

Ian did not agree. This "nothing" had been troubling Brownleigh for some months now. If anything, the man's face looked more ruddy every day. And he complained far more about his health that Ian could ever remember.

"Have you had another spell recently?" he asked.

The earl dismissed his question with a trifling frown. "It was more damned annoying than the last, I tell you, but means nothing. I am sure of it."

So Brownleigh had had a spell recently and refused to accept it. Again. Ian scowled.

"Perhaps Dr. Haney is not wholly incorrect," Ian said. "What did he suggest you do?"

"He wants me to give up brandy and walk the gardens for a quarter hour each day." The older man looked affronted. Ian did not think either suggestion untoward but knew the manner in which Brownleigh led his life was none of his affair.

"Perhaps the walking would be pleasant," Ian offered.

The earl shivered. "In this winter's cold, my boy? No. I fear catching a chill much more."

Ian nodded politely. "Still, I do not think your traveling to India would be wise."

"I am not an old man yet!" the earl insisted.

Suppressing a smile, Ian soothed the man. "No, but Lady Brownleigh would worry for you on such a harrowing journey."

"That is so," Brownleigh conceded, rubbing his chin.

"I can reach Juliana more quickly alone."

"You would fetch her for me?"

A more serious understatement Ian had never heard. Juliana was like a fever in his blood—a fever he had lived with for four and a half years. Yes, he would go. And this time he would take every necessary step to claim her.

"Indeed, I will."

"Splendid. Splendid," the earl mumbled. "But how shall we convince her to come home? She has some fool's notion of independence. What woman needs such a thing, I ask you?"

Ian shrugged. Juliana had always sought independence, necessary or not.

"We must give her a reason to return home," Ian mused.

"Well, if she's going to wed you, she cannot intend to remain in India."

"She may not choose to wed me," he said, working not to grit his teeth. "It would not be the first time she decided such."

Close to five years before, Ian had made mistakes in his suit, mistakes that had driven Juliana away. He vowed he would not make those imprudent errors again.

"Foolish girl," her father muttered, rubbing his belly once more. A moment later, he reached out with both hands, one toward Ian, as if to steady himself.

"Are you certain you're well?" Ian asked.

"Just tired, my boy." The earl sighed, then cast Ian a sideways glance. "You truly are concerned."

"Yes." Ian nodded, fearful the man was indeed ill.

The earl smiled, and Ian saw his devious thought before the man even spoke. "Do you suppose my wayward daughter might be equally concerned?"

Ian paused. It would work even though Juliana

distrusted him. Brownleigh's idea would be effective because, despite her resentment of the past she shared with Ian, Juliana had a caring heart where her family was concerned.

Besides, her father's illness was not a lie, not exactly. Ian feared the malady could be serious, even if Brownleigh himself felt more comfort in denying it.

Yes, he would bring her home, closer to her family—to him—then let Juliana and fate decide the truth.

And their future.

Ian nodded slowly. "I think she will be concerned, indeed."

As Lord Brownleigh and Lord Axton shook hands and congratulated themselves on a brilliant plan, the ghost of Caroline Linford hovered near the ceiling and watched the men plot. She could not deny they were cads, both of them. Still, if they saved Juliana from suffering the fate Caroline herself had endured, then perhaps she might be able to rest in peace—finally. Yes, and to ensure that headstrong Juliana understood what she must do, Caroline vowed to do a little extra haunting.

CHAPTER ONE

Bombay, India
May 1852

Juliana Archer had never liked surprises—too shocking by half. But the surprise on her doorstep stunned her beyond speech, beyond breathing ... beyond belief.

The past she'd escaped nearly five years earlier stood before her once more.

As she gripped the frame of the open door, the hot Bombay wind drifted through her widow's weeds, into her cottage, heating the air, her very skin. Juliana stared. Blinked. Resumed staring. Still, he stood there, tense, dark, tall. Had *he* come halfway around the world to see her?

"L-Lord Axton?" she stammered, stunned.

"Lady Archer." He grinned ruefully at their formality, then fastened his steady blue gaze on her face. "Perhaps you might call me Ian again, as you did when we were in the nursery? And I might call you Juliana once more?"

A thousand moments flashed through her memory, each captured like a finely wrought painting. Her childhood home, Harbrooke Manor, came first, followed by a vision of Ian in boyhood as they had romped in her gardens, when she had believed him to be her friend. The girlish bedchamber she'd slept in appeared next—and the very bed on which she'd cried, thirsting for adventure to color her gray country life. Finally came an image of her father and Ian together, faces smug as they announced Geoffrey's marching orders to India. And the worst, when they had done their best to deceive her ... As a blast of resentment rose, she shoved the remembrance away.

Still, she sensed five years had changed Ian in some indefinable way, as if he'd grown quieter. Or perhaps craftier.

Ian had changed physically as well. At twenty-two, he had been barely a man, too tall and too thin. At twenty-seven, he had grown into his prominent square jaw, which made a strong frame for his wide, firm mouth. He belonged in those broad shoulders and long legs. His piercing, vivid eyes suited him.

Awareness swept over her in an uncomfortable moment, for she saw him not as her manipulative neighbor but as a man.

That was not wise. So he was handsome. What of it? That only made him more disturbing and did nothing to erase the past.

"Jul—" Ian stopped himself. "Lady Archer, if you'd rather I not use your name, I will understand."

Would he? That implied he understood how wrong he had been in trying to stop her marriage to Geoffrey. That, she very much doubted, not after everything he had done to her.

Juliana bit her lip in consideration. It would not do to show him fear. Besides, Ian had merely asked for use of the name he had used freely the better part of their lives. That alone could not harm her.

Even if she didn't trust him, it seemed a bit churlish to refuse the simple request of a lifelong neighbor.

"Come in, Ian." She gestured into the house. "If you wish to call me Juliana, do so."

Upon entering, he paused and turned to her, waiting. Watching. He held something in his eyes—secrets, perhaps? Juliana met his stare. No matter what game he wished to play, she would not participate. Still, that stare roused her anxiety. Clearly, he had come for a reason.

She walked toward the parlor, desperate to fill the tense silence. Ian followed, watchful.

"I apologize for the laxity of my household. I keep very few servants. My *aiyh* has gone to market. Would you take tea?"

Juliana glanced back at Ian. Why had he come? His angular face gave away nothing.

"No, thank you." As he spoke, his familiar gaze touched her. Oddly, she did not hate his stare, not as she hated him.

Juliana looked away and led him to the parlor, an admittedly odd mix of eastern and western cultures. A small dark wood table and a shabby pale sofa of obvious European origin shared the airy room with native rugs in bright swaths of colors. Traditional Ian would think the room most odd. And she was strangely glad for anything that might keep him off balance. He had always been a man completely in control—of himself and everyone else.

She cleared her throat. "Won't you sit?"

"Thank you." He did as she'd invited, then balanced his elbows on his knees.

"Ian, I can scarce believe you're here," she said, striving for conversation. "How is Harbrooke? And my mother? I haven't received a letter from her in some months." Lately, Juliana had begun to feel the separation from her mother like an ache.

"Lady Brownleigh is as fine and sweet-tempered as ever."

A warm wave of relief slid through Juliana. "Splendid news."

"Indeed," Ian murmured. "But don't you wonder why I've come to India?"

Very much, yes. But could she trust anything he said? Uncertain, she cast a surreptitious gaze at Ian. At his reluctant, faintly sad expression, her unease returned.

"I do wonder," she admitted finally. "It's a long way from Devonshire to Bombay."

He nodded. "It was a three-month journey, yes."

Surprise lit her face. "Only three months? You took the land route through Egypt? Is that not dangerous?"

He shrugged. "I made port in Cairo and traveled over land to Suez. Though the area is somewhat policed against bandits, I would not recommend that route for many. But from Suez the journey by paddle steamer down the Red Sea was smooth."

He paused, then fixed his stare upon her, reminding her he could be a very determined man. Juliana met his stare. Not for anything would she convey the fact that he affected her, particularly since she was certain he had come to India with some purpose. Unease bit into her belly as she thought of the possibilities.

"So why have you come?" she asked finally.

Ian hesitated, face guarded. "Your father is ill."

As the shock bolted through Juliana, she gasped. Robust James Edward William Linford had fallen prey to some malady? It seemed utterly impossible, though she knew he approached sixty. It must be grave indeed for Ian to travel halfway around the world simply to tell her.

Or was this visit part of another conspiracy designed to control her future? Given Ian and her father, it was possible, if a bit far-fetched.

Perhaps Ian's assertion was true. . . .

Worry crept through her, insidious, consuming. She hated her concern for the old man, but she could not deny she cared. Despite his manipulations, Juliana had been unable to cut her father from her heart, especially when the last few years had proven his fears about her late husband so right.

"It's serious, then?"

Ian hesitated, glanced at his blunt, interlocked fingers, then raised his piercing blue gaze to her again. "He complains of abdominal pains, dizziness, and fatigue. He has gained a good amount of weight in the last few years and drinks too much brandy." Ian sat up. "He is hardly a portrait of health, Juliana. The physician fears it may be his heart."

That was grave news, indeed . . . if true. She closed her eyes in indecision. Ian coming to India to convey a falsehood about her father's health would be an awfully elaborate ruse.

But had their other lies not been equally clever?

Still, if the esteemed Lord Brownleigh was truly ill, she should return home. Posthaste.

If it was not true and she rushed to her father's side, he and Ian both would undoubtedly use their usual methods to try to control her destiny.

Juliana swallowed against a rush of conflicting emotions—yearning and fear.

"Juliana?" Ian called softly. "I see you are distressed."

Of course he did. Ian had never been thickheaded, just manipulative. She did not trust him, true. But in this instance Juliana was not certain she disbelieved him either.

Blast it, she needed answers to make the right decision.

"So, because of his illness, Papa sent you to fetch me home?" she asked.

Ian hesitated. "He sent me with the information. The decision to return is yours."

Shock stung Juliana anew. Her father would leave such a decision to *her* discretion? He had not demanded her return? If so, these past five years had changed Papa as much as they had changed her.

Had they changed Ian as well?

As wary hope sprang forth, homesickness filled her. She yearned to take tea again beside a cheery winter hearth at Harbrooke, stitch quietly beside her genteel mother. She wished again for her chamber. Juliana even recalled the manor's eccentric ghost with fondness, the beautiful specter who for years had sobbed in harmless gloom as she made her way about the upper floors—then disappeared into the walls.

Suddenly Juliana remembered one of the bitterest realities of her current situation.

"I haven't the funds for a passage home," she admitted quietly, staring at a black ruffle on her poplin dress.

Ian leaned closer. "He will gladly pay for your passage, Juliana. That is not the issue. He merely wants to see you . . . in case his illness is grave. And I suspect it is."

His manner appeared so forthright. Indecision tore at her.

Here lay her opportunity to leave this accursed country and its heat—return home to familiar places, things, and people. If she left quickly, she could be back in England soon—for Christmas even. What a joyous thought!

But could she entrust her future to the hope that her father's illness was no plot? Did she dare?

She must not rush to decide. Leaving India now would change her whole life forever. She could not forget the glaring fact that Ian and her father had lied to her before—and more than once.

But would she have another opportunity to leave Bombay and the disillusion it had wrought in her girlish heart?

"Perhaps you should consider his request for a day or two," Ian suggested, as if sensing her hesitation. "The next ship bound for England will not leave for two weeks yet."

Slowly, Juliana nodded, determined to temper her wistful yearnings for Harbrooke with remembrances of her father's myriad manipulations—including his attempts to see her wed to Ian.

"I believe that would be best. Thank you."

Ian nodded, his gaze drifting over her mourning attire. "My condolences to you on Colonel Archer's death."

That surprised Juliana. "You've heard? It happened only eight months ago."

He shrugged. "I still have contact with some of the East India officers in London."

Juliana stared hard at her guest. Yes, she had known for five years he had such contacts. Resentment churned in her stomach. And it was doubtful indeed that either her father or Ian regretted Geoffrey's passing. Neither had wanted her to marry the reckless officer, had done everything in their power to stop it.

And for the last three years of her marriage, her father's admonitions about Geoffrey had haunted her. To Juliana's distress, her father had been right. Geoffrey *had* been a greedy, worthless wastrel, far more interested in his amusement than a wife. Oh, life with Geoffrey had, at times, been agreeable. But more often it had been hell. And it chafed her pride to admit her father had been right.

Had Ian and her father truly seen through Geoffrey all along, or merely resented the fact the dashing colonel had thwarted their plans? It was irrelevant now, she supposed.

She glanced up, met Ian's searching blue eyes, remembering the evening he had proposed marriage to her . . . And she had refused him.

"Being a widow in an unfamiliar country cannot have been easy," Ian offered suddenly.

No, it had not been, and she was a bit surprised Ian recognized that fact—or cared.

"I have accepted my current state in life as the consequence of wedding a reckless man." Her mouth turned up ruefully as she gazed out the window, viewing the hot Bombay day. "My only surprise is the fact it took Geoffrey so long to find such a foolish way to die."

"Yes, I heard the details when I arrived today. Chasing tigers is an odd occupation for one's time."

"It was a dare," she offered. Maybe Ian would understand Geoffrey's rash actions, for she could not.

"Ah. One's manhood must be maintained and all that?"

Juliana shrugged. "I suppose."

Ian nodded solemnly, then stood. "Shall I return tomorrow, then? Will that allow you enough time to think things through?"

He was leaving? Yes, she had always found him intimidating—too domineering, perhaps. Manipulative. But he was her only contact with home other than her mother's letters. Besides, she sensed a change in Ian, and she was loath to see him go.

"You are welcome to stay for dinner," she offered.

Surprise darkened his gaze, followed by heat she could describe only as sexual. She swallowed at the recognition of it. He desired her still?

She took a wary step back.

"Not tonight," he demurred. "I've arrived just today, and I fear in my weariness I would make terrible company at your table. I'll come 'round again tomorrow."

With that, he made his way to her door. Juliana followed, bereft, suspicious, and confused.

Then Ian placed a warm hand over hers, his skin rougher than she remembered. Eyes like rich blue silk delved hers. The unexpected gesture caused a flurry of awareness of him as a man.

He squeezed her fingers in his, then withdrew. "It was very good indeed to see you again, Juliana."

With a crisp nod, he disappeared into the dusk.

The following afternoon, Ian made his way back to Juliana's modest cottage. He rubbed sleep-gritty eyes with a curse. Finally he'd had use of a bed not swaying with the ocean all night, and he had been unable to sleep. Juliana's face haunted him. No surprise, really. She had haunted him for five years—since the night she refused his proposal, told him she despised him, and eloped with that blackguard Archer.

This time, he vowed, would be different. This time, he *would* win her . . . no matter what.

Impatient to reach her, Ian watched the rented hack make its way through the city's teeming, dusty streets, closer to his goal, to Juliana.

He recognized that Juliana had been a girl five years ago. But the Juliana he'd seen yesterday was a woman, with a woman's eyes. Teeming with mystery, they beckoned. Sharp with knowledge, they called. He was more than willing to answer, eager to wrap his hands in her shining golden tresses and master her mouth with his own. He was eager, as he had always been, to call her wife.

Ian meant to make sure Juliana did not refuse him again.

The hack stopped before her home. With a quick toss of coin to the young driver, Ian stepped down.

Damn, his heart beat like a schoolboy's. Dragging in a deep breath, he made his way to the door and knocked. Within moments, an ageless woman with dark hair tightly wound atop her head opened the door and nodded. Without a word, she led him to her mistress.

Ian took in Juliana, seated on a yellow sofa with her legs tucked beneath her, book in hand. She sighed, and the sound called up lustful images he knew he had no hope of indulging soon. Still, he dragged his gaze over the smooth curve of her pale cheek, the graceful arch of her throat, the supple curve of her breast. She wore a simple black gown that did little to disguise her wondrous charms. No, she was not perfect. Some men would think her hips a bit too wide, he supposed. Not him. To Ian, she was daring, intelligent, self-assured. Those qualities drew him. He could not help but stare.

When the Indian maid announced his arrival, Juliana's head shot up.

"Good day. I did not mean to disturb you," he offered.

"Hello." She greeted him cautiously, setting her book aside.

He merely smiled.

"Please, sit." Juliana gestured to an old high-backed chair to her right, then returned to the small sofa. "I'm glad you've returned."

He'd been unable to stay away. "As am I."

"So," she began, "what do you think of India?"

Willing, even cheerful conversation. Before her elopement with Archer, she had refused to engage in that pastime with him. In her refusal, she had wounded his pride, true. But today her mood was too encouraging to dwell on the unpleasant past.

"It is . . . colorful." At her trickling laughter, he

responded with a smile. "The hotel fed me something for breakfast I could scarcely recognize. But the tea, that I would know anywhere."

Again she laughed, and Ian relished the beauty of her smile, the light in her hazel eyes. If she was grieving, the emotion did not torment her overmuch—a good sign for him, surely.

"And what of that breeding stable you longed to build? No doubt you finished it some years ago and have the best racing horses in England."

"Not yet. But soon."

"Really?" She frowned. "I confess some surprise. Your enthusiasm for the stable was always so high."

"It is still." He paused. "But as you well know, the venture is not a favorite of my father's."

"Ah, and so you must raise the funds yourself or wait until he dies and you are an earl?"

Despite the terrible clashes he and his father had shared on this subject, Ian grinned. "Indelicately to the point, as always, but something like that."

If he told Juliana that according to his father's dictates he must take a bride within seven months to receive the necessary funds, it would only confuse her about his intent. Ian wanted her to understand that he desired to wed her because he loved her. He always had.

Silence crept between them. Ian sat mute, fixed his gaze upon her, and waited. Juliana's smile disappeared, and he saw that she was a determined female with a matter on her mind. He felt certain he knew what that was.

"Ian, I realize you've traveled a long way—"

"You have questions."

She nodded. "Exactly how ill is my father? Has he suffered long? My mother did not mention it in her letters."

Juliana rarely minced words. Somehow Ian was rather glad Geoffrey Archer had been unable to change that, though he sensed the scoundrel had wrought other changes in Juliana he had yet to discover.

"Your father experienced several episodes in the four months before I left England, including one mere days before my departure. He is no longer a young man."

Juliana tapped her fingers on the arm of the sofa. "That is true."

"Yet you hesitate in returning. Juliana, why?"

She flashed him an astounded glare. Had he forgotten the past? "How can I know you're telling me the truth?"

Her words gave him pause; he must tread carefully here. "You think I would lie to bring you home?"

"I think you both would," she confirmed.

He held his grimace. "But I would not lie about something this serious."

Juliana remained silent. Ian let his hope grow that perhaps he had persuaded her to trust him. The victory would be sweet. . . .

But her hesitation remained.

"Juliana, you do not believe me?"

"I am not certain." She shrugged. "Besides, if I return to Harbrooke and my father is not seriously ill, his mere age and infirm state give me no assurance he will be a changed man. I won't forfeit my independence if I return home."

"No one has asked that of you."

"Yet," she retorted sharply.

"Your father is not a bad man," Ian pointed out.

Pique tightened her face. "He is not a kind one either, though I hardly expect *you* to understand."

Ian leaned closer. Part of him wanted to reach for her, but he refrained. Now was not the time. "Simply because I respect him does not mean I am blind to his flaws."

She sent him a gaping glare. "You can see his

flaws despite the fact they are so like your own?" she challenged. "Impossible. You are cast from his very mold. Had I not stopped you, the two of you would have planned my life with lies, seen me wed, bred, and silent until death."

Ian coolly returned her stare, despite the emotion churning inside him. No doubt, the past was haunting him now, and he feared it would be for some time to come. He wanted to defend himself, make Juliana understand the reasons behind his actions. But he knew her. If he gave in to his urge, she would only become more defensive.

Yet, neither he nor her father had anything but her best interest at heart. And she was angry with them for doing their utmost to secure her future. Why did she not see they both did so out of love?

"Five years ago, I had a far different picture of our life together. I rather wanted a wife, not a lapdog." The words came out more harshly than he intended.

"You expected a well-trained woman who would heed your every command, starting with the one to wed you."

"I did *ask* you to be my wife," he reminded her. "I did not demand it."

"And your shock at my refusal would have been amusing had it not been so foolish." She fixed a narrow gaze on him. "You honestly believed I would be happy to remain in Lynton, the wife of a staid country gentleman content to control my life, before I knew anything of what the world had to offer?"

Ian tightened his jaw, tensed his shoulders. "What has the world offered you, Juliana? What did Archer give you that was necessary for your soul?" he challenged. "From what you wrote to your mother, nothing but heartache, difficulty, and poverty. Is that the adventure you craved?"

Her mouth pursed with a frown. Disappointment at her mother's lack of discretion clearly needled her. The woman had always had difficulty keeping anything from Lord Brownleigh. Likely, Juliana had written to her mother in a moment of lonely weakness and wished now that she had resisted the urge.

"Geoffrey gave me almost nothing of what I wanted, but that was my choice to make. Neither you nor Papa understood that. It is entirely unclear you understand that even now."

She was wrong; Ian understood perfectly the choice had been hers to make. He had merely wanted to wed her himself, to spare her the trials he'd known Archer would bring her. Even now he wanted to spend the rest of his life helping her find both security and happiness.

Ian feared, however, that despite everything Colonel Archer had put Juliana through, she still was not ready to accept the life he sought to offer her.

He reined in his temper. "I have no intent to force you back to England. As I said, this choice is yours. I confess, I am not certain what here might entice you to stay, a widow with little pension in a foreign land filled with avaricious soldiers equally willing to take you for granted. But if you wish to remain, I will convey that to your father."

His brash concession seemed to deflate her anger. She sighed. "You've come halfway around the world as a favor to my family and I've been less than pleasant. I am sorry."

"In the past, I gave you little reason to trust me. I realize that."

Juliana stared at him in momentary surprise. She said nothing of his admission.

"Well, if this choice is mine, I must make it."

"Yes." He drew in an anxious breath.

She looked away, hands fidgeting. "I cannot continue to avoid home like a rebellious schoolgirl, I know. And if my father is truly ill—"

"He is, Juliana," Ian interrupted. "I would not lie."

"I could spend Christmas with my family." After a moment's hesitation, she confessed, "I cannot bear the thought of not seeing him again, even if it's only to tell him I care."

"Such words would please him," Ian assured her hopefully.

"I . . ." She sighed again. "I suppose I must return home."

Thank God! Ian released the breath he'd been holding and suppressed a smile. He worked hard to hold in his elation.

"But let me be clear." Her words sliced through his joy. "If I get home and discover he's not unwell, I vow you will not ever fathom the depth of my wrath."

Ian said nothing. Once she saw her father's decline in health, how could she doubt him? Brownleigh looked bad, and the physician thought the illness serious. Still, no one knew for certain. . . . No. In the end, Juliana would thank him for this.

And he would be happy. She was finally coming home—and would have to spend nearly six months on board a ship with him, day after day, as they sailed around the Cape of Good Horn, before she arrived back at Harbrooke.

He hoped it was enough time to convince her to marry him.

Bombay lay just two days behind them. The blue waters of the Arabian Sea glittered in the afternoon sunlight, the small crests of water like sparkling sapphires. Salt and crisp wind stretched the sails tight, while a coal-powered paddle sat behind the ship in case the wind should cease. An odd peace, lulled by the water's sameness, stole over Juliana.

This far from civilization, none of what had worried

her in Bombay mattered. She would not bother over her nearly nonexistent finances. Nor could she dwell on her father's illness or her widowed state. Oh, she must deal with them soon, but today the roll and rush of the sea set her at ease.

"Lovely, is it not?" Ian said, suddenly behind her.

She turned to face him and found his blue gaze roving the sea. Then he settled a warm, weighty stare on her.

This was troubling. The rest of her problems could wait until she reached Lynton—for she could do nothing about them here. But Ian . . . He was unsettling. Juliana had to resist the senseless, fluttery feeling his nearness roused within her. She was not a girl in her first season or a bride on her wedding night. Still, her stomach jumped in anticipation, almost as if she were. And it would not do.

She knew far too much about Ian to be anything but ill at ease with his presence so near. He was the kind of man who would lie to trap a wife. Somehow, she rather doubted such a shocking lack of integrity in a man could be cured.

"The sea is lovely," she murmured.

Beside her now, Ian cast a glance about the deck of the *Houghton*. Juliana followed suit, noting it stood nearly empty save a man in the rigging and the stout captain at the helm. Moments earlier it had been a swarm of men and activity. Ian did not look surprised by their departure, and Juliana's suspicions rose.

"I want to ask you something very particular, Juliana."

Shock froze her. The only other time Ian has spoken those words, a proposal of marriage had followed.

She raised a hand to stay him. "Ian—"

"Let me finish," he demanded. "I must say this."

Reluctantly, Juliana nodded. The strong square jaw relaxed, then tensed again. The carved hollows of his cheeks stood stark even as his eyes darkened with something that did little to comfort her.

"No doubt—" He stopped, his smile somewhere between angry and self-deprecating. "No doubt you know my intentions. I am not a man comfortable with words of poetry and love. But when I last asked you to be my wife and you refused me, I can truly say it pained me. When you eloped with Archer, you broke my heart."

The confession took her aback. Ian's heart had been involved? No! That seemed impossible. He had merely sought to please both his father and hers with an advantageous match among friendly neighbors. He must have wanted her father's money. Every suitor she had ever had, including Geoffrey, did. Though Ian was an earl's son, her family's wealth far exceeded that of most every aristocratic family in Devonshire. It seemed unlikely indeed that Ian had not been motivated by fortune as well.

He swallowed, then touched his fingertips to her cheeks. "Nearly the moment you left with Archer for Gretna, I realized my mistake. I never told you I loved you."

Juliana stood mute, a new wave of shock reverberating inside her, warring with caution. Ian was not the kind of man who often put sentiment into words, particularly such powerful, stark words. Why had he now?

If this was a lie, it was a potent one.

Lovely as they were, however, they were mere words. Ian's beautiful face could fool an angel. Even if she believed he loved her, Juliana doubted that his definition of love matched her own. In her mind, a loved one wasn't someone to be manipulated.

"You said nothing, yet you loved me?" she asked warily.

"Yes."

Juliana pondered his answer. She still did not trust him, nor should she care what his feelings were.

Love. She had craved it in her marriage. But she had wanted adventure too. Odd how she had assumed the two would fit together, like halves of a perfect whole. In Geoffrey she believed she had found the most wonderful man. Only for him, love would have dimmed the adventure. He had wed her, assuming her father would finance his exploits. When that had proven false, he had been much less taken with her.

Would she have chosen differently if she'd known Ian believed himself in love with her?

"How do you expect I should reply to that?" she asked.

He shrugged. The ocean breeze lifted the ends of his overlong dark hair and brushed them against the column of his neck. It was a strong neck, thick, and at the moment veined with tension. The sight of it, of him, suddenly made Juliana more aware of the fact that he was a man—and they were virtually alone.

No, no, *no*. No more awareness of his masculinity— or her reaction to it. Even if he'd come on a mission of mercy, he was a liar, her father's choice for her husband. She feared Ian sought to wrest the kind of control over her life that Papa wanted. If she let him, Ian would lead to her misery by stripping her of every ounce of freedom. She had known him too long to believe otherwise.

"Say nothing and let me speak," he implored.

Juliana's gaze snapped to his face, and his intense stare burned her. His next words shocked her again.

"I love you still."

Still?

"I have always loved you."

Always?

Whirling away from him, Juliana stared blindly out to the sea, which now seemed rough and tempestuous.

She could not hear this. She had no notion how to respond.

He loved her?

No. He could not. It was not possible. She did not care.

Blast it all, why did those words feel so powerful to her, despite the fact she did not want his love?

A moment later, the strength of his warm hands clasped her shoulders. His thumbs brushed the backs of her arms. At once, the touch was reassuring and alarming. This was her childhood friend, her lifelong neighbor, Ian.

Yes, but Ian had twice lied to her to separate her from the man she wished to wed, and now he told her he loved her. She must remember it was unlikely at best.

The timing seemed ironic as well. He had waited to tell her of his heart's devotion until their ship was too far from port to demand a return to India. Did he say it because he thought she wished to hear it? Had he said the words simply to soften her heart? If so, the lie was having its desired effect.

She let loose a shaky breath, and he eased her back against his chest, where she felt the steady rhythm of his heart.

"I did not speak of my feelings to frighten you, Juliana." His whisper in her ear both soothed and scared her. "I told you what is in my heart because I did not last time, because I did not realize you might care to know before we wed. I vowed not to make that mistake again."

Gently, he spun her to face him until they stood mere inches apart.

His blue eyes were more troubled and beautiful than the sea. And they looked so blasted honest. He eased her closer, until she rested flush against him, solid and broad.

Was it possible he really loved her?

"Juliana, marry me," he whispered. "I can care for you as no one else can. I understand your wishes and hopes."

Before she could reply—form a thought, even— Ian leaned in and settled his mouth over hers. She grasped his shoulders in shock, intending to push him away.

Then his mouth slid over hers, lips soft and persuasive with gentle pleasure. Velvet was no softer than the worship of his kiss. She froze.

With another brush of his lips, Juliana felt as if her mouth were melting into his, as if he had cajoled it into the mold of his liking with the skill of an artist, and resistance fled.

In the taut set of his shoulders, she sensed his desire to deepen the kiss. She wanted the same. Warmth flushed her, and Juliana felt her foolish yearning to continue the embrace.

He gave her another stroke of his lips, pressed a bit harder, teasing her with a flick of his tongue. Inhaling sharply at the sensations, Juliana felt lost in wonder at the dense heat—something like an ache— that sprang to life inside her. When Ian coaxed her lips apart moments later, she raised her mouth to his willingly. He thrilled her even more by angling his head to claim her with a probing, shockingly intimate kiss.

Suddenly, she was drowning in sensation.

Ian tasted like a lover, forbidden and exciting. Yet his utter familiarity soothed her. She would have known him anywhere, despite the fact he had never kissed her . . . until now.

The thud of her heart in her chest pounded in her ears. She felt her breathing shallow. As if sensing her surrender, he deepened the kiss again, his mouth captivating hers completely, his hands framing her face to keep her mouth at his.

This was Ian, the liar, the rogue. She kissed Ian!

Despite his poor character, the urge to give herself into his hands, experience the pleasure she'd always yearned for, stunned her. Suddenly, she could barely remember all the reasons she could not trust him.

His mouth moved with urgency, yes, but also with the care of one handling something rare and fragile. With his kiss, he made her feel cared for. Geoffrey never had. How tempting the thought that if they shared the intimacy of lovers, Ian could make her feel a wondrous treasure, at least for a moment.

But he would control her if she wed him.

I can care for you as no one else can. I understand your wishes and hopes.

A lie, surely. He understood nothing of her.

Juliana broke the kiss, calling herself every kind of fool for her body's mewling protest as she ended it.

"Stop. Perhaps you believe you care for me, but I do not need a keeper. I'm a woman grown, a widow of sense. As for my wishes—"

"Juliana?" A confused frown furrowed his wide forehead. As comprehension dawned, his jaw tensed and his shoulders turned stiffer than a towering oak. "You mean to refuse me again."

His expression, somewhere between masculine dissatisfaction and boyish puzzlement, tugged at her. Juliana looked away. She would not succumb to a worry for his feelings, lest she find herself wed again.

"I am still in mourning," she reminded him, though such was hardly her only reason for refusal.

"Naturally, I had no intent to wed you before we could do the thing properly."

"We will not do the thing at all! You say you understand my wishes and hopes, but you do not. You cannot, not when you think so like my father." She clenched a fist in frustration. "I will remarry *if* I wish and *when* I wish."

"Why would you wish to remain alone?" He sent

her a puzzled frown. "I will treat you well, provide for your security as Archer did not."

Would the man not understand? "I do not doubt that. But that is not my only wish in a husband."

"What do you wish in a husband, then?"

With a sharp stare, she quipped, "Not to have one at all."

Into Ian's morose silence she heaved a frustrated sigh. "You have ever been a good neighbor to my family, but far more my father's ally than mine. Perhaps you truly have some *tendre* for me; I do not know. But I am certain that if I wed you, you will oversee every aspect of my life: what I wear, who I see, when I eat. And Papa will help you plan it all."

Again, he frowned. "You make it sound as if we think you a prisoner instead of a genteel lady to be protected."

"I don't want protection. I want to live! And I cannot live, truly *live*, with a man of my father's choosing. I would never be free."

Juliana saw a flash of anger and disappointment cross his face, and she turned away quickly.

She had taken a mere two steps before Ian grabbed her arm and whirled her to face him again, her arm pressed to his chest now, his breath warm on her cheek.

"I am not your father. What I feel for you is more than a *tendre;* it is love. And, Juliana, be assured I will not give up until you agree to marry me."

CHAPTER TWO

Morning cascaded through the small window in the swaying cabin Juliana occupied. It was more sumptuous than she had imagined, containing a bunk, a round table, and a small settee, along with a few storage chests. Only the previous night she had learned Ian had handsomely paid both the purser for passage aboard the East India Company's ship, the *Houghton*, as well as the captain for use of his accommodations for her. The latter was an extravagant expense, but Juliana could not deny that she appreciated the privacy and comfort. Not enduring a leaking cabin on the second deck and soaked baggage because of it, as she had on her journey to India with Geoffrey, was indeed a relief.

She had never considered Ian a thoughtful man, but like everyone, Juliana supposed he could be kind occasionally—at least when it suited his purpose. The trouble was, his purpose had a fair amount to do with vows and a parson.

As she gathered her inkwell and her pen, then sat at the captain's small but sturdy table, she stared at the journal before her. She had begun the diary as a bride to record her adventures with Geoffrey. When the reality of her husband's ways had set in, she had used the little bound book as a confidante, pouring out her anger. When Geoffrey had been killed and she realized she was both poor and stranded in a country she had never liked, the diary had become like a friend.

Now that she would spend six months on a ship with Ian as her only familiar company, Juliana wondered which role the little journal would play in her life.

After dating the entry page, she wrote:

It is the fifth day of our journey, and already I do not know what to say to Ian. I must be polite at least, for he came halfway around the world to tell me of Father's illness. But I cannot let him close. He seems a changed man—or perhaps I am simply more aware of him. Yet there are times I fear he has not changed, not in his heart, but simply grown wilier with his words. What am I to believe of him now?

My ability to ignore him as I always did is much diminished, and now I must spend six months with him on this small ship. The thought is a bit daunting, I confess. Yes, I brought a maid, but she is no barrier against Ian's determination. He means to marry me. I have again refused him, but I do not believe he will give up. He says he loves me and always has. And I must be nothing but a fool, for his words caused such a flutter in me. If he should find out I am no longer immune to him, and the wonderful manner of his kiss, then I shall have no peace, indeed.

I have only left India, finally! Now I wish to begin a life of my choosing, to know that each day I follow no plan but my own. What I shall do for the funds for such a life, I do not know. But I cannot exchange my freedom for the comforts that marriage to Ian could

*provide. There is still something about him I do not
trust.*

Footsteps in the hall alerted her. The object of her
musings would knock on her door. It had become a
ritual of sorts, tea and breakfast. It reeked of intimacy,
of a wedded couple beginning their day together.
Still, he had persuaded her to indulge him in this by
pointing out they both had to eat. Why not together?

Why not, indeed.

Impulsively, Juliana snapped her fingers. Amulya,
her Indian maid, turned her gaze in her mistress's
direction. Juliana shook her head and pointed to the
door. As Amulya nodded her understanding, Juliana
then slammed her journal shut and dove for the bed,
settling her full skirts beneath the covers.

Ian knocked softly.

"Lord Axton," Amulya greeted Ian with a bob of
her dark head. "Memsahib does not feel well."

"Seasickness?" he asked.

Juliana heard the concern in Ian's voice and
cringed. She hated to lie.

The maid glanced her way. Juliana nodded.

"It is," Amulya said to Ian.

He sighed. "Tell Juliana I will consult with the
captain for a remedy and that I hope she feels well
soon."

More concern. As Amulya shut the door and turned
to face her, Juliana rose from the bed.

Hiding from Ian was childish, she knew. Were she
not discomfited by his determination and the
attraction she felt for him, Juliana would face him
again this morning. As it was, she could scarcely look
at him without remembering their kiss.

Foolish, considering that in their past he had
behaved unforgivably.

Amulya raised dark eyes of wisdom to her. "He
seeks to claim you. Would you spend your life alone?"

Is that what she wanted? Juliana frowned at the prospect. No, but she wanted a man who understood her independent nature, not one who sought to curb it.

"The matter is not that simple," she said finally. "I do not know what to do."

Amulya, ever observant, sent her a soft smile. "Your heart, it knows. It is your head that is not trusting him."

"My heart knows nothing. It ought to listen to my head!"

"If your heart did not oppose your head, you would be at ease."

Juliana could not refute that wisdom. She sighed. Of course it was not her heart that Ian engaged. With that powerful, fire-laden kiss they had shared, Ian had introduced desire between them. Now she felt that thirst of old, that need for adventure and thrill, even a burgeoning curiosity to know what kind of lover Ian would be. And she could not deny that on her doorstep in Bombay, he had looked full of male challenge, strong, unbendable—and dangerous. To say nothing of the feel of his mouth against hers, probing inside hers . . .

Stupid, stupid, stupid.

Juliana knew Ian would do his best to secure her acceptance of his proposal before they set foot in England—and still, the pull he now had on her senses stunned her. It was unacceptable. She must concoct a plan, something that would keep their rapport on the footing of friendship without giving Ian the impression she would wed him. And she must conceive of the plan now.

The only alternative was to trust her adventurous heart to his ironclad determination to tame her.

* * *

A week later, frustration racked Ian. Juliana was avoiding him. He could not deny that any more than he could deny his need to see her consumed his senses like a drug. That damned maid of hers gazed at him with stoic eyes each morning, even as she told him Juliana remained ill. He had brought Juliana remedies aplenty, concoctions recommended by the captain and several of the crew. None of them had had any effect on Juliana's rolling stomach, according to the maid.

Ian was not fooled.

So this morning he waited. At the far end of the corridor in shadows, he stood. Amulya would soon leave to fetch her mistress some tea. Then he could call her on this ploy. . . .

As if thoughts of the Indian woman had conjured her up, Amulya left the captain's cabin, her slender body swaying as if she alone heard some silent music and moved to its rhythm.

Once out of sight, Ian crept to the door and lifted the latch. Inside, Juliana sat at the room's small table, freshly dressed for the day, writing in a small book. The concentration on her face was somehow arousing, since he could well imagine her giving that much concentration—and more—to their mutual pleasure. Damn, but she looked beautiful.

Upon his entrance, she turned her head to the door. "Amulya, where is—" Her eyes turned wary as she spotted him. "Ian. I did not hear you knock."

"Because I did not bother." He speared her with a glare. "You have refused to see me each of the last six days."

"I have been unwell," she defended, slapping her book shut.

"Have you? None of those concoctions worked, then?"

She rose to her feet, wrinkling her nose. "They

smelled foul. And you had no right to burst in uninvited."

Ian might have laughed at her candor had he not been so angry. "My concern implored me to make certain you were improving. Indeed, you look very well today."

He let his gaze roam her body. She looked very well, indeed. Desire fueled his blood, doing its best to add a sharp edge to his mood.

"I believe I would like some fresh air. Shall we venture out onto the deck?"

Her voice shook, and Ian realized she did not want to be alone with him. True, in London society he could understand why she would not have dared to spend even a moment alone with him in her boudoir. But in the middle of the Indian Ocean, societal strictures merely chafed.

"A walk on deck would be nice," he conceded. "But I should like to speak with you first."

At that moment, Amulya returned, carrying a tray with tea. Surprise rounded her deep brown eyes when she spotted them together.

"Alone, if you please," he prompted.

Juliana hesitated, her gaze darting between him and her maid. Finally, she sent Amulya a slight nod. The Indian woman ducked out of the doorway and disappeared once more.

"You have your audience alone with me. Though what you have to say, I cannot imagine. I heard your proposal and declined it politely."

"Yes, you did. However, I must say I don't really understand why. I've explained my feelings—"

"Which I do not share," she railed. "You fail to see that in no way could you tempt me to the altar. It is nothing short of arrogant to assume that because you profess feelings for me that I will return them. Since turning seventeen, you, along with my father, have tried shameful measures of trickery and manipulation to run my life."

Frowning, Ian leaned closer, looming above her. "I asked you to do me the honor of being my wife. Perhaps my methods to persuade you once you'd refused me were not the best, but I cared for you and hoped you would come to return the sentiment."

Juliana glared at him, mouth agape. "You sent a woman—a courtesan—to Geoffrey's door, hoping he would betray me."

"Which he did, Juliana."

"Geoffrey did not touch her." She raised her chin in challenge.

"He told you that, and you believed him?" Ian asked as if mocking her trust. "Despite the fact you observed him button his breeches as he walked out the door?"

She faltered. Yes, Geoffrey had told her he'd remained faithful, and she had believed him. The woman had attacked him, Geoffrey had said. He had merely been righting himself. She'd loved him so badly that she had trusted his words.

"It hardly matters now whether or not Geoffrey partook of the woman—your own mistress, he later told me. The fact you sent her to him in an attempt to break us apart is despicable."

"You do not care that he bedded her two days before your marriage?" Ian challenged, eyes narrowed.

She flinched at his ugly words. "I hardly care what *he* did anymore. I care that you sent him a whore. That you did so with my father's approval only made it more vile. The whole incident was nothing but a manipulation."

Ian sighed. "Damn it, Seressia had no reason to be dishonest with me. She went to Geoffrey as a favor but not for money. It did not matter if she succeeded or failed. I only asked that she try, so we might judge

Archer's true character." Ian speared her with a glance. "He failed."

Juliana absorbed Ian's words, then swallowed the bitter pill. So Geoffrey had probably cheated on her as well. She was hardly surprised, given her husband's rash life. What alarmed her was that Ian's perfidy chafed her even more.

"That hardly absolves you of blame," she spat out. "Your behavior at every turn was contemptible. You tried to dissuade me in my choice of a husband by using your connections in the East India Company to have Geoffrey transferred to a regiment on their way to Bombay. When that did not work, you sent him your very own mistress! You had no interest at heart but your own."

"You did not belong with him," Ian defended. "Even you know that."

"That was not your choice!" She paced the small cabin. "And then came the compromise. Did you think I would not realize your plan when my father locked me in the library alone with you for over an hour? I am not brainless."

"I never believed you were."

"Had it worked, you would have taken a wife won by deceit?"

"Yes," he said without apology. "Given time, we could have been happy, I know. Marriages have been made on far less."

"Not mine."

He raised a challenging brow, working to contain his anger. "So you loved Archer? Loved him until his dying day, did you?"

Juliana paused, then admitted, "Geoffrey was a mistake."

Ian saw her hands shake, and something inside him softened. Juliana was struggling with herself, fearing she might again make the wrong choice.

"Have you considered the possibility I would not be

a mistake?" he whispered, then grasped her chilled hands in his.

"No." Her voice trembled as she pulled from his touch. "You are exactly like my father. The manner in which you seek to control me might differ, but your desired end is the same. Do you deny that?"

He gritted his teeth, tired of being cast as a villain in her mind. Indeed, he had not always shown her that he cared, nor was he a terrible beast for loving her. "I do not deny we both have your happiness in mind."

"Even if it is not the happiness I seek! No doubt, that is why he championed you as my suitor again and again. If he could not control me for the rest of my days, why not choose a husband who would do it properly for him?" she asked acidly.

Ian's temper surged, and he grabbed her arms. "That is unfair! We hardly forced you to wed me, then locked you away. We sought to save you from a dangerous attachment to a man destined to hurt you. We failed because your will was stronger than our insistence. We conceded defeat. We did you no harm."

"No harm? I chose poorly in Geoffrey, I admit that. But you made it impossible for me to trust either of you again."

Her words rang in Ian's ears. He was a man who prided himself on his ability to control his feelings, his temper. Around Juliana, he seemed to lose all such control, damn it.

"Stop insinuating your father and I have some grand scheme for your life other than to see you happy."

She shot him an incredulous stare. "Neither of you cares for my happiness, only that I wed you. I should be thrilled, indeed, if you both would leave me in peace!"

"By God, I am not your father!"

Juliana glared at him. "In every way that matters, you are."

Ian gripped her more tightly. "It is your own prejudice that casts such a shadow upon me. It is only because he wishes to see you wed me that you feel this way."

She gaped, openmouthed. "It is because you deceived me."

"I made mistakes, yes. But I love you—"

"I do not love you."

Her words felt like a blow. The force of them hit Ian squarely in the gut. No woman had ever affected his heart. He was considered a catch among the *ton*, and yet one female had held him in thrall since she was a green girl—and refused his every overture because her father approved of the match. Ian released her shoulders.

"You do not know me," he returned softly.

"I do—"

"No," he insisted. "You have no notion what I like, who I am beyond being the suitor of your father's choosing. You do not know what I want for you, for us. Never have you heard me on that score, Juliana. You do not know *me*, not inside." He paused, working to control the tangle of emotions she roused. "We were fast friends in the nursery. Once we grew and your father wanted me to join your family, you developed an aversion to me. I can credit only your rebellion for such a sentiment. I resorted to trickery, not knowing what else to do."

"Perhaps you might have simply accepted the fact that I did not want to wed you," she suggested.

Her voice chilled him. Juliana was angry. Indeed, Ian saw clearly that she had been angry for five years. He'd had little idea the incident would have such a lasting effect on her temper—or her hate.

"I cannot do that until you truly know me. Then,

if you can tell me you do not wish to be my wife, I will understand."

Juliana hesitated. A tangle of emotion shaped her eyes, her mouth, but they were too entwined to decipher. Now was as good a time for his gamble as any.

"I have a new proposal for you," he murmured.

Immediately, she shook her head. "I have no—"

"Hear me at least, Juliana. What can that harm?"

Reluctance turned her lush mouth down, hid her wide hazel eyes from his searching gaze. Damn, he wanted to touch her, ached to kiss her, possess her. How was it possible that this girl, his lifelong country neighbor, could tie his gut up in knots as no seasoned London flirt could?

Because he loved her.

"I am listening," Juliana said finally.

"You will have to wed soon, Juliana. You have not the funds to live alone, and you are too independent to share a roof with your father again, should he prevail over his illness."

She hesitated, biting her lip. Finally, she gazed at him and sighed. Clearly, she was loath to admit that truth. "What is your point?"

"You cannot husband-hunt before next season. Give me your time until Christmas Day, without thought to your father's feelings in our union. Let us learn about each other, see if the feelings deepen. If you can tell me then that you do not love me, I will never press my suit again."

Surprise crossed her delicate features. Her hazel eyes filled with questions, her berry lips parted. Ian wished like hell he could kiss her again.

"Never?" she whispered.

"Never. But you must give me until Christmas Day and deny me nothing that would not compromise you."

Her eyes narrowed with suspicion. "What do you mean?"

"See me each day. Talk with me about anything . . . everything." He paused, his hungry gaze unable to stay away from her mouth. "Grant me a kiss when you feel so swayed."

Juliana took a step back. "You ask for much."

"It is very little when you consider what this may mean to the rest of your life, Juliana. Think on it."

The following day, Juliana rose early and dressed, preparing for the assault of Ian's courtship. He did not arrive with breakfast and tea. Nor had she seen him by the time Amulya brought her lunch.

Instead, he sent a gift with her afternoon tea, a volume of Dickens's *David Copperfield* she had not yet read, along with a short missive. The volume was his, she surmised. Where else would he have found such an item on board the ship? That he had forgone its pleasure for this voyage and sent it to her surprised her—and truth be told, softened her anger a bit. The note asked only that she think of him.

Shortly before supper, Amulya entered the room with a ghost of a smile hovering upon her red-brown mouth. "Lord Axton is wishing to know if he may join you for dinner."

Juliana considered the request. In truth, she wanted the company, for she'd remained in her cabin nearly all day. Her wish for conversation, however, was not nearly as strong as her need to test him, to see if he could actually respect her desires. And that bargain he had proposed . . . It made her nothing short of uneasy. Juliana knew him; she was almost certain of that. Agreeing to it would mean granting him the necessary access to manipulate her, cajole her closer to marriage. History had taught her he would do his utmost to put his opportunity to use.

"I think not," she answered Amulya finally.

And so she ate alone.

The following day began remarkably the same. After taking breakfast and lunch alone, a bolt of spring green silk and another note arrived with her afternoon tea.

I found this silk in Bombay before we left. I knew right away how lovely it would look on you. Enjoy it.

Ian had signed the note "with love." He also asked to join her for dinner that night.

Should she comply or refuse him? On some curious level, she wanted both, but that would not do.

Juliana sighed. Despite his protests, she did not believe Ian truly loved her. She felt certain his "feelings" stemmed from the fact he could not control her. Certainly that had always roused her father's ire. Ian's polite show of asking to join her at dinner would turn to demands soon enough.

Again, she refused his request.

The following day saw another quiet afternoon, another gift, another request.

She countered with another refusal.

For the next two days, Juliana engaged in this odd dance with Ian. No doubt he would barge into her cabin at any moment and demand she consider their bargain, spend time "getting to know him," as if she had not known him most of her life.

What did he seek to prove with such an arrangement?

Dawn came swiftly in pink and vivid orange. With it came another bright, swaying day at sea, as well as a new gift. The latest demonstrated he was running out of items. A week after this charade began, he returned to her the gloves she had misplaced their first day aboard ship. The next day, he gifted her with a new inkwell for her journal writing. The day after, he promised to do his best to give her the moon, if only she would see him.

Juliana laughed.

"Lord Axton pleases you?" Amulya asked.

Reluctantly, she admitted. "He . . . amuses me at times."

"Does he wish to come to dinner?"

Nodding at the older woman, Juliana answered, "Yes."

"And you will refuse him again?"

Something in the woman's tone gave her pause. It was almost censure.

"You think I would be wrong to do so?" Juliana asked.

"It is not like you to spend so much time alone."

True, and the solitary existence had begun to wear on her nerves in the past few days.

"I am bored," she confessed. But worse, she *wanted* to see Ian in a way she had not anticipated and knew was unwise. She had not forgiven him, but she had to admit his unexpected acceptance of her refusals made her curious. Had he changed?

For eight days now, Ian had asked politely for her company. Even the simplest of courting allowed for visits of a quarter hour a few days each week. Yet he had not dismissed her wishes to be left alone. He had left her in peace.

Besides the grating boredom, she suddenly felt childish.

Ian had come to India as a favor to her family. He had given her an honorable proposal of marriage. While she did not want it, she could find no fault in the manner in which he delivered it. He had courted her while respecting her desire to be alone. And he had admitted that desperation had driven him to his rash acts of the past.

Was it truly possible he had changed?

Worse, was it possible her own unhappiness and frustration in life had blinded her to that possibility?

She could find out once and for all.

Juliana slanted a gaze to Amulya, who looked at her expectantly. At times Juliana swore the maid could read her mind.

"There is something you wish to say, memsahib?"

She smiled wryly. "Tell Lord Axton he is welcome for dinner."

CHAPTER THREE

Juliana's agreement to finally see him for dinner came as a surprise to Ian—and a relief. She had sent Amulya with a brief note regarding the time, and he finally had faith that Juliana was over the worst of her anger. Ian hoped his gifts to her had brought about her change of heart. Gifts were simple, and he could give her as many as she wished.

Instead, he feared his absence had swayed her. A hellish week, knowing she lingered mere feet from him yet wanted nothing of his company, had set his teeth on edge.

Ian had waited nearly five years for her, knowing another man called her wife. Waiting another day now seemed impossible.

He laughed. It wasn't like him to be so irrational. Juliana had that effect on him, made him believe that ignoring caution, logical thought, and decorum were splendid ideas.

But as he made his way to her cabin, that mad realization did not dim his mood.

Ian knocked upon her door. Amulya answered quickly and saw him in without a word.

The maid had already carried trays of food into the room. The fare was not fancy; his mother's French chef would have been appalled. But the rice, fish, and ale were adequate. Besides, he had not come to Juliana's cabin for the food.

Standing beside the small table, Juliana lingered, looking at him with a mixture of wariness and expectation. She had piled most of her glossy, pale hair on top of her head, leaving a few fat ringlets loose to frame her face and gleam with hints of white gold under the soft candlelight. She wore black again, and though she mourned a man Ian had hated, she still looked breathtaking. The dress accentuated her luminous ivory skin, brightened her hazel eyes, hugged her slender shoulders and the pert curve of her breasts. He wanted her so much, the force of it staggered him.

"Hello," she greeted him cautiously.

He smiled, hoping to ease her puzzling uncertainty. "Good evening. Thank you for allowing me to join you."

"You're welcome. Shall we?" She pointed to the table.

"Indeed."

Rounding the table, Ian made his way to Juliana's side. He placed a hand upon her back as he pulled out her chair. Even that simple touch left him achingly aware of the subtle lavender scent of her warm, silken skin, her lush mouth so near. . . .

Uncertain of her mood, he took his seat across from her. Amulya served them in silence before her mistress dismissed her.

They were alone. Finally.

Now, if he only knew what to say to persuade her they would be good—perfect—together . . .

Ian did his best to endure the silence. Forks clinked

against sturdy plates. The occasional flow of ale sloshed into a cup. Waves lapped against the ship's hull. Juliana's dress rustled against the swell of her breasts with every breath she took. Still, she said nothing.

His only consolation was that Juliana's eyes hardly left him. Not that her gaze was sexual. But she looked at him as if he were a puzzle she might solve if she stared hard enough. . . .

Finally she demanded, "I must know, did you travel to India merely to propose marriage again? Is my father's illness a ploy?" She gave him a hard stare. "I expect you to be a gentleman in answering me."

In other words, she expected complete honesty. Ian did not want to lie to her. Lord knew he could ill afford to rouse her anger again. Still, she would not speak to him again if he told the complete truth.

He paused. "Your father is ill. He hates to admit that, but I believe there is no denying it. As for marriage, I asked you again because I love you. I think I have made that plain."

"Yes, but I do not understand. Why do you love me?"

Ian almost choked on his ale. "How can I do anything less than love you, Juliana?" He sighed, fighting an urge to reach across the table and grasp her hands in his. "You are . . . different. You speak your mind. Your head is not filled with idle gossip or fripperies. You've no desire to conquer every male heart about you, though you do." He smiled wryly before his mouth fell by degrees into a thoughtful expression. "But it's more."

Ian searched his mind for all his words, for all he felt. "I admire your courage and daring, your strength, your willingness to fight for what you want in life."

"Despite the fact my wishes clash with yours?"

He smiled and shrugged. "Oddly, yes. I don't think

I could love a woman without conviction. Such women seem too ... weak, I suppose. No, you are something of a challenge."

"I am not your prize to be captured and hung upon your study wall," she snapped.

Her hazel eyes narrowed, and Ian realized he admired her defenses even as he wished he could scale them.

"I hardly think of you as some animal to display like a trophy caught on a hunting expedition," he chided.

"Perhaps, but I question whether you would truly continue with this devotion once I capitulated and the challenge no longer lured you."

"My, how cynical you are. Juliana, it's not just the challenge that appeals." He reached for her hand. "Yes, your stubborn nature adds to both my frustration and anticipation, but it is my heart that knows you and I are meant for each other. I have known it for years." He cast a searching gaze to her face, in time to see her expression soften with surprise. "I simply have not found a way to make you see that."

His last words were a mistake. Ian knew that right away when Juliana snapped back in her chair, shoulders squared, and retorted, "Perhaps you have not found that way because your heart is wrong."

Her doubt pained him like a knife in the gut, but he hid his emotion. "Do you truly dislike everything about me? I have never amused you, or helped you, or seemed your friend?"

Juliana hesitated, clearly gathering her response. He could count on her for honesty. That was paramount to her. But Ian knew her words might as easily bring more hurt.

"I do not dislike everything about you," she confessed, somewhat reluctant. "I recall you teaching me to ride after Papa had bought me that new pony for my eighth birthday. You consoled me after my kitty died a few years later.''

"I cared for you even then," he said softly. "But certainly you can recall some incident relevant after we left the nursery."

Juliana paused, then nodded as if conceding the point. "You listened when my father and I began to clash before my come-out." She sighed, and some of the anger seemed to leave her. "I admit you can be kind and, at times, compassionate ... so long as it does not interfere with something you want."

Perhaps that was true, Ian thought, but they need not dwell on it. "Have you felt only anger and dislike for me since we began this voyage?"

"No," she admitted slowly, then glanced away to her half-empty plate. "You have surprised me, I confess, both with your willingness to travel so far to help my family and the manner in which you respected my wish to be left in peace this last week."

"Yet I sense your hesitation."

She heaved a frustrated sigh. "You have no comprehension how vile I thought your treachery when you tried to end my betrothal to Geoffrey. That you can fail to comprehend how shaken you left me stuns me more. I trusted you."

Juliana frowned, eyes direct and unflinching. Ian resisted the urge to look away from that damning gaze.

"I believed you to be my friend," she went on. "Then to discover that you had plotted to destroy the bond between me and the man I sought to wed simply because I had refused you—"

"It was not a vendetta," he cut in. "I did it because I *knew* he would only hurt you. And watching your pain hurt me as well. Archer was beneath you."

"Just because he was not an earl—"

"No, because he was a blackguard whose sole interest in wedding you was your father's money."

"So you are a better man who has no interest in Papa's wealth?" The arch of her brow spoke much about her doubt.

Ian finally succumbed to the urge to reach across the table and snatch her hand. She struggled for release, but he held tight. "I like money as well as the average man, but that was *never* my motivation in offering for you. From the time you were fifteen, I waited for you, knowing in my heart we were meant for one another."

"That sounds awfully romantical. What facts do you have to support your theory?"

"Love needs no facts." He squeezed her hand, willing her to understand. "It simply is."

"Rubbish! I resist any notion that people are born for each other or—or fated to wed. I have more control over my future than that."

When she would have pulled away from his touch, Ian brought her hand closer to his body, until her fingertips touched his heart. Her gaze flew to his, eyes widening. How could she look both fierce and vulnerable at once? Her very nature intrigued him, and he could not imagine letting her go again.

"Ian—"

"No."

He reached a hand across the table to place a finger over her soft, warm mouth. God, he wanted to kiss her. No, he wanted more—to savor her taste, revel in the mewl of her surprise, before she melted . . . Hell, he wanted even more than that. But now was not the time to be distracted by his desire. He would wait, knowing she would be worth it, knowing someday he would have a lifetime to indulge his need for her.

"I know my behavior in the past was deplorable," he said, his voice candid but soft. "I know you think you will never be able to forgive me, to trust me again—"

"I won't," she confirmed.

Ian fought the urge to close his eyes and sigh in frustration. Juliana was a challenge, but he had known all along she would be.

"Only because you will not try to trust me," he countered. "I hurt you in the past, and that was not my intent. I have no thought to distress you again. Can you not try to have a bit of faith in me? At least enough to spend the days before Christmas with me? If you can tell me honestly that you do not love me by then, as I said, I will stop courting you."

Juliana hesitated. Ian watched a flurry of thoughts cross the smooth oval of her face. First came suspicion and irritation, then consideration, followed by something that softened her hazel eyes and gave him hope. Then she slid her gaze across the table to him. Her stare seemed to speculate about his intent, about him as a man. Finally, she looked away.

"You have nothing to lose," he pointed out.

"That is true." Juliana nodded. "Still . . ."

He hoped she would give him her promise now, even though he could see her mistrust and her logic fighting. Still, Juliana had always been one of the most logical people he had ever known. She could not tolerate illogical behavior in herself.

"Oh, bother," she muttered suddenly, then cast a glare in his direction. "I promise to spend the days before Christmas with you. I'm certain it will prove nothing and change nothing, but clearly you will not believe me until I play your game."

He smiled, relief swelling. Slowly, surely, he would break down her resistance, gain her trust, increase her awareness of him, and help her face the love they could share—if only she would let herself. His gut told him this plan would work.

"I think I might surprise you," he suggested.

Standing, Juliana rose regally to her feet. "Don't wager on that. You will most certainly lose."

* * *

Three evenings later, Ian again joined Juliana in her cabin for dinner. Since she had agreed to his bargain, he had seen her both morning and night. And still she held herself aloof, as if determined to convince him that his courting would never move her.

Ian was more determined he would affect her in every way he could conceive, particularly that stubborn heart of hers.

Tonight he had a plan he hoped very much would work. If he could not talk her out of her resolve, as he'd tried for the past three days, well . . . perhaps he could amuse it out of her.

After a quiet meal, Amulya removed their dirty plates from the table and onto a tray. In her usual manner, she whisked them away and exited the cabin.

Once they were alone, Ian set his gaze upon Juliana, taking in the rosy ivory of her cheeks, the splendor of her red mouth, the uncertain awareness she tried to hide in her hazel eyes.

He regarded her wordlessly, his smile questioning, challenging. He knew well his face gave away that he had a secret. And he waited, mute. A tense minute passed. Then another.

Juliana returned his stare measure for measure, her face not amused—yet. At first, her aristocratic features held nothing more than disinterest. For as long as it lasted, the expression was quite convincing. But Ian knew her well. Patience wasn't one of Juliana's finer qualities.

The silence ticked by. Ian watched her, aware of the moment her look changed from aloof disdain to impatience, characterized by the sudden tapping of her fingers upon the table. Within minutes, her expression turned to one of thin-lipped pique.

He only smiled wider.

She rapped her fingers more quickly upon the wood.

Color began to rise in her cheeks. Contrasted by her hated black bombazine gown, he saw the flush on her shoulders. The agitated lift of her breasts beneath her silky material, moving in time with her increasingly harsh breath, transfixed him.

Not only had this much proximity to the fair-haired minx he long craved left him hard and in desperate need for days, he felt keenly how much he had missed her in the last five years.

Still, he kept his smile in place.

Juliana's fingers tapped faster yet. Her stare became a glare. She bit her bottom lip in agitation, and, oh, how he wanted to kiss that mouth.

While thinking of that, his smile turned mischievous.

"Stop it," she demanded finally.

"Stop?" He pretended ignorance. "I am not aware of anything I have done."

She sighed in irritation. "You are toying with me."

"Am I?" He feigned innocence.

"Of course." Her pale brows slashed down in a frown. "What else could such a secretive little smirk mean?"

Ian shrugged. "Perhaps I merely find you enchanting."

She answered with a sound somewhere between a disgusted groan and an annoyed moan. "Ever the swain, aren't you? And do those foolish twits in London fall for that sort of rubbish?"

Ian tossed her a new, genuine smile and tried to hold back his laughter. In the end, he failed. "You don't sound respectful of your own fair sex."

"Perhaps if they simpered less and thought more, I would. Then again, their idiocy keeps rakes like you satisfied."

He leaned closer and whispered, "Unfortunately

not. My standards are higher, I fear." He winked at her.

She rolled her eyes, yes. But finally, he saw a reluctant smile tugging at the corners of her mouth.

He grinned back.

"You are smiling at me again, my lord."

Her tone reflected both exasperation and amusement. He decided to confuse her further.

"Do you enjoy singing?"

"Me?" Surprise widened her thickly lashed eyes. "You know my voice can hardly support a note."

He nodded, conceding the point. He remembered all too well the discomfort of listening to an evening's "entertainment" at Harbrooke as she learned the accomplishments of a lady, then proceeded to butcher most of them.

"We can content ourselves by listening to others sing."

Confusion pulled her face into a puzzled frown. Before she could interrogate him, however, Ian let loose a sharp whistle.

Not a moment passed before three of the ship's crew entered the small room. The first, a hulk of a dark-haired man, came in with a well-mannered bow, seeming at odds with his almost piratical mode of dress. " 'Ello."

The second, barely more than a boy, slinked into the cabin and nodded in her direction, not quite meeting her eyes.

The last, a tall man whom ladies all over the world would undoubtedly think handsome, strode into the small space with a confident air and a wink. He took Juliana's fingers in his and placed a brief kiss on her hand. Ian would have been much happier had the man kept the gesture to himself.

"My lovely lady," the charmer began. "Be our guest this evening and enjoy our song."

Ian cast a glance at Juliana. Her gaze drifted from one crewman to the other in a wide, startled stare.

The burly man at the back brought a violin beneath his beefy neck and began to play sweet melodic notes, a poignant movement of music designed to tug on the heart.

Again Ian looked to Juliana to see if she was influenced by the tune. The stunned expression remained on her delicate visage. Soon, however, something pleasant began to shape her slight smile. To the rhythm of the music she swayed just a bit, enough to know she enjoyed its rich flavor.

The others joined in, harmonizing the bittersweet melody as three distinct, rich voices filled the air. Carefully, Ian watched Juliana's face as the sailors began a new verse.

> *The dames of France are fond and free,*
> *And Flemish lips are willing;*
> *And soft the maids of Italy,*
> *And Spanish eyes are thrilling;*
> *Still, though I bask beneath their smile,*
> *Their charms fail to bind me.*
> *And my heart goes back to England,*
> *To the girl I left behind me.*
>
> *For she's as fair as Avon's side,*
> *And purer than its water,*
> *But she refused to be my bride*
> *Though many years I sought her.*
> *Yet, since to France I sailed away,*
> *Her letters oft remind me,*
> *That I promised never to gainsay*
> *The girl I left behind me.*

During the tune, Juliana's face brightened with surprise, then turned reserved with reflection. But as the last notes died and his gaze found her, silence fell over the room.

Her eyes narrowed, as if readying to defend her refusals of him. Damn, that ballad has backfired on him. He motioned to the burly sailor to begin another tune. With a smile and a raising of his hands, he asked for a brighter melody.

Giving a shout of jubilation, the hulk pulled his bow across the gleaming fiddle. Raucous music spilled into the room. The others began singing a naughty little ditty.

> It's a tale of a pretty fair maid
> As you shall understand
> She had a mind for roving
> Unto a foreign land
> Attired in sailor's clothing
> She boldly did appear
> And engaged with the captain
> To serve him for a year.

> She engaged with the captain
> A cabin boy to be
> The wind it was in favor,
> They soon put out to sea
> The captain's lady being on board
> She seemed it to enjoy
> So glad the captain had engaged
> A handsome cabin boy.

> So nimble was that pretty maid
> And done her duty well
> But mark what followed after,
> As she herself can tell
> The captain with that pretty maid
> Did often kiss and toy
> For he soon found out the secret of
> The handsome cabin boy.

Juliana clapped a hand over her mouth, eyes startled. Ian held his breath. Yes, he had meant the sailors to amuse her but not to shock her. He should have asked exactly what songs they planned to sing after that previous tune. . . .

Damn. Would Juliana denounce him as too forward and send him away? Cripes, what was he to do now?

Then he saw a reluctant smile tugging at her mouth. She looked at him with reproach, true, but that expression also contained mirth.

"That is a truly awful song," she said, then realized the singing sailors still stood beside their table. "Though well sung, I grant you, gentlemen."

"Thank you for your praise, lovely lady," the flirtatious sailor said, sidling closer to Juliana.

She gave the man a curt nod—and a curious stare.

Ian stopped the exchange immediately. "Thank you, gentlemen. Since the lady is suitably impressed, you may go."

The men filed out of the room slowly, the seafaring rake last, casting a wink over his shoulder at Juliana. Ian reminded himself to watch Juliana closely while she walked on deck.

As soon as the door shut, Ian looked back to Juliana, who now pressed a handkerchief to her perfect pink mouth. But her eyes danced with mischief, the roses in her cheeks in full bloom. She looked so exultant in laughter. He wanted to give her that expression every day for the rest of his life.

"That was shocking! My father would swoon to know you had hired them to sing such deviltry to me."

Her observation pleased Ian. Perhaps she would begin to see the differences between himself and Lord Brownleigh.

He shrugged. "A little wickedness keeps the soul honest, I always say."

She raised her golden brows at him, her expression intrigued. Yes, he had her attention now.

"I know you speak from experience. You've hardly been without sin your whole life."

"No one has," he returned smoothly.

She laughed. "Yes, but some of us have come closer than others. How could you let them sing such a song to me? If the *ton* knew, I'm sure it would be a decade before they accepted me in polite circles again."

"I won't tell if you won't," he teased, smiling.

Again, she laughed. "You are incorrigible. How am I to take you to task for such a song if you only twist my words to your advantage?"

"Perhaps you should try less to take me to task and try more to simply talk to me," Ian suggested.

He knew the proposition could backfire on him, but he was ill prepared for her swift retort.

Her smile crashed into a scowl. She stiffened in her chair and leaned in, looking suddenly as fierce as a she-dog ready to defend her bone. "You deserve every bit of chastisement I give you and more. Your efforts to charm me will not change the fact that your apologies for your past behavior mean nothing."

Ian frowned. "That is not true."

"If I had succumbed to your machinations as a younger woman, you would not have apologized once."

Ian paused. Truth told, he would not have been sorry in the least if she had wed him five years ago. Why should he? They would be happy now had she not been so stubborn.

"I knew it," she tossed at him. "Your face gives you away. I believe you are sorry your plot did not lead me to the parson. I do not believe you are sorry for the ploy itself."

What was the difference? He had her future happiness at heart.

"Juliana—"

"Good night, Ian."

It was a less than polite request for him to leave. He clenched his fists at his sides and restrained an urge to argue with her. Instead, he said nothing. After all, he had months ahead of him, during which he could convince her.

Refusing to be daunted, Ian rose from his chair and nodded. "Until tomorrow, Juliana."

The following night, Juliana sat alone at the dinner spread out before her—and the empty chair across from her. No, she had not wanted Ian's company this morning at breakfast or tonight at dinner. Yet she had counted on it. Solitude was not a state she favored, and having him near relieved that burden. For no other reason did she wish him to eat with her.

That explanation clarified her current pique.

He was not ill; she had asked Amulya to check on that.

Was he so angry with her accusations that he no longer wanted her? She found the thought vaguely disturbing, felt the discomfort of the possibility somewhere in her belly. Then she dismissed it. She did not miss Ian. Though his conversation was engaging, he incited her only to behaviors she did not understand in herself. For instance, laughing at the sailors' bawdy song about the ship captain bedding the girl disguised as his cabin boy. She flushed, merely thinking about it.

Still, he had surprised her.

Juliana recalled only a serious side to Ian. The glimpses she had seen of his nature since reuniting with her did not fit the mold of the man she remembered. Of course she had sensed right away that something about him had changed. . . .

Pushing away from her half-eaten meal, Juliana

rose to her feet. She did not want to consider that dinner was less palatable without Ian; she simply was not hungry.

Still, a restless mood prevailed.

Amulya came in to collect the dishes and glanced at Ian's untouched plate. Avoiding her maid's questioning gaze, Juliana wandered outside onto the deck.

The breeze lifted her hair into a dance with the wind. Night stars twinkled above as the sea lapped with soothing care against the *Houghton*'s hull, spraying mist and salt into the quiet evening.

She took in the night with her gaze—and was shocked to find Ian standing at the rail, staring out across the endless ocean. His wide shoulders seemed taut, his expression pensive. His profile revealed a razor-cut jaw, tense and unmoving. With his legs braced against the ship's sway and his hands clasped behind his back, he looked as formidable as any pirate of old.

Had he decided to cease his pursuit of her?

The thought filled her with both relief and vexation. Juliana could hardly tell what she should make of that.

"Ian?" she called softly into the wind.

He said nothing, gave no hint he had heard. Juliana crept closer, so close she touched her hand to his clenched shoulder.

Ian turned to face her abruptly. Startled, she gasped. She gasped again when he curled his fingers around her wrist, and a tingling bolt of fire shot up her arm, to her belly.

The look on his face could be described only as something between carnal and damning.

"I—I didn't mean to startle you," she stammered.

"You did not. I knew you stood there."

Juliana felt the silence as it stretched infinite and thick between them, broken only by her breathing and his touch.

She wanted to ask him why he hadn't come to breakfast or dinner. Yet she knew they would only spar if she did. The thought did not appeal to her.

Blast it all, she must say something! They could not continue standing here, breathless inches apart in silence. She could not continue to look into those blue eyes, not when she felt strangely as if she were sinking into them.

She cleared her throat and grasped the first innocuous subject that came to mind.

"Tell me what you plan to do about your breeding stables."

He hesitated. Juliana waited for him to turn his back on her or answer her or kiss her—something. Finally, he relaxed, released her wrist.

"I've been making financial arrangements with old friends and some new acquaintances. I have saved up nearly half the money on my own. The land I purchased two years past. Now all that remains is to build the manor house and stables."

"You don't want to live at Edgefield Park?"

"No."

"Never?" Juliana asked, stunned. Wasn't that his home?

He shrugged. "Perhaps someday. But this land I've bought ... If you could see it, you would understand."

Though she would never see it, Juliana found herself curious.

"Tell me of it."

"It's near Salisbury. I shall build the manor house upon a hill that overlooks a lush valley. In the summer, the saffron turns the hills a vibrant yellow. And it's more convenient besides, being closer to London. I shall have to go there frequently to discuss business, I should think."

"Indeed," she murmured, oddly numb.

The subject impassioned Ian, and Juliana found she could not be unmoved by his excitement.

"It sounds most lovely."

He nodded. "I hope to share it with you someday."

His words, his very ardor, jarred her from the lull of the conversation. Juliana stiffened, not just with his forward statement but with her own lack of rejection at the thought.

That would not do. "Ian, I—"

"Say nothing. I know I've given you until Christmas Day to answer my marriage proposal. I'll not push you to answer now."

The heated blue gaze touched her mouth, skimming as though he could touch her lips with his eyes. Juliana felt flustered by his expression.

She looked away. "I am not prepared to make any sort of decision regarding my future now. Geoffrey has not yet been gone a year and I"—she sighed— "I did not expect to be alone and childless at twenty-three."

Ian's gaze softened, and Juliana found herself absurdly glad for that.

"I know this year, and the past few, have not been easy on you. Archer was not the man you thought him to be."

"No," she murmured softly, reluctantly.

How did he understand that so easily, when it had taken her months to admit that to herself? And the fact Ian had correctly divined Geoffrey's true nature from the beginning made her both sad and agitated.

Juliana watched Ian, her gaze sizing him up. She *knew* who he was, the man made in her father's mold, the rogue capable of terrible manipulations. Though close to five years had separated them, it seemed likely he was that same man. People did not change that much, did they? Still, his sincerity confounded her.

Or could people indeed change?

Whether she relished the idea or not, she had made a promise to Ian to come to know him again. She owed it to him, and her odd sense of curiosity, to learn the answer to that question.

CHAPTER FOUR

"Lord Axton, he is coming for breakfast tomorrow?" Amulya asked late that night.

Juliana tried to stifle the strange sense of anticipation she felt at the thought. But no matter how she reminded herself he had lied and manipulated, the argument did not have as much impact as it once had.

Pushing the thought away, she nodded. "Yes."

Amulya looked as if she was in the mood to impart her sage advice. It was churlish, but Juliana was not in the mood to hear that she was not opening her heart and her mind.

"I will require tea when he arrives," she said. "That is all for tonight."

Her dark eyes revealing the knowledge that she had been dismissed, Amulya nodded. With a fat black braid swinging down her narrow back, the maid left.

Juliana heaved a sigh, sat at the little table, and reached for her journal, opening it beneath the warm glow of the candlelight. After dating the page, she dipped her quill in her ink once more and paused.

She wrote about the sea, the journey, about leaving India. Her thoughts of Ian were too confused to put on paper tonight.

With a sigh, she gave up trying and stashed the journal in her trunk. Then Juliana settled into the soft bunk and curled the blankets beneath her chin.

Her rebellious thoughts slid immediately to Ian, her friend, her betrayer, her would-be fiancé.

What on earth was she to do about his insistent pursuit—and her own weakening to it? Confused, she closed her eyes. . . .

Suddenly, Juliana found herself back at Harbrooke in the drawing room, sitting before a burning hearth. Ivy and holly decorated the mantel. Outside, she could hear the faint sounds of carolers. Ah, it was Christmas, her favorite time of year.

She glanced out the window. Snow fell. Peace blanketed the scene. She snuggled into the chair, watching the sunrise. Her parents would make their way to this room soon, where they would exchange gifts and enjoy the day.

Instead, Ian arrived, impatient as he blocked her view of the window. "It is Christmas morning, Juliana. I must insist you marry me."

His doggedness was both pesky and condescending. "I never said I would. In fact, I will not. And you cannot make me regret saying no."

"But I want to be with you," he cajoled.

This posed a problem, for lately Juliana had been enjoying his company. She had never liked the thought that she had lost his friendship. Could they not compromise?

"Certainly you do not require marriage for companionship. Let us enjoy each other without delving into matrimony."

Ian paused in thought. "Perhaps you are right."

"Of course I am. In no way can you change my mind

about your lack of character. But if we simply enjoy our time together, your visits will not agitate me."

"Won't they?"

"Indeed, I can be pleased by your company without taking your suit seriously."

"I'm not certain I like that idea," Ian said in her dream.

"You will," she vowed. "You'll see."

Ian's shoulders and face fell at once in a sad expression that made her immediately want to comfort him.

But he was gone before she could. Again Juliana found herself peering out the window at the beautiful white fall of winter blanketing the rolling countryside. She did her best to recapture the peace of the season.

Until the manor's ghost distorted her view.

"Why do you deny your destiny?" she asked, floating several inches off the ground, brocade skirt in one hand, lace trembling over the other.

"Destiny?" Juliana asked. "Certainly you don't mean Ian?" At the fair ghost's nod, Juliana said, "I am simply avoiding confusion. Ian does confuse me. He is full of surprises, like the sailors singing bawdy songs. Papa would never approve."

"But you like that."

"Yes," she admitted reluctantly, "he claims to love me and seeks to wed me, but . . ."

"Believe him and follow his wishes," the ghost advised.

"I cannot trust him though. He deceived and lied—"

"Perhaps not without reason," the ghost suggested, shimmering with brilliant light.

"I will not wed him. Ian is controlling. My future would hold mindless misery if I married the man. I would never be free to make a decision of consequence again."

The ghost scowled. Juliana felt her disapproval. It shamed her somehow, even as it infuriated her.

"Love him. Do not let him slip away."

"Slip away? I cannot shake him loose! He does not realize I mean to hold firm to my convictions and wed a man I choose, if I wed at all."

"Marrying another would be a tragedy," vowed the spirit. Then she was gone, evaporated like water on a scorching day. Juliana was alone again.

She awoke in a sweat, panting. She glanced around the cold, shadow-draped room. The captain's cabin aboard the *Houghton;* she recognized it now.

Still, she could not shake a sense of something peculiar, almost supernatural. Did she smell the faint scent of roses, the one that belonged to Harbrooke's ghost?

No, it was simply a dream, she told herself, trying to shake the feeling.

What could such a dream mean? Juliana played its contents over and over, until the images became hazy, its meaning even more muddled. Ghosts did not talk, did they? And never before had she dreamed of Harbrooke's haunt. Juliana frowned.

Only one part of the dream emerged with clarity and provided her the solution she'd been seeking for some days: How to deal next with Ian. She could enjoy his company, renew their friendship, and honor her promise to try to better acquaint herself with him, though she felt certain she already knew him far too well. Yes! She could do all that without feeling pressured by his proposal, for she would not change her mind. No amount of his cajoling would bring about that event!

A heavy burden of guilt and anxiety slid away, easing the knot in her belly. She relaxed against her pillow and sighed.

Why not smile and visit with Ian and enjoy his unexpected moments of amusement instead of worrying about marriage?

* * *

As Juliana considered her decision the following morning, Amulya entered the small cabin with the tea. A glance over her maid's shoulder revealed Ian stood just behind her. Tall and dark in the shadowed passage, she saw he wore a splendid but sober coat of deep blue that seemed somehow at odds with the silent hint of mischief in his eyes.

If nothing else, solving the puzzle of Ian's person might be entertaining. Juliana saw no reason not to enjoy that.

But she would not marry him.

She rose to greet him with a smile. Ian returned her silent greeting, his full mouth curling up in an expression that conveyed more than fondness. It was like silk, shiny and beckoning, rich and hard to ignore. Such a smile only enhanced the light in his eyes. What a flirt he was! How had she never noticed that?

Because she had been too busy worrying about his demands—but no more. Now the game was hers.

Her smiled widened. "Come in. Let us sit and eat. Then we shall have a nice chat about next to nothing."

Surprised, his warm gaze touched her cheek, lingered upon her mouth. He searched her eyes, as if looking for answers. Though Juliana did not understand why, her face heated under his appraisal.

Smiling, he murmured finally, "I should like that very much."

Ian sent a grin Juliana's way. He was vaguely aware of Amulya clearing away the breakfast dishes, but he paid the Indian woman little mind. His attention was focused on Juliana.

She seemed to glow this morning. Her cheerful nature, the one he remembered from her girlhood, had suddenly returned. He wondered what had brought about this change but decided not to question it too much. He was pleased.

As she'd nibbled on her morning meal, she had told him of her harrowing voyage to India five years earlier. She had loved the sea, the wind, the water, the seeming freedom. Unfortunately, her stomach had not always agreed.

Sea travel agreed with her today. Faint color bloomed in her fair cheeks. Her hair of multihued gold cascaded down her shoulders in a silken curtain, curling around her shoulders and elbows. And her red mouth lifted with a smile, so tempting to him. . . . He could not recall craving her touch with such urgency when he had courted her before her marriage. Then he had cared for her, known she belonged with him. Now she appealed to him in every way, and his gut tightened as he thought of calling her his wife—and finally claiming her as such.

"Oh, dear. You've gone silent on me," she said in mock concern. "I fear I've bored you to death." A puzzled scowl overtook her face, but the expression had enough play that he knew it as false. "Can a physician cure that? I wonder. And where would I find such a man in the middle of the ocean?"

He laughed at her teasing. "You shall have to use your sparkling words to revive me, fair lady."

"Sparkling? That is a tall order! Don't forget, I engaged in very little society in India. I'm afraid my sparkle may have blown away with the Bombay wind."

"I doubt that," he assured her. "Though the wind is fierce . . . Of course, I remember a worse wind. Do you recall that day—"

"The day I fished by the river and fell in? Goodness, are we to talk about that again? I vow you bring that up at every opportunity." She looked at him with mock censure in her eyes.

Ian tried not to laugh but could not help himself.

Juliana had been both reckless and brave even then. "I did save you that day, you know."

She gaped at him, her expression sharply skeptical. "I know no such thing, you impertinent man. If you had given me a few more moments to untie those sodden petticoats, I would have swum my way out of the river."

"That certainly didn't appear the case when you went beneath the surface of the water," he reminded her. "I pulled you out of that river and saved you from drowning. And for my trouble you kicked my shin so hard, it bruised for two weeks."

"You laughed at my petticoats as they floated down the river, you rogue! And when I would have jumped in to retrieve them, you prevented me. I think I must have explained that dilemma to my father for over an hour before he accepted it as truth. He was eager to believe I was traipsing around the countryside without the proper undergarments."

Ian's sound was one of disbelief. "Admit it, if you thought you could have done so without his notice, you would have."

"No," she protested. "I was quite the young lady then, nearly fourteen. I was determined to be a proper female."

"While fishing?" he teased her, then smiled when her cheeks flushed higher with color.

Flashing her a grin, Ian could not tear his gaze from Juliana. Yes, she was beautiful. In fact, he did not know when she had been more exquisite or when her mere words incited such an urgent need to claim her until they were both breathless. But she charmed him in other ways. He liked being with her as they shared a casual morning of tea and laughter. He liked *her*.

At times, Juliana set him at ease. Other times, she challenged, frustrated . . . even infuriated him. No matter what feelings she evoked, those she roused in him were by far more potent than any he had ever felt with another woman.

Across the table from him, Juliana gasped and pretended pique, her pout both mischievous and alluring. "I loved to fish. I could not bear to give it up."

"I recall. We fished together a great deal, at least until I realized that all your talking scared the fish away."

"That is untrue! And ungentlemanly of you to say so."

He shrugged, enjoying their mock dispute. "Perhaps, but when I fished alone I always caught more than I could keep."

"And you blame me for your distraction? I suppose next you will tell me you are a better card player when I'm not around."

He wasn't, but Ian refused to admit that, not when teasing her was so much fun. "Of course I am. Men fear me at the clubs, I can fleece them so easily."

"Easily, you say?" She scoffed. "I remember well why I refused to partner with you in whist all those years ago."

"At least I am not a sore loser," he quipped.

She lifted her chin as regally as good Queen Victoria. "And why should I be happy about not winning?"

Ian laughed at her again. "You're right. And the rest of us would do well to step aside and let you have all the spoils." He paused and let a moment of silence prevail. "What? Have you no answer to that?"

"You make me sound unfair," she objected.

He grinned. "Just determined. And I like that in you, so you've no reason to sulk."

"I do not sulk," she said, her mouth decidedly turned down.

A low chuckle escaped Ian before he could stop it. She did sulk—beautifully, like now. Still, it *was* sulking.

"As you will." She rose to her feet. "You may sit

here and laugh at my expense, if it pleases you. I am determined to walk on the deck in peace.''

Ian controlled the mirth and rose to his feet. Hope and anticipation brimmed inside him as he approached her. Juliana had spoken to him, actually been eager to engage in banter and remembrances. As a sign of things to come, it was a good one.

As they reached the door, Ian placed his hand at the small of her back to guide her out the door. Juliana did not stiffen or step away.

His spirits soared. Did she finally understand he posed no threat, meant her no harm? He would have to continue to woo her slowly, no doubt, by doing his best to maintain the rekindling of their friendship.

Juliana was not an easy woman to convince of anything; that he knew all too well. But saints above, was it possible she was coming to trust him once more? If his luck held, she could eventually feel a desire to deepen their friendship into something more, something lasting. He held in a heated sigh at the thought she might someday welcome his touch, call him husband. Not yet, he knew . . . but soon.

A week of companionship slid into two, then into a month. May became June; June became July. August saw a day's stop on the eastern cape of South Africa so they might gather fresh water and food before the East India Company's ship rounded the Cape of Good Horn.

Ian had suggested they go ashore for a few joyous hours of land beneath her feet, and Juliana had seized the opportunity eagerly.

She stood on deck, Ian at her side, as the *Houghton* sailed into Algoa Bay and the Charl Malan quay, as the captain had explained. From the deck of the ship it looked to be a lovely town with pristine white beaches. The day held a few clouds, but the weather was so temperate, the breeze warm. As land was only a short journey away, Juliana did not care about an imperfect sky. The opportunity to walk on solid land thrilled her.

After the captain went ashore for his business, he sent word back that they could disembark. With excitement, Juliana could scarcely stay still as she stood beside Ian.

"Did you not see Africa on your journey out?"

She shuddered. "Goodness, no. I was too sick by far."

Ian repressed a grin as he led her to land and changed the subject. "We are in Port Elizabeth, I'm told."

"Yes, the captain mentioned that."

"What do you know of the town?" he asked to make conversation. Hearing her voice comforted and aroused him, particularly since her banter now lacked a guarded nature, reminding him of the fun, spirited Juliana he'd known in youth.

"I know very little, I'm afraid. And you?"

He lifted a shoulder in answer. "I very much doubt the bit I learned will prove helpful, but I shall gladly share it."

"Yes, do," she replied, fingers clutching his arm as they left the docks behind and walked through the mild day.

To have her hand upon him, her hazel eyes beckoning him, her face so bright and unfettered by distrust, he would have told her anything she desired to hear.

For now he merely answered her. "According to the captain, the town was named in 1820 by one Sir Rufane Donkin for his late wife, Elizabeth. She had died in India two years previously."

Juliana nodded. "Such ill-fated occurrences are unfortunately not rare. Life in India can be harsh."

With a nod, he continued. "I'm told there are

several parks here, but the town is mostly known for its warehouses, wool washeries, and fresh water.''

"You are impressedly learned, my lord," she teased. "Shall we explore? I have the heart of a discoverer today."

"Then I must indulge you. What kind of gentleman would I be if I did not?"

"None at all, I am sure. Though that would not shock me."

"I am no reprobate!" he defended in mock insult.

"Not that you will admit to," she added wryly but could not stop her giggle.

"You know me too well, I fear."

With a wry grin, Ian placed a hand on her fingers, which lay curled around his arm. With a gentle squeeze, he led her away from the ship, through the throngs of dark-skinned Xhosa natives, large and bare-chested as they worked on the docks. The British officers, ill dressed for the warmer climate, stood over them, sweating and watchful. A few Xhosa women were about, selling fruits and handmade goods. Juliana gaped at the women, for they wore long skirts and turbans but absolutely nothing to cover their swinging, dark-nippled breasts.

A quick glance at Ian found him watching her face with a hint of amusement. She looked away and cleared her throat.

"That is shocking!" she whispered.

He shrugged. "Their culture is clearly much different."

"And these women are selling nothing more than trinkets and a few fruits?"

Repressing a smile, he whipped a sharp gaze down to her face. "And what would you know of women who sell more?"

She shot him a disbelieving gaze. "Ian, I am a widow of some years and experience. I know of such women."

"Gads, not very ladylike of you to admit that. Now it's certain we must spend all our time together. Neither of us is fit for polite company, it seems."

For an instant, the light mood vanished, replaced by uncertainty at his comment. Did he mean to raise the issue of marriage again? Juliana risked a glance in his direction and encountered only the most affable of smiles. No, a man with so carefree a face thought of nothing as momentous as marriage. In fact, Ian had not mentioned it once in weeks. Surely he only jested now, engaging in the light banter that was the hallmark of their rapport these days. And that was for the best.

Still, she was a bit curious about why he failed to talk of matrimony anymore. Had she succeeded in convincing him she had no interest in being his wife? Or had all his talk of love the first week aboard the *Houghton* been a lark? And if he had realized, as she had years before, that they were not suited to marriage, why should that put her ill at ease?

Suddenly, Ian peered at her carefully. "No frowning today, my dear. We are off to explore."

Determined to enjoy herself, Juliana nodded and let him lead her onward, away from the teeming activity and the half-covered women.

The port town was full of delights for a society so young and so far from its British roots. They visited the Cultural History Museum, built nearly thirty years before. It told her a great deal about the original four thousand settlers of Port Elizabeth.

Afterward, they stopped at an outdoor market run by an odd mixture of British and Xhosa, and purchased some fruits, cheeses, ale, and meat pies, along with a basket to carry it all. Ian also purchased a set of beautiful blue beaded combs for her hair that matched her dress.

Juliana smiled at his thoughtful gesture and

thanked him for the unexpected treasure. Ian really could be quite thoughtful. A good friend, indeed.

Only when hearts and futures were at stake was he dangerous. . . .

The makings of a picnic in hand, they walked deeper into the city, to Settler's Park. Juliana gasped at the flower house, which contained exotic flowers of lush, vibrant petals, the likes of which she had never seen so close. The humid air settled around these jewels of nature as they unfurled to perfection in every color imaginable. She smiled in wonder, then turned to see Ian's expression.

He watched her with quiet contentment on his strong face.

"They are so lovely," she whispered.

"Indeed, I had heard so. I thought you might enjoy this."

Surprise assailed her, followed by a touch of something warm that curled in her chest. "You planned this for me?"

The thought touched Juliana. Yes, that was the feeling beating beneath her breasts, increasing the rhythm of her heart. Geoffrey would never have done anything of the sort for her, and she was grateful to Ian for the day's adventure.

"I planned this for us," he corrected her.

His kindness, his patience, his friendship—none of it matched what she had expected of this journey. Again—indeed, daily now—she was moved to consider the possibility he had changed. In fact, changed a great deal. Beyond his newfound consideration, Juliana enjoyed the relaxed confidence he exuded. He looked now like a man at ease with himself, certain of his place in the world—and his appeal with women. Though she had no real interest in wedding him, she was not blind to that appeal.

Her gaze dropped to his mouth. The kiss they had

shared early in the voyage floated through her memory. . . .

Blue eyes, both piercing and captivating, slid over her face with a thorough stare so intent, it was like a visual caress. Juliana could not look away. Her breath caught; her heartbeat picked up a few paces. He stood closer than propriety allowed, close enough to smell bay rum, salt, and man but, oddly, not close enough to appease her.

"One never knows when the chance to explore something new will come. We cannot let opportunity pass us by," he murmured.

Though Juliana had never considered that possibility, she realized he was right. And the suggestive note in his voice, as if the attraction between them were an opportunity . . . Had he intended that? Or did some foolish part of her that she did not understand assume he had?

"No, can't waste an opportunity," she whispered into the tense silence. "A brilliant thought."

The breeze ruffled the glossy waves of his nearly black hair, brushing the back of his collar now from neglect with the scissors. Somehow, on him the look was perfect, as if he were a modern pirate. The desire to feel his mouth on hers again became a desire that defied logic. It was not rational, she knew, but it existed all the same.

Disappointment stabbed her when he turned away to retrieve the basket of their food. "Hungry?"

The low voice hinted at innuendo, yet his expression held nothing untoward.

She was no naive girl; she knew about men and sex. She recognized their flirtations. Still, Ian's ploy was so subtle, she felt trapped in a state of confusion. Something anxious gripped her, as if by not responding to Ian in kind she would run the risk of missing an adventure.

Juliana shook her head. Surely that thought was nothing short of ridiculous.

"Since it is afternoon, we should eat," she said finally and without suggestion to gauge his reaction.

"Let's find a place to settle." Nothing in his face betrayed displeasure in her answer, but something in his manner made Juliana suspicious he felt it all the same.

Placing her hand back on his arm, Ian escorted her down a bricked path to rock pools with stepping stones. Across the pools lay some grassy areas suitable for a picnic.

Venturing out onto the stones, Ian reached behind for her hand once more and guided her along, curling his fingers around her waist when she nearly slipped on the slick stones. The heat of his touch soaked through her dress as if she could feel him skin to skin. The effect was unsettling. Somehow in that simple touch, she became aware of the breadth of his body, of the strength of his hands.

Blast it, she must cease such thoughts. They had no purpose.

Birds flew above as Ian picked a secluded spot for their meal, away from two British women and their children. More of the lush foliage and tropical flowers separated them from the rest of the world, filling the air with the opium of their scents. Juliana felt as if they had stepped into their own personal Eden. Paradise could not have been more beautiful, serene, sumptuous.

What a lovely spot for a kiss, a tender brush of hands, heartfelt sighs, and . . . a gentle joining.

The thought shocked her, but Juliana could not shake loose the fantasy of making love here, surrounded by nature's glory and floral-tinged air. Fine ribbons of heat coiled in her belly.

She should not indulge in such wicked thoughts. Making love in a public garden with only the grass beneath her, the faint sounds and exotic scents of nature around her and her lover . . . A downright scandalous thought—but a tempting one somehow. The heat in her belly wound around her thighs and warmed everything in between.

And still the thoughts would not abate. Even more outrageous, when she closed her eyes to indulge for a moment more in the fantasy of a lover's silken caresses in sultry, perfumed air, she imagined sharing it all with Ian.

Ian? Dear Lord, what was she thinking?

She wasn't thinking, not at all, but her body had a life of its own. That low heat suddenly became an ache.

Juliana forced her eyes open and found Ian sitting across from her, gaze fastened on her with questioning intent.

"You're flushed. Are you feeling well?"

The polite question fell from his lips, but the tone . . . Yes, the tone invited her to share her thoughts, as he was perfectly aware of them, shared them even.

The ache became a throb.

"It is a bit humid," she observed, fanning herself. *Please let him ignore the thick air between us.*

For if he kissed her now, she felt certain her odd desire would overcome her jangled nerves and she would meet him halfway in a melding of mouths that would melt her better judgment.

"And hot," he added to her statement as he poured her ale.

Hot? "What? Oh, yes."

He fell silent, and Juliana did not encourage any further talk. Instead, she took the opportunity to breathe deeply.

As they ate, the occasional call of a bird or shriek of a child served as their only reminder they were not wholly alone. Still, the illusion they were remained alluring, and Juliana could not shake her intimate thoughts. And though Ian's face gave away little, she suspected by the watchful set of his eyes, the manner in which he leaned closer, that he felt them.

Why should she be so attracted to him now? Yes, she liked him. But she liked a great number of men, found them easy to converse with. Most of those men she had never considered kissing even once.

She shook her head. Likely the surroundings merely gave her odd ideas. With such a perfect display of nature at its most opulent, perhaps it was expected that hedonistic thoughts enter her head.

Still, unless she wished Ian to think she wanted to wed him, she would be better off to forget her daydreams.

After they finished eating, she and Ian reluctantly left their Eden but knew they must return to the ship.

On their way to the *Houghton,* the mood between them lightened again. But Juliana could not ignore the disappointment that pressed in on her when Ian offered her nothing more than an impersonal touch on her arm as an escort.

Such disappointment was both foolish and dangerous. Juliana shook her head. Clearly, they had been wise to leave the garden. The heady place had affected her better judgment.

"You are far too quiet," he observed with a falsely teasing expression. "The fresh air has befuddled your brain."

Distracted by his banter—and oddly grateful for it—she swatted his arm playfully. "Of course not. I find the fresh air quite useful for thinking."

He groaned. "Oh, I must worry now, for I can only imagine what's in your head when you fall this silent on me."

With a sharp stare, she asked, "And just what, pray tell, do you mean?"

"Have you forgotten your cousin Megan?"

Juliana frowned, trying to discern his meaning. "Of

course, I haven't—oh, you refer to her dancing."
Then, as she recalled the incident shortly after her
come-out, Juliana smiled, somehow thankful for
another direction in which to focus her mind.
"Nobody would dance with the poor girl. It took me
some moments to devise a plan, but I did not really
believe you would mind saving her from a danceless
evening."

"Normally, no. I admit, she was pleasant enough,
but she trounced my feet with all the grace of an
elephant." He laughed. "Admit it, you sought to
punish me."

Juliana felt her smile fade and her mood darken
as she recalled that evening. Ian had tried to dissuade
her from caring for Geoffrey by bringing up his lowly
birth and spendthrift ways. More surprising, Ian had
hinted broadly of his own marital intentions only the
day before. For some reason, the thought of wedding
Ian had frightened her beyond her wits. Juliana had
never understood why exactly. She knew only that
her feelings on the matter were somewhat different
now. How different, and in what way, she could not
say.

What would marriage to Ian truly be like? The
hell she had suspected before, or something quite
different? Lacking an answer for the question—and
any certainty she wanted one—Juliana pushed the
speculation aside.

Casting a thoughtful gaze at him, she admitted,
"You're right. I wished to punish you, though not
through poor Megan."

"My behavior warranted it, I suppose. But I did it
only because you deserved better than Archer."

Yes, she had. But Juliana had made her choice,
and she accepted that. She took responsibility for her
actions.

"I'm sorry my interference distressed you," he said
softly.

Something else inside her chest warmed, then melted. Maybe it was the sincerity in his blue eyes or the genuine regret in his low whisper. Whatever it was, she believed him.

Again, she felt compelled to consider that she had misjudged him. Perhaps she had misjudged him all along. Or maybe he had changed in the past five years. She had changed a great deal herself. Geoffrey, India, and disillusionment had altered her. Whatever the difference, their friendship now felt unlike it had before. Oh, she still took comfort in it, but it was not comfortable. Her odd awareness of him—his mouth, the way he moved his hands, knowing there was always something faintly sensual in his eyes—made complete comfort in their friendship impossible. But what they shared was special, more mature than the bond between them before her marriage. This time, she hoped, more lasting.

She offered, "I'm sorry for distrusting you so thoroughly when you first arrived in India. I confess, I'm very glad you came. In doing my family and me a great favor, I feel as if I've gained back the friend I lost years ago." She clutched his arm harder. "That is important to me."

Ian took her hand in his and squeezed it. Warmth curled through her fingers and up her arm. Not for the first time today, she wondered why she experienced these sensations with Ian and none of her other male acquaintances. In fact, she liked him in a manner she had not ever experienced before, a manner that defied explanation.

"I am glad to know that," he said softly.

He raised a hand to her face. Juliana held her breath. Would he kiss her now? Her heart beat hard, seemed to flutter in a way she could not fathom. Then his thumb brushed her bottom lip. Tingles erupted. His finger joined his thumb, creating a fray of sensation. He smiled, something so tender, the very softness melted her.

Then she realized he had captured a stray strand of her shimmering pale hair that clung to her mouth. He tucked the hair behind her ear and dropped his hand to his side.

"Your friendship is so very important to me," he whispered.

Without another word, he bid her good night and left her standing alone to be touched only by the night wind.

CHAPTER FIVE

As the days of the journey slipped past, a certain calm returned to her relations with Ian. Most days they now filled with chatter, an occasional game, and laughter, as if they were—and always had been—the best of friends.

But Juliana found she still thought of him in a different manner. She wondered about him as a lover, as she had in Port Elizabeth. Away from the sensual influence of the perfumed South African air, she had believed her thoughts would resume their decorous slant. That was not the case.

Still, she could not—would not—marry him. To give him any undue attention would make him think otherwise.

Such a resolution should have been enough to put him from her mind. It was not.

Six weeks after their last stop, the *Houghton* docked briefly again for provisions on the small island of St. Helena. Again, Ian and Juliana disembarked. The island treated them to a visual feast of rushing streams, lush, sharp cliffs, and thick forest. It was primitive and densely green—and unlike anything she had ever seen. Its exotic nature heightened her senses.

With this colorful atmosphere, Juliana could not ignore her ever-sharpening awareness of Ian, tall and male beside her.

As they wandered onto the island, he folded her hand in his, thumb brushing her hand in slow, rhythmic strokes. Aware of his movements, his very breath, they made their way through the small port town founded by the Portuguese some three hundred and fifty years before. From the looks of the port, little had changed, for the trappings of civilization were few.

At her side, Ian gazed at her with a riot of messages that matched the untamed land around them. And she thought of his mouth, found herself looking at his hands, large, square, containing such strength. Inside, she heated, felt alive and anxious, as if she waited for something. His touch?

Juliana did her best to shake away thoughts of intimacy, but as they returned to the *Houghton* in silence, she could not. Not with Ian's hand still firmly around her own.

Once on the ship again, Juliana fidgeted as she stood on the deck. The anticipation she'd been feeling for the past few weeks was growing. Juliana gazed at Ian intently, alternately willing him to understand and praying he did not.

The lush island slowly faded from view as the ship sailed. More lazy blue days passed. Then fall came, bringing crisp air as they drew closer to England.

More and more, Juliana found herself anticipating the days she spent with Ian. They talked nearly without taking a breath and played cards regularly. Ian did not seem perturbed to lose—though he did win far more than she remembered. He teased her about missing India's spicy foods, while she taunted him about the childlike amount of sugar he preferred in his tea. These days satisfied her. He made no mention of the painful parts of their shared past, said nothing of a future marriage between them. They simply behaved like chums of old, and Juliana found herself oddly grateful for the resurrection of their friendship.

All in all, she was pleased.

Well . . . somewhat.

She waited for the air between her and Ian to settle. And she waited. Despite the fact she and Ian were on happy terms again, an air of something . . . tense, too aware, lingered.

Finally, they reached the last night of their voyage. Juliana again stood at the ship's deck, feeling the chilly October wind play with the ends of her hair, which hung comfortably loose. That same evening breeze tugged at the hem of her gray serge dress as she looked out over the vast blue eternity of the ocean behind them. In her mind she saw a pair of eyes equally entrancing and blue.

Blast it, she could not deny that she had been unable to forget that disturbing kiss their first week aboard the ship. It replayed itself in her mind at the oddest times—as he sat across from her, expressive eyes laughing, dark hair ruffled by the wind. Or when he read to her from the volume of *David Copperfield* she had insisted they share. His thoroughly male face showed great pleasure in the tale, and questioning if he would bring the same vitality to a lover's bed roused her curiosity . . . and more. Or at night, when she lay down to sleep in her solitary bed, Juliana wondered if he remembered their kiss too, wondered if he too, thought of matters more intimate.

Heaven help her. Madness had finally overtaken her.

She was not disturbed that she liked him, for she had liked him very much as a girl. But this was different. Now she seemed to like him so well, she could think of little else.

A light touch upon her shoulder alerted her to Ian's presence. She turned to find him inches behind her, the settling dusk casting golden rays and intriguing shadows on the strong angles of his face.

"You look deep in thought," he remarked.

She had been, and about him, but sharing that with him seemed unwise. True, he no longer spoke of wanting her for a wife, but she could hardly bring the matter up without giving him the impression she might wish to find a parson.

Juliana purposely selected another topic. "The captain said we will dock in London tomorrow."

"Yes."

"I am eager to be home, I confess. After so many years away, I have little notion what to expect."

"Do not anticipate many changes at Harbrooke. That is ever the same."

Juliana nodded, pensive. "You are no doubt right. I—I simply hope I am not too late to see Papa. Do you think he—"

"We must believe he will be there for you," Ian soothed, clasping her shoulder. "Whatever was ailing him when I left did not progress overnight."

Placing her hand over his, she smiled into his eyes. "I hope that is the case. We . . . we have a great deal to talk about, I suppose."

"Yes, you do," he agreed quickly.

Juliana sighed, a sense of panic as she thought of facing her father again. Once, she would have never imagined that confiding in Ian would bring her comfort. Tonight, she wanted to confide in him so deeply, it surprised her.

"Ian?" The salty autumn wind stung her eyes. Certainly they teared for no other reason. "I'm frightened."

Concern stamped itself into the furrow between

his dark brows. He reached for her hand. "Frightened, why? Your father wants you home."

"And part of me—most of me—wishes to be there. But I worry. . . . What if his health fails? What if we cannot get along? I fear he will want to control my life again. What if—"

"Shhh," he whispered, slicking a soft hand over her hair. "Worry about that tomorrow, if you must. But think nothing more of it until you're certain you have cause to worry."

Slowly, she nodded. Ian brought her closer. Comfort assailed her, even as something forbidden sparked deep inside. She reveled in his strength, his light, even breathing, his solidity. Juliana laid her head on his chest, lulled by the steady beat of his heart.

Perhaps her father had changed, as Ian suggested. Ian himself had. Six months ago, she could not imagine allowing this contact, much less confessing her fears about her father to him. Somehow, doing so seemed . . . natural now.

"Juliana?" he called softly.

She raised her head, her gaze locking onto his blue eyes, rife with some expression she could not decipher, yet conveyed hunger. Everything within her became alert, leapt to attention. She held her breath. He reached for her.

Ian curled his hand around her neck, tilted her face toward his. She heard the thud of her heart.

"Juliana?" he repeated in a whisper.

"Yes." Her voice suddenly trembled.

"I know Christmas is seven weeks away, but your mourning is over. And this voyage has only deepened my feelings for you."

Surprise caught her breath in her throat. Yet she knew what he would say next—knew it for certain. And she did not know how to reply.

"You—you haven't mentioned marriage for months," she stammered. "I thought . . ."

"I wanted to give you time to know me again, to consider how right this could be."

Juliana could only stare in mute indecision. Ian's silence in the matter had persuaded her that he understood her position about marriage. And on the day she had promised to spend time with him, she had done so believing he could not tempt her in any way to want him as a husband.

Now uncertainty assailed her.

His rapt gaze fastened on her. The large hand clasped behind her neck tightened infinitesimally, then tilted her face up to him farther. His mouth hovered close. Juliana felt a warm flush across her skin, felt her heart beating, beating. . . .

"Say yes this time," he implored. "I will make you happy."

Juliana hardly knew what to say, with the warm rush of his breath against her mouth. The intensity of his blue eyes, the closeness of his body, slowed her thoughts. Marry him? She frowned, uncertain, nearly unable to think. She wanted him. Yes, she did, in a carnal way, with which she was ill at ease. But to speak vows with Ian? For forever? That she did not know. Dare she trust him? Did she even wish to wed again?

Before she could answer those questions, Ian dragged his thumb along her jaw. Tingles scattered along the surface of her skin. This she wanted. Confusion about marriage raged, along with a breathless expectation for his kiss. Ian's eyes narrowed, focused on her lips. Juliana quit breathing.

Just once more, she told herself.

Ian brushed her mouth with his.

Her heart surged with a thud against her chest as he feathered his lips over hers. Ian molded her response with the softest stroke of his mouth, cajoled her with a long, ragged sigh. She leaned into him, aching as she never had, wishing with all her might he would truly kiss her, claim her mouth has he had before.

Ian lifted his head to stare into her eyes. One breath, two. Silence broken only by his uneven breathing.

"Juliana . . ."

"Yes." *Kiss me,* she pleaded silently. *Again.*

Ian sought her once more, brushing a ghost of a kiss across her lips. She yearned for it even as frustration spiked within her. Desperation roused a moan from her.

Kiss me!

Pushing away Ian's hand from about her neck, Juliana seized his shoulders in a fierce grip and dragged him to her, pressing her mouth squarely against his. At once, she realized her kiss was dry and artless, full of more pressure than passion. It appeased her . . . yet it did not. Nor was it likely to tempt Ian.

She wanted more and moaned again in discontent.

Ian responded instantly. His hand at her hip slid around to her back, drawing her closer. He slipped his free arm around her shoulders, threading his hand into her hair, anchoring her face just beneath his. With a stroke of his mouth, he opened her lips to him.

Once inside, he conquered. The artless kiss quickly became a thing of burning beauty as his tongue swept through her mouth in a molten mating that reduced her to flushed dizziness. A breathy moan escaped her as she clung to him, fingers digging into the dark coat covering his solid shoulders.

"Yes. Yes . . ." he whispered against her lips before he plundered her mouth once more.

Stroking, seeking, giving her pleasure, he clasped her to him. Time slid away in a heated haze, measured by heartbeats and sighs.

Ian's fingers drifted down her back to the swell of her hip again. He nudged her closer to his body. Juliana could not mistake the thick feel of his arousal against her. She pressed herself against him.

The knowledge of his excitement stirred something illicit within her, something that begged for free rein, something she had never felt with Geoffrey. She had seen her husband's occasional visits to her chamber as her wifely duty, had never imagined the act would inspire anything more than tolerance. Ian's kiss stirred so very much more.

In fact, when he touched her like this, Juliana felt so swept away in sensation, she could scarcely think.

"Marry me," he said between panting breaths.

Juliana blinked into the twilight. All hint of sunlight was gone now, fallen from the sky in the minutes of their kiss, and she'd been oblivious. How disquieting that he had so much control over her mind when he kissed her. She could not trust herself to think clearly.

In fact, that realization was nothing short of disturbing.

She stepped away. The night breezed over her heated body, cooling it, bringing focus back to her hazy mind. Stance guarded, Ian watched her.

He had proposed marriage again. She sighed, torn. Yes, she had come to like Ian. He no longer appeared to be the manipulative cad who had done his best to send Geoffrey thousands of miles away from her. She could not imagine the man before her would send his mistress to Geoffrey to prove her betrothed's faithlessness.

But Ian *had* done those things. Juliana knew she must not forget that. She must be careful of giving him her trust.

"I cannot answer you now."

Instantly, his face tightened, became a glower of anguish and rejection. "Juliana, say yes. I will stand by you, no matter what. I will wait, if need be. But give me hope, love."

Juliana had a difficult time resisting such an entreaty as she reached out and touched his arm. "Please understand," she whispered. "I cannot yet. Let me spend some time with my father. I've scarce finished my period of mourning Geoffrey; give me enough time to be certain I will not be mourning my father as well. I have promised to answer you on Christmas Day, and I shall."

Stillness and silence fell between them. He frowned, looking so painfully alone—and so temptingly handsome.

"Ian, I'm sorry. I—"

"I understand," he cut in. "I want you to be certain when we exchange vows. I shall await your answer on Christmas Day."

His gaze caressed her cheek an instant before his palm did. As his fingers slid down the side of her face, he turned away.

An unsettled week later, Juliana sat atop her mount, taking in the familiar sharp cliffs and wooded valleys surrounding Lynton. Ian sat silent at her side. They had long since left behind the carriage carrying their trunks in the hands of Ian's servants so they might hurry to Harbrooke.

As they neared her home, the weak afternoon sun filtered across the landscape, shedding light on the last of the rich reds, golds, and russets that signified the decline of the year. The trees lining the dirt road swayed with the early November wind, teasing her with images of Harbrooke between their dancing branches. Juliana caught a glimpse of a chimney here, a window there, had an overall impression of the manor house's cream-colored facade.

Her heart accelerated, and near bursting with

impatience, Juliana nudged her horse with her heels. A clippity-clop behind her told her Ian followed. Cantering down the road, she reached the mouth of the lane to her house quickly and rounded the bend.

Harbrooke came into full view in all its exquisite beauty, revealing itself in a gasp of perfection, made more vivid by the explosion of fall colors.

Welcoming steps led up to a series of Doric columns in the Roman fashion that supported a stately pediment carved with heroic battles. The surrounding cornice was fluted and elegant. The door stood open in welcome. The rest of the manor house rambled behind it, a testament to the many times her ancestors had expanded Harbrooke, adding their own touch. Windows gleamed like watchful eyes, as if signaling the fact it, and everyone within, had been waiting for her arrival.

The mount galloping beneath her, Juliana ignored her breathlessness and reveled in her sense of belonging, of home, that stole through her heart in a warm taking.

At the top of the stairs, everyone she loved dearly stood. Her mother at the edge of the porch, arm wrapped around a wide column, smiled in greeting with suspiciously tearful eyes. A smattering of servants from her girlhood stood just behind her mother. Smythe, the butler, along with Monsieur DuVires, their chef, waved eagerly in the cluster of familiar faces.

Her father, the esteemed earl, sat in a chair near the door and eyed her with a guarded smile. Her heart stilled.

He was alive!

Juliana could not reach the first of Harbrooke's steps fast enough. As she vaulted off her mount, her mother awaited her, nearly shaking with excitement.

Lady Brownleigh had aged in the last five years, her hair now mostly gray, soft lines framing her brown eyes and fading mouth. Her shoulders looked some-what stooped, and she was too thin. Such reminders of time passing made Juliana fiercely glad that Ian had persuaded her to come home before it was too late.

Her mother met her with a quiet, fierce hug. Juliana embraced her, eyes squeezed shut, feeling the rise of hot, joyful tears, a fierce sense of homecoming.

"Mama, I've missed you so," she whispered.

"Not as much as I have missed you, dearest." Her mother's voice cracked. "Oh, how I've wanted you home . . ."

At her sides, Smythe and Monsieur DuVires appeared.

"Good to have you home, my lady," said the butler.

"*Oui*, very good," agreed the chef.

Still wrapped in her mother's embrace, she smiled at each of them. "Lord, it is good to be back. I missed Harbrooke."

"I understand. I know you disliked India."

She had written as much to her mother in a moment of weakness. And Juliana wasn't pleased her mother had passed that information along to her father, and in doing so, to Ian. But what was done was done. Knowing Mama had a soft heart, Juliana was not surprised she had been unable to keep such a secret in the face of Papa's persistent questions.

Papa . . .

Juliana's gaze snapped to his chair. It stood empty now. Backing away from her mother's hug, Juliana looked about, only to see him standing a few paces behind her, shaking Ian's hand. The two men shared a low-voiced exchange and smiles.

She watched them carefully. Papa and Ian were neighbors, and her father would naturally be grateful that Ian had expended nine months to fetch his only daughter home before he ailed permanently. But something gave her a moment's unease.

Stepping toward her father with a thudding heart, Juliana regarded him. As Ian had said, Papa had put on weight in the last five years. No denying that. But his color looked fair, if a bit rosy. And he smiled like a man without a care.

He turned his hazel gaze upon her and reached out to her in invitation. Juliana went toward him, hands outstretched as well. They clasped fingers. Her father squeezed her hands in his warm palms. Juliana, lost in the moment, refused to dwell on the reasons she'd spent the last five years cursing her sire. She chose to recall the fact he had given her life.

A fresh wave of homecoming, of gladness at her return, swept over her as they clutched hands. And he looked quite good, robust even. It relieved her. Oh, he had aged. Like her mother, his hair had grown gray. Wrinkles had grown more prominent around his eyes. The walking cane nearby suggested he did not navigate the many stairways and long halls of Harbrooke with the ease he once had.

But he looked so much better than she had dared to hope.

"Juliana," he said, clasping her hands all the tighter. "Finally, we have you back in England, where you belong."

Though Juliana did not want anyone—most of all her father—believing he could tell her where she did or did not belong, she said nothing. After all, he was an older man now and still of frail health certainly, even if he did not much look the part today. No sense in arguing the point this instant, for England, indeed, Harbrooke especially, was where she most longed to be.

"It is good to be home," she whispered.

An instant later, Ian and her mother joined Juliana and her father in a tight circle. Her father clapped Ian on the back. Ian sent her father a smile that looked oddly stilted. She wondered why but realized he must be as tired as she.

At her side, her mother gasped suddenly. "My, I did not mean to leave you standing outside in this chilly wind. Oh, and you traveling in it. I hate to think of that. You two must come in and take tea."

Juliana nodded, eager for the warmth it would bring as well as the ease of her rumbling stomach.

"Thank you," murmured Ian. "After a day with very little food to recommend itself, I happily accept."

"Come in, then. It's been prepared for you."

With that, Juliana's mother turned to her father and offered her one arm. His free hand clasped the cane. Did he need both her mother's help and the cane's to balance? Juliana doubted her fragile mother was up to the task of supporting the robust Lord Brownleigh.

Once more, Juliana felt a glad feeling steal through her. She had come home in time. If her father was fading, he was doing so slowly enough that Juliana would still have some days, perhaps even weeks or months, to be with him before something should happen.

She reached up to pat his shoulder.

Before she could, her father handed the cane to her mother, who alternately hobbled on it and leaned against her father's tall figure all the way back to Harbrooke's foyer and beyond.

Juliana could only stare in stunned silence.

Two days later, Juliana entered the breakfast room to find her father reading the newspaper and indulging in a plate of eggs and pastries after a surprisingly late night of cards with neighboring Lord Bouston. Her mother imbibed at tea and dry toast, the cane at her side. The scene pierced her with a sense of uneasiness she had been fighting almost from the moment she arrived home.

Her mother—not her father—looked horribly frail. Faded, even. While, in her estimation, her father looked quite well for an ailing man. In fact, she had seen him look nothing but the image of health. He carried few pounds too many—and more than she remembered—but so did many men his age. That alone should alarm no one.

So why had Ian been so alarmed?

Suspicion reared its head. Had Papa persuaded Ian to lie to her so she would return here, where together they could do their utmost to control her future? Could the Ian she'd come to know on the journey from India betray her in such a fashion again? Juliana closed her eyes. She did not want to believe he could lie to her while his actions bespoke friendship and his eyes shone with devotion. But the possibility could not be overlooked. And it hurt her like a kick to the belly.

Papa stuffed a scone in his mouth and gulped from his teacup as he rose. "I must shove off. I promised Reverend Collins I would drop in to discuss the church's repairs."

Juliana regarded him dubiously. "Whatever for? You are not his patron. Lord Chatfield has that honor. Let him take care of that."

"Everyone knows Chatfield hasn't the sense to rub two rocks together. Besides, Collins and I plan some hunting as well."

Hunting? A man with a supposedly serious heart problem felt well enough to hunt?

Juliana shifted from skeptical to disbelieving.

"Hunting." Mama shuddered, frowning. "Did you remember to walk this morning?"

"What?" He sipped his tea again. "Oh, yes. Damn and blast, that foolish physician. I'm certain all I shall receive for such trouble is a chill."

Her mother sighed in frustration. "James, have you not been feeling better in the three months you've been walking?"

He opened his mouth and hesitated. He cast a quick glance in Juliana's direction, then closed his mouth once more.

With his guilty pause, Juliana felt even more certain that her father was not actually ill. Had he ever been?

The suspicion she'd been fighting since her first night home strengthened their roots and began to grow.

Her father cleared his throat. "It was all well and fine in the September sunshine. But now . . ." He shivered. "The air is crisp with the coming winter, and I'm certain no one in his right mind would continue traipsing out of doors once snow falls. I certainly do not plan on it! We knew all along Dr. Haney might be wrong. He was a young pup anyway."

"So you're feeling better?" Juliana asked, skewering her father with a direct stare that demanded an answer.

Again, he paused. "Somewhat. Though your mother and Ian—and I daresay even myself—feared the worst for a bit, I'm feeling improved."

"Because you've done a bit of walking?" Juliana did not believe him, and it showed in her voice.

"No, no," he blustered. "Walking is mostly for nannies and children, eh?"

Juliana did not respond to her father's jest.

"He has cut down on brandy," her mother offered into the silence. "And begun to eat a lowering diet. More fish and less lamb is good for nearly anybody according to Dr. Haney."

Excuses and half-truths, that's all she heard. And the fact that Ian had made himself scarce less than an hour after delivering her to Harbrooke, into her father's hands, only added to her misgivings.

"Indeed," she murmured instead, staring with a speculative eye at her father.

As if he sensed the nature of her thoughts, he walked toward the door. "Well, I must be off. Can't keep Reverend Collins waiting."

Something was definitely suspicious. Juliana was almost certain of that now. "Hunting is strenuous. Is that wise in your condition?"

"What do you imply with your tone?" her father barked as he whirled to face her.

So, he wanted to take the offense. Once he did, Lord Brownleigh would be much more formidable. If she were going to prove her suspicion, she could not use her father to do it.

Juliana risked a glance across the table. If her father had used her mother to obtain information about his daughter in faraway India, why should she not return the favor and have a go wheedling information out of her mother?

"I meant nothing at all," she lied smoothly, smiling. "I didn't sleep quite well. I'm sure you understand."

Her father scowled as if he didn't quite believe her. *Good, now the feeling is mutual.*

"Get some rest, then," he ordered gruffly and left.

As soon as he quit the house, Juliana turned to her mother, who even now made to rise. Normally, Juliana did not invite confrontation. But in this case, where her very future hung in the balance, she required some answers.

She must know if Papa—and Ian—had duped her again.

"Mama, sit down. Why rush around? Can we not talk?"

Nodding slowly, her mother stared at her hands, folded tightly on the table before her. "Juliana, do not stir up trouble with your father."

"Would that be bad for his health?"

She sighed tiredly. "Although I am quite concerned for family harmony at this moment, that is possible as well."

"And what of your health?" she asked softly.

Her mother's gaze snapped up, and she reached a bony hand across the table to grasp Juliana's fingers. "Oh, you mustn't worry, dearest. Nothing is amiss with me. As I told you, I simply fell down a few stairs and hurt my ankle. I spent more days in bed than was good for me and I am just now regaining my strength. Do not worry for a moment about me."

Juliana hoped that was true as she squeezed her mother's hand before releasing it. "I'm pleased to hear you're recovering. I hate to think of you both in ill health," she said. "Though I feel much better now that I understand what's ailing you. But what of Papa? I'm curious about this illness of his. Ian described it as being related to his heart."

"Dr. Haney rather feared it was," she murmured.

"How awful! Did you agree?"

Her mother shrugged. "Juliana, I am hardly a physician."

"Naturally, Mama. I am merely concerned. Is Papa truly ill?"

"Though he is much improved now, earlier this year he suffered so from fatigue and dizziness."

Juliana frowned. "Might that have been an influenza?"

"Oh, no," her mother assured. "Your father's ailments lasted for months, much longer than influenza."

"So you believed Papa's illness was nothing minor? That it might pose a risk to his very life?"

Her mother shrugged, suddenly enthralled by the half-eaten piece of toast on her plate. "We were not certain. Such episodes are so difficult to understand or predict."

Perhaps her mother spoke the truth, but her explanations sounded nothing less than weak. Juliana's suspicions grew.

"Did Papa think of himself as being gravely ill?"

"You know your father; he hates to be even remotely fallible."

True, but the explanation still bothered her.

"He is stubborn, isn't he?" Juliana affected a laugh, and her mother seemed to relax. "Well, when did Papa start feeling better?"

"Oh . . ." Her mother stared at the ceiling, as if trying to recall. "A few months after Ian left for India, perhaps in July or August."

Juliana pondered the answer, wondering if it wasn't a bit too convenient.

"What a relief that must have been for you."

"For us all." Her mother nodded.

"Indeed. But he looks rather well now." She paused. "In fact, he looks remarkable for a man nearing sixty."

Her mother's brown eyes widened, and she looked away. "You know your father. He's always taken pride in his appearance."

Juliana sighed. She had tried every way she could think of to persuade her mother to tell her of any ploy Ian and her father might share. But if her mother had one downfall, it was her unswerving loyalty to a man who neither loved nor appreciated her. Only the direct approach would suffice.

"Indeed, but I must confess to a moment of cynicism."

That brought her mother's gaze up once more. "Cynicism?"

"Papa and Ian have been known to hatch schemes in the past to mold my future."

Her mother hesitated, then looked away, saying not a word.

Juliana's suspicions grew again. "Did they, perhaps,

decide to embellish Papa's illness and use it to bring me home?''

Her mother said nothing for a full minute. A clock in the nearby study chimed. A bird sang its song outside the window. Lady Brownleigh sighed.

"Mama?" she urged.

Folding her hands in her lap, her mother tilted her head, clearly choosing her words with care. "I know your father wanted you home, as did Ian. We feared for you in India all the while you lived there. But without the protection of a husband—even an absent one—we fretted you might be overtaken by one of the natives, or fall prey to another blackguard."

As answers went, her mother's was incomplete. But it hinted that her suspicions had been true. Still, Juliana wanted—no, *needed*—the truth about Papa's and Ian's intentions. Especially, she felt an urgency to know if Ian, whom she had come to truly trust during the last half of their journey together, had lied to her once more.

"Mama, does that mean yes or no?"

Another long pause. Her mother began wringing her hands. "Juliana, perhaps you should speak with your father about this."

"Yes or no?" she demanded, unmoved.

Her mother bit her lip and toyed with a ruffle of lace upon her sleeve. "He did not know for certain if his illness was grave when Ian left for India. Embellished is a strong word."

"Is it? Ian told me Papa's ailment would likely end his life, despite being less than certain apparently. I think that qualifies as an embellishment."

"They were merely concerned for you, dearest." As she wrung her hands again, Mama's voice pleaded with her to keep the peace and say nothing.

Concerned, my corset! Fury burned in a white-hot ball in Juliana's belly. They had duped her, just as she'd suspected, using her innate concern for her family to control her—again. She had never trusted her father and was no more than mildly surprised by his part in the deception. But Ian . . .

He had betrayed her horribly—again.

His perfidy cut deep, slashing into her like a knife. He had smiled at her, kissed her, and cajoled her trust. And he had been less than honest all the while. The damned blackguard! Words alone could not describe how vile she considered his behavior.

Despite her mother's wishes, there was absolutely no way she could let this manipulation pass without a word.

In fact, she had many words she wanted to express, and she would speak with her father when he returned from cowering with the good reverend.

Ian, however, she would confront without delay.

CHAPTER SIX

Ian approached the door to Edgefield Park's coziest drawing room, anticipation surging through him like the most potent brandy.

Juliana had come to him—finally.

The three days he had given her alone with her family had been difficult but necessary. Absence made the heart grow fonder, or so someone had said. He'd gambled on that being true. So when his butler, Harmon, had announced Juliana's arrival, Ian prayed she had come because she'd missed him.

As he entered the softly shaded, book-lined room, he knew instantly he had been gravely mistaken.

Fury bounded in her hazel eyes, and his anticipation died.

With dread sinking in his stomach, Ian suspected his worst fear these last few days had come to pass: Juliana had discerned his scheme with Brownleigh.

Damn the man for not having the wits to at least look sick when Juliana arrived home. It was clear she thought the worst.

Panic, then denial, crept in. His optimism crumbled. Now she would give him hell. And he could only hope to find ways to diffuse her anger, convince her that he had acted in her best interest, not in duplicity.

"You slithering cad." Her voice vibrated with anger.

Ian tried not to flinch at her ferocity.

"How can you sleep, knowing you are more slippery than the lowest serpent?"

He contemplated pretending ignorance. In the end, he respected her intelligence too much. She knew the truth; he could not deny that. Doing so would only infuriate her more.

"Juliana, I did not intentionally lie to you."

"Damned if you didn't! You said my father was *dying.*"

"No," he refuted. "I never did."

Would she never believe him for more than an instant? Ever trust him? Bloody hell, why wouldn't she try at least? Stubborn chit.

"You said exactly that!"

His anger peaked. "Damn it, I told you he did not look well and that I was concerned. That was not a lie!"

Another burst of rage tightened her pink mouth to a white line. "Then you claimed the ailment was serious. And what was I to make of that? Together with your sudden appearance in India, I could only assume he had one foot in the grave."

"I understand your assumption," he soothed, moving closer. He ignored the narrowing of her eyes and pressed on. "I told you exactly what the physician had told your parents to that moment, that your father may be suffering from a heart condition. That is and always was true."

Juliana leaned in and growled, "Then why is he out *hunting* today? That is certainly not the sport of a dying man. He does not look as if he's near the grave either. *If* he was ever ill, it certainly was of little consequence. And you used it to deceive me! You two vultures preyed upon my fear to bring me back here, where you *think* you can control me. Think again.''

Ian reached out, clasping his hands around Juliana's slim shoulders. She wrenched away from him, her eyes spitting fire.

"Do not touch me," she warned.

He sighed. He had seen Juliana angry on more than one occasion. Hell, he remembered the night she realized that he had both obtained Archer's marching orders to India and sent his mistress to her betrothed's bed. He had thought Juliana's fury could not be exceeded after that.

Clearly, he had been wrong.

"Your father looks better than he did when I left for India," he offered quietly.

Gaping, Juliana rolled her eyes. "Have you any clue how inane that sounds? As excuses go, it's dreadful." She made a sound of disgust. "You've always been a skillful liar. I'm surprised you could not do better this time."

Her sarcasm and accusations riled him. Was it his fault he had to drop a few less-than-true words here and there to protect her from her headstrong ways? In her rigid mind, yes. Now it was up to him to divert her energy until her temper cooled.

"Juliana, I have no defense except the one I've given you. It appears that your father finally started listening to the physician and it has brought results. I congratulated him on his improvement the very day of our arrival."

Disbelief shaping her lovely face, she sneered. "Oh, I saw you two, all handshakes and smiles, no doubt congratulating one another on dragging me back to Lynton. My father clearly wants me back under his control. And you?" She laughed. "You need to go to this length, sail around the world and lie in order to win a bride? And here I thought with your looks and charm you might win a woman without trickery."

"I want *you*," he countered. "Damn it, I want only you."

His soft, honest sentence had no impact other than to strengthen her resolve. "You will not win me. That scheme you and my father shared ensured that neither of you will win your way." Juliana snapped her reticule back around her wrist. "I have no need to wait for Christmas. Let me assure you now that I will never wed you."

Ian sucked in a breath. Anguish and horror pounded him. Blindly, he reached out for her, grabbing her arm and bringing her closer.

"No," he nearly pleaded. "Listen, you've been home but a few days. Perhaps your father is having a good spell. Perhaps he's truly recovered. But he *was* ill when I left."

"Stop with your lies!" she demanded. "Do you have no notion when to quit?"

"Juliana, you're angry and confused—"

"And it's your fault!"

He tightened his grip. "Listen to me. I know you think I've dealt you some untruths—"

"You have," she rejoined, pulling away from him.

Ian let her comment pass. "No matter what you feel, you must know I love you."

"I cannot believe that either. If you truly loved me, you would have come to India with something other than deceit in your plans."

He grasped her shoulders again. "Would you have come home if I had said your father was mildly ill with something the physicians can't name, and that I desperately wanted to marry you? No."

She wriggled away from his grasp, eyes narrowed. "So you lied to get what you wanted. How typical of you."

"That is not so!" Ian's blue gaze drilled into her.

Juliana held her ground, fury swelling, seething, giving her strength. "How can you say—"

"What if your family and I *had* treated his illness as nothing, decided to inform you by letter—or not worry you at all?" Ian paused, raising a questioning brow. "What if the illness had been serious, even grave? Can you not say you are glad to see your father once more?" He paused, hoping his words would move her. When she said nothing, he added, "We erred on the side of caution, Juliana. Neither of us wanted you to be too late, just in case."

"My, how pretty you make that sound." She tilted her head, her expression tinged with regret. "And if you were anyone else, I might believe it."

"Don't—"

"Don't say another word," she demanded, jabbing a finger into his chest. "Do not contact me. Or court me. Do not bother returning to Harbrooke to see me. I will refuse you."

"No, Juliana. I—"

"Nothing you say will sway me. You have done your best to deceive me every time I trusted you, and I am finished. Consider our little Christmas arrangement at an end."

"That is a breach of your promise."

Juliana stopped, her cheeks red and her fists clenched, looking like she wanted to hit something— or someone. "Waiting six weeks will change nothing I say to you. If you intend to hold me to that promise, then I shall spend my time searching for a husband who does not lie to me with every breath."

Before Ian could argue that she had agreed to spend time with him, Juliana brushed past him and out the drawing room door. He stared at her departure, dumbfounded, haunted by her soft scent.

So she planned to refuse him, after he'd given up nearly a year of his life to bring her home? Despite the fact he desperately needed a bride to see his breeding stables come to fruition? Even though he loved her completely?

No. Juliana might refuse to admit him to her home, but he would make certain he was never far from her thoughts.

Ian stared moodily into the fire, a fresh glass of brandy in hand. He took a healthy swallow, wishing he could forget the last hour. Juliana had been gone only minutes, but he feared his feelings for her, no matter how unrequited, would last a blasted lifetime.

Damn.

"I'm told Lady Archer left here moments ago, her temper piqued," said a familiar voice from the door.

Ian whirled to see his father standing there. A short man Ian had towered over since age fourteen, Nathaniel Pierce always felt the need to be right and have the last word. He possessed no heart and seemed happily unaware of the fact.

They could not have been more opposite if they had tried.

Normally, Ian dealt with his father by ignoring him. Tonight, however, Ian was a jumble of despair, anger, and frustration. Nathaniel would get the fight he so desperately sought.

Tweaking his wiry mustache, Ian's father shut the door softly behind him. The click of the latch resounded in the silence.

"Juliana's temper is my concern," Ian said, then downed the last of his brandy.

As he reached for more, his father sent him an angry scowl. "Your refusal to find a bride affects us all. Do your duty, damn it! I'm asking very little of you to acquire a fortune."

Sarcasm vibrated in his father's every word. Ian felt

each sound like a blow as he poured his brandy. He clamped his teeth together to prevent lashing out.

"I've found a bride," he said, refusing to admit defeat where Juliana was concerned.

"Find another," his father snapped back. "She does not want you, you idiot. Get you a pretty, docile creature of good family who will let you bed her silly until you get a child on her."

Ian's stomach clenched. His father never thought with anything other than his prick or his pocketbook. And the older Ian became, the more he understood why his mother had spent the last twenty years away from home, refusing to see her husband at every opportunity possible. They both took lovers as often as a fashionable lady changed gloves.

Together, they made a mockery of marriage. Ian was determined to have more.

"I can find a pretty, docile creature to bed anytime I want. Juliana is far more interesting. Soon she will admit she wants to wed me."

His father spit out a mean laugh as he dropped onto the sofa. "You must be blind. If you could not woo her five years ago or seduce her when you were alone on the sea in six long months, why do you imagine you will suddenly succeed?"

Ian refused to wince. His father's words eerily echoed his own thoughts in moments of defeat. But he could not listen. He had traveled all the way to India to claim Juliana. Giving up now was not an option.

"I know women," Ian said simply. "And I know Juliana better than most. She will relent."

"But not before the new year." Buffing his immaculate nails on the front of his coat, his father remarked, "It's just as well you will remain unmarried, I suppose. I can't abide the thought of my money financing that damned breeding stable you're always talking of. A waste of money, if you ask me."

Ian had not asked him, but he knew that did not matter. His father was always ready with an opinion.

A dangerous surge of temper gripped Ian. With a hard swallow of brandy, followed by a deep breath, he forced it down. Contradicting Nathaniel on this score would only lead to a verbal clash neither would win. No, best wait until he could show his father the profit to be had in the business he loved.

Buying time with another sip of brandy, he studied his father's smug face over the rim. How best to get the man to leave and forget this marriage matter? In good time, Ian knew he would win Juliana, and therefore have enough of his father's money to open his prestigious stables. Eventually, he would prove his father wrong.

Before he could say anything, Nathaniel went on. "And Juliana Linford—oh, Archer now, I suppose, is hardly the best choice. She was married for five years and never conceived. What if she is barren?"

Ian brushed aside the ridiculous notion. "Archer was a colonel in the East India Army. I doubt he was home very much so that Juliana might conceive."

His father shrugged, as if conceding the point. "Why bother with a woman who not only does not want you but eloped with a man so far beneath her? Even though her father is quite wealthy, I daresay you can do better."

Ian smiled and couched his phrase in a way his father could understand. "I consider it a challenge."

Nathaniel actually stopped to consider that. After a few silent moments, his father shrugged. "Assuming *any* woman exists who is a worthy challenge, I cannot imagine why you feel the need to test yourself just now."

Ian smiled. "Perhaps it's you I'm testing."

Something like approval crossed his father's aging face. "So long as you understand that you'll have a bride by the new year or be penniless."

"You've made that perfectly clear," said Ian, gritting his teeth.

He searched for a way to understand his father. As men went, he was a bastard. Cold and manipulative and damned proud of it. Nathaniel would never understand—much less admit to feeling—any emotion that resembled love. How could Ian possibly explain his devotion to Juliana? The way in which he knew their hearts were entwined?

Impossible.

"Why are you so eager for me to take a bride?" he asked, annoyed.

"You're approaching thirty."

"That hardly puts me at death's door," Ian drawled.

His father puffed out his chest and snapped the lapels of his coat against his chest. "Someday, perhaps sooner than later, *I* will find myself at death's door. I want to know my line is ensured before I do."

Ian closed his eyes in an awful moment of understanding. His father, vain and self-concerned as always, wanted immortality the only way he could achieve it—through the begetting of future generations. At that moment, Ian wished he could deny the pompous demand, but he wanted children with Juliana.

So he simply nodded. "I understand."

Nathaniel smiled. "Good. I'll be expecting a bride by the new year . . . or else."

I am so very angry. Furious, really! That man is—

Juliana gripped her pen as it hovered over her inkwell, scouring her mind for the perfect word to describe Ian. *Cad* and *serpent,* which she had called him to his face when she'd last seen him two weeks ago, were far too kind.

Moonlight and the candle's glow illuminated the

paper before her. Winter's bite seemed to creep through her window, slipping under her wrapper. Juliana rubbed her feet together for warmth and swung the heavy curtain of pale hair behind her shoulder. Yes, she should go to bed. But blast Ian, she was too enraged to sleep.

Gripping her pen with renewed vengeance, she pressed on, writing in the faithful pages of her journal.

> *Polite ladies cannot use the words necessary to properly express Ian's low character. I can safely say he makes the darkest of blackguards look pious.*
>
> *He lied to me yet again. I am thoroughly disgusted with my own surprise. How gullible he must think me! Never again will I allow the charm of his smiles or the warmth of his kisses to lull me. I know who Ian is and what he is. That will never change, I am certain of that now.*
>
> *He lied by not telling me the entire truth. Ian had no more thought my father ill before he left for India than he thinks my father ill now. His soft words of devotion and love are no different. He is a—*

A brash knock sounded at the door, startling her. She rattled in her chair, spilling ink across the corner of her page. Frustration heated her sigh.

"Juliana?" her father boomed on the other side of her door.

She held in a curse. He was the other person she had no wish to see, would never believe again. She was furious with him as well but not surprised. She expected trickery from her father, as she should have expected it from Ian. It was her misfortune that she had come to trust the worthless rogue again during their voyage. Perhaps the sea had affected her mind. . . .

"Yes, Papa," she answered tightly.

"Open up, girl. I want to talk to you."

She had no wish to talk to him. He would only irritate her more with pointless, haughty excuses. "I'm quite tired. Can it not wait until tomorrow?"

"I'll be but a moment. Open up."

Blast him! Knowing he would only insist until their encounter turned ugly, Juliana blew on her ink to be certain it did not smudge before closing her journal and tucking it away inside a thin drawer of her desk.

"Juliana, now," her father ordered.

Lord, she hated that voice. Zeus himself could not have patronized the mere humans with a more bloated tone than her father possessed.

Heaving a sigh that matched the rolling of her eyes, Juliana rose and padded across the room. "I'm coming."

She wished again she'd taken time to don her slippers. St. Andrew's Day would arrive tomorrow, and the air reflected the coming of winter, smelled of an early snow.

Reluctantly, Juliana pulled open the door but did not stand back to permit her father entrance.

He brushed past her without an invitation and paced to the center of her room. When he puffed out his chest with a deep breath, Juliana feared she was in for a long evening.

"I've just learned that you visited Ian earlier this month." His brows fell into a scowl. "Though I want you to wed him, you know I do not condone you traveling to Edgefield Park alone, even if you are a widow."

Apparently, it had escaped his notice that she had spent six months alone on a ship with Ian. If she had wanted to tarnish her eternal soul and good reputation with sins of the flesh, she could easily have done it by now.

"Our conversation was brief and chaste, I assure you."

The scowl deepened to include grooves between

his brows. "Not everyone will see it that way, young lady. Neighbors talk. Don't give them scandal. Already they say you and Ian should have wed long ago out of familiarity alone."

And what did familiarity breed? Juliana wanted to point out she had plenty of contempt for Ian but knew her father would only talk until he argued his way to Ian's sainthood.

"You should marry Axton. He's a fine man. A very fine man," her father blustered.

But he is an even better liar.

Pasting on a polite smile, she replied, "Papa, Geoffrey has scarce been dead a year. I have no wish to rush to the altar again."

He grabbed the lapels of his coat and tried to fit them around his protruding belly. Did he think that made him look important?

"A smart move, girl, not wanting to make a mistake again. But you can trust your papa's judgment. Ian will see you happy. He truly does adore you."

Even if it was true, Juliana found she was too mad to care for his feelings. What about hers, of betrayal, of fury? No one cared about those, least of all her father.

"I should like to take some time to reacquaint myself with other men in Devonshire before I decide upon a husband. Surely Ian cannot be the only fine man in the district."

Her father frowned, as if considering the prospect. "I daresay you're right, but since he is so fine and cares for you so well, why look for another man? That would only be a waste of time."

Perhaps, but it was her time to waste. . . .

"Papa, what reason have I to hurry? I'd rather be certain of my happiness before I wed again."

"Ian will make you happy," he assured, as if her concerns were no more trifling than the weather. "Besides, I've looked into your finances. Without a husband you'll not last long. You must be practical, girl."

"You looked into my finances?" Anger etched her voice with a harsh edge. "I gave you no permission—"

"I am your father," he said in his Zeus tone again.

Didn't he think she knew that by now? She sighed.

"You listen to me," he barked. "As your father, it was my duty to look into your situation, since you have no husband. Now that I have seen how pitiful that lowborn buffoon Archer left you, I must insist you wed. Ian is a prime choice. Quite the bachelor."

Yes, and quite untrustworthy too.

"I shall consider it," she lied, then took her father by the arm. "Now I'm quite tired and require my bed."

He whirled on her, shot her a narrow-eyed stare of scrutiny. "See that you thoroughly consider wedding—and soon."

Juliana nodded, then her father finally left.

She threw herself across the bed with abandon, then rolled to her back, staring up at the intricate ivory carvings on the blue plaster ceiling.

Groaning, she murmured, "Well, Papa, Ian may be quite the bachelor. He is welcome to change his state with some other bride, but it will not be me."

A faint weeping filled the air a moment later. A chill passed down her arm, her thigh, to her already icy feet. The heavy scent of roses lingered in the air.

She knew the sensations, had grown up with them since her youngest years. And as she sat up on her bed, her suspicions were confirmed.

At her feet floated the weeping ghost of Harbrooke.

Whoever she was, she had been a small woman. Nearly transparent and so very frail-looking, she wept, sorrow pouring silently from her eyes as it had every time Juliana had ever seen the spirit. She wore a wide, billowing gown common during the Restoration, nearly two hundred years before. Thick in textures, dozens of bows dotted the sleeves, even as lace dripped at the ends, all the way to her fingertips, in which she clutched a red book. Her hair hung in an array of fat curls upon her neck and shoulders. With her wide mouth and graceful shoulders, the woman had clearly been a beauty in life.

As she had since her youth, Juliana wondered who the ghost was and why she cried.

"Thomas."

Juliana heard the whisper—hadn't she? Yes, but where had it come from? Certainly not the specter. But it matched the anguish in her eyes.

No. Ghosts did not talk. Did they? At least this one never had before.

But who else would have spoken?

No one else was about.

She sat up straighter. Well, the ghost had never spoken to her before. Why had she chosen to do so now? Who was Thomas, and why did the spirit speak of him?

"Thomas," she heard the agonized whisper again. "My love, forgive me. . . ."

The specter wore such torment on her translucent face. Had she ever hurt that badly? Juliana wondered. Yes, when she realized that Geoffrey had no real interest in her, despite wedding her and taking her with him to India. And again today when faced with the depths of Ian's manipulations. All too well Juliana understood the despair dealt women by a handsome face with no true heart beneath.

But what did the ghost feel she needed to be forgiven for? Juliana wondered.

Without thought, she found herself reaching out to offer the small, exquisite spirit comfort.

As Juliana reached to her—through her—the ghost faded away.

Juliana blinked. Then she blinked again. But the

spirit, and her rich rose perfume, had gone as suddenly as she had come.

She stared into the empty space before her, trying to decipher what had just taken place. The ghost had spoken; well, whispered anyway. But who was she?

Always, Juliana had been interested in learning the specter's identity, but no one had known for certain. They had their share of tragic ancestors, as did most families who had a long lineage steeped in history.

"Forgive me ..." she heard softly again behind her, so close, goose bumps broke out on the nape of her neck.

Juliana whirled to the sensation but found only the rest of her bed and another blue wall.

Curiosity to know what had doomed the dead woman to cry for eternity pierced Juliana. Perhaps that pursuit would distract her from the fact she needed a husband to counter her dwindling funds and help her forget the fact the man offering for her hand was deceitful enough to lie his way out of hell.

CHAPTER SEVEN

As luck would have it, snow fell that night. That meant their neighbors to the south, Lord and Lady Bouston, would host an impromptu gathering at their manor, as they did each year after the first snow.

Perhaps, Juliana mused, this would give her the opportunity to reacquaint herself with the gentlemen in the district. Not that she had any burning wish to wed, but she had few options if she wished to escape her father's iron rule. Society allowed a woman so few options in which to support herself. As her father had so bluntly pointed out, her funds were running thin. And under no circumstances would she accept money from him.

Without references, finding a job as a governess even would be unlikely, particularly after her somewhat scandalous elopement with Geoffrey, a man most viewed as a social inferior. Nor did England's law permit her to own property or a business in her own right. She had few choices and even less freedom. Mary Wollstonecraft, the famous advocate for the rights of women, would be appalled with her logic.

But Juliana was, with the exception of her disastrous marriage to Geoffrey and her odd attraction to Ian, deeply practical.

"Are you ready to leave, dear?" her mother asked on the other side of her closed bedroom door.

Glancing at her image in the mirror, she noted the way the gaslights shone on the resplendent moss-green gown. She could not recall the last time she had felt so feminine.

She called back, "I am ready." *More than her mother knew and her father would approve of.*

Tonight she would hunt for a husband—one her father had not selected for her, one who would not deceive or confuse her, one who would demand nothing more than a good hostess for his home and a mother for his children.

Juliana's subdued green taffeta gown moved with three shimmering flounces. Lace trimmed the wide sleeves and low bodice. White gloves completed the look. The ensemble belonged to her mother, who had not yet worn it. Juliana had not the means for such a lovely gown in years.

The ride to Lord and Lady Bouston's was filled mostly with silence, although her father reminded her of Ian's sterling qualities as they drew closer to the party. Juliana believed Ian's finest talent was his ability to lie, but she kept the opinion to herself. Her father would never understand.

They arrived at the party within a half hour. Since the snow had fallen and left no more than a festive dusting of white in its wake, no one had difficulty reaching the gathering, which was already quite lively when they arrived.

Everywhere familiar faces abounded—including Ian's.

Light glinted off the inky sheen of his rich, dark hair, and his blue eyes shone with a dangerous flare. Shadows clung to the aristocratic angles of his face, accentuated the breadth of his wide shoulders. Her gaze seemed disinclined to leave his intriguing countenance.

How foolish! She was angry with him. Furious. She *was*. Why, then, could she not stop staring at him? And why did she always feel some unseen impact when she looked upon him? No matter what she could say about his character—and she could say plenty—she could no longer deny how powerfully he drew her.

Spotting her, Ian walked toward Juliana, an uncertain smile on his wide mouth. "Good evening. You look lovely."

He raised her gloved hand to his lips. She did not fight him. In fact, she did not even think to deny him until the deed was done. Why, despite his repeated perfidy, did she respond to him more each time she saw him?

Because she remembered his warm, sweeping, tempting kisses.

Lord, she had to stop such ridiculous pining. And she absolutely had to find an undemanding husband who roused no more than polite feeling in her.

"Find some woman who wants your attention. I do not," she snapped, then turned away.

At that moment, their hostess, Harriet Radford, Lady Bouston, rushed over to greet her. "Lady Archer, what a lovely surprise! I heard only this morning that you've returned from India. And a widow, you poor dear. Oh, what you must have suffered alone in such a strange country."

Juliana shrugged. "At times, I—"

"Never fear," Lady Bouston rushed on, "we have much here tonight to keep you diverted. Any number of people are already gathered with their families for the holidays or in preparation for a quick trip to London for the last of the Little Season. I daresay you shall have plenty of conversation."

As her hostess trilled with laughter, Juliana merely nodded and smiled. Once Harriet started talking, everyone in Lynton knew that stopping her was near impossible.

"And Lord Axton," she went on. "How lovely to see you."

Juliana scowled at him over her shoulder. He stood there, staring at her with something terribly resolute in his eyes. Certainly a man with his fine face could find a woman here who wanted his attention. Why did he persist in following her?

Harriet babbled on. "I understand you traveled all the way to India to bring our fair Juliana home. Such devotion," she cooed, speculation ripe in her gaze. "Perhaps we hear wedding bells in your future?"

"Perhaps," said Ian.

"Never," insisted Juliana.

She glared at him again. Ian said nothing, but his piercing blue eyes were full of challenge and displeasure. Juliana felt certain he still had not given up on wedding her.

"The course of love never did run smooth," Lady Bouston quoted, laughing again in a high-pitched bray. "Until you decide for certain about another trip to the altar, Lady Archer, come meet my cousins, recently arrived from Yorkshire."

Juliana nodded, eager. Anything to get away from Ian and the hungry, determined way he watched her. Thankfully, Harriet took her from Ian's side and through a swelling sea of people. Along the way, her hostess stopped a passing waiter and thrust a glass of sherry in her hand.

"Can't have you thirsty," Lady Bouston all but sang as she made her way across the lively room, past a group engrossed in a card game, away from a young girl torturing the guests with her burgeoning skills on the pianoforte.

Having so few options, Juliana drank her wine and followed.

But when she turned back, Juliana noticed Ian had already worked his way through the room and now stood a handful of steps away from Lady Bouston's family and Yorkshire cousins. Blast him! What did he intend to do, listen to her every word?

At the edge of the gathering, three men stood deep in conversation, and a very bored young woman clung to the arm of the eldest one. Lord Bouston busily argued, his face reddening with each word. No doubt, the debate centered on politics, Lord Bouston's first love and only concern. The older man listened, occasionally shaking his head in disagreement. The pretty girl, a waif of a redhead barely out of the schoolroom, clung to his arm, obviously ready to end the heated if pointless discussion.

Ian stood on the fringe of the group, with his back half turned to Lord Bouston. He chatted with a dowager countess whose name had escaped Juliana's memory.

As Juliana passed Ian and approached the small group, the young red-haired woman tugged on her father's arm. "Papa, can we not talk of something else?"

Both he and Lord Bouston paid the girl no notice.

Also standing in the semicircle with the men was the Radfords' son, Byron, an intelligent but painfully shy man who danced without a shred of grace. He smiled in her direction.

In the last five years, he had changed, settled into the angles of his face. No longer was it gangly, but now long and elegant and reasonably pleasant. His strong, sloped jaw led to a thin dusting of a beard. Byron Radford, Lord Carlton, had always been exceedingly kind.

Wondering if he had married, Juliana smiled in return.

Encouraged by her greeting, Lord Carlton broke from his small crowd and made his way to her. He reached for her and placed an enthusiastic if careless kiss on her hand. Juliana was all too aware of Ian half turned to her a mere step away.

"Lady Archer," he greeted, bowing to reveal a head of severely shorn blond hair. "I heard you had returned."

"Indeed." She smiled, determined to ignore the manipulative cad behind her. "How have you been?"

"Quite well. And you? You must have suffered in India."

Juliana shrugged. "India is so different from England. At times, I feared I would melt from the heat."

His mouth pursed with disapproval. "Archer should not have taken you to that barbaric land. How awful it must have been."

Apparently, Lord Carlton misunderstood. India had not always been awful. At first, it had even seemed an adventure, at least until she realized Geoffrey did not love her.

Lord Carlton met her gaze shyly from behind the spectacles perched on the long column of his nose. His eyes were sharp with intelligence. And unlike Ian, he was uncomplicated.

Yes, here was an undemanding man. With such honest brown eyes, she doubted he would spend his days concocting lies to tell her. He was of good family and pleasant disposition. While not very wealthy, he was comfortable. The fact he incited not a shred of emotion in her made the whole thought of marriage more palatable. He would not tempt her to behave irrationally. As husbands went, he would be livable, far more so than Ian. Perhaps he would do.

Brightening her smile, Juliana gazed into his kind face.

"Have you married, my lord?"

"Is *this* your idea of husband-hunting?" an all-too-familiar voice taunted behind her as he turned his head toward her ear. "You cannot be serious."

Ian. Damn him!

She felt him again, intent male, inches behind her. He splayed hot fingers at the small of her back, onto her hip, in a purely possessive gesture. Likely no one saw in the crowd.

But she felt it acutely.

Drawing in a deep breath of air, Juliana willed herself to ignore him. Almost instantly, she cursed her weakness. Tumult crept through her. No, it could only be irritation. Certainly after all he had done to her, his touch did *not* incite a thrill.

Juliana stiffened and refused to deign his presence with even a glance. "Go away."

"I—I'm sorry," Lord Carlton apologized, his gaze flitting to her face, then to his polished shoes. "Of course you don't wish to talk to me. I'll leave you—"

Juliana grasped his hand. It was smooth and a bit cold from the winter's chill.

"You must do no such thing," she insisted to Lord Carlton. "Of course I want to talk with you. I should like nothing more." Juliana smiled for effect.

"If you're certain . . ." Lord Carlton began.

Where was the man's confidence? She didn't have much time to ponder the question, when she felt Ian at her back again.

"Would you truly consider wedding *Byron*," Ian insisted.

"Why not?" Juliana snapped, anger with Ian mounting.

Byron shuffled in place. "Well, my life is not *very* interesting, not like yours, I am certain."

Now Lord Carlton was admitting he was boring? If he had any interest in forming a cozier acquaintance, as his gaze said, why would he not keep such a thought to himself?

"No, your life is perfectly interesting, I have no

doubt." Juliana insisted, "Go on. Tell me everything."

"You've always called him Boring Byron," Ian whispered, taunting. "As a girl, you never liked him because he understood insects more than humans."

"People can change," she shot back, wishing Ian would go away. Thanks to him, she was finding fault with Lord Carlton where certainly none existed.

Byron hesitated. "Well, I—I suppose I could try to be more interesting."

Juliana somehow managed not to roll her eyes. If Lord Carlton thought he had to *work* at that, he must be boring indeed. And though she had come tonight seeking the safe and staid, now that she had found a prime example, she could summon no interest.

"You're satisfactory as you are," she said absently. "Could you excuse me for a moment?"

Lord Carlton hesitated, and Juliana hated the confused hurt in his expression. It was just one more reason to loathe Ian.

"Of course," Byron murmured, and began to turn away.

Tentatively, she touched a hand to his arm. "I shall join you for that chat shortly, if you'd like."

He smiled again. "I would."

Juliana thought Byron might leave then. Instead, he caught sight of Ian just behind her, who now faced his way, and smiled.

Blast it all, why wouldn't Lord Carlton leave so she could really give Ian a good dressing-down?

"Ah, Axton," Byron said, holding out his hand. "I've been looking for you."

Ian shook it, sandwiching Juliana between them in the crush of the crowd. "Home from London for the holidays?"

Byron nodded. "Yes. I just arrived. And I have the information you seek."

Edging closer into the small circle, Ian's face brightened with interest. "The horse breeder?"

"Yes, his name is Fergusson. He says he has a prime Thoroughbred stud for sale."

Smiling, Ian said, "That is splendid. I shall contact him when next I am in London."

"I told him to expect your visit after the holiday."

Ian slid his gaze to Juliana suddenly, then took her hand and placed it in the crook of his arm. His fingers closed over her own possessively.

Lord Carlton took in the gesture with disappointed eyes but said nothing. Juliana scowled and did her best to pull away from Ian, with little result.

"I should be able to meet with Fergusson then," Ian said.

Frowning, Juliana stared at Ian, puzzled. Why would talk of a horse prompt him to reach for her hand so suddenly?

Who could understand the vagaries of the male mind?

Rolling her eyes, she tugged again on Ian's grip. She felt him tense and she shot him a glare. Instantly, he released her.

"Splendid news." Byron nodded. "Fergusson will be pleased." He turned to her, subdued once more. "Good evening."

Lord Carlton walked away, blending into the crowd.

Juliana opened her mouth to give Ian the sharp side of her tongue, but someone equally odious interrupted her.

"Ian, my boy," said his father as he approached the two of them. On his arm was Harriet's pretty redheaded cousin, who had apparently been relieved of her boredom from her sire's and Lord Bouston's political discussion.

"Father," Ian replied tonelessly.

"Good to see you, Lady Archer. I trust you are

happy to be home from the hellish environs of India?'' asked Lord Calcott.

"Quite. I thank your son for his assistance."

"Yes, well, I am glad you're home safe, but that boy should have more sense than to run off for months simply to chase a woman. Foolish," his father said, cutting his gaze to Ian. "He has pressing matters to attend, as he well knows."

Before Juliana could even gape at such a rude reply, Lord Calcott thrust the Radfords' cousin in Ian's path.

"Son, this is Lady Mary Crenshaw of Yorkshire. She is visiting Lord and Lady Bouston for the holidays after spending the fall in London."

"How do you do?" said Ian politely, lifting the young woman's gloved hand to his lips.

Lady Mary sighed and gazed at him with blue eyes, fixed and dewy. Clearly, she liked what she saw. All charm, Ian smiled.

Annoyance hit Juliana. Why, the lady's expression indicated a full swoon might soon come! Did men enjoy such rubbish?

"My lord," Lady Mary breathed, her eyes riveted on Ian.

"How do you find Devonshire?" he asked, his voice low.

"Simply wonderful," she cooed.

Lady Mary's response left little doubt the girl complimented Ian and not the shire. Juliana's irritation multiplied. And despite his words to the contrary on the *Houghton,* Ian's warm smile seemed to prove he found favor with Lady Mary's dim-witted behavior. And why not? Such drivel clearly fed his bloated self-confidence.

"Splendid. I'm certain we shall see each other again." Once more, he smiled, then bowed.

"I shall look forward to it."

Juliana frowned at the young woman. Did she realize how brazen she sounded?

"Would you excuse us, good lady?" Ian asked.

Before Lady Mary could utter a word, Ian grabbed Juliana's hand again, tucked it upon his arm, and whisked her away.

Glancing around to see if they were noticed, he led her to the family drawing room, just down the hall. Once alone, he shut the door and turned to her.

"You cannot mean to consider Byron as a groom," he barked.

Oh, yes. She could. She might not want to . . . but she could if Ian pushed her.

Finally free to give Ian a much-needed tongue-lashing, Juliana happily indulged. Suddenly, she was glad he had dragged her away from the gathering like a brute so she could put all her anger into voice.

"When will you understand I do not want to see you?" she demanded. "Lady Mary clearly desires your company. Perhaps you should—"

"Why are you hunting for a husband when I've offered to marry you and laid my heart at your feet?" Ian's eyes devoured and accused her at once.

"Yes, you love me so much, you needed to lie to me—repeatedly," she spat out.

"I did not lie to you. Your father's condition has vastly improved since I left for India, and—"

"Do you have nothing original—or believable— to say?"

"I'm speaking the truth," he growled. "Stop thinking about your poor put-upon sensibilities and start thinking about the people who love you and are glad you've returned home."

How dare he! After lying to her to get her home and lying to her about lying, now he chastised her for her feelings of betrayal? It would be sad—if she weren't so furious.

"Other than my mother and a few of the servants, there is no one I am glad to see in Lynton. It's only a matter of time before you and Papa try to direct me to the altar so you can spend my life telling me what to say, where to go, how to behave." She drew in a deep furious breath. "It will not happen. I'm not the young, naive girl I was before."

Ian scowled, his mouth tightening. "We have no thoughts of treating you like a child. We only want to see you well cared for, well settled."

"And without a single decision of my own."

He hesitated, then grabbed her arm and leaned closer. His face turned taut with anger.

"Perhaps you need no decisions about another husband. Geoffrey Archer was hardly a prize."

Her fury soared until she heard a roar in her ears. "I'm no longer eighteen and foolish."

"No, you are twenty-three and stubborn. That combination, too, will likely see you with an equally abysmal husband."

Juliana refused to consider his words. She would *not* make that mistake again. Geoffrey and Ian had taught her too much.

"Could anyone be more wrong for me than you?" she challenged, a slim brow arched in a way that had infuriated him for fifteen years.

Ian locked his jaw, his eyes spitting blue fury so hot, it could have blistered her. "Byron would give you no firm hand."

She gaped at him. "I do not require one."

"He would provide no challenge," Ian went on. "No excitement."

"Nor would you!" she lied. "I would simply go through my days—"

"As I would," he cut in. "In anticipation of the nights, when I would twine your fingers in mine"— he grasped her hand, pulled her closer, and nuzzled her neck—"breathe in the scent of your bare skin, and make love to you so completely that you can no longer remember your name."

Juliana was too stunned to move. His behavior was improper, to say the least. But his words incited a lightning-quick flash of desire in her blood. The arousal warred with her fury, leaving her somehow more clutched in the thrall of both.

Ian kissed the side of her neck, nipped at her earlobe, fitted the hot breadth of his palm around her nape, and breathed her name. Juliana began to quiver.

No. There were reasons she should resist his seduction.

"Stop this. Now."

He went on as if she'd said nothing. When his mouth moved with slow precision across her jaw and hovered inches over her mouth, her thoughts and protests began to dissolve.

Suddenly, Juliana feared Ian could make good on his threat. Already he was making her lose her mind.

Reeling, melting, Juliana closed her eyes on a moan, erased the distance between their mouths, and kissed him. Ian met her halfway, his lips against hers greedy and open, instantly commanding as he molded her mouth to his. He entered her mouth, swept through like a hurricane, and enthralled her senses. Every bit of her body felt alive, alert to his touch high on her waist, just beneath her breast, to his brandy-rich taste, to his subtle male scent that seemed to feed her hunger.

Ian took deeper possession of her mouth, fingers clutching her nape. Juliana responded without hesitation, driven to know more of the sensations only he gave her. She tightened her grip around his neck, her fingers filtering the silky, newly shorn hair. She felt his moan arrow down through her belly, to her toes, making everything between tingle.

Pulling her tightly against the solid length of his

body, Ian plundered his way inside her mouth as a pirate would his treasure cove. He touched her completely as his tongue stroked hers, engaged her, filling her with a delicious, urgent need.

Ian lifted his thumb a fraction, brushing the underside of her breast in a soft stroke. Sensation burst through her chest, centering in her pebbled nipples. Juliana arched into him. Desperation to have his hands on her body seized her very mind. She drew in a ragged moan of need.

Juliana felt Ian back away from the kiss and grabbed his shoulders all the tighter. But she could not stop him.

When his lips left hers, she felt somehow cold and empty, bereft even.

In heaven's name, why did Ian's kiss do this to her? In her pleasure-hazed mind, she had no answer.

He did not move far away. Rather, he curled his hands around her heated cheeks, pressed his forehead to hers, breath coming deep and hard, as was hers. A moment of silence passed, and Juliana felt how difficult a task it had been for Ian to end the kiss.

She took a deep, steadying breath. With it came her sanity—and mortification.

"You make me lose my mind, Juliana," he whispered, echoing her thoughts. "I nearly forgot we are at the Radfords' party."

His words bounced Juliana back to reality. She had forgotten that fact altogether. That was a very bad sign. . . .

"But I could not pass up," he went on, now stroking her cheek with his fingertips, "an opportunity to touch you in any way you would let me. I know you're angry with me." He backed up a fraction so that she had little choice but to peer into the endless blue of his eyes. "But I truly believed that, just in case your father's illness was serious, you would wish to come home. It is our good fortune that he is on the mend."

Yes, here was the reason she wasn't speaking to him. He had lied—again. Juliana blamed him for his duplicity, for trying to direct her life after his wishes and assuming she would not mind. She was also angry with herself for believing a word out of his manipulative mouth, for trusting him even an inch, and for allowing him to kiss her into forgetting.

Anger rushed through her at his words, settling in her belly like a cold stone. She was *not* the kind of weak-willed woman to tolerate such management. If she had not made that clear to Ian before, it was high time she did.

Thrusting his hands away from her face, Juliana made for the drawing room door. "You are right; I am angry. The fact you cannot understand why and persist in believing that you might kiss the fury out of me is insulting. I will not be maneuvered to the altar. I thought I had made that perfectly clear when last I saw you."

Ian rushed to her side. "Wait, Juliana! Give me time to—"

"To lie to me some more, to find some underhanded way to convince me that you did not hope your scheme would affect the rest of my life?" she yelled. "No."

"Shhh. The party goes on right outside this door."

Tensing, Juliana chastised herself. If members of the party had found them in here, alone together, her lips undoubtedly swollen from his kiss, she'd be ruined and forced to wed him this very day.

Juliana nodded crisply. "Thank you for reminding me."

At her tone, frustration stamped Ian's features. He grabbed her hand, surrounded it with both of his, and took a step closer. Blast him, his eyes turned soft, persuasive. His voice became a pleading whisper. "I have not always made the smartest choices in proving that I love you, I know. But I do love you."

Juliana steeled herself against his lie. Perhaps he believed it in his demented mind. But she did not, could not. Ian had convinced himself of this love he claimed because she continued to refuse him. For if he truly loved her, how could he lie to her repeatedly?

"It's of no concern. I don't—"

"Give me until Christmas Day before you answer my proposal."

Juliana started to reject him that instant, until he said, "We had a bargain, Juliana. You promised."

At that, she gritted her teeth. Lord, she hated such a reminder. But she *had* agreed; there was no denying it. Fair was fair, even if she disliked it. But come Christmas morning, she would give him the set-down of his life for coercing her into coming home and agreeing to this bargain.

"As you wish." She broke away from his hold and brushed past him, heading for the door. "I shall see you on Christmas morning. But the answer will be no different."

Ian stopped her with an arm around her waist— and his soft lips against her nape. Her pulse soared, and she closed her eyes, looking for some way— any way—to fight the shiver of sensations winding through her body.

"The bargain was that you would spend time with me."

His whisper caused her stomach to flutter. She swallowed. No doubt, he was sincerely good at seducing a woman. She must remember that such temptations were merely a game to him.

"I did that every day aboard the *Houghton*. You proved nothing except that you are the same odious man I've always known."

"Was I not all that is considerate and polite?"

Juliana was not fooled by his innocent expression. "Indeed, even as you fed me your latest deception."

Behind her, he sighed. "That is your assumption, not the truth. Spend time with me, Juliana. Do not resign us both to a loveless life before you do."

How prettily he pleaded, and if she stood here long enough, she feared he would find some way to convince her he was right. And she knew well—too well—exactly what manner of man Ian was.

"I will never love you," she said.

Then she slammed the door between them.

CHAPTER EIGHT

The very next morning found Ian on the prowl once more, Juliana decided. She had plans for the day—major ones to begin her search for a husband—none of which included dealing with the honeyed cajoling of Ian's lies.

But at nine o'clock, a messenger arrived bearing a small card in an envelope and informed her that he was to await her answer. Frowning, Juliana paced to the end of the foyer for a bit of privacy and opened the envelope.

Inside lay a Christmas card, printed on a stiff, dark reddish-brown cardboard. She had heard of such things. Select lithographers in London had been printing them for nearly a decade, but she had never received one. It was lovely, depicting a family party in progress.

A Merry Christmas and a Happy New Year to you had been engraved into the crisp surface just beneath the picture. *Published at Summerly's Home Treasure Office, 12 Old Bond Street, London* lay at the very bottom.

As sentiments went, it was nice and, admittedly,

thoughtful. Juliana had always appreciated the Christmas season far above others. If Ian did as well, good for him. But the thought did not soften her anger toward him. Well ... maybe a little. As long as he demanded nothing of her—

Before she could complete the thought, a white linen note spilled from the envelope, drifting to the floor like a feather lost without a breeze. Frowning, Juliana retrieved the note.

Ian, in his own scrawl, had written:

> *Christmas is a season for forgiveness. Please accept my apology and allow me to see you today. I seek your absolution so we might save our friendship and see what our future holds.*

He did not sign his whole name, only a large, slanted letter *I* beneath his request.

Juliana wadded up the page in a tight fist.

Anger hit her like a solid force. Ian played upon her weakness—her grief at losing their friendship. Then he made it sound as if its future lay in her hands, as if he had not jeopardized it with his actions. How lacking did he think her mind? Surely he must know she wasn't so mutton-headed as to fall for a manipulative ploy like his?

The fact he believed she would made her even more furious.

With small, efficient steps, Juliana returned to the waiting messenger's side.

"My lady?" the young man asked, white wig comically askew.

Juliana had no urge to laugh. "Tell him—" She paused, searching for the perfect retort. "Yes, tell him that I would rather spend my time in Harbrooke's barn, since I prefer the company of an ass that cannot speak to that of the ass who can."

* * *

Ian received the messenger's reply an hour later. Fury churned like lava in his blood. Though he wondered if he ought to stay at Edgefield, leave the stubborn woman be until she began to think with her mind instead of her temper, he couldn't. Eruption of his anger was too imminent.

Without wasting another second, Ian made for the stables and saddled his bay, then charged off to Harbrooke.

Damn her! It was past time Juliana stopped blaming him for everything wrong between them. He wouldn't have to speak anything less than truth if she would see what was in front of her face. They had known each other their whole lives. She had trusted him as a childhood friend. Why in bloody hell could she not trust him as a mate? Why had she never tried?

Winter wind whipped through his hair, stinging his cheeks, freezing his nose. Snow lingered on the ground and glistened in the trees from several days past. The discomfort riled him. If he were a less rational man, he'd blame it on her. Hell, he just might anyway. If it weren't for her mulish ways, he would not be racing through the early December wind just to satisfy the urge to speak to her.

A half hour's ride in the cold had done little to chill his temper when he arrived at Harbrooke. Climbing the stairs and striding between the stately columns, Ian cursed with the effort to keep from banging on the door.

He rapped politely and waited. Soon, the staid butler, Smythe, greeted him, led him inside, and went to fetch Juliana.

Ian paced the drawing room, his long strides eating up the floor rapidly before he turned and repeated the process. "Damn woman," he muttered.

Was any woman worth this hell?

Though he hated to admit it, Juliana was. Somehow she complimented him, made his shortcomings seem less severe. She was the voice of reason at times, when he was scattered by indecision. He appreciated her calm logic, her clear insight.

He did not, however, appreciate her obstinate temper.

The butler entered the room a moment later, hesitant. "Lady Archer is indisposed at the moment, my lord."

Ian knew well the translation for that; she simply did not want to see him.

"Perhaps you would like to leave a card?" the servant said.

A card? No, that had started this whole mess, his attempt to wish her a happy Christmas and see if they could not recover the sentiment between them, in the spirit of the coming season.

The anger housed inside his chest thickened, tightened, crept up his throat, closer to eruption. That damned woman was likely to be the death of him yet.

Two things, that's all he wanted in this life: His breeding stables established and Juliana at his side. Why were acquiring both proving to be so bloody difficult?

"Thank you," he said stiffly, then slipped past the butler, slamming his way out the door.

Fine. If Juliana wanted to play unfairly, he would oblige her.

Making his way around to the back of the manor house, Ian looked up and spotted the window that belonged to Juliana. Yes, she was in her room. He saw the gaslight, saw her shadow moving around. She seemed to be carrying something.

Dismissing the observation, Ian eyed the trellis that scaled the side of the house. Yes, it had been fifteen years since he climbed it, only to put a frog in her bed. Hopefully, it would prove equally sturdy and handy today.

Grabbing one rung of the trellis, he pulled on it as hard as he could, testing it. The trellis hung steady. He added the other hand and repeated the test, with the same result.

"Why the hell not?" he muttered, then shrugged.

Ian began climbing. He was as agile as always, and though the vines climbing the wooden structure were considerably thicker than they'd been fifteen years before, he still made it to Juliana's window with ease.

He thought to knock but feared she would only hold the window shut so he couldn't enter. And Ian would not give her the opportunity to thwart him again. He had something to say, damn it. The willful woman was going to listen for once.

At the top, he slid the window open with one hand, while bracing himself with the other. Moments later, he grabbed the sill of the window and hauled himself through the opening.

The winter wind blasted in with him. Juliana turned at the intrusion, took a step toward the window. When she saw him, she gave a startled gasp and froze for an instant. Only an instant.

Then heated displeasure stormed her hazel eyes, firmed up her sharp jaw. She was going to scream; he was nearly certain of it. Damn.

"Juliana, sit down," he commanded quietly before she could unload her anger on him.

"Do *not* think you'll sneak into my room like a thief and tell me what to do." She stepped closer, her tirade already gaining strength in her furious whisper. "And you wonder why I don't want to marry you, Ian. You apparently have no respect for my wishes, my privacy, or my independence. You—"

"If you'll recall, I tried twice to see you politely. How do you expect we'll work through our differences if you won't speak to me?"

"I'm sure you'll disagree, but the fact that fair means are not working gives you no right to use foul. There is a reason I did not receive your call, and I don't wish to see you now."

Juliana turned for the door with a decisive stride and walked away. Realizing she meant to leave the room, Ian lunged in front of her and blocked the door.

"Damn it, you are *not* leaving."

She leaned closer, very close. Fury clenched her face, flared in the scowl of her narrowed eyes. "Move now or I will scream and bring the whole house here."

He hesitated, then smiled, leaning against the door, arms crossed over his chest. "I wish you would."

Juliana opened her mouth, lungs ready to bellow. Abruptly, she snapped her mouth shut. Loosing her anger would bring the entire house running—and send her father after the parson.

"I'm sure you would like that very much," she snapped.

Flashing her a lopsided grin, he taunted, "Are you certain you can hold that scream in?"

With a sound of disgust, she turned away. "Since I don't wish to find myself engaged to you this very hour, which my father would doubtless insist upon, I think I shall refrain."

"If you're certain you can curb the indulgence—"

"I can," she insisted.

"Then let us mend our differences in this friendship."

Juliana threw her hands in the air. "I am not certain we can."

The downturn to her mouth showed him that notion disturbed her. Good. It should, for her logic disturbed him too.

"I don't believe that any more than you do. You're angry with me. I understand. Talk to me, but do not hide."

"I am *not* hiding!" The suggestion clearly incensed her.

"Of course you are. You tell yourself you are punishing me for my bad behavior, but you are hiding from me because you might have to admit you've been hard on me, because you might actually have to bend that inflexible skull of yours."

"Admit you've been right?" She sounded appalled. "Oh, that's rich. Next you'll be telling me you've been visited by fairies."

"Clearly that is more likely than you ever apologizing."

Blinking, gaping, Juliana was stunned speechless for a full five seconds. *"Me* apologize to *you?* What the bloody hell for?"

Ian raised a brow and tried not to laugh, despite the gravity of their argument. "What lovely language for a lady."

"Bugger off," she muttered.

At that, Ian howled. He couldn't stop. Although they'd resolved nothing between them, Juliana always found a way to reach him, to get him beyond a moment, to another place that reminded him why he loved her. She was ... so herself.

"Quiet down," she commanded. "Someone will hear you!"

"It's a shame they won't."

Juliana bit her lip, swallowed, and frowned fiercely. No doubt, it was killing her not to scream. "You are an evil man."

Stifling his mirth, Ian quietly said, "No, I am in love. I came her to see if we cannot find some compromise. I have spent years trying to find a way to prove that my heart is yours. At every turn, you reject and deny me. Can you not understand?"

She crossed her arms over her chest and cocked her head. The glint of the afternoon sun slanted into the room, lighting her fair hair with rich strands of gold and sunlight. Despite the brutal sun of India, her skin still looked as fair and pure as an angel's wing, like gossamer. A yearning to touch her kicked him in the gut.

"I understand perfectly. Even my mother seems to think you and my father embellished this illness in order to coerce me to return. And you want an apology. Should I say I'm sorry for believing you?"

Ian paused, fighting an urge to yell. That was the problem; his whole world was more passionate around Juliana. He could scream as quickly as he could laugh. He could feel lust for her even more quickly. The tempestuous rapport they shared enflamed him. If she would ever admit it, their relationship did the same for her.

"No, say you're sorry for not believing me for more than a moment. Have you never heard that many medical conditions can be grave one day and greatly recovered another? Yes, you have," he answered for her. "How was I to know when I left that your father would look the picture of health when we returned?"

Juliana paused, mulling over his words. Her teeth worked her bottom lip. She was deep in thought, he knew.

"Perhaps. But can you honestly say you had no thought of using the illness, whether grave or not, to bring me home?"

He sighed. "We both thought it was time. You were alone in a foreign country where rumors of revolts abound and they worship animals as gods. Their temples are filled with deities copulating in every conceivable position. The heat and disease kill people. Why do you imagine that we would let you remain there unprotected?"

"What are you saying?" Her eyes narrowed.

"Your father being ill, perhaps even seriously, gave you the perfect reason to come home, in case your pride would not stomach a return simply because you wished it."

His words only inflamed her. Ian cursed as Juliana fisted her hands and started toward him with murder in her eyes.

"So you admit it. You lied to me!" she accused Ian.

"I protected you," he contradicted.

"That's bloody rubbish! I trusted you against my better judgment. Knowing how I felt, you deceived me anyway."

If the heat of anger could produce fire, Juliana would create an inferno with every syllable. He had never seen her this furious, all tense mouth, flushed face, and eyes spitting hate. If she had been a man, she would have done her best to beat him senseless, draw and quarter him—or both.

Ian gritted his teeth. She had to be the most stubborn woman God ever put on this earth. He'd given her logical reasons for their ruse, if it could be called such. And she was furious. Most of the time, Juliana was refreshingly logical, but not once her temper got in the way. So, until she might calm down and find reason, he had to find a way to retract the statement or turn it around so she might see it as less damning.

"Juliana, I—"

"Never mind." She spun away. "This is my fault. I knew better than to believe you, and I did it anyway."

She muttered the words nearly to herself. Ian listened to them with a sinking stomach.

Then he noticed the half-packed trunk at her feet.

Alarm made his stomach plummet to his toes in a heartbeat.

"I had an instinct," she continued, "and I went against—"

"Where are you going?" Ian asked.

"Can you not even be bothered to listen to the reasons I'm angry?"

He pinned her with a gaze that contained his every possessive, protective impulse. All too well, Ian feared he knew where Juliana was going—and why.

"I understand your anger. I have heard your reasons," he said in a low voice, using a tone one might to calm a beast. "Please tell me you are not planning something rash because you're angry with me."

Juliana stiffened, bristled. "I don't regard finding a husband in London as a rash act."

Ian bit back a curse. Exactly as he expected—and feared. "You cannot mean to go."

"Why not? I am a widow now, with a bit of money, so I *can* go," she countered. "There is at least a week of the Little Season left. Before everyone begins to return to the country for Christmas, I'll take in polite society and do my best to find a husband who appreciates an independent woman and will take me far away from you and Papa."

"Damn it, Juliana! Do not go alone. The rakes in London will eat a naive girl like you alive."

She laughed softly. The bitter sound reverberated in Ian's ears, multiplying his concern for her.

"I think not," she said, straining to keep her voice down. "You've taught me far too well what to expect from rogues and rakes. Now get out!"

Ian paused. Juliana was much too angry to reason with. He could see that. Heeding her demand would make her feel a bit of needed power. He would let her win the battle, so long as he won the war.

"As you wish." He turned and headed for the window again.

"No argument?" she challenged, surprise coloring her face.

"No."

Ian could almost feel her gaze narrowing on his back. Even in retreat she didn't trust him.

No doubt, he had well and truly destroyed the

strides he had made aboard the *Houghton*. What the hell was he to do now?

"You're not going to fight me?" Juliana asked.

He told her the truth. "Not now."

She peered at him, open suspicion in her eyes. Then she heaved a sigh of frustration. "But you have no intention to leave me alone, have you? You still plan to pursue me."

Despite the fact she read his mind far too well, Ian smiled and turned to her. "Until the day you say 'I do.' "

London was cold. It was the temperature as much as the people, Juliana decided four days later.

She did not have much wardrobe to recommend itself, just what she could borrow from her mother, who had handed over her frocks with a worried smile. The journey had been lonely and oddly long. With each mile, she felt as if she were forgetting something, leaving something valuable behind. What that was, she did not know.

After her surprise arrival at her parents' town house, Juliana made a few calls on friends and acquaintances from the days of her come-out. To her dismay, most had retired to the country already.

One of her dearest friends from her debutante days, Lady Clara Wimsett, had wed an earl. Clara herself had retired to the country for her upcoming confinement. Because the child was not due until February, Clara's husband, Lord Tothbury, had received her with all kindness in London and procured her invitations to the few remaining gatherings of the season. Lord Tothbury's brother, Mr. Peter Haversham, had agreed to be her escort so that Lord Tothbury could return to Clara's side.

Most promising, since Mr. Haversham was, as yet, unwed.

Juliana quickly decided he was an affable man, perhaps thirty, with a smooth face and idle hands. Well-shorn hair in a shining shade of gold complimented his fair complexion and mischievous blue eyes. True, they were shades paler than Ian's rich, complex blue—

No, she would not think of *him*. No sense spoiling her trip.

As they stood at the top of the stairs, above the evening's soiree, Mr. Haversham smiled at her. "Are you ready?"

"As I shall ever be." She took a deep breath.

As a debutante, she had done well enough. Indeed, she had collected more than her share of suitors. Somehow, Geoffrey had caught her attention far more than the young gentlemen her parents had deemed acceptable. Now she wondered if everyone would remember her elopement to the untitled Archer—and hold it against her.

Thick perfume wafted in the grand house's air as she and Mr. Haversham were announced. A few heads turned, a few eyebrows lifted. If Peter noticed, he gave no indication.

Descending the stairs into the crush of people, Juliana looked about her for familiar faces but found precious few.

"Oh, dear. I've been in India far too long, I suspect. I know almost no one."

Peter patted her hand and flashed her an impossibly white smile. "Don't worry, my dear. We'll get on just fine."

His confidence fed hers. "Of course you are right. I'm simply concerned my polite manners are a bit rusty."

The smile on Peter's face became an indulgent grin. "Well, polite company is overrated anyway. Why don't we dance, and once everyone sees how fetching and graceful you are, you will be quite sought, I'm sure."

"You are all kindness," she murmured as he led her to the dance floor.

When the music began moments later, Juliana discovered Peter was a polished dancer. He was charming and attentive, and if he had heard of her disastrous marriage—and no doubt he had—he made no issue of it.

As he smiled down at her, Juliana detected more than a hint of interest. A mixture of relief and confidence began to make its way through her, infusing her movements with a surety she had not felt upon entering the room.

Here was a likely candidate for marriage. He seemed too relaxed to bother telling her what to do. Clearly, his biggest concern now was enjoying the party—and perhaps, judging from the warm expression on his patrician face—courting her. Juliana returned his gaze with a coy one of her own as the dance ended and Mr. Haversham escorted her off the floor.

Could finding a husband be this simple? She had hoped to meet a man who might be smitten enough with her in a week or less to ask her to wed. Deep down, she'd feared it wasn't possible. But with the Little Season dwindling, so like her funds, a week was all she had.

What if Mr. Haversham was the answer to her prayer?

Oh, would she love to see Ian's face upon announcing her engagement—

Wait. She peered across the room. That *was* Ian's face.

Dear God, he'd followed her to London!

And judging from his stride as he charged closer, he wanted to have a few words with her.

"Blast him," she muttered.

"You know Lord Axton?" Peter asked, spotting Ian.

She sighed. How on earth was she to explain that she had a man chasing her across the countryside to marry her, when she was looking for a husband? How was she to keep Peter interested in her once he discovered that tidbit?

"Yes, he is my neighbor in Devonshire," she offered.

"Oh." Peter frowned. "He looks angry, my dear."

"Eternally. It is my misfortune to live near the ogre."

He hesitated. "Well, if you don't wish to see him . . ."

She didn't, but Ian was looming close, and an encounter was unavoidable.

"I shall be fine," she murmured. "Perhaps if you fetched me a glass of wine, it would make the meeting more bearable?"

Peter cocked a brow at her suggestion. He knew he was being dismissed. Rather than being put off by her behavior, he merely smiled wider.

Quite a polite fellow. That was a point in his favor. And now to the irascible one . . .

She turned to Ian.

"Juliana." His greeting was terse, his movements agitated.

"Ian." She bowed her head, more for the curious partygoers around them than for Ian himself. "Now that we've done the polite, you may leave me in Mr. Haversham's capable hands."

"Unless you wish to learn about his capable hands sooner rather than later, I suggest you come with me."

Juliana did her best not to openly gape at Ian. "What are you suggesting, you—"

"He is a cad."

"And what does that make you? You are nothing

but jealous. Mr. Haversham has been all gentlemanly politeness. And *if* I wished to learn about his capable hands, well, that would be my affair, wouldn't it?"

To Juliana's surprise, Ian tightened his jaw but made no reply. His silence startled her, until she heard Peter clear his throat behind her.

Mortification swept over her. Please God, don't let him have heard the remark about his hands. . . .

Trying not to cringe, she turned and accepted the proffered wineglass. "My thanks to you."

"It is my honor to make certain you are cared for."

To her left, Ian glared at Peter.

"Axton," her escort greeted.

Ian merely nodded, then returned his attention to her. "Dance with me, Juliana."

"I appreciate you gracious invitation," she murmured acidly. "But I've no further interest in dancing tonight."

Mr. Haversham smiled. "Would you like to leave, my dear?"

She sent Ian a smug expression. "I would like that above all things. Thank you."

"Then go we shall. Good-bye, Axton."

As Juliana turned away, Ian grabbed her hand. His earnest face nearly gave her pause.

"Please let me take you home," he whispered.

"Mr. Haversham brought me here; he will escort me home."

Closing his eyes, Ian sighed. "I shall call upon you tomorrow afternoon to make certain you are well, then."

"If you wish. But do not expect you will be the only caller there."

CHAPTER NINE

Morning mist began to dissipate over the rolling green field as the sun rose a notch higher in the English sky. The magnificent stallion romped across the grass, tossing his head, as if demonstrating his superiority to the mere humans who watched. Powerful hindquarters and long hind legs gave him speed. The deep girth boded well for his lung capacity. His long, sloping shoulders lent him superior equine grace.

Ian had to admit he was impressed. Damned impressed.

Byron Radford had told him that Fergusson had the perfect specimen with which to begin a solid breeding stable for racing horses, but this glossy creature was far beyond Ian's expectations.

"Well, what do ye think of me horse Bruce?" asked the short, rough-hewn Scot by his side.

Ian nodded, reluctant to take his eyes off the horse. "He is remarkable."

"Ye didna think I was lyin' now, did ye, my lord?"

Ian could not appreciate the man's attempts at

levity just then. He had the perfect horse—and the perfect woman—in his sights, yet had not the ability to claim either.

"No," he murmured to Fergusson. "How old is he?"

"He's five now. Well past his racin' days but young enough for yer needs, eh?"

"You say he won races?"

The Scot puffed out his chest. "Aye, any number of races, including Ascot."

Ian was suitably impressed. "And has he sired any foals?"

"Aye, that he has. Two in the last year."

Smiling, Ian nodded. At a mere five, Bruce would have many active years as a stud. Excitement hummed through Ian at the thought of all the foals Bruce would sire, how sleek they would be. Equally exciting, Ian knew how prestigious his stables could become and how much money he could make.

The Scot spit in the dirt beside him. "I hiv others interested in Bruce, mind ye, but I can tell by the look on yer face that you'll treat him well."

"That I will." *If I can raise the money.*

Ian had not given more than a passing thought to his father's ultimatum that he marry by the new year or lose his inheritance. But thinking of Juliana with Peter Haversham and of the fabulous stud Bruce would make for the opening of his breeding program, he could not help but panic.

He held in a curse. If Juliana would only stop with her stubborn ways and agree to marry him by Christmas, they could all be happy. He would have the funds to buy Bruce and the means to show Juliana he was the best husband for her.

As it was, he had no idea how to get her away from that rogue Haversham.

Ian suspected Haversham's intent was not honorable. Whispers held that he would likely offer for

the daughter of a marquess, who happened to be a
political chum of his father's, when the chit came
out next spring. Gossip also indicated that he had
no mistress at the moment. And Ian knew from his
rowdy London days that Haversham had never been
a monk.

That Juliana was his target Ian could not prove . . .
but felt sure of it.

How the hell could he persuade stubborn Juliana
of the man's lascivious intent, when she would not
even talk to him?

"How long before you must sell Bruce?" Ian asked.
Though Byron had given him an indication, Ian
prayed his neighbor had been wrong.

Fergusson buried his fingers in his oily brown hair
and scratched his head. "I tell ye, I canna wait any
longer than a bit after the Twelve Days. Bruce here
will bring me money I need for spring."

Early in January, as Byron had said. He had a month
at the most to find the money somewhere—or persuade Juliana to marry him. He had not the faintest
clue where to begin.

Three days later, Peter, as he had requested Juliana
call him, sat across from her in her town house's
drawing room with a cup of tea on his lap, gazing
intently upon her face.

"Have you had a chance to read the book of poetry
I sent you?" he asked. "I think the verses wonderful
myself, but I look forward to your opinion."

That was what she appreciated about Peter. He
valued the fact that she had a mind of her own. And
while she felt the poetry he had sent her the morning
after their disastrous encounter with Ian was a bit too
indelicate, she could find no fault with his thought-
fulness. He had even sent a lush bouquet of hothouse

flowers that must have cost a small fortune along with the book.

"I'm still browsing," she demurred, not wishing to offend him. "If you chose them, I'm certain they will be lovely."

"Indeed." He smiled, looking pleased. "And you're wearing the earbobs I sent yesterday. How thoughtful."

Self-consciously, Juliana raised her hands to her ears to feel the perfect pearl drops attached there. They were stunning, and for him to give so generous a gift after so early an acquaintance either said a great deal about the depth of his pockets or the measure of his growing affection—or both perhaps. Accepting them wasn't entirely proper, but she could not afford to insult him. Besides, if they wed soon, who would know?

"Your gift was all that is generous. I again protest such extravagance—"

"Please, no. They are best worn on a woman of your perfection. No more protests, my dear, or you shall break my heart." He gave her a mock pout.

Put that way, Juliana thought it impolite to hurt his feelings. Perhaps he'd gone a bit too far with the gift, but he had meant well. And Peter was on the shy side. It was entirely possible he did not give many young ladies gifts and had been uncertain about what was appropriate.

"Very well," she relented. "I accept them with all appreciation."

He patted her knee. "As long as you enjoy them half as much as the time I spend with you."

Juliana opened her mouth to protest his touch, but Peter withdrew and changed the subject.

"Did you enjoy the opera last night?" he queried.

"Quite," she answered, relaxing once again.

She had enjoyed it up until the moment Ian had arrived and done his best to again convince her

Peter's only intent with her was nefarious. His accusations were rubbish, born of his obsession and jealousy. Peter was far too polite and respectful to have lascivious notions, she was sure. But her friendship with Ian had been further reduced by the event, a fact that both distressed and saddened her.

Once Peter had taken her home, he had kissed her as if he held a great measure of passion for her. Juliana was flattered by his attention, even if it wasn't entirely proper. But as a widow, she could be allowed one kiss without social harm. And she was too eager for what she hoped would be a forthcoming proposal to turn him away.

What disturbed her, however, was the fact she had been oddly removed from Peter's pursuit. Perhaps because she knew Ian was somewhere near and she could not abide another confrontation with him. She must concentrate on Peter and begin forming romantic feelings for him, for she suspected he was growing an attachment for her.

"I've always liked the opera," he said, interrupting her reverie. "I find it so stimulating."

Juliana shrugged at his description. She thought it pleasant, but opera clearly affected Peter in a way she had not experienced.

She shrugged. "Well, it's been an age since I've seen good opera or theater, or even been to a large social gathering not made up of military officers and their wives. I've appreciated all our outings, since the entertainment in India was limited."

"So I've heard," he mused. "And with your husband frequently away, I suppose it was even more difficult to bear."

Toward the end, Geoffrey's absence became a blessing, but Peter needn't know that fact now. Too many explanations would be required. So she merely nodded.

"You've been alone for so long," he murmured, setting his teacup aside.

He eased himself closer to her, his long fingers moving to caress her cheek gently. He trained his gaze upon her. Juliana thought the gesture forward, since she had known him but three days. But he had devoted himself to her entirely during those days, and she sensed more out of attraction than any obligation his brother may have placed upon him.

If Peter offered for her, she would most likely accept. In fact, she could not think of a reason she should not. He seemed kind and well placed in society. He was attentive and intelligent. He had his odd moments, but she suspected everyone did. She had no grand passion for him, which meant she could keep her head in the midst of their union. Most of all, he valued her opinions and her independence. He would never try to control her as Ian did.

"You don't have to be alone any longer," he whispered, then placed a soft kiss on her cheek, close to her ear.

Juliana let him, alternately gladdened and concerned that his urbane charm and golden perfection did not move her the way Ian's hot, piercing gaze did.

She closed her eyes, trying to block thoughts of Ian. Why could she not get the cad out of her head?

Peter kissed his way down to her jaw, nibbled a path to her neck. She felt the shock of his tongue graze her skin, his sigh in her ear. She stiffened and backed away.

"Peter?"

He lifted his mouth from her and sat up, taking her hand in his. "I'm sorry, darling. Of course you wish to wait."

Juliana offered him a stilted smile until she realized what he had said. He wanted to wait for intimacies! He could only mean until their nuptials. Had he made up his mind so quickly to offer for her? Her mind raced. If so, her problem would be well solved—and sooner than she had hoped. Her relief grew, for already the funds from Geoffrey's pension were diminishing.

"Indeed," she said. "Your understanding is most gentlemanly."

Peter laughed. Why, Juliana could not imagine, but he did.

"Well, if you are up to an outing this evening, my dear, I have a party I should like to take you to. And while we are there, I have a matter I am most eager to discuss with you."

Could he mean marriage? Oh, how she hoped so! A slightly odd place for such a conversation, but perhaps he had a reason.

Juliana released a shaky breath and smiled. "I should be delighted, Peter."

"It starts late, so I shall be here at eleven. These are very particular friends of mine. We must come in costume and mask. It enhances the mystery of the games we shall play."

Juliana had not been to a costume ball in years. She had always enjoyed them, however. So the evening's entertainment sounded delightful to her. Except the fact she had no costume.

As if he had read her mind, Peter said, "I shall send you a costume this afternoon, if you don't mind. It will compliment mine so that everyone knows we are together."

Was that important to him? The thought it might be made a heady ease slide through her in thick waves. Her days of fighting her father and Ian for the control of her life would soon be over!

"That would be lovely. I look forward to the party."

"As do I," Peter murmured. "If the costume seems a bit different, don't worry. It's all in good fun."

Smiling, Juliana shrugged. If he thought it would

be fun, well, she had no reason not to trust him. "I shall be waiting."

Juliana and Peter arrived at a darkened house on the outskirts of London after midnight. Other than the coaches parked around the dwelling and the drivers milling about with bottles of spirits, she would have thought the house devoid of people.

"It's so dark," she whispered, grasping her cloak tightly around her small, spangled costume.

"Part of the atmosphere." Peter slid his arm around her waist and gave her a squeeze. "You'll see. Put your mask on, my dear."

Easing away from Peter's somewhat familiar touch, Juliana all but ran through the crisp December night to the door, wanting the promise of warmth inside. The costume Peter had sent was that of a harem girl to compliment his sheikh disguise. Her outfit was more than a bit daring—and brief. Still, she lifted her demi-mask near her face to appease her escort.

"No," he reprimanded, his voice sharp. "Put it on, truly."

Juliana frowned. She had been to a number of masquerades during her come-out. No one had actually worn their mask for long, as there was no need; everyone knew everyone.

"Peter, why?" she asked as apprehension began prickling at the back of her neck.

He hesitated, his grip on her arm tightening. "You'll see once we're inside."

As they reached the door, Peter knocked twice, then paused. He raised his hand above the door to knock again. Before he could, Ian stepped out of the black shadows and approached.

He was dressed in black, his hair freshly cut and combed away from his face. His tense posture and angry eyes let Juliana know he had come with confrontation on his mind.

When would the blackguard understand she had refused him?

"Go away, Ian!" Juliana demanded. "I neither want you here nor appreciate your interference in my life."

Ian ignored her and directed a killing stare to Peter. "You're not taking her through that door, Haversham."

"I am," Peter retorted. "I asked her to come with me tonight and she agreed."

Ian leaned closer and growled, "She has no idea what she agreed to."

"Of course I do!" Juliana protested. "It's a masquerade."

Ian finally looked her way. In fact, he drilled her with a furious stare. "Yes, where wealthy men bring their mistresses for all manner of lewd exchanges."

"That is a lie. Blast you, you're revolting!" cursed Juliana. "How did you find me anyway?"

"I bribed one of Haversham's servants to tell me his destination tonight. I've been here ten minutes, which is nine minutes longer than I needed to be certain exactly what kind of gathering this is."

Juliana could not believe, refused to believe, that Peter would bring her to such a party. Surely Ian misunderstood—or, worse, deceived her so she might leave with him.

"Stop it! Lying to malign Peter just because I prefer his company to yours is despicable."

"Is that what you think?" His eyes were a fierce blue.

"Isn't it the truth?" she countered, refusing to flinch from his angry, wounded gaze.

Cursing, Ian turned his attention back to Peter. "Tell her everything, Haversham." When her escort hesitated, Ian barked, "Now, damn you! You know she does not belong here."

"She is free to make her own choices."

"Thank you, Peter, for understanding that. Ian, I'm afraid, never will. You'll talk to a wall with more success."

"Tell her the truth," Ian barked to Peter.

"She's not a dewy-eyed virgin who needs your supervision," Peter hissed.

Juliana's mouth dropped open. While she agreed with Peter's sentiment, it was highly indelicate for him to discuss her chastity before they were married.

"She isn't wise to the mate swapping and voyeurism that goes on in there so she can make a decision," Ian asserted. "She's not a part of the demimonde."

"Peter never thought that," she yelled, then turned to Peter himself. "Did you?"

"I did not imagine you were part of the demi-monde," her escort said, his voice quiet.

A bit of ease slid through her.

"But you wanted to make her one," Ian accused.

"Enough, Ian!" Juliana demanded. "Peter's behavior has been beyond reproach." *Well, mostly.* "And he had never once mentioned any dishonorable intention. I intend to go to the party tonight and enjoy myself. If I choose to wed him over you, you will have to stop haunting me and start accepting it." She turned to Peter, who looked oddly stiff. He released her suddenly.

She sighed. "Think nothing of Ian. He's been plaguing me all my life. Let us go."

"Juliana, do not go in there. You'll ruin your reputation and your life," warned Ian.

She gritted her teeth. "Stop being so dramatic. It's a small gathering of friends, nothing more. And if you don't cease hounding me, I will forget we were ever friends and vow never to speak to you again. And I mean that."

"Have them answer the door," Ian said to Peter. "And do not consider for a moment taking her more than an inch inside."

Peter did not knock. "I intended to have a few minutes alone with Juliana first, to lay forth my . . . proposal." He withdrew a small box from a pocket within his cloak and laid it in her palm.

Juliana closed her eyes, not certain she wanted to open the box. Suddenly her doubts crept in. Peter had been oddly forward at times and given her an expensive gift two days after their acquaintance. And her costume tonight, why was it so brief? The house he'd planned to take her to stood silent and dark. Why wouldn't he knock on the blasted door? Juliana looked down at the box in her hand. What did it contain?

Slowly, she opened the gift to reveal a stunning emerald necklace. Its worth easily tripled the funds Geoffrey had left her to sustain herself for the rest of her life.

"I will be good to you," said Peter quietly. "I will never control you. I appreciate your strength and your mind. You arouse me as no one has in years."

A chill that had nothing to do with the weather shivered through her. Outside, she felt numb, incapable of the betrayal most women would feel. Inside, a core of seething molten fury rumbled through her. But she'd be damned before she would deign to show Peter or Ian her emotions.

"But you had no intent to marry me?" she asked Peter.

He paused, the breeze tugging at his turban. "I cannot. I must have an impeccable woman of quality. Please understand—"

"I am an earl's daughter!"

"Who eloped with a commoner. Everyone imagines you are free with your favors because of it," he said with regret. "I'm sorry."

Peter's words stung far more than she thought possible. The bastard. The cad!

"And because I wed an officer instead of an earl, that makes me damaged goods? So much that you would insult me with an offer to be your mistress?"

He grasped her hand, squeezing gently. "I meant no insult. I simply wished to be with you."

"You meant no insult?" she said, incredulous. Then she looked down at the necklace in her hand. It twinkled even in the dark, heavy and valuable and cold.

Finally she had found a man who appreciated her as she was, only to discover he did not think well enough of her to make her his wife. She swallowed, trying to force down a rise of humiliation, of angry tears. Peter would see neither of these. Juliana never wanted him to know how deeply he had shattered her illusions—and her future.

Calmly, she wrapped the necklace in her fist. "What manner of party is this?"

Peter looked away to the endless empty field about them, securely wrapped in night. "Juliana, I never meant—"

"What manner of party, you rogue?" she demanded.

Peter said nothing, did not look at her.

"Tell her," Ian prodded from behind her.

She felt his protective hand upon her shoulder a moment before he wrapped her in his cloak, still warm from his body. At the moment, she was achingly grateful for both.

But she hated the fact Ian had been so terribly right about Peter's intent.

"She deserves the truth," Ian added.

Slapping an absent hand against his thigh, Peter still did not acknowledge their requests.

Juliana's temper snapped. "What makes you so hesitant? Open the damned door!"

With a heavy sigh, Peter lifted his mask to his face. Remembering his warning, Juliana followed suit. Peter knocked twice on the door, paused, then knocked twice again. A woman with round brown eyes opened a small slat.

"What're ye wantin'?"

"A mutton pie in the garden," he muttered, clearly uncomfortable.

Juliana's confusion and trepidation rose. Was Peter's nonsensical reply some sort of secret password? Was the party so tawdry that it required such?

The woman behind the door laughed. "Aye, there be plenty of pies in the garden to choose from, me fine gent."

With that, she rammed the slat home. A click followed. The door swung open. The trio stepped into the vestibule, Ian blocking the door so no one could shut it and trap them inside.

Words could not prepare Juliana for the sight that greeted her. Shock uncoiled within her when she spotted a dark-skinned woman with rouged nipples and a shaved mons. The woman had been tied to the wall, naked and spread out. Her eyes were glazed and heavy-lidded, her smile crooked.

"Oh, dear God," Juliana gasped, backing away from the image into Ian's protective embrace. She did not know what else to say.

"She looks to be under the influence of opium," Ian whispered in her ear.

Juliana bit her lip to hold in a gasp. The depravity of the sight stunned her beyond speech. She looked away, turning her head to the left. That vision only horrified her more. She espied a room full of naked, twisting bodies, entwined together in clusters of three or four, reaching out with hands, tongues, genitals.

She gaped in shocked silence, then clapped a hand over her mouth. Never had she seen anything so depraved and immoral. Never had she imagined people would enjoy this manner of congress. Oh, she had heard of such things in India, but to see that dissolute conduct occur in London . . . She had never imagined it possible.

"And you sought to bring me here?" Juliana managed to force past her tight throat as she glared at Peter. "You thought I belonged here? You believed I would participate in—in this—"

"Orgy," Ian supplied from behind her.

Juliana shuddered. Even the word was hideous. "I want no part of such debauchery. Why would you bring me here?"

"I thought you understood, truly," Peter said finally, his voice almost pleading. "After hearing gossip of the poor state of your widowhood and your refusal of Axton's marriage proposal, when you arrived in London, well, I—nearly everyone assumed you meant to find a protector. And for a woman who had married as you once did . . . It was ambitious, despite your beauty, to think you would easily snare a titled husband."

If Peter had dealt her an ugly truth, society had slapped her with such insulting assumptions. What was she to do now?

Juliana knew only one thing: She was too proud to be any man's mistress.

"Sweetheart, shall we leave now?" Ian asked softly.

Furious and humiliated, she nodded, threw the emerald necklace back at Peter, then ran away from the house as if hell were at her back. She welcomed the biting wind, for it reminded her that she had escaped the horrors inside the house. Ian followed her, a supportive hand between her shoulders.

He took her to his coach. Once the door shut behind them, Ian sat beside her. He loomed close but did not attempt to pull her near. Juliana appreciated that Ian understood she preferred to release tears when she was alone.

But right now, those tears were terribly close.

Instead, he simply held her hand, his thumb brushing the top of it. "I'm terribly sorry, but I could not allow him to hurt you."

The damnable tears stung her eyes, nearly closed her throat. She sank her teeth into her lip to hold them at bay.

Blast it all, she hated that someone with intentions as vile as Peter's had shattered her plans, her hopes. And barring Ian's interference, she would have had no notion of his terrible intent until it was far too late. That disturbed her immensely. Why had she not guessed what Peter planned?

Worse, she did not want Ian to understand how distressed she was. If he understood her desperation for a husband, he would only press his suit harder. And blast him, she did not want to admit he'd been right any more than Peter had already forced her to. Besides, showing Ian her tears, her weakness, would only add to her humiliation tonight.

But, oh, how her throat ached with the effort of holding it all in.

"Why should you be sorry?" she answered in a tight voice. "You did me a great service tonight, for which I am obliged."

"That is utter rubbish. You're angry with me for being right. But I should rather have your fury and your pride bruised than to have you in Haversham's hands behind that dark house's door."

Ian was right. And worse, he understood her.

The tears rushed up again. Juliana swallowed, nodded. She couldn't manage more.

Silence ensued. Ian clearly waited for her reply. But emotion seized her voice, and she found she could not force words forth.

A minute ticked by. Another, broken only by the *clop* of the horses' hooves, the leaves dancing about to the music of the night wind. Warm bricks at her feet and blankets wrapped around her made Juliana feel safe. No, knowing Ian sat beside her gave her that sensation.

Peculiar, really. She didn't trust him with her heart, but she did with her life, her comfort, even her sense of happiness to a degree. It really made little sense.

But there it was, true and unchangeable.

Beside her, he sighed, a clear sound of frustration. "Splendid. Hate me if you wish." He spat out a sarcastic sound that in no way could be called a laugh. "You will do as you please anyway. For now, I am relieved beyond words to know you are safe."

He grabbed her hand and squeezed it. When he would have released her, Juliana held on.

The tears surged again.

And this time, she couldn't stop them.

Knowing that Ian cared more for her safety than virtually anything, even her opinion of him, added both relief and turmoil to her beleaguered mind. For she had no doubt he cared deeply.

The first sob came in a great burst, a rush of grief. The second came on a jagged breath that seemed to tear its way up her throat. Before the third came, Ian put his arm around her and slid her onto his lap.

And even though Juliana remembered next to nothing of the words he whispered in her ear over the next half hour, she remembered the tenderness of his touch and the understanding in his voice.

Damn him for caring! But she couldn't hate him anymore.

CHAPTER TEN

"*Memsahib?*" her Indian maid, Amulya, called from the door.

Juliana looked up from the mesmerizing flames of her hearth, pushing aside the confusing circle of her thoughts.

Two days had passed since the disastrous night of the lascivious costume ball. Since then, Juliana had been unable to shake her anger. Humiliation plagued her, as did a grief she did not understand. What did she have to grieve? The potential loss of her reputation? It had not come to that. Rather, the simple future she'd thought she could share with Peter was now a shattered illusion, one that disheartened her.

And what if her father learned of her near disgrace?

"Yes," she answered Amulya, rising to her feet.

"Lord Axton is sending packages for you."

Surprise took her aback. "Now? Why, it isn't even Christmas yet."

Amulya merely shrugged. "A man is delivering them. Do you wish that I put them in your chamber?"

"That will be fine. Lord Axton is not here himself?" Juliana asked, not certain if such would bring relief or disappointment.

Ian had come to see her twice since the final incident with Peter. Uncertain what to say, she had refused to see him both times.

"No, he has not come today," Amulya replied. "Not yet. Will you be seeing him if he does?"

She hesitated. Though Ian had been her saving grace that terrible night, memories of the unstoppable tears she had shed in his arms now made her feel weak and embarrassed. Yes, he had comforted her, and in those moments he had been the friend she needed. But the knowledge that he had used superior judgment was evident, and Juliana was loath to face that fact.

"I think not," she answered the Indian woman. "We must leave early tomorrow for Harbrooke."

Her actions were cowardly; Juliana was well aware of that. After all, she would have to face Ian someday . . . but not today. She still had no notion what to say to him.

At Amulya's censuring stare, Juliana knew the maid understood—and disapproved. It only added to the guilt and tumult she could not shed.

Worse, her usual Christmas cheer was absent, lost in a sea of impotent fury and a strange hopelessness. The thought this season might be doomed in her heart only depressed her more.

"Have you finished packing?" she asked the maid, more to distract herself than to learn the answer.

"Yes, memsahib. All but whatever Lord Axton is sending."

Juliana nodded. She should have known Amulya would be ruthlessly efficient as always. "Yes. I shall see to Lord Axton's delivery."

A few minutes later, Juliana trudged upstairs, not certain what she would find. Once in her chamber, she stared at the white boxes stacked on the serene green carpet beside her bed and frowned. Goodness, he must have sent ten boxes—and not small boxes either. What could Ian possibly have bought her?

Tied to the top of the first stack, Juliana found a sealed envelope bearing her name. Inside, Ian had written:

> *Think of the other night as a moment in which you would have seen the truth soon and saved yourself. I was there only to help, as friends do. It was simply another windy day at the river. And if your father should take issue with you, show him the contents of the boxes. This time, you can prove you lost nothing. Please see me when you are able. I miss you.*
>
> > With affection,
> > Ian

Juliana frowned, confused. She read the card again. What did he mean?

With a frown, she reached for the first box. She was stunned to realize it had come from an exclusive lingerie shop. Had Ian done something she would not have thought even he would dare; had he sent her unmentionables? The thought both troubled and intrigued her.

Grabbing the fat blue bow that secured the first box shut, Juliana yanked on the end. The ribbon flew off, and she all but ripped the lid of the box away.

Inside lay a frothy, lacy, bright red petticoat.

A smile tugging at the corners of her mouth, Juliana pulled the confection from the box and held it up. Layer after layer of dyed lace and ribbons fell from her hands to the floor.

The next box revealed a petticoat startlingly similar but in black. Two more came in white. She found others in blue, in green, in a soft pink, still another in horsehair.

Bemused, she read Ian's note again. The message made perfect sense this time.

The day she had fallen into the river and discarded her petticoat to prevent drowning, she had endured her father's displeasure at what he was certain was her hoydenish disregard for propriety. If she'd only had a petticoat to show him, it would have saved her an hour's worth of a tongue-lashing.

Juliana laughed. Ian had the most unusual sense of humor as well as a keen ability to amuse her.

Her dark mood began to lift as the elaborate underthings transported her back to the day Ian had fished her out of the cold river. She did not like to admit it to herself, much less to Ian, but he *had* saved her that day.

Her father had been displeased that she'd been fishing, as no proper lady would. He'd been angry that circumstance had forced her to remove her petticoats where anyone might have seen. And the fact that Ian had seen her naked legs in the melee ... well, she remembered the disgrace her father had tried to heap on her. Meanwhile, Ian had stood outside Harbrooke's study window, behind Papa, and made silly faces.

And while a petticoat would not save her this time if her father found out about the disaster Peter had nearly led her to, well, Juliana understood Ian's message: He would be there for her, help her however he could.

And she could not help but be touched.

Once back in Devonshire, Juliana made the trip to Edgefield Park alone, perhaps because she knew her father disapproved. The first week of December had drifted into the second, while cold descended over the landscape with all its white glory, crisping the air, clinging to bare tree limbs. Normally, she appreciated winter's show of splendor. It reminded her of Christmas. At the moment, she cared for none of it.

Ian had refused to give up on saving her from Peter Haversham's debauched intent despite her own shrewish behavior toward him. Then he had sent her a gift both sentimental and humorous because he knew she would feel awkward about the tears she had shed onto his shirt in great, heaping sobs.

Even if he had manipulated her back to England, she admitted—reluctantly—that she appreciated being home. Ian had been her friend since they had been old enough to filch apple tarts. At the very least, she owed him a few words of thanks.

Upon reaching Edgefield Park, her footman helped her from the carriage. Ian's butler, the stony Harmon, stood ever-waiting to receive her.

"Lady Archer," he greeted, admitting her into the house.

"Hello, Harmon. I should like to see Lord Axton."

"He is with Lord Carlton at the moment, my lady. Would you care to wait?"

Since Ian and Byron had been friends from the cradle, their visit could be long. An odd disappointment weighed on her buoyant mood. She did not miss Ian, of course, but was frustrated she could not relieve herself of her debt of gratitude.

"No, but I think I shall spend a few moments warming myself before I brave the cold once more."

"Very good." Harmon gestured up the stairs. "Follow me."

The butler took her to a cozy library she knew well and had played in many times as a girl. Ian used it frequently, probably because his father never did.

Smiling, she made her way over to the blazing hearth and gratefully held her icy hands near the flames.

The murmur of male voices reached her a moment later. Juliana paused and cocked her head toward the sound, centered in the drawing room on the far side of the room's other door.

"Splendid news that your visit with Fergusson went well," said a voice she recognized as that of Byron, Lord Carlton.

"Quite. Bruce will make an excellent stud," said Ian. "And when I inquired about Fergusson in London, everyone agreed he was every bit as respected as you said. You have my thanks, and if I can repay you for the tip, let me know."

"You can," Lord Carlton interjected. "Explain your behavior toward Juliana Archer at our first snow party."

Ian responded after a moment of silence. "I have again asked her to marry me."

"I see. And how did she answer?"

He paused once more. "She has not—yet. She has promised me a reply on Christmas morning."

"You don't sound terribly optimistic," observed Lord Carlton quietly. "Do you think she will refuse you again?"

Ian sighed. "Unfortunately, yes. She has given me every indication she will, but still I hope."

"Why do you believe she will reject you?"

"She's angry with me for doing my utmost to prevent her marriage to Archer, though I acted with her best interest in mind. For that, she views me as manipulative and controlling."

What other way was there to see him? She rolled her eyes. Why did Ian never see logic where she was concerned?

"Perhaps she's simply not the woman for you, old boy."

"She is the only woman I wish to wed," Ian stated with conviction. "But I persuaded her to leave India by telling her that her father was ill. I'm glad for his returned health, but she looks at his hearty visage now and assumes I lied."

"Really?" Interest held the emphasis in Byron's voice. "For some months, Brownleigh looked terrible. Even my father remarked upon it."

Juliana started, then wandered closer to the cracked door. Her father truly had looked ill? Had *everyone* noticed it?

"And I tried to explain that to her," said Ian. "I tried like hell to clarify my personal concern for her father's health, but to no avail. She trusts neither of us."

At Ian's words, shock vibrated through her. Her mouth fell open. He *had* been concerned about her father. Oh, my. If that were true, he had not lied completely. She felt faint.

Perhaps not, but he had also embellished the truth, by his own admission.

But he had done so with good intentions in his heart, she argued with herself. Did that not count for something?

Worse, she had wrongly accused and upbraided him.

Again, Lord Carlton laughed. "I begin to think you will never learn. Well, if Lady Archer rejects you again, my cousin, Lady Mary, the girl you met at the party, would be most willing to accept the very proposal you put to Juliana. Mary is very much hunting for a husband, and I have from the lady herself that she found you quite handsome and thinks you are all that is—how did she put it?" Byron paused. "Ah, yes, 'all that is agreeable in a man and husband.'"

Juliana found herself gaping. The daze-eyed chit had discerned all that after a mere two minutes? She knew nothing of Ian, of what he wanted or needed. Who did the brazen girl think she was?

"No offense to your cousin," Ian began, "but my mind is set upon Juliana. If she rejects me, I'd rather you ply me full of whiskey, as you did the last time."

"And if I'm not available for that arduous task? How will you survive? I think you should keep Lady Mary in mind."

"I would rather ride hell-bent to find you and that whiskey," quipped Ian, but his voice sounded hollow.

"Well, I suppose I can stay close, in case."

"Do," Ian said. "I may have need of strong drink by Boxing Day."

After Byron left, Ian sank down to the sofa, his mind heavy with thoughts of Juliana.

With Christmas just over a fortnight away, he could not disregard the worry for his future. It crept in insidiously, like a spider. Ian felt like fate's fly, ready to become prey.

Until now, he had assumed that Juliana would recover from her pique of temper and realize they could make a perfect marriage. But he had not seen her since revealing Peter Haversham's lewd intent. Not even the petticoats had warmed her to him, it seemed, for she had said nothing of them before leaving London. He had no notion how to convince her that he would stand beside her, that she need not be embarrassed by the tears she had wept. That he loved her.

Ian thought of losing Juliana not only as a wife, but as a friend. And he despaired. He was also painfully aware that every day made his hold on Fergusson's fine horse, Bruce, increasingly tenuous too.

Damn! His every dream in life was slipping away. What the hell could he do to stop it?

"My lord?" intoned the aging Harmon upon entering the room.

"What is it?" Ian muttered, fearing his father wanted to grill him on his failure to procure Juliana as a wife—or any other wife—while in London.

"Lady Archer has been waiting for half an hour to see you."

Surprise replaced Ian's downtrodden mood in an instant. Hope came hard on its heels. "Here? For me?"

"Indeed, my lord. In the library."

"Thank you," he murmured as he bolted to the connecting door.

When he reached the library, he paused, then flung the ajar door wide open, his heart pounding with excitement and apprehension. Dear God, he hoped she had come to listen to him, that he could talk some sense into her stubborn hide and persuade her to marry him.

Juliana stood frozen in the middle of the room, wearing a stunned expression. She looked incredibly fetching in a gown of pale green, complimented by small pink roses dotting the neckline and sleeves. The rich mass of her fair hair lay atop her head, framed by a few shining ringlets about her face. Cold had nipped her cheeks and the tip of her nose with color.

Ian ached to kiss her again.

But she already looked quite wide-eyed and confused.

"Juliana? Are you well?" When she did not reply, he frowned and trod closer. "Can I get you some—"

"I overheard you with Lord Carlton."

That took him aback. "I see." Mentally, he replayed the conversation, trying to discern what might have stunned her.

"My father truly was ill?" she asked.

Automatically, Ian nodded as his memory of the conversation with Byron returned in force. Yes, even their neighbor, whom Juliana had no reason to distrust, had believed Lord Brownleigh ill. How fortuitous that she had overheard! He could not have planned this better if he had tried.

"Juliana, I told you the truth as I believed it. Your father did not look well to me. I had every hope he would recover, but I also had every hope that you would agree to come home because of it. I had no way of knowing how long, or even if, he would live."

She blinked, turned slowly, moved as if in a trance over to the settee. Ian trailed behind her, standing beside her as she sat. Finally, she looked up at him with wide hazel eyes that held both bewilderment and regret.

"I—I hardly know what ... I can only say I'm sorry."

Juliana looked down, where she clasped her hands tightly. Ian knelt before her and lifted her chin with his finger.

"It's all right."

Seeming to wake herself from the odd trance, she focused on him with a sharp gaze and gave her head a decisive shake. "No, I've been unfair. I thought I had you all figured out. You were made in my father's mold, right? And you would manipulate me to the position you wished me to occupy, then ignore me until you needed me again."

"Shhh. That is not so." He caressed her cheek. "I could never do that to you. How can I prove how much you mean to me?"

"I let my fear of being controlled color my behavior," she offered. "Whatever the case, when I'm wrong I try to admit it."

Hope swelled within him. Maybe now she would agree to wed him. Now that she believed he had only her best interests at heart, perhaps she would cease fighting him.

Ian clasped her hand in his and squeezed. "I'm simply glad that you're no longer angry and that we can be friends again. We can, can't we?"

A faint smile lifted the corners of Juliana's wide pink mouth. "We always have been. And I came today to thank you for being a friend to me in London. I—I was wrong there, as well, not to listen to your warnings about Peter Haversham. I never believed anyone would think so little of me. And it was all too easy to believe you would lie ruthlessly to get your way. I painted you very black in my mind, I'm afraid."

"And now?" Ian asked.

His heart was racing, speeding toward an explosion of hope and anticipation. More than anything, he longed to hear her say that she would wed him, but he knew he must tread carefully. Any hint of more than gentle persuasion would send her running like a skittish mare.

"I realize I'm lucky to have you as my friend. Not everyone would have continued to help me while I treated you as less than a gentleman."

Ian smiled. Friendship was good, a start. She was moving closer to him. Yes, he wanted more, wanted it so badly, his whole body ached. But from the manner in which she had previously kissed him, he felt certain she found him somewhat appealing. Perhaps with a bit more time she would adjust to today's revelations and finally decide to trust—and marry—him.

"That is what friends do for one another, love. I like to think you would have done the same for me had I found myself in trouble."

"I like to think so too," she said with a smile. "But I am not certain whether I should thank you for the scandalous gifts you sent me in London or scold you for such roguish thoughts. A gentleman would not think of my undergarments."

"Considering I watched them float down the river, I think we are far beyond that, don't you?"

"Perhaps." She laughed. "But don't think I won't keep them—and use them too."

He laughed. "I should be most honored if you did. Perhaps you might think of me on such occasions?"

"I'm sure you wish I would," she scolded playfully.

"Indeed, I do," he agreed, sending her a message of solemn desire, of intent.

She responded with a fixed stare, a smile that slowly fell.

"Juliana . . ."

Ian lifted his hand to her face again, curled his fingers around her neck and inched closer. He gave her plenty of time to back away. Instead, she met his stare measure for measure, her face reflecting something tender and breathless. She closed her eyes moments before their lips met.

He took her mouth gently, careful not to frighten the wary woman, alternately brushing and melding his lips with hers until she sighed in contentment.

Moving closer, Ian kissed her with reverence, worshiping her mouth, savoring her response, given in honesty and trust. Nothing was ever so sweet as her tentative surrender.

Again, he deepened the kiss, taking her mouth in slow sweeps, angling to fit her perfectly, opening her lips slowly to take her all in. To his every subtle cue she responded, granting him all he asked and more.

Beneath his palm he felt the pulse of Juliana's heartbeat at her neck. It accelerated with each kiss. He urged her lips to open to him completely, and she complied. Her heart picked up speed. Their mouths mated. Ian swirled his tongue around hers, tasting her essence. Her pulse beat harder. He swept his other hand up her arm, caressed her shoulder, then sent his fingers down, down, to brush the swells of her breast. When he traced the shadow of her cleavage, Juliana's heartbeat hammered out of control.

With his fingers, Ian brushed the tips of her breasts. Right away, he felt the peaks hardened from their kiss. His own heartbeat erupted, roaring in his ears.

Caution fled his body as lust and need bellowed through him, stripping his mind of rational thought.

Moaning, he cupped her breast in his palm and brushed his thumb over its peak. Once more, he seized her mouth in a hungry kiss, drunk with the taste of her, the possibilities that lay before him. Never had he wanted her so badly. Hell, never had he wanted anyone this much.

Juliana answered his fevered kiss, her breath turning short, her lips meeting his more than halfway. She arched into his hand as he continued to fondle her with needy fingers.

Wanting desperately to take her in—all of her— Ian kissed a heated trail down the softness of her jaw to the dewy skin at her neck. He plied his lips there with fervency, with a single-minded drive to possess her, please her. Juliana sighed raggedly and angled her head to provide him better access to the sensitive place between her neck and shoulder he knew would smell as spicy and intriguing as she always did.

Laying her down on the settee, he leaned over her, into her, placing his mouth on just the spot he sought. He inhaled her, nearly dizzy with all she did to him.

"Juliana," he rasped, then nibbled on her neck, her lobe.

She shivered and clasped him tight, gasping when his mouth found a responsive spot behind her ear.

Ian explored there, sighed there, kissed there. The swells of her breasts began to flush and dampen. Tightly, she clasped him, until he lay on top of her, his thigh resting between hers. Lightly, he pressed against her sex. She moaned his name.

Never had he heard a sound sweeter.

And he was driven to taste more of her feminine mystery, all she would allow, absorb her into his memory, learn her every pleasure with the hope they would become spouses and lovers.

Kissing a heated path down her neck, Ian lifted her breast from the confines of her gown. Rosy, taut, and hard, her wide areola beckoned him. He obliged the urge, savoring her with a sweep of his tongue, followed by a full possession of his mouth.

Juliana called his name again, this time fisting her fingers into his hair.

Heated beyond endurance, lust burned inside him. He needed her, knew they were right together. Now he began to truly hope she saw it too.

Again, he explored the kernel of her breast with his tongue, gently grazing it with his teeth. He pressed his thigh into her sex again, rhythmically, until she began to move with him.

She whispered his name once, twice.

The desire he felt was like an inferno. He wanted Juliana naked. He wanted to send her over the edge and watch her face as she found that perfect pleasure. He wanted to be inside her, feeling her take him in, accepting him, opening to him in love.

Reaching down, he lifted the hem of her gown in his hand and gave the voluminous skirts a ruthless shove up past her shin, to her knee. His greedy hand left the dress, fastened itself on her thigh over her stocking. He followed the scrap of silk to its end, where only the softest of flesh burned against his hand, beckoning him with her feminine heat just inches away.

In a well-practiced motion Ian unsnapped her stocking and thrust it down to her knee. With his thigh wedged between hers, he parted her legs farther, then touched his way up her inner thighs with a feathery caress. Within moments, he could feel her damp heat. His belly clenched. He was long past mere arousal, yet at the thought of touching her most intimately, he hardened unbearably and moved to settle his palm over her mons.

"No," she breathed, panted. "Ian, this is not right."

Above her, Ian stilled. Frustration tore through

him, but he would not do anything she did not want
as badly as he.

"This is right," he argued. "We are right together."

"I—I . . . This is too much. I've never felt so melted
and—and wanton."

He wanted to ask why Archer had never seen to
her pleasure, but he knew she would say nothing.
More, it pleased him to think he might be the first
to give that gift to her.

"I feel the same way," he assured.

"Anyone can find us here. I'll be ruined!"

He sighed. "My room is not far. No one will look
for us there." When she hesitated, he said, "Come
if you wish, but remember we are grown adults capable of making decisions for our lives."

Unable to resist the disheveled sight she presented,
Ian trailed his fingers across her cheek and pressed
his mouth to hers.

Instead of responding, Juliana sat up and righted
her clothing. "Nothing is that simple. Do you not
see? I made a rash decision when I wed Geoffrey. I
cannot rush into such a decision again. I cannot risk
doing so again. I—I'm simply not ready for that."

Ian closed his eyes and swallowed the bitter reality
of her words. No amount of coaxing or cajoling would
change her mind. Oh, she might give in to his seduction. But she would only hate him for it tomorrow.

"I understand," he said, rising to his feet and
righting his coat and cravat.

"Thank you," she murmured as she adjusted her
clothing.

She was shy now, clearly a bit ill at ease with the
intimacies they had shared. Indecision he understood; discomfort he would not have.

Sinking his fingers into the luxury of her gilt-hued
hair, he tilted her lips to his for a soft kiss. "Think
about how good we are together. Think about con-

senting to be my wife. Promise me you will consider it again before Christmas Day."

Ian heard the pleading note in his own voice. He'd never been reduced to begging for anything in his life, but somehow with her, his pride took second place to his need to wed her. Perhaps he was obsessed. . . .

"I promise," she whispered.

At the end of the day, those two words were all that mattered, for Juliana always kept her promises.

The following morning brought a pair of odd occurrences, in Juliana's estimation. Harriet Radford, Byron's mother, called upon her. Not upon her mother but specifically upon her. And she stayed a full hour. Polite society dictated the length of the optimal call was fifteen minutes. Because they kept country manners in their small corner of Devonshire, no one thought much of a visit slightly longer.

However, a call from a bachelor's mother that lasted such an inordinate length of time was bound to raise brows and set tongues wagging in Lynton. The fact that Harriet Radford could speak only of Byron's merits and ask thinly veiled questions about her feelings toward Ian incited both her curiosity and apprehension.

Shortly after Harriet left, Byron himself arrived, looking as well—and as nervous—as she had ever seen him. He held a box of candies and cakes.

Holding her curiosity, the two of them took tea together in the drawing room before the fire. He said nothing for fully three minutes. Juliana's mind raced, wrestling to discern the reason for his visit. He behaved as if he were . . . courting her.

"You look quite—quite—" He stuttered, stopped, closed his mouth, and opened it again. His fair skin turned red. "Very lovely today. Yes."

Juliana smiled. Byron would never change. He was shy and kind and clearly uncomfortable. "Thank you."

"How do your holidays progress?"

He nodded emphatically. "Very nicely. And yours?"

"They shall be quiet." At least until her father confronted her about her plans to marry again. "We haven't the family staying with us, like your Yorkshire cousins."

Again, Byron nodded. "Oh, yes. But that may be a blessing. My cousin Mary, if you recall—you do recall her?"

Juliana found herself gritting her teeth. "Of course."

"Perhaps she and—and Ian will . . . become friends. Maybe more? Mary is already half smitten, I daresay. And why shouldn't Ian find such a charming girl . . . well, ah, charming?"

Chewing on the inside of her cheek, Juliana considered how best to respond. But her thoughts were interrupted by bursts of anger at Lady Mary, the little hussy.

The girl wanted to be Ian's *friend,* did she? His wife, in truth. Juliana rolled her eyes. It was no surprise, really. An insipid country miss with one foot still in the nursery would have to be blind not to notice a man of Ian's qualities.

Yes, he had them; even she had to admit that. Ian was, of course, handsome, provided one liked men with hair a most touchable black, wide foreheads, firm jaws, cheeks seemingly carved from stone. Impossibly wide shoulders, yes—and an unyielding body with gentle hands. But that wasn't so unusual, surely. Ian's eyes were pleasant, quite nice even, expressive, and incredibly, fathomlessly blue. Juliana shook her head to clear her thoughts. Lady Mary could undoubtedly be attracted to Ian's title, his family wealth, his well-spoken manners—and that seductive quality in his voice, as if he spoke to a woman, and to her alone. And his kiss ... Certainly Lady Mary suspected how potently it affected a woman.

"Lady Archer?" Byron said. "Do you disagree that Ian might find Lady Mary charming? Perhaps you find him ... pleasing?"

Juliana ignored Byron's last question. "I fear it may be premature to discuss Ian's sentiments for your cousin. They've met but once. Is that not right?"

Byron nodded his pale head. "Yes, but Mary says she's never met a man quite so charming and believes he presented himself with such charm for a reason."

Holding in a sigh at the girl's naiveté, Juliana smiled instead. "I am convinced that Lady Mary finds Ian to be admirable. If you've come to ask me about Ian's feelings for your cousin, I can only say I do not believe he is equally inspired."

With a downward glance to the hands he wrung in his lap, Byron said, "That is not why I have come. I—I wished to thank you for your kindness to me at the first snow party. We never had the opportunity to talk, as we agreed."

So Byron *had* come to pay his addresses to her.

Juliana did not particularly believe that she and Byron would suit, but she did not know for certain. After all, their conversation had been unfairly cut short at the first snow party, thanks to Ian. In light of that fact, she thought it wise to spend at least a few moments with Byron. No need to rush to decision about marriage. She'd acted rashly with Geoffrey and earned little more than misery. Besides, why should she limit her choice of suitors to Ian alone so soon?

True, he had not lied to her about her father's illness. But did that mean Ian had changed, and she could completely trust him to be all honesty now? Somehow, Juliana found herself skeptical. And how could she possibly trust Ian when she couldn't even trust herself around the man? Succumbing to the pleasure of his kisses yesterday had been both dizzying and foolish.

A moment later, Juliana heard her name. She looked up to find Byron peering at her, a question in the sedate eyes behind his spectacles. She sent him a contrite smile she hoped didn't look as awkward as it felt.

As they began a chat about her days in India, Juliana studied him, his too-short hair, his intelligent eyes and kind face. He would make a fine husband. And while he provoked no reaction in her, she had to remind herself she'd been hoping for a man very much like this to wed. If he lacked self-confidence in public, surely he would feel at ease with her over time.

Still, she tried to imagine him approaching her chamber on their wedding night—and could not.

A short ten minutes later, Byron rose and made to leave. Juliana smiled, oddly relieved their visit was over. In truth, Byron was everything she could want in a husband—docile, wealthy, polite. Clearly, he held some measure of interest in her. Why, then, was she not thrilled?

"May I—I come to, ah, that is . . . may I come calling tomorrow?" he asked, tongue-tied once more.

Juliana found it both endearing and irritating at once. Still, regardless of her odd impulse to refuse him, she must not yet eliminate any potential husband who presented himself. "That would be lovely."

He left with flushed cheeks and a wide smile on his face.

CHAPTER ELEVEN

The following afternoon, Lord Brownleigh raced to Edgefield Park as if the devil were at his heels. Ian received Juliana's father instantly, fearing something had gone dreadfully wrong.

He was right.

"Byron is courting Juliana?" Ian asked once her father had finished explaining. "Byron Radford?"

"Yes! He's been to see her twice in as many days. This morning, he stayed more than half an hour. And when he left, they both were smiling as if they had a secret."

Ian sighed against the tightening of his gut. It was not his place to tell Byron whom he could woo, but damn it, the man—his own friend—had known Juliana was considering his proposal. Why would he press his suit to her now?

That was but a minor consideration, really. More urgently, Ian wished to know if Juliana welcomed Byron's suit. Pain tore through him at the thought she might, especially after the intimacies they had shared just a few afternoons before.

Sinking down onto the sofa, Ian wondered what he should—indeed, what he could—do about this distressing turn of events.

"I begin to think you have not been properly motivated to win my daughter's hand," Brownleigh cut into his thoughts.

Ian would have laughed had he not been so disheartened. If he had been any more motivated, surely it would be illegal, immoral, or both.

"I assure you, I am all eagerness to win Juliana's—"

"Truly, I'd believed she would be so thrilled to see you in India that she would agree to your proposal on the spot."

The earl spoke as if he were the only one in the room, so Ian saw no reason to respond. Anyway, he had not proposed to Juliana again until they were aboard the *Houghton,* but why correct Lord Brownleigh's error?

"And I very much thought you could persuade her during the voyage back," Brownleigh blathered on. "If nothing else, seduce her, compromise her. You know how to do that, man."

Not for lack of trying, but this was *not* the conversation Ian wanted to have with Juliana's father. Besides, he made his affection sound so calculating. All Ian wanted to do was touch Juliana, feel her acceptance, sink into her essence, and drown.

"Your daughter is a stubborn woman—"

"Who needs the firm hand of a man to guide her through life," the earl cut in, his cheeks turning red. "Good God, you cannot lose her to Byron Radford. He is a terrible cardplayer and even worse at managing his estates. He'll let Juliana run wild because he is too meek to temper her strong impulses."

Impulses? Juliana did not have many of those, only strong opinions.

Ian frowned at the earl's disturbing words. He

wanted to marry Juliana, not parent her. And while he agreed she needed a strong husband, he believed it because she needed the challenge, an equal, not because she needed to be told how to run her life.

"I assure you, I will do everything in my power to win Juliana. I love her, and she knows it. We are, I think, coming to understand each other. I very much hope it won't be long before she relents."

"So you've said before." Brownleigh sniffed. "It's clear you need an incentive to advance your pursuit. Didn't take you for a man who would be bothered by competition, but you don't always know about these things."

"I am not bothered at the thought of competition," he said through gritted teeth. Well, he was bothered but not scared. He had no intent to back away. Juliana was *his*, even if she stubbornly refused to acknowledge it.

With a sigh, Brownleigh ignored Ian and peered at him with a cunning scowl. "How much more money do you need to see that breeding stable completed and the manor house built?"

The question took Ian aback. "In addition to the money I shall receive from my father once I wed?"

Was the earl talking about an incentive of that proportion? Ian frowned. Did Brownleigh mean to tempt him to take a bride he yearned for with the whole of his heart? It seemed impossible the old man would believe him insincere, but he must.

With an impatient gesture of his fleshy hands, the earl brushed his question aside. "Yes, after that, how much do you require?"

"A-about ten thousand pounds." Damn, he hated the shaking in his voice. But he wanted it all—everything, especially Juliana—so badly.

"Done," Brownleigh snapped.

Ian's conscience prickled and poked at him, but he thrust it aside. He hardly needed such inducement to pursue Juliana, but the earl had offered it. Why turn it down? He would do his utmost to wed Juliana either way. Obtaining what Brownleigh offered would only enhance their future together.

"But it will be yours only if you can persuade my daughter to accept your proposal by Christmas. And I don't have to remind you of the consequences if you should fail, do I?"

Ian clenched his jaw. The earl needn't say a word.

"I see you understand me. Now, get to winning her hand before that slobbering prick Radford beats you to it."

As quickly as he had blown in, Brownleigh left. Ian sighed with relief and sank to the sofa.

Dear God, had the old earl lost his mind? He and Brownleigh had always had an amiable rapport, but today Ian had felt distaste for his neighbor's suggestions and posture on the subject of his daughter.

Still, they wanted the same end, even if for differing reasons. And he could not afford to turn down Brownleigh's "incentive." With his help, he and Juliana would have a grand home of their own almost right away.

That Juliana would be furious with this agreement went without saying, but Ian did not intend that she learn of it. She would only misunderstand why he had agreed.

In truth, his every instinct urged Ian to go to Juliana and find some way—any way—to convince her to refuse Byron's court. But if he did so, Ian had no illusions; Juliana would welcome Byron more just to spite him. No, that wasn't the answer.

But he believed he knew what was.

Decided, Ian turned for the stable and ordered his mount saddled. He and Byron would have a chat, man to man.

* * *

The next day snow fell fiercely. Christmas drew closer, and while her weather-induced captivity indoors would have been the perfect time to finish making the gifts she planned to give her family, Juliana found she could not concentrate on tasks that left her hands busy and her mind idle.

Pleading a headache, she took to her room and withdrew her diary. She had been avoiding it lately, she realized. She hadn't known what to say exactly.

Still, she retrieved the small book that carried years of her innermost thoughts, sat at her small secretary, withdrew her ink and pen, and sighed.

> *Just when I think I know Ian for the cad he appears to be, he surprises me. I had no notion until I overheard him talking to Lord Carlton that most in Lynton truly thought Papa ill while I was in India. Since that is true, it appears I've been wrong about many things, Ian in particular.*
>
> *He asked for no apology, though I offered one. It was only fair. Instead, Ian asked that I consider his proposal of marriage again and answer him on Christmas Day. With less than two weeks before I must reply to the query, I do not know what I shall say.*
>
> *Can I trust him? Perhaps more than I thought. Even when I believed him a duplicitous rogue, I could not deny an attraction to him that befuddles me. He possesses more capacity for tenderness and forgiveness than I. And still he wants me.*
>
> *While I am flattered by Lord Carlton's suit, I am unmoved. He is everything my mind tells me I should want and everything my heart rejects. Even writing this, I feel foolish, but it's true. The kinder Byron is, the more I grit my teeth. Or maybe it is my yearning*

*for Ian that prevents me from enjoying Lord Carlton's
company in any but the most platonic manner.*

*I can no longer deny that I should consider marrying
Ian. He claims to love me, and I have no reason to
disbelieve him. Do I love him? I'm not certain. I think
about him far too much, can scarce resist his kisses,
and I enjoy his laughter. Is that love? I am hardly
an expert on the subject, I fear. I thought I loved
Geoffrey, and yet I came to thoroughly loathe him.*

On that sour note, Juliana put the book aside and
rose, restlessly pacing.

Was she really considering Ian as a husband?

If she had to ask herself the question, clearly she
was. And why wouldn't she?

Could she see him approaching her chamber on
their wedding night? Yes, he would barge through
the door if he must. And she knew from his kisses,
his shocking, hot mouth upon her breast, that he
would have no hesitation in doing much more than
necessary to consummate their marriage.

The thought made her flushed and restless all over.

But it was the man himself who drew her. He had
such capacity for feeling that always enticed her, daz-
zled her, made her feel alive. She had seen him flash
with anger and laugh with mirth. He was caring at
times, impossible at others. He made her *feel.* Some
days, she hated him for it because her emotions were
always such a jumble. At other times, she blessed him
for the penchant because it kept her heart beating
human.

At the center of her reality, however, lay the fact
that her mind dwelt upon Ian with the stubborn hold
of a vine clinging to a tree.

Perhaps he would make a good husband. Maybe.
The question was, did she want to take the ultimate
chance, which would bind her for the rest of her life,
to a man with a history of lying, to find out?

* * *

The following day brought yet another surprise: Ian's mother. Despite the fact they were neighbors, Juliana had seen the woman only a handful of times. She generally stayed wherever her husband was not, which usually meant London.

Juliana stared at the pale, thin woman whom age had scarcely touched and wondered why she had come.

"The expression on your lovely face tells me you wonder why I've called on you," said Ian's mother.

"No," she lied. "I'm delighted to have the company, Lady—"

"No formality, please. You must call me Emily."

Such a familiar invitation after so long an absence between their acquaintance? Juliana tried not to frown in thought. But one question ruled her thoughts: why?

"Thank you . . . Emily. Call me Juliana."

"Of course. Thank you."

A smile turned up the corners of Emily's small mouth. Juliana imagined that many would think Ian's mother a cross between an angel and a sprite, with her pale complexion and bright blue eyes that held more than a hint of mischief.

"You've returned home?" Juliana said, trying to make polite conversation.

"For the holiday. Ian so enjoys Christmas. Since he is my only child, I cannot deny him such a small request."

Juliana frowned, her thoughts following the trail Emily had laid about following her son's requests. "Naturally. And did Ian also send you here to speak on his behalf?"

Emily smiled, her dark hair shining in the winter sun that streamed through the windows. Her eyes held years of experience Juliana sensed had come at great cost. Her only two wrinkles lay between her brows, where it appeared she frowned often.

"Ian said you were still forthright, even as a woman full grown."

"I'm sorry if I offended you." Still, it did not escape Juliana's attention that Ian's mother had dodged her question.

"No," Emily assured her. "It's refreshing."

"I have never been afraid to express my opinion," Juliana murmured in self-deprecation. *Just ask my father and your son.*

Emily reached for her tea and sipped delicately. The woman studied her with an earnest gaze, assessing and dissecting her. Juliana did her best to meet the woman's stare squarely, chin raised.

"Then I shall not be afraid to express mine," said Ian's mother.

Her smile disappeared. The frown that engaged her two wrinkles appeared. Again, Juliana was struck by the notion that here sat a woman who understood well life's joys and sorrows.

"Ian is a good man." She smiled and paused, as if determining how best to go on. "I've heard it said children are a blend of both parents. I'm sure you're aware Ian's father and I have not been on . . . polite terms for some years, so naturally I never wanted Ian to possess any of his father's qualities. But he has Nathaniel's pride. I like to think he took intelligence and patience from me."

Emily smiled sadly. Juliana hadn't the faintest clue what to say.

"But from each of us," the woman went on, "he received some gifts that make him better than either of us alone. His father gave him great cunning and strength of conviction. It's what makes Nathaniel both a shrewd money manager and such a bastard."

Emily's statement stunned Juliana to wide-eyed silence. The woman was so honest about the state of her marriage—and so impassive. Yet the sadness in her otherwise pixieish face told a story different than her voice and words.

"I've shocked you. I am sorry, but hear me out." At Juliana's nod, Emily went on. "Ian has his father's only good qualities, and they are tempered by the heart he inherited from me. If my son says he loves you, he does."

Juliana sat back against the sofa and swallowed. At times, she believed that, yearned to. At other times, she wondered how a man who loved her could want to deny her the independence that allowed her soul to breathe.

Exhaling, confused, Juliana had no notion how to respond to Emily. Perhaps the woman did not truly understand Ian's controlling nature.

Or had she herself completely misunderstood it?

No. Juliana only needed to remind herself of Ian's many attempts to prevent her marriage to Geoffrey. Right or not, the choice had not been his. And though he admitted that now, his tendency to take matters into his own hands remained. Or had he truly changed in the last five years?

Emily sipped her tea again, easing the cup down gently. "Ian can be a tyrant, I know. But he is not unreasonable."

Raising a brow, Juliana studied the older woman. Emily believed what she said. Clearly, a mother's love is blind.

"You've brought a simple solution to a matter that is anything but," Juliana said. "Sometimes I fear there may be too much history, too many lies, and too much distrust between us. My father would like to see my life controlled by a 'strong' husband from the day I wed until the day I die. He's chosen Ian for the task, and I have no illusions why. They are quite the same creature in their ability to wield power. I was born to my father, so I could not help that as a child. But I am a widow now. Let me assure you, I will not easily turn over my autonomy to a man who seems an awfully lot like my sire."

Emily gave an airy laugh and reached out to pat her hand. "Dear, Ian does not want to control you. His stern behavior is born of fear."

Juliana found herself thoroughly confused. Either the woman was quite daft or simply brilliant. "Fear?"

"Of course. Fear that you will not give him a chance to win your love."

"I have given him chances. Too many, most likely."

"And still you feel nothing for him."

I wish I could, she thought, closing her eyes and praying for strength. "Unfortunately for your son, my childhood trust and adoration gave way to adult reality when he lied to me to stop my marriage." She paused at Emily's faintly censuring expression. "I grant you, he's done a great deal for me since, and I am trying to trust in him again. I am considering his proposal. But at nearly every turn he infuriates me and tries to bully me to the altar."

"The fear," said Emily as if it were obvious. "He has not yet learned the secret that women have known for centuries: It's easier to catch flies with honey than with vinegar."

Now she was thoroughly confused. Juliana squinted at Emily as if she'd lost her mind. "I beg your pardon?"

Again, Emily laughed. "He's quite afraid of losing you, I think, that plain courting and common courtesy have not really crossed his mind. So in his fear he resorts to the male response: He demands and connives. But underneath, he merely wants to love you—and win your love in return."

Was that true? Could Ian's behavior be explained so simply?

"Think on it, my dear," Emily said. "If you're so inclined, I should love to welcome you to our family."

Then, before Juliana could question Ian's mother, she was gone. Still, Emily's words echoed in her mind all day.

The afternoon only grew more strange. Not half an hour after Emily's departure, Juliana sat staring into the blazing hearth, trying to discern Ian's true motives toward her, when her butler announced Byron's arrival.

He came bearing no gift this time, which she found slightly odd. Still, she looked forward to his chatter more than the gifts, so his lack of a present meant nothing to her.

"Lord Carlton, how good to see you," she greeted.

He looked down at his boots. Juliana held in a sigh.

Truly, she had thought he had passed his shyness with her, but this posture only proved she'd been wrong.

"I—I'll stay only a moment. I do not want—that is, I will not bother you for long."

Juliana frowned at her shy suitor. "You are no bother at all. Sit down and—"

"No," Byron shook his head. "No, no. I merely came to apologize."

For the second time today, she began to feel as if she had missed a relevant conversation or two. Not only was she confused, she was bloody frustrated.

"You have nothing to apologize for," she said. "You've offended me in no way, I assure you."

Byron lifted his serious face to her once before he dropped it again. "I—I thank you for your kindness. And I vow that I did not mean to interfere in your courtship with Ian."

Never mind having missed a conversation or two; maybe she had missed an entire day or two, for she had no notion what Byron rambled about.

"Interfere? Heavens, what gave you—"

"Ian told me of your promise to answer his marriage proposal by Christmas. I am most honored to court you, but—"

Alarm spiked her formidable temper. "Ian *told* you about that promise?"

Byron lifted his head and sent her an uncertain glance. "He merely asked me, man to man, to allow you a few weeks to fulfill your bargain so he might have this chance to win you before I called on you again. To be fair, I agreed."

Fair? Where was it written that she could have no other suitors until she had given Ian her final answer on Christmas Day? Nowhere but in Ian's twisted head! And Byron thought *he* was interfering? If anyone was, it was that conniving neighbor of hers!

"You look angry. Oh—oh, no. Oh, my. I said the wrong thing," he lamented.

Holding in a sigh of frustration, Juliana tried not to glare at Byron. No wonder the rat had so smoothly talked him into giving up his suit. Ian had the velvet-tongued dance of persuasion down to an art. Byron hadn't stood a chance.

"I thought I had the opportunity to court you only because Ian said he felt certain you meant to refuse him." Byron's shoulders sagged. "But Ian is entirely right; it was unfair of me to rob him of his last chance with you before you properly decided upon that course. If—if in fact you decide that course."

Byron gave a nervous smile. Juliana tried to match it with an understanding one of her own. She feared her face looked more temper-flushed and furious than sympathetic.

"If you decide not to wed him, I should like—that is, I will pay my addresses to you again after the new year. With you-your permission, of course."

The man couldn't be anything other than what he was: shy, kind, uncertain, and polite to a fault. Though it was unlikely she would wed Byron—as foolish as ignoring her logic was—Juliana opened her mouth to invite his pursuit now.

But she saw expectation shining from his direct, intelligent eyes and knew that giving him false hope would be cruel.

They would never suit.

However, that did *not* mean she wasn't screamingly furious with Ian.

"Thank you, my lord, for your honesty. When I'm ready for another suitor, I'll know just whom to call upon."

A reserved smile creased his long face. "Thank you, Lady Archer. I hope to see you then. Have a wonderful Christmas."

"You do the same, and wish your family well for me."

He nodded. "Good-bye."

And then Byron was gone. Just like that, her only other hope for a husband left. And she had let him.

Why?

And why had Ian driven the man away, if not to limit her choices?

It couldn't possibly have anything to do with fear, as his mother tried to bamboozle her into believing. Ian feared nothing. No, he had an agenda to win her, and a fierce one it was. He was willing to lie, trample on friends, send his mother to her door. Why? Juliana held no illusions about herself. She was a poor widow of very average looks. Ian was wealthy, witty, desirable—he could have his pick of London beauties. Why did he continue his relentless pursuit of her and her alone?

Juliana searched for an answer but could not find one.

Rising, she chewed off the corner of a ragged fingernail. If he actually loved her, he would allow her free choice. He would deal with her honestly.

Heaving a frustrated sigh, Juliana made her way out of the drawing room and up to her chamber.

Damn Ian! Just when she seemed to understand him, believed he might be worthwhile as both a man and husband, he did something that made her furious and gave her fits trying to understand. Besides manipulating her, he'd taken the fragile trust she had been building after he rescued her in London and sent her the petticoats, then he spit on it before trampling it with both feet.

"Ugh," she sighed as she paced before her window. She wasn't even going to try to comprehend his logic.

No, now she was only going to worry about finding the best method in which to show her extreme displeasure.

The following morning, Juliana sat in the drawing room, trying to calm herself with the scent of the pine wreathes around the room. Dried berries and pinecones dotted the festive decorations, as did shimmering bows and ribbons. She and her mother had laid out the nativity scene her German grandfather had carved from smooth pine wood many years before. Sprigs of mistletoe dangled from the mantel, and snow covered the ground in white. Christmas lay all around her.

So why wasn't she in the spirit?

Damn Ian for wringing that promise from her. In many ways, she dreaded answering his marriage proposal. No matter what she said, Juliana feared she would either surrender her independence to a crafty man whose seductive kisses muddled her mind, or lose all ties with her lifelong friend through her refusal. She had no palatable option.

Rising, she paced to the fire, turned, then paced back to her chair. No matter how hard she thought, no option came to her that would avoid both consequences.

Blast it all, she was not an indecisive person!

Still, with Ian's manipulation of her courtship with Byron, Juliana saw almost no way to trust him enough to marry him. He would only maneuver her until her life was no longer her own but what he wished it to be. That realization infuriated her all over again. Why must he manage everything?

"Dearest," Mama said from across the room. "Please sit."

Unwilling to distress her mother, Juliana did so.

"Goodness," she exclaimed. "What has you as anxious as a debutante upon her come-out?"

Juliana looked to her mother's softly lined face, the wreath of her pale hair sprinkled with gray, the kind brown eyes, faded now with age. Peace had always emanated from her mother, as if the troubles of the world could not touch her. As a child, Juliana had found the quality soothing. Today, it chafed. Did nothing bother the woman? How could her serene mother possibly understand her plight?

"Silly of me," Mama cut into her thoughts. "You must be considering Ian's proposal."

Slowly, Juliana nodded. "I am confused. You are happy with Papa's strong influence over your life. I would find such treatment like a harness."

She shrugged. "I regard it as the way of a woman's life. Ian loves you. But if you truly want to wed him, you'll find the means to compromise."

Her mother's calm smile nearly made her scream. "Can you not see? Once the wedding vows are spoken, Ian no longer has to compromise. He *owns* me. He can tell me what to do every day, and I will have no means to stop him."

Mama advised, "Ian would never play the ogre with you."

Juliana nearly jumped from her seat. "He just convinced my only other suitor to end his addresses until next year. If he cannot refrain from managing my affairs now, I have no hope he would do so after we wed."

Her mother laughed. Actually laughed! "Juliana, from the time you were very small, I realized how much like your father you are. Both of you are prone to worrying, often about matters that never come to pass. I doubt Ian would treat you as callously as you fear."

Was her mother right? Juliana did not know. Nor was she willing to take that chance. "You wish me to marry him?"

Her mother shrugged. "I admit I like the thought of you being loved, but if you do not believe he will make you happy, tell him so and be done with it."

"But I shall lose his very valuable friendship." A keening note crept into her voice.

"I would hardly give up on that so quickly," she offered.

Her mother was wrong! The friendship would end, for she did not see how it could survive mistrust. But she could not argue that point with Mama. "And I do not know where I shall find another husband before Geoffrey's money runs out."

"Your father will hardly turn you out to the streets."

Perhaps not, but with every extra farthing he spent on her behalf, Juliana knew she'd be beholden to him that much more. And he would exact his price. He always did.

"That was not my concern, Mama," she answered.

"I know, but this is one of the choices you must make in life. You won't always get your way, dear."

Her mother made everything sound so succinct and simple. Usually, Juliana herself filled the role of the logical mind, and she wondered why she could not manage that feat now.

She plopped herself down on the sofa beside her

mother, who set her embroidery aside. "I think it's the waiting I cannot tolerate. Christmas is a full ten days away."

Frowning, her mother reached out and gave her a quick hug. "Dearest, if you're certain your answer will not change between now and then, simply give him your reply today."

"I promised I would wait until Christmas to answer him."

Mama shrugged. "Do you wish to marry Ian, yes or no?"

Did she? "I think not. No, definitely not. He's too difficult."

"Then tell him. What matter if you tell him today or Christmas Day?"

"It matters, unfortunately." She had promised. Ian would hold her to every one of the days between now and Christmas. "But when Christmas comes, I shall be good and ready to tell him exactly how I feel."

CHAPTER TWELVE

Clutching her note in his hand, Ian comprehended Juliana's message all too well.

As he wandered about the grounds between Harbrooke and Edgefield, he cursed. Had she really said that? Perhaps he had misunderstood. He read the missive again:

> While I have promised to wait until Christmas to answer your proposal of marriage, I see no reason to subject myself to your intolerable presence until then. Do not call upon me before that time.
>
> *Juliana*

That was all. No explanation. No reason why she had refused to see him.

She simply told him to bugger off—and in a sealed note delivered by her butler when he had called upon her minutes earlier.

Damn it. Damn *her!* Why? No matter what he said or did, Juliana was never pleased. She's always preferred perfection. While Ian . . . well, he liked whatever was easy and fun. Why couldn't he love a woman with such wants as well?

Because life was never that simple. Because he did not find such women intriguing. They usually came with giggling mouths and empty brains. Their major concerns tended to be owning the perfect dress, knowing the latest *on-dit,* having the right acquaintances. He preferred Juliana's keen intelligence, her forthright ways, her logic. She made him strive to be a better man, if only to equal her integrity.

How the hell could she refuse to see him? It was very nearly breaking her promise, something she *never* did.

Crushing the note in his fist, Ian turned his mount around and headed back to Harbrooke. It was past time he and Juliana cleared the air. He intended to march to her door, climb up to her window again if he must. But she would bloody well give him the time of day.

Fortune smiled upon him when he trotted his mount into Harbrooke's stable and found her there alone. From the looks of it, she had just finished her own ride, and a fairly hard one at that. A thin sheen of perspiration covered her forehead. Vigor flushed her cheeks, while her pale curls skipped around her shoulders with abandon. Her shallow breaths made her pert breasts rise and fall rapidly.

Would she look like this just after they made love?

Blood rushed from his brain to parts south, where it would do him no good today. He cursed as lust replaced anger. Even now she held an earthy honesty that roused him.

Ian looked around for the groom. Quickly, he discovered they were alone.

Finally, his first reason today to smile.

On silent feet, he approached her, watching her take a cloth to her damp forehead and rosy cheeks, still oblivious to his presence.

After no more than three steps toward her, however, she paused, lifted her head, and gazed straight at him.

A gamut of emotions passed across her face, surprise, then anger. When he sauntered closer, her note in his hand, she showed her fist signs of both fear and defiance.

"Are you so daft that you do not understand my message?" she snapped.

Ian stepped closer still, so close now, he could inhale that slightly musky scent on her skin—the one that drove him insane to taste her.

"Perhaps I am. Explain it to me," he challenged.

Juliana lifted her chin. My, she was good at superiority. The thought of her surrendering her feminine power to his male hands in their marriage bed made him so hard, he ached. How satisfying to see her drop her barriers, to watch her whimper and writhe in passion. He did not want her to surrender her assurance. No, it made her far too alluring. He just wanted to rattle her enough to strip it temporarily.

"I dislike whatever expression you wear on your face."

"And what expression is that?" He flashed her a wolf's smile and waited for her response.

"As—as if you should . . . as if you seek to devour me."

His smile widened. He concentrated his stare on her mouth. "I would very much like that."

Juliana's eyes flared. Her lips parted. Her breathing became more erratic. Yes, they would be good together. Blood coursed violently through every part of him; he felt so incredibly alive. He'd wager she felt much the same, even if she would never admit it.

"You scound—"

"But not now," he said before she could finish

insulting him. "At the moment, I want an explanation about your missive."

"I have nothing more to say," she snapped, and started past him, toward the stable door.

Ian seized Juliana by the arm and urged her back into the wall.

"Let me go," she demanded through gritted teeth.

He hesitated, taking in her narrowed eyes and flushed cheeks. Slowly, he did as she wished. "Stand here and explain it to me."

"I see no reason why I should do any such thing. You had no right to ask Byron to stop calling on me. Our courtship is none of your affair. If I wish to wed him, you cannot stop me."

"And you want to marry him, do you?" he challenged.

"Perhaps," she lied.

He smiled. "Sweetheart, I know you too well. Byron, as kind as he is, would bore you quickly. You're not such a green girl that you don't realize it too."

Juliana tossed her towel aside and made fists with both hands. "But that was *my* choice, just like Geoffrey. And again, you did your utmost to take it away from me. You don't bloody listen, and you do not respect me in the least!"

Ian paused. From her words, he gathered Byron had told her all about their man-to-man chat. He had not expected Byron to go to Juliana and actually explain the situation, but apparently he had. Sighing, Ian feared the best he could do today was temper Juliana's anger, retreat, and return another day.

But the days before Christmas were both precious and numbered. And he was damned tired of being her whipping boy.

"You ask me repeatedly to consider your sentiments. I try, damn it," he growled. "But you never consider mine. You do not listen to me. You do not understand me. Hell, you continually misconstrue all

I do." He cursed. "And you never give any consequence to the fact that I love you."

She shot him a biting laugh. "If there is anything you love, it is manipulating me. Do you enjoy seeing if I'll act the perfect puppet every time you pull my strings? I cannot imagine any other reason you would, so—"

"I did not intend to remove your choices as much as I asked Byron to be a friend and a gentleman and bow out temporarily until you and I were certain we did not suit. If you refuse me come Christmas, why, I'm sure he'd be happy to cement your engagement on Boxing Day." Ian forced the words out on a harsh breath.

"I am capable of considering two men at once."

The thought carved a gash in his composure. He felt a muscle tic in his cheek as he tried to control his temper. "But that does not honor the spirit of your promise to me."

"Blast that promise!" she shouted. "You will never let me forget it, will you?"

"At the moment, it's the only hope I have of eventually persuading you to be my wife."

Juliana snorted. "You delude yourself if you think you have even that."

He ignored the pain in her stinging remark. "Until Christmas, I will do all I can to change your mind."

She cast a stormy gaze up to the ceiling, then, after biting her lip, drilled a hole in his heart with her angry stare. "Why? So you may continue to manipulate me? Can you not simply be my friend again? Can't our relationship be as it was when we were children?"

Ian took the final step toward her. He ignored the way she stiffened. Instead, he brushed a wild lock of hair away from her cheek. Then he allowed himself the luxury of running his thumb over the red silk of her mouth, remembering the soft taste of her, the surprisingly untutored enthusiasm of her kiss.

Gently, he took her chin between his thumb and fingers. "We're no longer children, and what I feel for you is far more than friendly. If you're honest, you feel the same. I know change can be hard to accept. But it's come, and now you must face it and decide."

Before she could say a word, he took her face in his hands and leaned in to stroke her lips with a brush of his mouth. He inhaled her, trying to soak her in like fine perfume.

Against his mouth, she trembled. She stood so still, so tense. He peeked at her through half-closed eyes to find her frowning, fighting herself.

Such restraint on her part he would not tolerate.

When he grazed her lips with his once more, she still remained unmoving but resistant. Ian's heart cried out. He could not leave her to hate him, could not bear to feel rejection in her touch.

Ian whispered to her in a reverent caress, "Juliana, give me a chance, love."

Again, he took her tender mouth in a soft, imploring rain of kisses that spread to her cheeks, her forehead, her neck. Ian clutched her face still, willing her response.

Juliana shuddered, cried out. "No!"

Then she pressed her mouth to his with artless fervor.

As soon as he responded with a hungry kiss, she opened her mouth beneath him.

Elation soared through Ian. He accepted her invitation, marauding the inside of her mouth. She was perfect, her taste addicting, like her scent. She was never sweet or cloying. Even her essence was like her—unique, sharp, sexual, yet always that of a lady.

A sigh of need shivered its way through his chest.

He savored her acceptance for a long while, broken only by the neigh of his mount. He lingered at her enchanting mouth, soft and beckoning. With a final glide of his tongue against hers, he released her, leaving her with closed eyes and harsh breathing.

"You'll not find that in the arms of another man," he said. "Because we were meant for each other."

Then he did one of the hardest things he had ever done. Shaking, he turned away, certain that if he kissed Juliana with too much possession, as he ached to do, his weak resistance would collapse. He would use any persuasive means available to make love to her. She would believe he forced his will on her again. Then her anger would have far more lasting effects.

As his leaden feet took him from her, she shouted, "Damn you! Why must you do that?"

Ian did not answer. He was not certain if she asked about his kiss or his retreat. No matter, really. Perhaps someday she could appreciate the whys of both.

"You arrogant rogue! If you cannot read between the lines in my note to determine what I shall tell you on Christmas Day, then you are even far more dense than I imagined!"

Closing his eyes against the pain, Ian cursed and forced himself to continue out the door. No matter how she responded to his touch, she was determined to hate him. Stubborn woman. He had no notion how to change her mind, but he must think of one— and fast—before he lost her forever.

Juliana pouted the remainder of the day. Nothing pleased her. Dinner was not to her liking. The book she was currently reading had grown tedious. Fate had even seen fit to send a torrent of icy rain across the land, forcing her inside with only her thoughts.

And still, she did everything she could to avoid those. If nothing else, she desperately wanted to forget that anytime Ian's mouth touched hers, she seemed to lose all grasp on reality. His kiss was too persuasive, the temptation too powerful for her to resist.

Blast him. Why couldn't Byron have had this effect on her? Or someone—anyone—else?

Night fell, and Juliana prepared for bed. She dismissed Amulya after the maid helped her to disrobe. The Indian woman seemed only too happy to leave her foul temper behind. The thought only made her sulk more as she sat in front of her dressing table, took down her hair, and ran a brush through the long, golden-pale strands.

In the mirror, beyond her right shoulder, she noticed a hazy white spot. A moment later, she heard the faint sounds of weeping. As she gasped, the lamps in the room were suddenly extinguished, as if they had all been turned off at once.

Somehow, the hazy white image in her mirror grew brighter, took shape.

Harbrooke's resident ghost glimmered in the dark glass, clutching her red book, her small fingers working at the lace hanging from her sleeve.

"Why?" the ghost moaned.

Curiosity roused Juliana from her mood. She was not scared but somehow felt as if her blood had stilled in her body. The air just behind her felt eerily frigid.

Transfixed, Juliana watched the apparition in the mirror. Again she wondered who the ghost had been in life and why she remained at Harbrooke.

"Why did I not believe?" the ghost's faint whisper floated through the air.

Then the ghost turned an angry gaze forward, looking directly at Juliana.

Chill bumps erupted on her body.

The ghost held up the book angrily, as if in display. "Read my thoughts."

As soon as she uttered the words, the spirit faded. Chill bumps erupted all across Juliana's skin and she sat wide-eyed in shock for a long while.

She had dreamed of the ghost speaking to her aboard the *Houghton,* but never before had she believed it would truly happen.

Why would the ghost speak to her? Why today? What had it said? Juliana frowned as she replayed the scene. "Read my thoughts," she murmured. "What thoughts? I do not read minds."

Yes, but the haunt had been holding up a book.

How was she to read the book? Juliana wondered. Grab it from the spirit's hands next time she appeared? *If* she appeared. That would hardly do.

Still, she felt certain the ghost was trying desperately to tell her something. The question was, what?

Juliana could not elude the spirit even in her fitful sleep. In the morning's early hours, she finally drifted off, wondering about the ghost's message. She awoke three hours later, before the servants even rose, surprisingly refreshed.

Her dream, which had featured Harbrooke's haunt, was fresh in her mind. And in that dream, the specter had been writing furiously in that red book she always clutched, glancing guardedly around Harbrooke's library. At least Juliana believed it was Harbrooke's library, for the room and its features were those she knew, but the furnishings were of another time.

Suddenly, the ghost began weeping with utter tragedy on her tear-ravaged face, then stashed the little journal in a niche between the bookshelf and the wall, near the floor, where plaster was cracked. Then she stumbled out of the room.

None of the dream made sense to Juliana, least of all why she could actually feel the ghost's despair. It moved her in some odd way she simply could not ignore.

Wrapping her dressing gown around her to ward

off the morning chill, Juliana rushed downstairs and hurried into the library. The embers in the grate had died to ashes during the night, and the room was utterly chilled. And no wonder, for it was snowing once more. But Juliana was determined.

She lit the gas lamps in the room, then cast her gaze at the walls of books. More than likely, her imagination toyed with her, teasing her with the location of the book. Surely finding it could not be this simple.

Bending down, Juliana began fitting her hand in the small, shadowed space between the wooden ledges that held centuries worth of fine books and the freshly painted wall.

She found nothing. Goodness, she could scarcely wedge a hand between the bookcase and the wall, which certainly had been long repaired since the days of the Restoration. The paint alone proved that.

Sighing at her own stupidity, Juliana sat on the floor and heaved a sigh. Why had she believed the ghost tried to tell her something anyway? The spirit had always been harmless and seldom seen. She had never even asked her parents if they had noticed Harbrooke's haunt. She'd always feared they would laugh at her if she mentioned it.

Grasping the edge of the shelf, Juliana used it to pull herself to her feet. A piece of the shelf gave way.

Reluctantly, yet with a racing pulse, she peered into the small, dark hole she had created. She almost expected to see that red book.

She found nothing.

Laughing at herself, she turned away to find her bed again.

A rustling noise behind her caught her attention.

Juliana whirled to the sound. She saw nothing. The sound stopped. She frowned. Perhaps it had been only the wind outside.

After turning away again, Juliana took another two steps. The sound filled the empty room once more.

Not only did it sound familiar, it sounded like a crackle of paper.

Pivoting slowly, she paused when the sound stopped.

Juliana scanned the bookshelf and the wall again. As before, she saw nothing. Stillness pressed heavily against her, and she felt as if she was not alone.

She laughed in the stilted silence.

Then a wave of cold pervaded the air, assaulting her face and shoulders before retreating again. The pungent scent of roses wafted to her.

The ghost?

Juliana swallowed, unwilling to believe her senses. The spirit had visited her more in the last few weeks than she had in the last ten years. Why?

As if it could read her thoughts, the rustle sound cut through the quiet morning again. It was definitely paper, and it was coming from a dusky crack in the wall she had not previously seen.

Staring at the wall as if it might grow horns, Juliana crept toward the crevice, which sat lower on the wall than she had been searching. The spot had been shoddily painted.

Juliana knew she was not in a trance. A trance would not have been this frightening, this exciting. Whatever she felt, it induced her to move slowly, with care, toward the spot of the disturbance.

As if the spirit was mollified, the insistent crinkle stopped.

Heart pounding in a fierce rhythm now, Juliana reached a trembling hand down into the dark, her fingers fumbling with the opening of the little niche. The chill gusted hard between her fingers. The piquant odor of the rose perfume she'd come to associate with the ghost made her stomach quiver each time she inhaled.

There, between the crumbling folds of the furrow

in the wall, she felt something, part stiff and thin, part wilted.

Apprehension rang in her head more loudly than church bells. With impatient fingers, she fumbled around for the edge of the object. When she found the sagging corner, she tugged gently, by degrees, afraid to rip it. Plaster trickled down the wall to the floor. The air around her swirled colder, more choked with roses. Juliana's heartbeat sounded thunderous in her ears.

With a final tug, the item fell from her fingers to the carpet, damp and musty and amazing.

It was a small journal, bound in red.

She swallowed with disbelief, with anticipation, as she reached a shaking hand out to the volume. With her hand half extended to the book, she hesitated. Was this real? Was this foolish? Was this a coincidence?

A moment later, a strong blast of frigid wind blew the book's cover open.

There was not a single window open in the room.

Again came the gale, flipping a page, then another, and another.

The gust ceased at that moment, but the chill settled around her. Though Juliana could not see the woman's ghost hovering, she felt it, felt its impatience.

It seemed unwise to argue with a specter.

Trembling, Juliana clutched the book and began to read.

It was mid-morning before her mother joined her in the library. By then, Juliana's feet felt like blocks of ice and she was sadly out of place in her dressing gown. But she had not moved from her place on the floor since opening the book.

The story the woman—the ghost—had written in

the precise flourish of her script had given Juliana chills.

"Heavens, dear," her mother exclaimed, entering the room. "What are you doing on the floor?" She frowned upon noticing the object in her daughter's grasp. "Wherever did you find that relic of a book?"

Juliana raised her gaze to her mother in wide-eyed silence. What could she say that anyone would believe? Certainly not the truth. Her father would think her addled for certain.

"I—I found it . . . unexpectedly." She glanced from her mother's expectant expression back to the book. "It appears as though it belongs to one of Papa's ancestors."

"It must be interesting reading to keep you engrossed in this cold."

"Quite," she murmured, then swallowed.

Part of her wanted to ask Mama if she'd heard the story inscribed herein. The other part wasn't sure she believed all of this herself. And she could find no simple way to explain to her perfectly rational mother that a specter had led the way to this volume. People whispered about such occurrences, but did anyone believe them without recommending a long stay at Bedlam?

"What manner of book is it?" her mother asked.

Juliana rose to her feet and tucked the book against her chest. "A journal. It was written by Lady Caroline Linford, a many times great-aunt on Papa's side of the family. Do you know anything of her?"

"Heavens, yes. She was practically a legend in Lynton when I was a child. Have you seen her ghost?" her mother added in a hushed whisper.

Shock sizzled through her, as hot and sudden as lightning. She answered her mother with an excited bob of her head. "Have you?"

"Not in some years. After your father and I first wed, I saw her quite a bit. I always speculated she

disliked not being the only woman in the house."
Her mother smiled. "What does her journal say?"

"That her father wanted her to marry a man, a
neighboring earl, Lord Grantham. Lady Caroline
refused him." She swallowed, finding the next words
difficult.

"Oh, yes," her mother recollected. "Lady Caroline
never did marry, as I recall."

Juliana nodded. "You are right. She had refused
him three times, much to her father's vexation. Lord
Grantham went to London and found himself a
bride." She paused, biting her lip, clutching the
book, still recalling the chill bumps she'd gotten
when she first read Caroline's weeping words. "Once
he was beyond her, she realized she loved him."

"I remember now." Her mother's expression
turned thoughtful. "Lady Caroline refused him to
spite her father. She died before age thirty, a broken-
hearted spinster pining for a married man."

With a sober nod, Juliana turned frightened eyes
to her mother. "She never examined her true feelings for him until it was too late." Again, she swallowed. "Mama, Lady Caroline visited my room and
my dream last night. She stayed in the library with
me until I found the book. She showed me where it
was." Juliana looked heavenward, as if divine inter-
vention would help her sort through the muddle of
her thoughts. "I scarce understand it, but I believe
she wanted me to read this."

Her mother cocked her head, her brow furrowed
with concern. "That's a bit fanciful."

"Why else would she hound me about this book?
This is not the first time I've seen Lady Caroline since
I've been home either. I saw her rarely as a child,
but now . . ."

"You truly believe this?" her mother asked,
astonishment gathering her face into a guarded
smile.

"I realize it sounds mad, but the similarities between Lady Caroline's courtship with Lord Grantham and mine with Ian is so eerie— What else am I to believe?"

Her mother shrugged. "Perhaps you're right."

"I think I am." She blinked, stared at her mother, tried to catch the whirl of her thoughts. "I understood her perfectly. I knew why she refused him; she could not give her father control of her life through her husband."

"Apparently, Lady Caroline decided she was wrong."

Juliana nodded slowly. Tears welled in her gritty eyes, as they had when she had read the entry Lady Caroline had written shortly after Grantham had brought his bride to Lynton. "Even when he could no longer marry her, he came to her and told her that he had always loved only her. Then he vowed never to speak of it again so he would not dishonor his wife." She sniffled. "How terrible to realize too late that he had not wanted her father's money or power over her."

"He simply wanted her love," her mother said, her voice hushed.

"Yes." Desperation clawed at her throat. "Yes."

With a considering expression, Mama enfolded Juliana in her arms. "If indeed Lady Caroline wanted you to have this information, what shall you do with it now?"

Juliana sighed. Paced. Worked a nervous rhythm with her fingers against her thigh. "I'm not certain. I *know* all the ways Ian has connived to drag me to the altar in the past. He maintains he did so because he loves me."

"Do you believe him?" Her mother sat on the sofa, never taking her gaze from her daughter.

"I never have, not really." She threw her hands in the air as she made another trek across the carpeted floor. "How could I believe such a thing, given all his lies and machinations. He seemed to want what *he* wanted, regardless of whether it pleased me." Juliana ceased pacing and sent a supplicating stare her way. She whispered, broken. "Now I wonder if he loves me but . . . but simply does not know a—a good way to express it."

"That is possible. Men never know their own hearts, dear, until you tell them."

At that statement, Juliana sat on the sofa, shoulders sagging. "He said I never understood him. That I never listened." She cast another confused glance at her mother. "I've always known my own mind. But this . . ." She sighed. "I cannot seem to swim through the tangle of my thoughts. I've always feared believing him. Now I fear not doing so."

"Love is not meant to be easy, Juliana. If it were, everyone would find it and keep it forever. It requires respect and trust—"

"He appears to have no respect for me, and I have no trust in him," she snapped.

Her mother acknowledged her words with a quiet nod. "Perhaps. But have you considered that you may be able to rectify that quite simply?"

Juliana scowled. "Respect and trust are no easier to come by than love." She shook her head. "Maybe this matter is hopeless. I'm so angry with him for dissuading Lord Carlton's suit—"

"Would you have wed him?"

She rolled her eyes. Must everyone ask her that? "No, but it should have been my choice to send him away, not Ian's."

"Yes," Mama conceded, then with a wave of her hand said, "But men like their superiority. They like believing they know better. How do you know that, in his mind, he was not saving you from another impetuous marriage that would only make you unhappy?"

She didn't know that, not for certain. Oh, Ian said such things. She had never believed them. How could he look at her and think her incapable of making such judgments? Did he have no faith in her?

After her debacle of a marriage to Geoffrey, why should he? Juliana pushed the pesky thought away.

"What should I do?" she whispered finally, deeply, dreadfully confused.

"Go to him. Spend time with him. Try not to let your temper or your past interfere with your decision. Ask yourself if you enjoy being with him. Discern whether he makes you laugh and glow on the inside. See if you can find care in his eyes."

Put that way, it all sounded so logical. Perfectly logical. She would want a mate whose company she enjoyed, who could lift her spirits. A mate who loved her as she was. Had she ever really looked for those qualities in Ian?

Sadly, no. Instead, she had looked at him as her father's choice of a husband, as the man who had done his very best to deceive her all the way to the parson's door. She had never worked past her pride and her temper—or her fear of being controlled by another strong-willed man.

"I think I shall get dressed now and ride to Edgefield," Juliana declared quietly.

Her mother smiled brightly. "A splendid idea."

CHAPTER THIRTEEN

Ian stood at the top of the hill above Edgefield Park, staring at the gray sky. It would snow again, probably within an hour or two. Cold hung in the air, gusted in the wind.

Huddled in his greatcoat, distracted by thoughts of Juliana, he felt very little of the chill.

How could he win that obstinate, aloof heart of hers?

Ian grimaced, not at all certain he could.

With a sigh, he wandered the hilltop, feet crunching in the snow. He ducked beneath the spindled branches of a winter-bare tree and gazed down at the chilled blue waters of the East Lyn River that lay a score of paces away.

Asking Byron to postpone his courtship of Juliana had been a tactical mistake. He had panicked, he admitted, fearing Juliana would find his friend a more logical option. She had no passion for the man; of that, he was certain.

But that fact made him more fearful, not less. He

knew too well that Juliana shied away from her emotions more often than not.

Perhaps he should stop trying so hard to make her feel. And then what? Be content to remain her friend only? Never.

Would he be better served to seduce her into marriage and let her sort out her heart later?

Ian paused, drawing in air so cold, it hurt his chest.

The idea had merit, he supposed. It was underhanded, however. He hated to resort to more deception, but the headstrong hellion had left him few options. After all, Juliana was fighting herself—and him—foolishly. Her body responded to him. In time, after their vows, she would realize she could trust him with their future and her heart.

Toying with the idea of coaxing her sensual surrender to claim her as his wife, he turned back to Edgefield Park. Perhaps he should simply venture to Harbrooke today to see Juliana. Maybe some other way to win her would present itself.

If not . . . well, his seductive scheme was always available.

Ian started down the peaceful white hill, eager to reach Juliana, only to discover she had already come to him.

Bundled up in mittens and a dark fur-lined cloak, she rode her gelding toward his stables. His interest and hope both peaked. Had she come to talk sensibly with him? Could he persuade her to enjoy the chemistry of their kisses again?

Probably not, but a man could hope . . .

The groom came out to claim her mount. She left him and began a trek to Edgefield's door.

"Juliana!" he called.

She whirled around to face him. A tentative smile curled the corners of her mouth.

It might as well have been the heartiest of laughs. Her face, her mouth itself, welcomed him. Holding in a holler of triumph, he sprinted down the hill toward her.

"Hello," he said, trying to gauge her mood, her purpose.

"Hello, Ian."

Juliana said nothing more. She looked as if she had more to say, was perhaps gathering her thoughts. Still, he saw no anger on her face, only a great number of questions tumbling inside her direct hazel eyes.

"Are we still friends?" she asked quietly.

Ian hesitated, wondering what had prompted the question. Sensing she had come with a purpose in mind, Ian trod carefully. "I've made no secret that I hope to make you my wife. Even if that happens, I believe we shall always be friends." He smiled and teased, "What other man would give you undergarments without the specific intent to seduce you out of them?"

Her answering smile acknowledged that. "The same man who prevented me from making another poor choice in London."

"I'm not a hero," he said softly. "I did that because I care for you."

She peered into the chilly wind, hesitating, sighing. "Remember when I was six, and you and Byron and all the servants' boys spent afternoons climbing that tree over there?" She pointed to the towering oak on the far side of the river.

"Yes, you were afraid of heights."

Juliana nodded. "And you did your most to cure me of it, insisting the tree was harmless."

"It was."

"Perhaps, but I was afraid, and you coaxed me into climbing it."

He smiled. "And then I helped you down when you screamed your throat raw."

Her answering smile oddly sad, she nodded. "I was too frightened to climb down myself."

"I hardly minded saving you," he said, wondering where on earth this remembrance was headed.

She turned to him with a probing gaze. "Why did you help me?"

An odd question, he thought, frowning. "Should I have let you fall?"

"No." She paused, oddly pensive. "I think the better question is why did you convince me to climb the tree at all?"

Another odd question. He shrugged. "Because I knew you could. You were too brave to be so frightened. I—I felt certain that if you tried it once—"

"It was my choice to stay frightened," she cut in with a censuring frown.

This argument about her choices had a familiar ring. They had it each time Geoffrey Archer's name and the subject of marriage arose.

He scowled, alarmed and saddened at once. Did she seek to widen the chasm between them? "Did you come today to argue about an incident that is nearly twenty years old? Can you possibly imagine that we do not have enough between us already?"

"No." She smiled wryly. "We have plenty of discord, I agree. The point is, even as children you liked to decide what I needed, what was best for me. At that time in my life, I did not doubt you cared for me."

What was her point? Ian resisted the urge to change the subject or kiss her out of this conversation. Perhaps he should seduce her and be done with it.

But Ian found he had little enthusiasm for tricking her to the altar. Instead of conceiving how simple such a solution would be, he was aware of how much she would dislike him for it. Damn it, why did he reject such a painless resolution?

Because she was not angry. Because her smile had been welcoming. He sighed. Perhaps he should be a bit more patient.

"I still care," he assured her softly.

Juliana hesitated, her gaze moving across the mantle of white around them. "I think I believe that."

Relief rolled through him, thick, like honey dripping downhill. But something in her thoughtful expression did not set him entirely at ease.

Shut your mouth, he told himself. *Don't ask.*

"Then, what troubles you?" he questioned anyway.

"You say you love me—"

"I do." He grabbed her gloved hands and squeezed. "I do. Whatever you think, never doubt that."

"I am actually beginning to believe that as well." With a gentle pull, she extracted her hands from his grasp. "It is the manner in which you demonstrate affection I find troublesome."

He scowled at her. "What do you mean?"

"I've realized that the more you care for someone, the more you interfere. One of the other kids was afraid to climb that tree, yet you never once challenged him to conquer his fear."

"What does it matter?" Her logic baffled him.

"That is my point. You did not care about him, so he did not matter. You cared about me and my fears. You wanted me to defeat them, so you pushed me to climb the tree."

He peered at her frosty-pink cheeks, saw her breath in a cloud each time she exhaled. Her eyes were so earnest, willing him to understand. It only confused him.

He pressed a spot between his brows where a headache began to throb. "What are you saying?"

"I think the only way you know how to love is to control. I will not abide that." Her soft oval face was excruciatingly honest.

Did she mean to refuse his proposal now? Had her welcoming smile been an illusion?

"Do you think me so heartless that you feel nothing

for me?" His heart pounded in apprehension. What would he do if she said yes?

She laughed at him.

"If it were that simple," she said, "I should have refused you long ago. But nothing about this is simple."

"No," he agreed, relieved. "It is not."

Still, his heart would not slow. He wondered if this conversation would bring great triumph or utter defeat.

"I would be dishonest if I said I did not care about you," Juliana murmured.

"We are, if nothing else, friends," he said, trying to hide the bitter note from his voice. He wanted to be much more to her.

"But you were right yesterday when you said that something between us has shifted, changed. We have become . . . more."

Ian held his breath as he peered into her beautiful open countenance. Finally, she was acknowledging something in their rapport beyond that of childhood playmates.

Perhaps this was the appropriate time for his seduction. Maybe she meant to encourage him in that regard.

"You respond to my touch," he whispered, leaning closer.

Immediately, Juliana backed away, looked away, across the white peace of the landscape again. "Yes. Even when I should not. I confess marriage did not prepare me for the manner in which you affect me."

He grasped her shoulders, turning her to face him. Did she mean that? He scanned her face and again, found nothing but truth. "Oh, Juliana—"

"It is not something to celebrate," she chided, pulling away. "It only muddies the waters of this decision I must make."

So she had not decided about their marriage yet.

That could be good—and bad. Ian frowned. Maybe he should kiss her, distract her, compromise her now. Somehow convince her with his touch how much he cared. Certainly she would see what he felt, then. Or would she?

Suddenly, snow began to fall in large flakes, sweeping with the gentle wind across the afternoon sky to fall softly to the ground in silence.

"Let us go inside," he urged, knowing he could not possibly seduce her in the snow.

Juliana hesitated. "No, I find it peaceful here. I remember the Christmases past when we went caroling in the snow. This is the first moment I've felt joy at the coming holiday."

Ian knew that was important to her. He took her hand and smiled. "I am glad. We can go inside and sing—"

"You need not always alter things in an attempt to make them better. Let me enjoy the moment as it is."

He shrugged. "I merely wanted to add—"

"I understand." She held up her hands to ward off further comment. "That is what I've been explaining. When you care about someone, you challenge them to feel, want them to fall into your thoughts, your rhythm of life. Perhaps such makes you feel closer to them; I do not know. And the more you care, the harder you try. That is what I cannot live with." Her face took on conviction and passion. "I can consider your proposal seriously if I feel certain you will allow me my own thoughts and cease trying to change my actions. Please understand that even if we act in different manners, perhaps those manners compliment one another."

Ian held in a smile. Leave it to Juliana to overthink a thing. He simply wanted to help, that is what friends—and mates—did. He did not want to change her or mold her to the—what had she said? Yes, the rhythm of his life. Rubbish! He merely helped when she feared and cajoled when she resisted.

"You have been giving matters a great deal of thought."

Juliana nodded, her expression rueful. "You have no idea."

That sounded promising, indeed. Ian sidled closer. "Knowing you, I think I do. However, I appreciate your thought. Truly." He smiled. "Now, are you interested in giving that active mind of yours a rest yet?"

She raised a dark brow. "After everything I said, you aren't suggesting we go inside to sing carols, are you?"

"Something better," he said, his voice coaxing.

"Better?" she repeated, smiling as she bent to pick up a handful of snow from the top of the barren hill. "Unless you mean a snowball fight, I cannot imagine what would be better."

Juliana hurled the loose white ball toward him. It landed with a splatter on his chest and fell apart into a stream of white powder.

"You minx," he accused, grabbing a hunk of snow in his grasp. "You understand this means war."

"I am prepared for battle," she assured him, chin lifted.

Quickly, they both reached down and grabbed handfuls of the white powder. Juliana was quick, firing off the first shot and grazing Ian on the thigh. But Ian was methodical, patient. His large hands molded the snow tightly as he advanced on her.

Laughing, she streaked past him, across the valley, heading for the cover of thin trees. He pursued. He had no doubt she heard him close behind when she bent to scoop a handful of snow, then tossed the hastily made weapon at him. It missed.

"Running off the battlefield?" he taunted.

At that, she stopped long enough to grab another chunk of the cold white stuff and fling it at him. It fell apart harmlessly when it landed inches from his feet.

With a dastardly smile, he chased her again, now past a large boulder, as he molded his large, lethal snowball.

Shrieking, Juliana whirled to her left and sprinted through a flat, snow-covered field toward the stables. Ian put his long legs in motion, bounding after her. Close, so close, he could smell the musk of her skin, almost like cinnamon and pure female mixed.

With another lunge, Ian looped his arm around her waist. They tumbled to the flat ground in a tangle of limbs and laughs. With superior strength, he rolled Juliana beneath him. Her shoulders shook with her giggles and deep breaths.

"Do you surrender, minx?"

"Never," she declared.

"You leave me no choice but to fight to the death."

Before Juliana could utter a protest, Ian slapped his fat snowball on top of her head. It crumbled apart in a shower of icy powder, into her hair, across her face.

She came up sputtering, wiping snow from her eyes and laughing again. "You fight unfairly, sir!"

"I fight to win," he corrected her. "Now do you surrender?"

"I will not!"

And before Ian knew what she was about, Juliana reached up, looped her arms around his neck, and fit her body against his. That instant, his heart began to pound, the blood pumping through his body in a violent course. Every muscle in his body clenched with want. She had aroused him fully.

Juliana sent him a sultry look, playful and inviting, alluring as hell. Yearning for a taste of her, he bent to take her mouth, claim her.

She shoved a handful of snow down the back of his shirt.

With a shout against the shocking cold, Ian leapt up, his back arched. He yanked his shirt out of his breeches, trying to clear the snow of his skin.

"You vixen!" he accused as she rose to her feet, dusting off snow from her riding skirts and fitted sleeves.

"Do you surrender?" came her self-satisfied question, her brow arched smugly.

He advanced on her, his face a mask of mock evil. "It will take more than a little chill to defeat me, good lady. The day is not done yet."

Juliana giggled. "You look foolish."

"Ah, yes. But I made you laugh."

"True." She conceded the point.

"And you had fun." His tone challenged her to refute him.

"That too," she admitted.

"That is victory enough for me. I am beyond cold and ready for something warm. Come inside and take tea," he invited.

Inside the cozy library, with its low ceiling and roaring fire, Juliana admitted she was quite warm. The teacup in her hand, filled to the brim, had chased the chill from her fingers.

Ian himself had somehow warmed her heart.

She could not deny she had fun with him, enjoyed his company—at least when they did not argue. But today had been nearly perfect. She had explained her fears for the future. He had listened, seeming to consider her point, then lightened the mood, gifting her with the first real laughter she had experienced since returning from India.

Lifting her gaze to Ian, Juliana found herself studying the firm set of his carved features, the full bounty of his mouth, the impossibly wide shoulders that conveyed his male strength.

Funny, when she was not angry with him, she found it impossible to ignore him as a man.

"I plan to start the breeding stable next year," he said suddenly. "I've finally found the perfect stud to start with."

As she processed his comment, one fact became clear. "You will be moving away?"

He peered at her as if he wished he could read her thoughts. "My land is near Salisbury. I shall build a manor house there. Perhaps I will call it Hillfield Park, for it sits high up on a hill, overlooking a field."

Juliana swallowed. The thought of him leaving here, leaving *her*, was . . . inconceivable.

"Soon, I shall be putting forth my ideas to an architect I recently met named Cockerell. He's quite brilliant."

"Wonderful," she said. But she did not feel it. She missed him already.

"I could use your help, however."

"Help?" she echoed numbly.

"I cannot decide between Greek Revival or Palladian style. Or perhaps something a bit more Georgian? What is your favorite?" He looked genuinely perplexed.

He wished her opinion of his house? "Oh, if it were mine, I should prefer something with columns, so Palladian is always a favorite. Or—or Baroque."

Curiously, Juliana studied Ian. True, he had asked her to marry him, but the manner in which he had sought her judgment had seemed very much off-handed, like he was soliciting opinions so he might consider all options.

Why should he care what she thought? Unless he wanted her input on the house he hoped they would one day share.

The thought warmed her, softened her. Maybe he did care for her opinions if he would build a house to please her as well. Suddenly, a tenderness she could not suppress glowed in her heart.

"Yes. Palladian or Baroque. That is a smashing idea," he said as if she were a genius.

She smiled. "I'm fond of porticoes as well. While I adore tall ceilings for looks, they are not practical in winter's chill."

"Of course not. Your sensible observation is most appreciated."

"And I adore windows—lots of them. But not facing north, where coldest winds blow in. Or in east-facing bedrooms, where the sun assaults the eyes before the civilized rise."

Ian laughed and walked to a writing desk. To Juliana's surprise, he began to jot notes. "Excellent notions."

Liquid pleasure flooded her. He truly did care for her opinions, for once wasn't trying to alter her opinion to fit his mold. He simply listened.

"You wish me to share that house with you, do you not?"

Chagrined, he nodded. "You could tell, could you?" He crossed the room to her and knelt at her feet. "Yes, I want above all for you to share this house with me, as my wife."

When Ian palmed her nape and kissed her softly, she did not resist.

"Thank you for asking my opinion. It means a very great deal to me."

Wryly, he smiled. "Just in case you are so moved to marry me, I shall tell Cockerell to make certain the house has everything you want."

Juliana wondered if she had gone completely mad, but at the moment she was feeling very moved.

CHAPTER FOURTEEN

When Juliana arrived home, her father was waiting for her in the library. He wore a serious expression on his ruddy face, one she loathed. His scowl said that, although she would soon be twenty-four, he was still the parent, she the child. And she had better listen.

"Good evening, Papa." She was determined to be polite.

"You traveled to Edgefield Park alone again."

It was an accusation, not a question. Juliana saw no reason to deny it. "Yes."

"People are sure to talk," he chided, swirling brandy in the glass he held. "Such behavior makes you look fast."

"Hmmm." She tapped her chin as if deep in thought. "I thought I might be viewed as independent."

Her father loosed an ugly scoffing sound. "Who values that in a woman? Always leads to trouble."

Juliana clenched her teeth and refused to rise to his bait. He wanted her to fight with him so he could point out all the reasons he was right and force her to listen. As a young girl, she had fallen for the trick every time. Today, she knew better.

Her father took a long swallow of his brandy.

A pale brow arched, she asked, "Should you be drinking that?"

"Hush up, girl. Changing the subject will not save you from explaining yourself."

Eyeing the uneven pallor of his ruddy face, she sent him a censuring glare. "Seems as if you are avoiding the more important subject. You've ceased walking each day, have you not?"

"Too blasted cold, not that it's your affair," he bristled. "I've come to talk of your improper traipsing about Lynton."

"I thought you wished me to spend time with Ian," she offered innocently. "Have you changed your mind?"

He scowled at her strategy. "No. He's a fine man, and he will make you a fine husband too."

"Perhaps."

Juliana knew her noncommittal answer would drive him half mad. She held in a smile at the thought.

"No perhaps about it," he blustered. "You've gone to him twice now completely unchaperoned. The two of you are spending a great deal of time together. People in Lynton all assume you mean to marry him, as you ought." He took another drink of brandy. "When will you stop leading him on this merry chase, set a wedding date, and be done with it?"

After today, she might well do that . . . soon. She and Ian had honestly discussed her concerns. He had listened, nodded, then turned the mood lighter again so that nothing oppressive hung between them. She appreciated that he knew it would discomfit her. And then they'd had fun together, laughed with utter abandon. He had pressed her for nothing, asked for nothing she had not wished to give. Already, she was seriously considering the notion of wedding him.

But she would rather cut out her tongue than give her father the satisfaction of knowing that now.

Tapping down her ire, Juliana shot him a brilliant smile, then reached for her favorite Dickens novel. "You will know my choice on Christmas Day, after I inform Ian. Not before."

Her father's face turned a blotchy, thunderous red. He leaned in and grabbed her arm in a rough grip. The scent of brandy haunted his breath, strong and unavoidable. Anger and alcohol teamed together to narrow his hazel eyes.

"You will marry him, Juliana. I'll not have everyone in Lynton whispering about you—about your mother and me—again. You're only refusing him in a stubborn pique, like a child. Make the mature choice this time. Marry your social equal, a man of means."

"What if I don't wish it? What if I wish to wait until the coming Season to snare another husband?" she baited him.

He shot her a contemptuous glare. "You had no luck in London earlier this month. I have no reason to believe waiting another few months will change that. To everyone who matters, you are a woman of good fortune and family who *eloped* with a commoner. Your marriage was no less than a scandal. No man of Ian's caliber will have you but Ian himself."

Her father's mean words too closely echoed those uttered by Peter Haversham in London to be anything but truth. She wanted to blurt out that perhaps she would marry another commoner, this one with money. Some thriving merchant perhaps. Such a pronouncement would infuriate her father, set his proud heart spitting fire. But her threat would be an empty one. Any common man who married her would likely be doing it for title and coin, not because he cared for her. Juliana refused to have another indifferent husband like Geoffrey.

"I will marry the man of my choosing," she answered, brimming with defiance and a need to throw something at his wretchedly demanding face.

Her father thrust a sharp finger in her face. "You'll marry Ian or I'll make certain you regret your defiance."

In a small show of rebelliousness and a need to escape her father after last night's row, Juliana rose early and left Harbrooke for Edgefield Park and Ian.

Odd, but she felt certain the very man causing dissension between her and her father could comfort her. The thought had no logic, but she could not shake the conviction.

She arrived shortly after noon, to find Ian inside, reading and sipping coffee. He looked every inch a gentleman in a double-breasted swallowtail coat the color of the ocean—the color of his eyes. His silk cravat was a muted blue. His crisp white shirt possessed a high collar that hugged the masculine width of his neck, while his narrow tobacco-colored trousers and gleaming black boots finished the elegant picture. The glossy waves of his dark hair drew her gaze. His long, square fingers and big hands made her stomach flutter.

"Juliana, how wonderful to see you again." He rose to greet her. "I did not expect— Are you well?" He frowned, brow furrowed in concern.

Mortified that he'd caught her staring, she jerked her gaze away and pretended interest in his coffee. "My—my father and I, we fought."

"I'm sorry." He crossed the room to her side and seated her on the sofa. Moments later, he sat beside her, holding her hand as if she were a child in need of a loved one's comfort.

"I'm a fool for coming here, to talk to you when you are the very reason we fought." Suddenly, tears invaded her eyes. Juliana could not remember a time when she had felt so alone. "But you are my only friend."

Her world became a watery blur, and Juliana turned away.

With gentle fingers, Ian pressed a handkerchief into her palm. She dabbed at her eyes, cursing her sudden weakness, when he touched her face and returned her stare to him.

"No need for tears, love. Your father is a bit like you." He smiled softly. "He's stubborn but will see logic when it has been presented to him."

She shook her head before he even finished speaking. "I have given him logic. I've told him I wish to choose my husband, wait until I am ready to take one." She sighed, disheartened, and her stomach ill at ease. "He is determined to see me wed now and is equally resolute that I wed you."

"I know." He took her hands in his. "He simply wants to see you settled and cared for."

Juliana withdrew her hands and rose. "Coming here was a mistake. I should have expected you to take his side."

With a firm tug on her arm, Ian brought her back to the sofa beside him. "I am taking no side. I am explaining your father's wishes to you. Perhaps your anger will be reduced if you understand his motive. He wishes only the best for you."

"Why has he never considered that I may know that far better than he?"

"That is not male logic," he teased. Then his face sobered, as if he willed her to understand. "Men are taught early in life it is their duty to see after their family. Your father knows he cannot cheat death forever. Each day brings him closer to that in which he will leave you to this world and fate. I believe he wishes to know you are with someone who can and will care for you until you leave this earth too. If you must blame him for something, have it be caring too much. I assure you he has no other, more sinister motive."

Easing onto the sofa, Juliana stared absently with the flounces on her violet and lace dress. She tried to put herself in her father's place. She could see his logic ... somewhat. But in demanding that he see her settled, he did so with the assumption she was too obtuse to care for her own future.

It did not flatter her in the least.

"I understand his motive is not sinister," she said finally, raising her gaze to the concern on the strong angles of his face. "But that does not lessen the degree in which he impacts me."

"Close your ears to him," Ian suggested with a shrug.

Juliana felt her eyes widen, her mouth fall open.

Ian laughed. "Do not be shocked. I am merely suggesting that you think less of your father's wishes and look deep into your heart. Think about the ties destined to last you a lifetime. If you choose to wed me, let it be because you care, not because your father has pressured you."

She could not have been more stunned if Ian said he'd been beheaded yesterday. It mattered to him that she marry him because she cared? Not because he and her father demanded it? Never had she thought he would express such a sentiment. Ever. Had she completely misjudged him—terribly this time?

Those dratted, embarrassing tears returned again, stinging her eyes. Lord knew her nose was probably turning red.

"Let's have none of that," he whispered. "Here I try my utmost to honestly make you happy and you cry me a well of tears. What am I to do with you?"

Juliana laughed despite her confusion. "Since you are my only friend, you shall have to tolerate my odd moods, I fear."

"True. As odd as they are, who else will?"

"It is ungentlemanly of you to tease me so."

He thrust wide fists on his narrow hips. "You like that about me. Admit it."

"Never." She stuck her chin in the air.

Ian laughed again. "Do you feel better, love?"

Her serious mantle returned, but in truth, she *did* feel somewhat eased by their talk. Confused about her opinion of him, yes. But less distressed by her father's words.

She nodded.

"Very good." He took her hand in his again. "Juliana, this decision is between you and me. I know you must make it, but I want you to be certain you understand I love you and have no intent to see your freedom curtailed or your opinions overlooked. They are part of what makes you so intriguing to a man, me especially."

Did he mean that? Any of it? Hope made her heart leap for a moment, and she studied him with a serious, fixed gaze. "Why, then, have you always tried to mold me to your wishes?"

Ian smiled. "Can you blame a man for trying to take the easy way? Waiting out your stubborn mind can be quite a task."

She swatted his shoulder. Inside, joy began to take root. She had leapt to the wrong conclusion about Ian after she had returned from India to find her father looking healthy. Since then, Ian had been nothing but fair and kind. Oh, he'd been high-handed. Nothing would ever change that, she feared. But beneath his bluster and force, he possessed an essentially good heart, something Geoffrey never had. Something her father did not even understand.

Juliana valued that far more than she ever thought possible.

"My stubborn mind and I thank you for listening," she said finally.

"I awoke with no other thought today but to see you happy."

He spoke with an edge of laughter, but his face held no hint of mirth. In fact, he looked as if he truly meant each word.

She smiled. "You may have succeeded, at least for the moment."

"I feel fortunate, indeed." He reached for her hand and squeezed it. "Some days you look so lost, like a little girl who cannot find her doll."

Before she could comment, Ian stood suddenly. "Oh, yes. Dolls. Perhaps you can help me. Stay here."

With that, Juliana watched Ian dash out of the room. She frowned. Certainly Ian had not taken an interest in dolls!

But three minutes later, he returned with a doll in hand. His large hands dwarfed it. Wearing an elaborate velvet dress of blue and a matching tall hat, the brown-eyed bisque doll was about eighteen exquisite inches long. She even wore shiny kid shoes and pale stockings. It was the kind of doll every little girl dreamed of.

"What do you think?" He handed her the toy.

She frowned, inspecting the lovely plaything. "It's beyond lovely. But aren't you a bit old for this sort of thing?"

Juliana worked to keep the smile from her voice and her face.

Ian grinned. "She is the only female who listens to me."

"Only because she cannot talk."

"I had not thought of that." He pretended dismay. Together they laughed. A richness, a contentment, began to infect her mood. Juliana felt herself relax into the sofa.

He took the doll back in his grasp and set it on the sofa beside him. "I bought her in London for my aunt Georgiana's daughter, Laurel. She just turned four last month. I don't believe you've met her."

"I haven't. Does she live in Cambridge?"

"Indeed. I mean to give her this doll as a gift from Father Christmas. Do you suppose she will like it? The shopkeeper said—"

"Put yourself at ease," Juliana assured. "Little Laurel will love it. What fanciful girl wouldn't?"

Ian smiled, looking genuinely relieved. He cared this much for a child's happiness and good opinion? He'd thought enough to give such a splendid gift to a child he probably scarcely saw more than once a year.

A heartless man would not care half so much for the little girl. Juliana's own father certainly would not have given the child's Christmas gift a thought.

"Thank you." Ian cut into her thoughts. "I feel much better knowing I did not guess badly."

"Not at all. In fact, you guessed quite . . . wonderfully."

Of her own accord, Juliana reached across the small space separating them and took hold of Ian's hand. His fingers were warm as she slid her own around them. His palm was slightly hotter but dry. Nor was it too soft. They were perfect hands for a man. She had heard of the things a man could do to a woman with such wonderful hands. Geoffrey never had done anything so giving for her.

Still, she heated at the thought of Ian doing so.

He squeezed her hand. "Wonderful, am I?" He cradled her cheek with his free hand. "No, I'm certain that is you."

* * *

Four days passed; December twenty-third arrived. Juliana had found her Christmas spirit the day she spent with Ian. Yet the realization that the holiday would be here in two days—and that she would be bound to give Ian an answer to his marriage proposal—filled her with anxiety. She wanted to say yes. Something held her back. Perhaps it was her father growling that she had best marry the man. She wasn't certain.

Still, when Ian invited her for dinner with his parents that evening, she thought it best to go. Perhaps she would clear her confusion and decide today.

Heedless of the gently falling snow, Juliana jumped into the carriage and settled in for the peaceful ride to Edgefield Park. The fields normally lush with heather and gorse were blanketed in snow. It had been an unusually cold winter on this mild coast, but Juliana did not mind. Far too well, she recalled the hellish heat of India.

Ian greeted her moments after she arrived with a searching, gentle expression. "You came. Thank you. I feared the weather would be impossible."

"It is no worse than yesterday," she assured him.

He looked unconvinced but shrugged. "Supper is nearly ready. Are you hungry?"

A suggestive smile accompanied the low-voiced question. A leer followed.

She laughed. "Stop. I will not admit to being hungry when you behave like that."

"A shame. I suppose I shall have to be satisfied with Christmas pudding."

"Indeed."

A few moments later, she joined Lord and Lady Calcott, his parents, who waited in silence around the ornately set table. Servants floated around the room with all manner of dishes meant to tempt the palate. Celery and winter vegetables complimented the roasted duck and baked haddock. Juliana ate until she thought she might explode.

"Save room for pudding," Ian whispered, leaning closer.

"I need nothing more," she murmured back. "But if you do to be satisfied, you mustn't pass it up."

"Pudding will do." *For now,* his eyes said. But clearly, he was interested in much, much more.

When the confection was brought out minutes later, Juliana's interest surged. When the chef came out to set the dish on fire and decorate it with a holly sprig, her mouth watered despite her full stomach. The scents of raisins, nutmeg, and cider hung thick around the dish. She accepted her serving with relish.

After they had finished the dessert, the men departed. Juliana faced Ian's mother. "Your chef did wonders with the entire meal, the pudding especially."

Emily smiled. "I am so happy you're pleased. Ian asked if we could have the traditional meal tonight so he might share it with you."

Soft surprise warmed her heart. Christmas was a blessed season, and Ian had wanted to share its traditions with her? She must be important for him to want thus. She had always believed that to him she was merely an object to attain. Maybe she had been wrong. Perhaps her wishes and feelings mattered. Hopeful and warmed, Juliana suddenly knew of no one else she would rather share the day with.

Clearly, since he had arrived in Bombay all those months earlier, he had become equally important to her.

"I am flattered," Juliana said finally.

"He is enjoying himself. When Ian is done with his brandy, we shall decorate the Christmas tree, play snapdragon, hang our stockings, perhaps carol a bit."

"Will your husband not join us?" she blurted out.

When she saw Emily's pained expression, she wished she had not.

"There is no avoiding it, I fear. At least for now."

A few minutes later, the men rejoined them and escorted the ladies to the drawing room. Even as Ian stroked the fingers she laid upon his arm, Juliana noticed his parents did not touch.

Inside the drawing room, the makings of a Yule log lay just outside the fireplace. Someone had draped the stockings along the back of the sofa for hanging at the mantel. A stout, undecorated fir stood in the corner beside the frosty window. A glance at the night outside confirmed that snow had fallen all through dinner. All in all, it seemed a perfect Christmas picture.

Juliana cast a warm glance at Ian. His eyes were on her, roving, restless, incredibly blue. Care resided there, as did hope. She also saw hunger for far more than pudding, and she felt an answering pulse within her.

"What shall we do first?" Emily asked the group.

Ian's father, Lord Calcott, lounged in a fat chair, holding a brandy. His expression was nothing less than bored. Clearly, he would offer no suggestions.

Ian looked at her expectantly. "Juliana?"

"How about the stockings?" she murmured in the tense air.

"Smashing idea," Ian said quickly.

They went about their work, and hung each up with care, just as *A Visit from St. Nicholas* said they should. Beside her, Emily hummed "O Come, All Ye Faithful." Ian joined in. Juliana wanted to do the same but knew her voice would only spoil it. She listened with pleasure instead to their deft singing.

"There," Emily said as she stepped back to survey their handiwork. "Now if Father Christmas drops any gold coins as he comes down the chimney, these will surely catch them."

Lord Calcott snorted. "You're too old to believe in such nonsense. Besides," he said, standing, "this one is crooked."

As the dispirited man made his way to the stockings, he took hold of one and set it to rights, grumbling all the while.

"You two are below the mistletoe," Ian said to his parents.

Juliana looked up and realized that was indeed the case.

Suddenly, his mother looked nervous. "Where did that come from?"

"I hung it earlier today," Ian confessed.

"I can be festive," Lord Calcott insisted, then leaned toward Emily, his gaze on her mouth.

She turned away at the last moment, so her husband found only her smooth skin. When he had placed but the briefest kiss on her cheek, Emily stepped away and toyed with a locket around her throat. "Well, you two are standing nearly beneath it. Perhaps you should indulge in a holiday kiss?"

"We are not yet beneath it. That would be cheating," Juliana asserted, reluctant to kiss Ian while his parents watched.

"True," Ian whispered to her. "But the night is not over."

A rush of surprised tingles spread their way throughout her body. Juliana glanced over her shoulder to find Ian there, a promise on his face. The tingles became warm flutters.

A taut moment later, Emily suggested they play snapdragon.

They called to the servants, who brought a large silver bowl and filled it with brandy and raisins. Emily set it on the table between the sofa and chairs. Everyone sat and watched as Ian set the brandy aflame with a candle and his flourish.

As one, Juliana and Emily began, "Here he comes

with flaming bowl, don't he mean to take his toll. Snip! Snap! Dragon!''

Then Ian joined in. "Take care you don't take too much. Be not greedy in your clutch. Snip! Snap! Dragon!''

"Go ahead, Juliana," Emily encouraged. "Go first."

They continued to sing as she reached into the flaming bowl and snatched a raisin, also on fire. Quickly, she thrust the heated fruit into her mouth and closed it, putting the fire out. Tastes and textures burst into her mouth—sweet, hot, succulent. Her fingers sizzled.

"You shall have to be a bit quicker next time," Ian said.

"And you can do the thing faster?" she challenged.

"Watch." His nod was annoyingly confident.

Ian stared at the bowl for a moment, into the flames. Then, in a blur of motion, he reached in and plucked one of the flaming fruits out, dropping it through the air into his mouth.

"See." He held up his hands. "No burned fingers."

"How superior you are, my lord," she cooed, batting her lashes in mock adoration.

"Well . . ." He laughed. "If you are at ease admitting that obvious fact—"

"Can we send him to Bedlam this close to Christmas?" Juliana asked his mother. "Or should we let the poor thing enjoy his delusions a bit longer."

"Let him stay," Emily said, stone-faced. "He's proven harmless so far."

Juliana could not resist smiling. "So far. We shall have to watch him closely."

"Indeed," Emily agreed.

"Enough!" Ian burst out. "Let us resume the game."

The trio played until all the raisins had been consumed. Lord Calcott looked on with disinterest that Juliana did not believe was entirely real.

When snapdragon ended amid giggles and vows of retribution, Emily suggested they begin decorating the Christmas tree. Juliana readily agreed. Trees were her favorite symbol of the season, bright and crisp-smelling, a symbol of nature, of peace.

"We shall need your assistance," Emily said to her. "This is our first tree, and since you have a German ancestor, you know far more about this than we."

Juliana nodded. "It seems difficult to believe this is a new tradition in England. I've been decorating trees all my life."

"Just another nuisance we have Prince Albert to thank for," muttered Lord Calcott.

"No, you have me to thank," challenged Ian. "I wanted a tree. Juliana enjoys them."

More soft surprise assailed Juliana at Ian's words. He had brought a new holiday tradition into his home simply because she enjoyed it? Tears pricked at her eyes. She willed them away.

Ian had such a giving heart. It made her own suspicious one feel dark and Scrooge-like. She reached for his hand and clasped it, wanting his warmth and closeness.

"You should spend less effort on such frivolities," admonished his father, "and more on seeing to your future. The new year is coming very soon. You are wasting precious time."

Suddenly, Ian tensed. His stance became aggressive. He thrust her behind him and faced his father. "It is my future and my time."

Lord Calcott shrugged as if he did not care. Juliana knew better, saw determination on his face.

What he was determined about in Ian's life, she had no notion.

"If you have any intent to marry this oaf, save us all, particularly Ian, a great deal of headache and do it very soon."

With those cutting words, Lord Calcott left the

room. Juliana stared after him in stunned silence. Neither Emily nor Ian seemed shocked in the least.

"He dislikes the holidays and seems to delight in crushing others' enjoyment," said Emily matter-of-factly.

But Juliana could see she was shaking with fury.

Ian, on the other hand, pretended nothing had happened. "What shall we use to decorate the tree?"

"W-was the tree cut today?" Juliana asked, trying to forget the episode with Ian's father.

"Indeed. I did it myself this afternoon."

He looked quite pleased with himself. Juliana, determined to forget Lord Calcott's rude outburst, smiled at Ian. "It is beyond lovely. And since it is so fresh, we can decorate it with candles. If you've baked gingerbread men, we can string them together." At Emily's nod, she went on. "And ribbon—red if you have it. That's always lovely."

"Red, Mother?" Ian asked.

"I think we can manage that." Emily smiled indulgently.

Within minutes, servants had gathered all the necessary supplies, and the trio began decorating. Ian, being the tallest, worked at the top. Emily and Juliana shared the fat sides of the bottom half of the tree.

Laughing, they strung gingerbread men and ate their broken arms and legs. Ian admonished them for gluttony, even as he did the same. Finally, the tree stood tall and bedecked in holiday splendor. Ian handed Juliana and his mother each a candle, and with his own, lit theirs. Then they turned to the tree and began to illuminate the miniature candles attached to the branches.

Emily began to sing.

> *Silent night, Holy night*
> *All is calm, all is bright . . .*

Juliana felt the force of the season completely infuse her. Peace rolled through her veins like molasses, reminding her of why she liked this season so much. It was a time to forgive. It was time to give to loved ones, especially those she had not shown much affection during the year.

She cast her gaze to Ian as he joined his mother in song. They lit the last few candles on the tree and stood back, as if paying homage to the glorious sight with their song. Quickly, Juliana blew out her candle and rushed to the nearby pianoforte.

As she completed that carol and began to play "God Rest Ye Merry Gentlemen," the peace sank deeper into her bones, digging out anger and resentment. The squabbles of the year ceased to matter. This shining moment was perfect. No matter the means Ian had brought her home from India or the purpose, she felt an explosion of happiness now and was overjoyed to be with him. She wished this moment could go on always.

As the last notes of the carol ended, Emily smiled at them both. "Merry Christmas."

With a kiss to Ian's cheek and a gentle hug for Juliana, Emily quit the room, leaving the two young people alone.

His blue gaze settled on her, sparkling, earnest. Her heart seemed to melt further. "Thank you for sharing this evening with me."

"Thank you for thinking of me." She felt shy suddenly, and knew her face reflected her sudden reticence.

He took her hands in his. "I would not dream of sharing it with anyone else. It was perfect." He swallowed and looked at their joined hands. "I could almost imagine spending each holiday—and every day between them—with you."

Ian's words moved Juliana so deeply, she nearly could not breathe. Everything today had been perfect. She, too, could see a shimmering future, filled with his love, their shared joy.

Was it possible that she could know this kind of happiness, this sense of being complete, if she accepted his proposal?

A moment later, Emily gave a soft knock and entered the room again. "Juliana, I don't mean to distress you, but I fear the snow has fallen frightfully hard since the sun set. I do not think you should travel back to Harbrooke tonight."

Frowning, Juliana raced to the window. Quickly, she realized Emily was right. Pure white covered every object in sight, lay inches high on the railing just outside. Snow still fell in earnest.

"Of course you are welcome to stay here," Emily continued. "I will have a chamber prepared for you and send a man to your parents first thing in the morning so they do not worry."

Stunned but accepting, Juliana nodded. "Y-yes, I thank you for your hospitality."

Emily smiled, her eyes wise and serene. "You are always welcome with our family."

With that encouragement, Emily left again.

Juliana mused with some confusion that she felt as if she belonged with this family.

CHAPTER FIFTEEN

Juliana retired to her chamber, thinking of Ian and the soft kiss he had placed on her cheek moments ago.

He had been perfect these past few days. They had talked, laughed, played, shared. He had done his utmost to please her and hadn't pushed the issue of marriage once.

Still, Juliana considered very seriously that she ought to marry him. Oh, she would like to refuse to spite her father and teach Ian a lesson about meddling, but if all her days with him were as sublime as this . . . How could she refuse such happiness?

Leaning against the chamber door with a sigh, she pressed her fingers to her lips. Though it scared her, she could not deny the possibility she loved him as he claimed to love her.

A knock interrupted her reverie.

With Juliana's permission, a maid entered with a swish of the door against plush carpet and a curtsy. The silent little woman assisted her out of her clothes into a lace-edged white nightrail Emily had thoughtfully provided, then brushed out her hair before leaving Juliana alone with her thoughts.

Should she marry Ian? She wished she had her diary to confide in. Despite their troubled past, Juliana could now find no solid reason to refuse him. What he had done to prevent her imprudent marriage to Geoffrey had been foolish but well meaning. Nor did she think the Ian she knew today would engage in such behavior. He had not lied about her father's illness. In fact, since her sire had given up walking and began drinking again, he'd begun to look bloated and red. She could see why Ian had been concerned. Yes, he had asked Byron Radford to cease courting her. But if Byron had truly wished to wed her, he would have ignored Ian's request.

She'd always known Ian was high-handed and tended to dictate before he listened, but he had a good heart and a keen sense about people. After all, he had known of Peter Haversham's intentions. When he cared, he cared completely. He did not hide his regard, and Juliana admired his open feeling. She did not believe she could behave with such candor unless she felt absolute trust.

And therein laid her question: Did she trust Ian?

Mostly, yes. Almost certainly. With very little reservation.

But it disturbed her that she had any reservations at all.

Juliana knew herself too well to be anything but honest. Had she yet to fully recover from Ian's perfidy five years ago? Perhaps it was the seemingly suspicious nature of the events since he had arrived in India that cast doubt in her mind. While he had been vindicated in the matter of her father's illness, there lurked a bit of uncertainty . . . somewhere.

Or perhaps she did not trust herself. Such an intense reaction of her body, mind—and even her heart—did not put her at ease. She enjoyed self-control, and yet with Ian it slipped away readily. His kiss alone made her forget her goals, her fears, propriety in general. Such vulnerability could not be good for her soul.

Despite the logical plan she had held for some time, she could not bring herself to wed another man, one for whom she felt only polite affections.

With a sigh, Juliana crossed the room to the fireplace and stared into the low-burning blaze. How was she to answer Ian's proposal in less than two days? Could she wed him and take the chance he had deceived her or that he would control her future? What if she refused him and he walked away, or, worse, wed another? Juliana feared she would become like the ghost of Caroline Linford, her heart bleeding for what might have been.

Another gentle tap sounded on her door. She felt certain it must be the maid returning, until an altogether different voice echoed through the portal.

"Juliana, are you awake?" Ian whispered.

She stared at the door in surprise. Had he not retired? What did he want? What *could* he want at this time of night?

"Yes."

As if he had heard the suspicion in her voice, he offered, "I forgot to give you your Christmas present."

With some surprise, Juliana realized she had not given her gift to him either. She looked around and spotted the blue-silk-wrapped package on the dressing table, next to her reticule. One of the servants must have brought it to this room before she retired.

"We can exchange gifts in the morning," she suggested.

He hesitated. "I would rather not have my parents looking on. May I give it to you now?"

An imploring note resounded in his low whisper. Knowing the contempt his father seemed to hold for the holiday, as well as the disdain he would have for the gift she had procured for Ian, Juliana decided she preferred to exchange their gifts alone too.

But it would not be proper—or wise—to invite him into her chamber. She was much too aware of Ian as a man.

Opening the door a crack, she peered into the darkened hallway. Ian was at one with the shadows. Gray and black tones contoured the angles of his strong nose, his lean cheeks. But his eyes, so blue even in the dark, met her gaze with an earnest wish to please—and something else tightly leashed and dangerous.

Definitely, she could not let him in. He could not be allowed to satisfy her curiosity—or any other ache.

Gone were his cravat and coat. He still wore his crisp white shirt, but the top buttons had been loosened, revealing an intriguing glimpse of taut golden skin rippled with sinew and muscle. He had rolled back his sleeves, baring brawny forearms lightly dusted with dark hair. His brown pants fit snugly over narrow hips and muscled thighs as he leaned against the portal, watching her.

Juliana swallowed. Since Ian had appeared in India nearly seven months ago, she had found denying his masculine charm difficult. Tonight, cloaked in darkness and the hint of intimacy his casual attire implied, she found it impossible.

As his blue gaze roved her with a hot caress, Juliana realized she wore nothing more than a nightrail so sheer that if he touched her, she would no doubt feel the heat and texture of his hands through the fabric. She swallowed.

"We—we cannot stand here like this. Someone will see. The servants—"

"Have all sought their own beds. It is after midnight."

"Yes, of course. If you will hand me your box, I shall hand you mine and we can—"

"Juliana," he called. He spoke softly, his voice rife with allure, with male persuasion. "Come into the hall at least. I shall do my best to restrain any ... urges I have to ravish you."

She heard the wry humor in his voice and could not help but smile. "If you're certain?"

"I can control myself for the time necessary to watch you unwrap a gift, I think. But if you take too long, I may be compelled to ravish."

Juliana laughed softly into the night as she opened the door farther and stepped into the hall. Bless him for lightening the thick air between them.

"You are incorrigible," she chided.

"I can tell it bothers you a great deal."

At his lazy smile, warmth curled inside her. Juliana enjoyed teasing him so, and this seemed to add another dimension to their perfect day together.

Turning, she retrieved Ian's gift and handed it to him. "Open it," she invited. "I had this made for your future."

Ian shot a questioning gaze to her, his eyes sharp, before he delved cautiously into the wrapping. She watched with anxiety as he lifted the gift free of the box. Would he like it? And why was it so important that he did?

He held up the gift, a placard in brass and warm woods, and peered at it in the dark. He squinted and frowned.

"You do not like it?" she asked, more than faintly disconcerted by that prospect.

"I cannot read it," he corrected her. "It is too dark."

Juliana hesitated, then opened her door a bit farther, gesturing to the desk just beyond the door. "My lamp there is still on."

He shot her a fleeting smile as he brushed past

her. He bent close to the low, golden light. After a moment, his fingers brushed over the brass, traced the horseshoe above.

"Hillfield Park." He looked up at her, holding the plaque tightly in his large hands. His eyes showed appreciation and admiration at once. "You remembered that name."

"Of course. I know how important dreams are when you feel as if you have nothing else."

In silence, he nodded. "I cannot thank you enough. Your belief in me is—" His smile was wistful. "I find myself moved. I will value this not only because it will decorate my future, but because you said you understand my goal. For too many years, I have yearned to begin breeding the fastest horses, on land I purchased myself. Someday, soon I hope, I will have it. And this will be the first thing I hang. Thank you."

His eloquence warmed her as much as his honest appreciation, perhaps because they both stemmed from his heart.

"You are most welcome," she said softly, and meant it.

Setting the box and the placard aside, Ian approached her with serious eyes, holding a small square box out to her.

"Merry Christmas," he murmured.

But his eyes seemed to plead for her approval.

Slowly, Juliana removed the bright red bow and the white silk wrapping. Inside lay a box engraved with the name of a prominent London jeweler. With a gasp stuck in her throat, she lifted her gaze to Ian's taut face.

"Open it," he encouraged.

With suddenly shaking fingers, Juliana lifted the lid. The gold of the gas lamp shot a gleam into the delicate gold necklace in the box. In the shape of an oval, her name was engraved on the front. It was stunningly lovely.

She lifted it from the velvet cushion on which it rested and held it up to the light. Then she saw it was not just a necklace, but a locket. She opened it to find a miniature of Ian and a small lock of his hair—in keeping with the current custom many brides received from their affianced grooms.

Before anger at his presumption could hit her, Ian offered, "If you choose not to wear this as an acceptance of my proposal of marriage, wear this in friendship. I shall be happy to have you think of me at all."

The rasp in his voice hinted at emotion both raw and real. His face revealed the same, and Juliana found she could not be angry with him.

"You would truly be content to remain my friend if I refused your proposal?" she challenged.

Sorrow cascaded over Ian's features as he closed his eyes for a long moment. "If that is your wish. I will not like it, but I will respect it. As you say, it is your choice."

Shock hit her in the chest. She lost her breath. He understood—finally! An intense wave of something she had no name for swept through her, bringing with it a pang of yearning. Caution crept in a moment later, trying its best to temper her response. For once, she shoved it aside.

She leaned into Ian and wrapped her arms around him instead. He did not hesitate for a moment before he enveloped her in his embrace, holding her firmly against him. In that moment, Juliana experienced closeness to Ian, a sense they were somehow bound. For once, she did not avoid it.

Into her ear, he whispered, "Perhaps I've never been good at expressing it, but having you in my life seems to lighten me, make me whole."

Ian had captured perfectly the sentiment she had been trying to describe these past few days.

"I feel the same way," she said, her lips inches from his musky, golden neck.

Scents of wood and brandy and man enveloped Juliana, tangling with the glow of tenderness in her chest. An urge to touch her lips to the bare warmth of his throat seized her. For a moment, she stood frozen, fighting the urge. Would he think her forward? Would she find it pleasing?

Into her panicked indecision tumbled one thought: Ian had kissed her—and taken other liberties—more than once. Certainly she could be permitted this one chance to assuage her urge.

Blocking out further thought, Juliana leaned in and pressed her moist lips against the forbidden flesh somewhere between his ear and his collarbone.

Against her, Ian stiffened. Beneath her lips, his pulse began to race. His fingers tightened at her waist.

Intrigued by his reaction, Juliana kissed his neck again.

At first, Ian said nothing, did nothing. Finally, he eased back enough to look at her. Not just look, however. His gaze delved into her eyes, her soul, desperately seeking something.

Uncertain what he wanted, she smiled shyly.

Before she even finished forming the expression, Ian brought her back against him, flush to his hard length. Then Juliana felt his hot mouth behind her ear, at the curve of her neck, on her jaw, melting her.

Finally, he hovered just over her mouth.

"Juliana?"

His whisper asked nothing in particular, yet everything in its breathy plea. But she did not want to talk or answer questions. For now she wanted only to feel the security and exhilaration that came with his closeness.

She closed her eyes and pressed her lips to his.

Their mouths met in a rush of breath. Ian curled his hands around her head, fingers invading the braided mass of her hair, as if trying to bring her closer. He urged her lips apart with a persuasive brush of his own, and his tongue swept into her mouth, finding her, encouraging her—igniting her. He was around her, his taste on her lips, his scent exploding in her mind. Juliana kissed him back without hesitation, withholding nothing of the desire bubbling inside her.

She felt as if she were swelling, unfurling with the need to feel him. It was an unfamiliar sensation, but the innate female within her recognized what the swirling, growing urge meant.

One of Ian's hands whispered down her neck, fingered her spine, caressed the curve of her waist, curled about her hip. Everywhere he touched her skin felt alive with tingles, awakened and amenable to the whims of his touch.

Restless, his mouth left hers and traveled with persuasive power to her jaw, then just beneath. A sigh caught in her throat. But he was not finished. She realized the depth of his insistence when he pressed his lips to her neck, pulled gently on her lobe with his teeth, then settled into the crook of her nape. His exhalations swept across her skin.

She felt alive. Truly alive. Her heart raced. Blood pumped through her as she felt desire pooling where one very wanton part of body wanted him most.

With warm fingers, Ian pushed aside the lace edging of her nightrail and planted a series of kisses on her shoulder. His teeth nipped her. His tongue lapped the tingling spot.

Juliana had never felt anything like it in her life.

Never comfortable with a passive role, she resolved to do the same to him and brought her mouth to the exposed side of his neck. As she neared, she again smelled the musk of man, the musk of desire.

Entranced, she teased his flesh with her teeth and tongue.

"Yes," he breathed, urging her closer.

Then he was bending, his hands working at the small buttons of her nightrail until he created a deep V that exposed the inner swells of her breasts. Aware of the night whispering across her flesh and Ian's gaze heating it, Juliana's breathing turned ragged.

"You are so lovely," he whispered.

Then he lifted a hand to her and palmed her breast, cupped it, lifted its engorged weight. Between his thumb and finger, he gently squeezed the aching, distended tip. Like lightning, the sensation tore through her belly and lower.

She arched into his heated touch, her head tumbling back on a gasp. Ian was like an inferno raging as he molded her body to his, setting his hungry mouth to her neck and shoulder as his thumb brushed the hard length of her nipple.

Juliana scarcely felt her nightrail fall off her shoulder, exposing one breast entirely to the golden lamplight and his possessive gaze. He looked directly into her eyes. She met his blue stare, saw the question in his hungry expression. It was a question she did not know how to answer; she knew only that she didn't want to give up the wonder of his touch yet.

He reached behind him to shut the door. It closed with the barest of sounds in the winter eve, a dim disturbance of the silence.

As the sound registered in Juliana's senses, Ian's hand found its way to the other shoulder of her nightrail. He lowered it until the lace-edged neckline caught on the swells of her breasts. In his scorching gaze, she felt the heat of his desire and frustration; she shared his sentiments when he cradled her breast in his hand again, the thin fabric a barrier between them.

Ian made a sound of protest in his throat, one she

felt through her entire body. She *needed* his hand upon her, touching bare flesh, assuaging the ache.

Somewhere in the hazed whirl of her mind, Juliana knew this was not proper. But she could not care now. She had been so alone for so long and she trusted Ian as she had never trusted Geoffrey. More, what Ian made her body feel—her heart feel— seemed so right, so necessary to her.

And Juliana realized that at some point she had fallen in love with him. She could bear separation no longer.

With a cry, Juliana took the nightrail in her hands and pulled it down, until it skimmed her hips, caressed her thighs, brushed her knees, fell to the ground.

She stood naked.

Ian's hand fell away from her. But his eyes . . . Oh, those blue eyes did more than stare; they touched her, devoured her, made love to her as if she could feel their every move.

His face ablaze with possession and determination, Ian stepped back. Before disappointment could flay Juliana, he pulled his crisp white shirt over his head and tossed it to the floor.

She stood in mute awe. Carved and solid, he was taut-muscled beauty. A fine dusting of dark hair in the shadowed valley between his brown male nipples somehow added mystery. A fierce desire to solve him, to touch all his golden flesh and please him, buffeted her.

Juliana reached out, until the shaking center of her splayed hand touched his chest. As she suspected, the flesh beneath her palm was heated and hard. Her mind began to race more quickly, along with her heart. The secret place between her thighs pulsed with desire.

She feathered her fingers across the raised muscle of his chest, over his nipple. It hardened. She watched in fascination, then glanced up into his face as it tightened too. She repeated the process. Ian hissed in a breath.

Then he grasped her wrist and set her hand at her side. Uncertain, aroused, she complied with his silent wish. He curled his hand around her waist, to her back, and began drawing her near. Her heartbeat exploded against her chest. With a brush of fingertips, he caressed his way down to her buttocks and pulled her flush against him. She felt every inch of his arousal against her belly, firm and silently demanding.

Juliana opened her mouth, to say what, she was not certain. Ian ended the dilemma for her by covering her mouth with his in a blistering kiss that both coaxed and insisted. She lost herself in its rhythm, his taste, the heat they created. Wanton ferocity boiled within her as she swirled her tongue around his, not just answering his kiss but matching it and demanding more.

Ian answered her every wish, burning her up from the inside out. Her skin was alive, excruciatingly alert to his barest touch. She gasped into his mouth when his fingertip circled the tip of her nipple, teasing, making her endure.

Wild and enthralled, Juliana whisked her hands from his shoulders down to his linen-clad backside and urged his hips to hers. The wide ridge of his shaft pressed against her core, digging the abyss of need deeper inside her. She cried out.

Ian answered with a groan amid his harsh breathing. "You feel . . . so, so perfect, like every fantasy—"

"You are unlike anything I imagined," she whispered. "Wonderful."

Again, their mouths met. She swayed in his arms. Juliana felt the bed at the back of her knees. She sank to its soft comfort, pulling Ian down with her, grateful for a place where she could hold him close, give free rein to the maelstrom inside her she could no longer control.

Then Ian was on top of her, enveloping her in his heat and spice. He planted his hands on either side of her face and settled a series of demanding kisses on her bare shoulders, nipping at her collarbones, the hollow of her neck. Down, down, his mouth caressed her skin until she was certain it must pulse with want.

An encouraging half-whisper escaped Juliana. She found herself opening to him. She flung her arms wide, arched to him, her every lustful impulse firmly in control of her mind.

Ian seized each opportunity she granted, starting with a lazy tongue lapping at the peak of her breast. Once again, he laved her distended nipple until she felt its silent cry for more. As if he heard the sound, he slid a hand beneath her shoulders, lifted her up to him as if she were a feast for his taking. He gorged until she turned breathless.

Slowly, he made his way down her body, kissing as he explored, to the soft surface of her abdomen, into the shadowed curve of her waist. His tongue swirled in her navel as he caressed the full swell of her hip.

Ian's thumb swept across her hipbone. A melee of sensation made her hiss in a breath. Juliana felt certain nothing could arouse her further.

He brushed his fingers over the burning core of her mons, and she knew she had been wrong.

Every part of her roared to furied life then. At once, she was fire and ice. She wanted—Lord knew how much. With his every touch, she only became more heated, more out of control.

His finger probed her gently, touching her in a way she had only distantly suspected a man might, but never actually known. Against his fingers, Juliana felt the extent of her moistness, and his murmur of approval gratified her—at least until his touch,

centered on her most sensitive spot, took her near
the edge of explosion. Sweat broke out in a fine sheen
on her skin.

At that moment, she wanted nothing more than
to have Ian fill the emptiness yawning like a chasm
inside her.

She reached down to tug at the waist of his
breeches. He stilled, then caressed her hair from her
face, holding her gaze on his. That blue stare probed
deep into her eyes, searching.

"Are you certain?" he asked, voice low and
strained.

"Yes." Even her whisper seemed to ache.

He smiled with such tenderness, Juliana's heart
reveled in his care. "Truly?"

"Yes." She kissed his warm mouth. "Yes."

He rolled to her side for a moment. In the faint
golden light, she watched as he doffed the last of his
clothes. She caught little more than a glimpse of his
stiff male flesh and muscled thighs before he rolled
over, covering her once more.

Nothing seemed more natural than opening her
thighs wider and letting him settle in between. Sensation ruled then, the light abrasion of his hair against
the tender inside of her thighs, the solid blaze of his
chest against her, the shallow breaths he took, his
mouth searching for hers. . . .

Juliana felt each inch of him pressed against her
with excruciating clarity. Still, that emptiness deep
in her core railed at his absence. She lifted herself
to him, knowing she behaved shamelessly and not
caring—as long as he assuaged the need.

"Easy," he whispered.

A moan of protest slipped from her throat until
Ian gripped her hips in his hands and guided her
up to him. Breath held, she waited—one heartbeat,
another, another. Finally, Ian braced himself against

her swollen entrance and began to slide himself inside.

A pleasant burn suffused her as she stretched to take him fully within. But he was moving with such care—so slowly, Juliana thought she would expire before he was totally sheathed. With impatience, she lifted her hips up to him, taking every last inch of him in one sharp stroke.

Unprepared for the sensations, she gasped at the tingling bliss. Ian groaned, his fingers tightening around her hips.

"You're likely to kill me," he whispered.

Normally, Juliana would find some quick reply. But when Ian withdrew and filled her again, then again, she found she could not form a single thought. She was too busy matching her body to his rhythm, meeting the mating of his seeking mouth.

They fit together perfectly. She had not have imagined such bliss could be found from an act that had never before inspired more than irritation. But this rush of blood, of sensation, to the place where their bodies lay joined, confirmed that the way Ian touched her was wholly new—as was her urge to please in return.

Above her, he continued to thrust into her body, his movements growing less cautious as his breath grew more labored. Juliana shared whatever he experienced, for she felt on the edge of something she had no name for but wanted badly.

Suddenly, Ian removed his hands from her hips and slid his arms beneath her shoulders, drawing their bodies together at every point—breast, abdomen, thighs. Juliana sucked in a sharp breath at this new, seemingly ultimate closeness.

"Tilt up to me," he whispered raggedly in her ear.

Juliana did as he said, and when he plunged into her again, she thought she would explode from the sheer intimacy.

But it was the pleasure that overwhelmed her.

Suddenly, she felt a cry escape her throat as a sensation unlike any other she had ever felt raced up her thighs and between. Filled with heat and pressure, it spiked deep within her core until she felt herself pulsating in pleasure.

Above her, Ian stiffened and moaned, then called out her name as he thrust into her with swift, urgent strokes that only heightened her satisfaction. He gave a long, guttural cry, then stilled above her, skin slick, heart racing.

Touched inside, outside, and deep in her heart, Juliana felt the urge to cry. As tears filled her eyes, Ian lifted his head to look at her.

He brushed a damp strand of hair from her face. "Love, don't be upset. I—"

"I'm not," she whispered between quiet sobs. "I don't know when anything has felt more right."

"Because it *is* right." His voice was low with conviction and feeling. He punctuated the vow with a tender kiss.

Juliana could not stop her tears, nor did she try, safe while Ian held her until sleep came.

Dressed for the day ahead, Ian crept from his own room an hour after sunrise, eager to see Juliana. Today, they should agree on a wedding date. The thought made him smile.

God, she had been magnificent last night, her body so candid about her desire and pleasure. Their joining had held some spark of magic, as if fate had ordained it with blessing. He could scarcely wait to hold her again.

But wait he would.

The previous night had been one of the most astonishing of his life, but certainly they could not again risk her conceiving before they spoke vows. She had been talked about and maligned enough by Devonshire society. Yes, he and Juliana had allowed their passions to carry them away, but responsibility would have to reign until they were man and wife.

On their wedding night, however ... His body hardened as he imagined all he could show her, all they could share, all through their life.

Ian made his way into the kitchens. Too excited to sit for breakfast, he grabbed a spot of coffee and a scone, then made his way to the library.

While he tried his damnedest to concentrate on the newspaper, Juliana wandered in, looking excruciatingly young and hopeful and uncertain. His heart swelled.

He rose and walked to her side, taking her hand in his. "Good morning. How are you feeling?"

She flushed. "A bit sore, but well rested."

He smiled at her honesty. "Not wholly unexpected."

With a shy nod, she asked, "When did you leave?"

"Shortly after you fell asleep," he whispered. "I did not want to risk someone finding us together."

Relief crossed her pale face, taking the tension from her body. "Good notion."

He tucked a strand of hair behind her ear. "No need in giving anyone something to whisper about before the wedding."

The smile dropped from her face. A furrow took up residence between her brows. "Wedding? But we ... I—I did not agree to any marriage."

Ian reared back and stared at her with growing confusion. "Last night, we— You can't mean to— You are not the kind of woman to share a man's bed without marriage, Juliana."

She hesitated, her thoughts clearly racing. "No, but nor am I the kind of woman to be pushed to the altar."

"Pushed? I simply assumed after what we shared that you would demand I do right by you."

Something ugly and suspicious crossed her face. "Or did you simply hope that if you bedded me, I would have no choice?"

Turmoil and hurt squeezed at his heart. Yes, he had once thought of such a plan, but last night had been wholly spontaneous. "That is unfair! You kissed me first. You—you never once protested. I even asked if you were certain and you said you were. Twice! What was I to think?"

"That I wanted a lover, perhaps," she challenged.

Ian threw his hands in the air. "Why would I think that? If you merely wanted a lover, you had opportunities, I am sure, to take one in India. Or to tell me you sought only a lover from my company aboard the *Houghton*. But you went to London to find a husband. You refused Peter Haversham when he would have paid you to be his lover. You are a decent woman who has never taken a lover in her life. Why did you assume I would believe you had done so now?"

"I was simply ... with you last night," she said finally, "without thought to any particular outcome or consequence."

Juliana was the least impulsive person he knew and he did not believe her for an instant. "And speaking of consequence, what if you conceive?"

Juliana paused, her mouth pursed. "We shall talk of that if it happens."

"No," he argued, grabbing her hands. "I want to marry you. After last night, I cannot turn my back on what is right."

"Release yourself from your overdone notions of duty," she snapped. "There will be no wedding unless I say so."

Ian opened his mouth to speak, but a knock on the door filled the room instead.

"What is it?" he growled.

"Lord Brownleigh is here to see you, my lord."

Ian hesitated, rubbing a hand over his suddenly tired eyes. He glared at Juliana. How could she not want to marry? He'd been so certain that last night was her way of accepting his proposal. All the joy he'd known in the hours since holding her was gone, buried in a shallow grave marked "hope."

"My lord?" Harmon called through the door.

"Damn it," he cursed. "Show him in."

Juliana rounded on him. "You can say nothing to my father of last night."

"You think I would?"

She gave no response to his indignation except to face the door in silence. Ian felt more insulted than if she'd slapped him.

Lord Brownleigh filled the space moments later, his face ruddy, gait labored. He looked at the two of them with a long stare.

"Good morning, Ian. Juliana," he greeted them.

"Papa, are you well?" A frown gathered between her hazel eyes, and Ian could see why; Brownleigh looked haggard.

"As fit as I can be, considering your absence. But I see you're both well despite the snow."

Ian nodded to his neighbor.

"How did you travel here?" Juliana asked.

"My mount. Girl, I think we must seriously discuss the prospect of you wedding Ian. Spending the night here will only ensure everyone in Lynton will gossip about you again."

Juliana frowned. "Why? His parents were here, who are perfectly acceptable chaperones. There were servants—"

"That is true," he conceded, clutching his stomach. "But—"

"Papa, are you certain you are well?" Juliana could

not hold back the question. Her father looked flushed and tired.

"Do not change the subject, young lady. You have been spending a great deal of time with Ian. After last night, everyone will assume you two will wed, and if you do not, they will whisper in speculation."

Anger surged up from her belly to her throat. "I will not wed someone just to quiet wagging tongues. What has one to speculate about? Can a man and a woman not be friends?"

"Not if they are both unwed."

Her father was cynical, but in society's eyes, he was right. Juliana knew it, but it chafed her all the same.

Still, after last night, weren't she and Ian more than friends? She should wed him; she knew it. But it seemed as if Ian and her father both were, once more, doing their best to rush her to the parson. And she refused to be rushed.

"I will not take no for an answer, Juliana. Not this time. Your mother cannot endure more gossip."

Juliana gaped at his manipulation. Of all things, bringing her mother's fragile sensibilities into this was most insidious.

Then Papa turned his attention to Ian. "See that you bring her home shortly. Help her return our coach to Harbrooke. Perhaps you can talk some sense into her along the way."

With a wink at Ian and a stern look at her, he was gone. Juliana felt ready to scream.

She turned to Ian, incredulous. "Nothing he does should shock me, but it does. And you . . . you said nothing to him!"

"What would you have me say? I think he is right."

Fury tumbled in her gut, merged with shame and betrayal. "Yes, you would," she sneered. "You are just like him. Take me home. Now."

* * *

Silence gathered like an impenetrable wall between them as the coach glided over the fresh snow to Harbrooke. Juliana crossed her arms over her chest, clearly sulking.

Ian gritted his teeth—and not from the cold. He was past understanding, past listening to her woes and suspicions. He presented her an honest offer of marriage, then insisted standing by it once he had compromised her. Most women would be relieved, thrilled even. Juliana? No. She accused him of rushing her into marriage, then dug her heels in more stubbornly than an old mule.

Damn, the woman made no sense.

"What is truly stopping you from marrying me?" he said, tearing down the invisible wall between them. "After last night, it's clear you do not hate me. You are not in the habit of taking lovers upon a whim. And I'm certain that, despite what you told your father, you do not want everyone in Lynton gossiping about you. So why do you continue to refuse me?"

Piqued, she lifted her sharp chin in his direction. Her eyes were a hazel chill, matching her pursed mouth. "I should hardly be surprised you don't understand. How quickly you rushed to play the gallant and assure me that you would wed me after I'd become a fallen woman. Did you plan to seduce me?"

He glared at her. "Do you recall kissing me first?"

If anything, her eyes turned icier. "A kiss is hardly an invitation to share my bed. No, you did admirably in wheedling your way there once I gave you an opportunity."

"Wheedling? *If* I'd plotted to seduce the woman I love, it would be to share the joys of lovemaking, not to trap you. You are being both stubborn and unrealistic. What if, upon your awakening this morning, I had told you I no longer had any interest in marrying you? You would have thought me the worst cad."

"But at least you would have been an honest one."

Her words sliced Ian to the core. Nothing he said or did would reach this woman, ever. Not his love, for she'd disdained that often enough. Not sharing special holiday traditions with her, for she seemed to have forgotten the bond they'd forged. Certainly not lovemaking, for she was determined to litter their special night together with suspicion and accusation.

No more.

"As you wish. I give up. Forget I ever proposed marriage to you. Forget it completely. At least this way I shall finally have some peace, rather than being accused of lying, of being made in your father's mold. I tried to love you, help you find the best path in life. You couldn't discern the difference. So I quit."

Juliana stared at him with narrowed, angry eyes.

"Do not look at me that way," he spat out. "This is no ploy. I am finished. Until you can make peace with your father, you will never believe that we are not dominating fiends. And I will not share a life with someone so blind and mired in fear."

"I am *not* mired in fear," she shouted. "When have you ever given me a reason to trust you? When? You lied to me every time you thought it convenient or helpful. If I distrust you, it's because you taught me to."

Anger and sadness both invaded him, weighing down his heart. She would never love him or trust him or believe he did things in her best interest. She would never wed him. He'd wager she had never forgiven him for trying to dissuade her from marrying Geoffrey Archer. Stubborn woman.

He had always wanted to marry her, but not with distrust an anvil between them. He'd be better suited to forget her, turn his attention to someone uncomplicated, like Byron's Yorkshire cousin—what was her name? Margaret? It hardly mattered. Whatever her name, he could marry her, start Hillfield Park, and forget the willful Lady Archer even existed.

As Harbrooke came into view, Ian turned to her with a sneer. "You never could see that I simply tried to guide you away from trouble. You saw only the lie, never mind the reason behind it." He shook his head. "Last night, I thought we were perfectly suited. I see now I was bloody wrong." With an angry sigh, he gave a careless wave to gesture toward her house. "Go. Live your life alone if it pleases you. I am finished with trying to win you."

CHAPTER SIXTEEN

When Juliana arrived at Harbrooke, she immediately sought refuge in her chamber. Ten restless minutes later, she left the small domain, her mind in a blur of shock, and ambled through the house aimlessly, toward the drawing room and the soothing sight of their Christmas tree.

Ian had withdrawn his proposal of marriage. After years of seeking to make her his wife, he suddenly surrendered the fight? That simply? Somehow she had pictured him chasing her until they both had one foot in the grave.

Juliana frowned. She might believe his angry words were a ploy, except for the genuine anger and anguish on his face. Certainly if he had chosen to back down as a means of cajoling a rebuttal, his manner would have been smooth, less agitated. No, he had truly withdrawn his proposal, and the realization sat like a hard lump of confusion—and perhaps despair—in her belly.

"Damn it, man! She does not want to marry me,"

she heard Ian shout, his voice carrying through the closed door of the drawing room.

She hadn't known he was still at Harbrooke.

The murmur of another voice, which certainly belonged to her father, sounded in an unintelligible mumble.

The two of them, together as always. She groaned in disgust. They enjoyed each other's company well enough and thought eerily alike. Too bad they could not wed one another.

"No," Ian shouted again. "I cannot tempt her into marriage. I cannot cajole, coax, or otherwise persuade her. She has quite decided against the idea. It is time and past we left her to the fate she chooses."

Juliana blinked. Had Ian really said that? *Ian?* And meant it? Surprise thrummed through her. Did he finally, *truly* comprehend that she disliked being manipulated? That she had no intention of marrying a man she could not trust?

Flashes of memory, of his gentle touch, his wicked smile, the mountain of petticoats he had sent her, the doll he had bought his cousin—all these plagued her. Beneath his faults, he was a good man, an even better friend. . . .

Oh, rubbish! She could not possibly miss the man. He had not yet left her house, for pity's sake. Nor could she afford to be swayed by these illogical feelings.

Her father rumbled a reply once again, and drat, she could not understand him. Why could he not cooperate and shout as he did on every other occasion?

Creeping closer to the drawing room door, she heard Ian bellow once more. "It is not that simple."

The next sound—a scoffing noise—came from her father. "Of course it is, Axton. You simply have not asserted yourself enough with the silly girl. Is ten thousand pounds not enough incentive for you to be creative in pressing your suit? Certainly you can manage to woo her for that amount of blunt."

Shock blasted Juliana in an icy gust. Her ears buzzed. Blood drained from her body. Blinking, speechless, she stared at the closed white doors, heard Ian shuffling behind the door. Still, she could scarce comprehend.

Ten thousand pounds to wed her. She inhaled raggedly.

Juliana had no trouble believing her father had made such a appalling offer. The question was, when? Had Ian accepted the devil's bargain before she married Geoffrey? Geoffrey had wanted to wed her only for her father's money. Why not Ian too?

For some time Juliana had believed Ian thought himself in love with her, though in his own controlling way. Had love for money, not for her, prompted all his courting?

She had no proof of that . . . but she had no proof it was not true either.

Rage invaded her every muscle then. By God, that pair of cads deserved the sharp edge of her tongue— and every blade in the house. She reached out, ready to shove the doors open.

Her father's cutting words stopped her.

"Have you lost your ballocks, then? Think of all you stand to lose besides my ten thousand."

"Damn it, don't you think I know," Ian growled.

But Papa wasn't listening. "Remember that stud you've been so hell-bent on buying will be beyond your reach. What kind of breeding program will you have without him, eh? It will be years, if ever, before you can build a house on your land. And there is your father to consider. . . ."

Sounding dull and defeated, Ian answered, "I remember quite well that he plans to disinherit me if I fail to take a bride in a week's time."

Anger trampled Juliana's defenses again, deliv-

ering another jolt of shock. Ian stood to lose his
inheritance if he failed to wed?

Was that, coupled with her father's outrageous
offer of ten thousand, the reason he had come to
India nearly the minute he had learned of Geoffrey's
death?

Likely, yes. Juliana felt every inch the fool. Ian had
led her to believe at every turn that he loved her and
wanted no other bride.

Of course he wanted no other bride. Few came
with so large a fortune to recommend them.

"Believe me, I know all too well what will happen
if I do not wed within the week. I'd planned to call
upon Lord Carlton today. His young Yorkshire cousin
is seeking a husband. My father would be willing to
put up the money to make her amenable to a rushed
wedding, no doubt."

"The little redheaded thing?" her father asked.
"You truly wish to marry Lady—what is her name?"

"I do not recall." Ian grunted in frustration. "But
I must either wed her or give up everything I've ever
wanted."

And to gain Hillfield Park and his stud horse, he
would wed that brazen, pasty creature from Yorkshire? Without thought? Without even knowing her
name?

Juliana swallowed. Pain and anger vied for control
of her head. Ian's own words indicated she was little
more than the means to his dreams. Likely, if some
other girl's father had put up ten thousand to see
her wed, Ian would have asked her as well. And she
hated him for that. Not just for the lies and manipulations he had told to win his way. No, now she loathed
him for all the recent days he had called her friend
and done his best to build false trust in her, hoping
to shove her to the altar so he might claim her father's
bribe.

Her rage heated, surged, peaked, pushing the pain

aside. Juliana grabbed the door latch once again and gave it a hard shove.

She crashed into the room and stalked toward them. "You two are deplorable!" Then she focused her stare and her fury on Ian. "How long have you plotted to make me your docile, unsuspecting bride?"

Ian said nothing. He merely looked at her with guilty blue eyes and a jaw clenched so tight, it must hurt.

"How long?" she shouted.

"Juliana, I . . ." He frowned, searching for words. Likely the words with which to deceive her again.

"Bloody hell! You plied me with your false words of love, and I nearly believed them." She gave a sharp, self-deprecating laugh. "And now to discover you did it—came to India, proposed and coaxed me, told me you cared—all for my father's dirty money. Blackguard is too polite a slur for you, my lord."

"Juliana, that is not true!" Ian defended. "Listen—"

She held up a hand to stay further denials. "Save your words. I am certain your ploy is all I imagined and more."

"But you do not know what is in my heart," he protested. "You've never listened and never believed me."

"All you ever did was lie!"

"Juliana, damn it, the money your father offered me meant nothing. I wanted to wed you anyway. It would not have mattered if you'd come to me penniless. I simply wanted you as my wife."

Even through the thick wall of her anger, his words cut her. It pained her to hear him continue with the same trite excuse. How could she trust him now? But her heart ached to believe his every word.

No. She was finished being his fool.

"And what of your father's threat? You love me so much, you're willing to wed a green girl whose name you cannot remember. Why? If you cannot have *my* father's blunt, you'll at least have *your* father's?"

Again, Ian stared at her with burning eyes and a clenched jaw. "You do not understand—"

"When did your father threaten you? I'll wager it was before you left for India to find me. About the same time my father made his offer to you, no doubt." Derision dripped from her voice.

"No, Juliana. Stop and listen to me. I've known for some months that my father would disinherit me if I did not wed by the new year, but neither your father's money nor my father's mattered to me as much as you mattered."

"Enough!" That was all Juliana needed—or wanted—to hear. Shockingly, she felt tears sting her eyes, then hover at the corners, threatening to spill and humiliate her.

"Damn, you stubborn girl," her father shouted. "Hear the man out!"

"Stay out of this! You've done far too much already," she snapped at him, stunning him into momentary silence.

Juliana turned her attention back to Ian. "You have lied at every turn, at every moment. Worse, you preyed upon my memories of our friendship and used them to make me beholden to you in every way you could. No more! Bow to your father's money and marry that Yorkshire chit; I do not care. Just do not ever speak to me again."

Juliana turned to leave. Ian grabbed her arm.

His fingers tightened around her soft flesh. Heated memories flashed through her mind. A traitorous tingle assailed her. Even faced with the ultimate revelation of his deceit, her body responded, remembered his big hands upon the damp, needy places of her body.

"Let me go," she ordered, her voice low, breath shallow.

Ian ignored her. "You are ever willing to believe the worst of me. When I said I loved you, immediately you looked for ulterior motives. I made mistakes in the past, yes. But you have *never* forgiven me for them." His stare drilled into her. "Geoffrey Archer was your choice, and I swallowed that bitter pill eventually. Since the day I heard you were widowed, I wanted nothing more than to claim you as my own wife. My father's threats and Lord Brownleigh's offer meant nothing except the means to see my dream come true and build a future for us away from Lynton, a future completely our own. And you assumed only that I had some master scheme to trick you into wedding me so I could spend my days gleefully manipulating you. Do you think I have nothing else to do with my time?"

He grunted, a sound of irritation and frustration. "I cannot marry a woman who refuses to trust me. I cannot even talk to such a woman." He released her and stepped away. The hollows of his face seemed carved from granite, his blue eyes lay flat, cold . . . utterly empty. "I have withdrawn my proposal of marriage. Now I shall withdraw from your life."

Ian spun away and charged toward the stairs leading to Harbrooke's front door. Suddenly, Juliana did not know if she should applaud his departure or mourn it.

"Are you completely daft, girl?" her father shouted, his face a fiery purple-red.

Did his anger cause that odd pallor? Perhaps she looked a similar hue. Lord knew she was furious too. And that heartsick feeling—no, she refused to give in to that. At least not now . . .

"You only wished I was daft," she shot back. "That way, you and Ian could have easily duped me to the altar. But I am through tolerating these manipulations. I well know my finances make me beholden to you for my necessities, but I am no longer a child.

My dependency hardly gives you the right to decide my future for me. I am a grown woman—"

"Grown, perhaps, but not responsible," Papa growled.

Juliana thrust her hands on her hips, her temper soaring like a locomotive. "Suffering marriage with Geoffrey taught me a great deal, chiefly to be careful in choosing the man with whom I tread to the altar. Ian and I—"

She started to say they did not suit, but that was not entirely true. Some moments stood out like golden beacons, shining and hopeful—their snowball fight, the Christmas celebrations he had chosen to spend with her, the hours afterward he had loved her thoroughly. If he weren't so deceptive, so controlling, if he had meant even a moment of it, perhaps they could suit.

No, impossible—regardless of the wistful thought. Striving to change the low qualities in Ian was like wishing to change the color of the moon.

"You and Ian are far more suited than most well-bred couples who marry," her father asserted. "You know each other well. The match is an excellent one in every way, and it is nothing more than your stubborn nature that prevents the union. In that head of yours, you believe yourself to be intelligent and independent. I've seen nothing more than a headstrong hoyden much too concerned with her own thoughts to care for anyone else's!"

Papa would never change, neither his mind nor his ways. Juliana knew that, knew she should hold her tongue and stop wasting her breath. In the end, she could not stop her words.

"I am protecting my future so it will be what I wish. And how dare you scorn my behavior! At least I never *paid* anyone to manipulate you. That is one of the most vile acts I can conceive of."

Papa frowned and put a hand to his chest, as if

wounded. Good. She hoped her words hurt him as much as his actions had hurt her. Perhaps then he would consider how she felt, cease any further management of her life.

"Do you care how inferior that makes me feel?" Juliana went on. "I doubt it."

Her father staggered back a step, then another.

"Are you leaving now that I have a few words for you?" she challenged. "Are you so cowardly—"

"No . . ." her father groaned, closing his eyes and clutching his chest.

Then he fell to the ground in a heap.

He writhed on the burgundy carpet for a moment, moaning in pain. Something was wrong, Juliana realized as she knelt at his side. Truly, dreadfully wrong. The unholy grimaces on his face and awful moans from his throat bespoke terrible pain.

Had her father's heart given way? Horror of the possibility robbed her of breath, of thought.

Juliana screamed.

Ian returned from Harbrooke in a foul mood. He rode his gelding too hard, marched into Edgefield Park, tromping up the stairs with no thought to the noise or mud he left in his wake.

He knew his behavior was petulant and he didn't bloody care.

Upon reaching his chamber, Ian slammed the door behind him. He went straight for the brandy on his small secretary. After pouring the liquor to the rim of a glass, he threw it down his throat, glad for the burn it caused. He would have thrown the unsuspecting glass at a wall just to hear it shatter had he not wanted another brandy.

Damn woman! Bloody stubborn, beautiful wretch.

Why did everything have to be so terrible between them?

Ian poured another brandy and tossed it back as quickly as he had the first. And he waited for some comfort, a small measure of numbness to overtake his whirling mind or breaking heart.

Nothing. Not the smallest spot of relief. He frowned. Odd, for brandy usually cured the occasional foul mood. Granted, this mood was more foul than most. But did that matter?

"Bloody hell," he cursed, then poured and drank once more, hoping for better results.

Still nothing. Odd, indeed. Damn it all, now what?

An experiment? Yes. How many drinks would he need to see his memory diluted? How many would his body require until he found the bliss of sleep?

Ian did not know for certain, but there was one way to find out. He poured another glass and raised it to his mouth.

The liquid burned his throat as he swallowed. But Juliana was still there, stubborn even in his mind. Damn, why had the woman refused him? Would she never see that everything he had done, while perhaps underhanded, had only been to help her?

When Ian heard footsteps approaching his door, he paused in his experiment. Who had come to ruin his scientific endeavor?

Without a perfunctory knock, his father made his way into the room, disheveled and flushed. But his stance was that of a calm man. Ian frowned.

"My boy." Nathaniel edged close, clapping him on the back.

As soon as his sire moved within a foot, Ian detected a strong scent of jasmine, just like Ellie, the upstairs maid wore. As he watched Nathaniel adjust his jacket and smooth back his dark, ruffled hair, fury hit Ian. Could the philandering jackass not keep his prick out of the servants on Christmas Eve?

Ian stepped away from Nathaniel. "What do you want, Father?"

He shrugged, the picture of nonchalance, his wide shoulders bobbing in his sober gray coat. What a bloody lie!

"Tomorrow is Christmas Day. Need I remind you that you have a week to wed? You have yet to announce your wedding plans to . . . anyone. Do you simply not care for your inheritance?"

Ian wanted to shove it all back in his father's face, but Hillfield Park beckoned, reminding him of his future and all the reasons rebellion would be ill advised.

Tossing back another brandy, he said, "My bride has proven reluctant thus far, but I have a week remaining before the new year. I have another plan still."

Ian refrained from mentioning the pursuit he plotted of Byron's cousin. What *was* her damned name? No matter, he decided, shaking his head. On Boxing Day, he would visit the Radfords and pay his addresses to the redheaded girl.

But he had no enthusiasm for the idea. None at all. Damn his unruly heart.

"Reluctant?" his father echoed, clearly surprised. "Still? How can that be? You finally used that brain of yours and seduced the girl last night. Tupped her in her own bed."

Dismay washed over Ian in hot waves, yet he felt a distinct chill. He did his best to hide his reaction and the truth. "You are wrong. We exchanged Christmas gifts, nothing more."

Nathaniel shot him a leer. "And that took you nearly five hours, did it?"

Five hours? Yes, from the time he had entered her room at midnight, the hours during which they had made love and dozed, before he had awakened near dawn. How in the hell did his father know that?

"I saw you knock on her door as I went up the servants' stairs. When I returned to the hallway some hours later, you were creeping out of Lady Archer's room in nothing but your breeches," his father offered smugly.

Ian did not have to guess what his father had been doing in the servants' quarters in the middle of the night. No doubt the same thing he had been doing a quarter hour past. His anger surged once more.

"What Juliana and I do is none of your affair."

Nathaniel rolled his eyes. "Think for once, boy. You tupped her. And now you have a witness of her indelicate behavior. Me. What good lady would not wish to protect her reputation if you let her know that you may not be able to keep such knowledge to yourself?"

Disgust bit into Ian's gut. "I would never do that to Juliana. It is nothing short of manipulative and despicable."

His father rolled his eyes. "Drink another brandy and numb your conscience, please. Life is not about fairness. It is about winning. Her own actions have condemned her; you are simply using them."

"No."

Nathaniel cocked his head in a show of disbelief. "I can help you achieve everything you want. You will have your bloody foolish breeding stables and the wife of your choice. Why turn me down? It is a bit late to be so fainthearted."

"I will not have Juliana's name dragged through another scandal—"

"It will not come to that, boy. As soon as you tell her all of Devonshire will likely learn of your liaison unless you wed, she will comply immediately. Everything will be solved."

His father spoke as if such a solution abounded with common sense. And in some twisted way, it did make sense. But Ian could not remember the last time he had heard such stupidity.

"Nothing will be solved! She will hate me forever."

"Whatever her feelings are will cease to matter then. The thing will be done—in more ways than one."

Again, Nathaniel gave him a smirk that sent Ian's temper soaring.

"I said no, damn you. I meant no."

His sire's friendly demeanor disintegrated instantly. A hard mask of anger and impatience overtook his wide, still-handsome face.

"I hardly need your permission to start a rumor."

The silky threat turned Ian's very blood to ice. Juliana would loathe him until the day she left this earth. And he doubted she would marry him, despite the dishonor. Lord and Lady Brownleigh would be none too happy to have their only child's name associated with another such scandal.

"Stay out of my life," he growled. "You cannot force me to deal in so underhanded a manner with someone I love. You cannot plan my future for me. Nor can you make it what you wish. Have you no notion how much I despise you for your constant interference and management of my life? Surely even you are not *that* insensitive."

His father reared back, as if surprised by his vehemence. "Despise me, do you? I realize you don't fancy the notion of telling Devonshire that you bedded—"

"No, I do not fancy the notion in the least." Ian slammed his brandy glass down on his secretary. "And I would appreciate it if you would keep all such future notions to yourself and allow me to run my own life."

"I want grandsons, damn it!"

"And you will have them someday, hopefully soon. Until then, do nothing to come between Juliana and me." The chasm was already wide enough, but he need not admit that.

Worse, he barely understood it.

Nathaniel shrugged, clearly pretending to be

unruffled. "If you would rather lose your inheritance—"

"That is my choice!"

"Stupid boy, I am trying to help you. Can't you see that?"

No. All Ian saw was a mean-spirited, scheming cad. He would not allow his father to choose for him or "help" lead him to the decisions he did not wish to make. Juliana, on the other hand—

Juliana had tried to tell him the same things. Everything he said now to his father she had said to him— repeatedly. Assuming he had known better, known they were destined for marriage and bliss, he had trampled over her feelings without a thought.

Oh, God in heaven. Juliana likely saw him in the same ghastly light in which he saw Nathaniel.

Denial shoved its way into his mind. That could not be so. Everything he did to Juliana was done with the best of intentions.

Would not his father give the same excuse?

Ian heard a terrible buzzing in his ears. On leaden feet, he trudged to his bed and sank to the soft surface.

He had tried to take Juliana's choices away over and over—when Geoffrey Archer had begun to press his suit, in London when he had forced his knowledge of Peter Haversham upon her. Hell, even coercing Juliana into her promise to answer to his marriage proposal by Christmas had been dastardly. And he cringed to realize all the controlling ways over the years in which he had tried to "help" her, starting first with the tall tree beside the riverbank, as she had mentioned, to his assumption she would indeed marry him after spending a night in his arms.

In every way that mattered, he had behaved like his father.

The realization made his stomach roil and heave.

"I do not see that your scheming ways have helped

me in the least. Ever," he said to his father. "Cease
them now, before I make very certain you know how
wretched it is to feel like a bloody marionette."

Nathaniel scowled, stiffened, tugged on the lapels
of his coat. "Ungrateful cur. Just remember if you
do not marry the wench by New Year's Day, you will
be disinherited."

A lightness, a sense of pure freedom, overtook him.
By allowing what his father—and even himself—had
assumed would be the worst to occur in his disinher-
itance, Ian would finally be free to create his own
destiny. He would be penniless, but he would be
beholden to no one.

And maybe, just maybe, Juliana would someday
trust him enough to risk a friendship with him again.

But if she did not, that was her choice . . .

Ian shot his father a grim smile. "Father, I suggest
you prepare to lose a son. I will not force Juliana to
do your bidding. Or mine. Now, get out."

CHAPTER SEVENTEEN

In her father's chamber, Juliana stood beside her weeping mother. She clasped Mama's icy hand in her own, and with dry, aching eyes watched the young physician bend over Papa's still form.

With a sense of unreality, Juliana saw the doctor sigh, shake his blond head, tousled, no doubt, from his quick ride to Harbrooke. Her mother shuddered with renewed tears. Juliana blinked once, again, hoping she would somehow wake from this painful nightmare.

When she opened her eyes once more, the young man still stood at her father's bedside, then gathered up his instruments.

As soon as he tucked them away in his bag, he paused, then looked toward her and her mother with obvious reluctance. His gray gaze flitted over Mama, who had all but buried her agonized face in a sodden handkerchief. Pushing the ache in her chest aside, Juliana faced the doctor's grim countenance. Pity for Mama flashed across his broad face.

With a slight nod to the physician, Juliana led her

mother into the adjoining lady's chamber, decorated in her favorite lace and lavender. Urging Mama to lie down, Juliana leaned over the frail, grieving woman and kissed her forehead.

"Let me speak with Dr. Haney," she whispered. "For now, Papa is alive. That must give us hope."

Her mother closed her eyes and curled onto her side, sobbing once more. "Leave me," she whispered.

Biting her lip in worry, Juliana complied. On leaden feet, she crossed the threshold from one chamber to the next. Her thoughts whirled, illogical, incongruent. Yet each met in one point: Papa could not die.

He could be a bastard of the first order, yes, but beneath her animosity, she loved him. Flaws in character and lofty demands—her father specialized in those. And somehow she had come to both despise their terrible arguments and relish the challenge of besting him. God could not see fit to take him from her now, not when so many unresolved issues and sentiments lay between them. Not on Christmas Eve.

Blast it, no one died on Christmas Eve.

Softly, Juliana shut the door between the chambers and looked at the sober young physician expectantly. "My mother is resting. Now you may tell me what . . ."

She tried to go on, truly. But Juliana felt tears rising, closing her throat, drowning her words in salty sorrow.

"I fear your father has suffered a major episode with his heart. I cannot say when—or if—he will recover." Dr. Haney sighed. "That will depend partly on him. And on you. He must stay in bed for now. You must not give him anything more than broths and juice during this time. Absolutely no brandy."

Glad to have direction, Juliana nodded. "Broths, no brandy. I understand."

"If he has another episode, send your man for me at once."

Juliana responded with a shaky nod. "Thank you for coming tonight. I know it is Christmas Eve—"

"I have no family." Dr. Haney lifted his bag, then looked at her with bleak eyes. "Today, and tomorrow for that matter, are like any other days to me. If the holiday is your only concern, do not think twice about summoning me."

Pity and concern hit her like a hot wind, robbing her breath for a moment. The doctor had no one with whom to share this special, reverent day? Even if he seemed not to care, Juliana felt sad indeed for him.

"Doctor, why don't you stay with us?" she offered, her voice gentle. "The weather is frightful, and we've plenty to eat. You could stay near my father."

She wanted to tell him no one should be alone on Christmas but knew somehow that her pity would only sting his pride.

The young doctor saw through her ruse. "I appreciate your offer, but such charity at Christmas is unnecessary. I am accustomed to being alone. Call upon me if your father's condition takes a turn for the worse."

With a smart click of his boot heels and a flash of black coat, Dr. Haney exited the room. Juliana stared after him, a weighty sadness denting the armor of numbness around her mind. He would spend Christmas alone, without a thought of whether he must work or not? Such a reality seemed altogether wrong to her.

Still, she understood the good doctor's lack of Christmas spirit. Spending the season without loved ones made it truly depressing, like the sharp jab of a blade into an already lonely heart.

Suddenly, Juliana understood the feeling all too well. Her father was gravely ill, her mother incoherently distraught over the fact. Ian no longer spoke to her. Juliana felt little like celebrating herself, particularly when she could not ignore the fact she may never have the chance to speak to her father again.

And for the first Christmas ever, she would likely spend the day alone, fighting both tragedy and sorrow, her hopes for the future destroyed.

Afraid and overwhelmed, Juliana sank to the plush carpet, grasping the thick quilts of her father's bed in her white-knuckled fists, and cried.

Darkness filled every corner of Harbrooke by the time Juliana sought her bed. Assured that her father rested comfortably, and settling her mother into slumber with a brandy, she finally sought her own chamber.

The clock in the hall chimed twice. Was it that far past midnight? Rolling her tense shoulders, she admitted the day had passed so quickly, it has seemed no more than a few instants long. Was it just last night that she and Ian had made love so tenderly, she swore she could feel her heart melt? In other ways, the day had seemed a painful eternity filled with betrayal and loss.

Now Christmas was upon her.

Juliana sighed, sadness and confusion weighing upon her very soul. Sleep would not be soon in coming, she knew. Yet as she disrobed, minus Amulya's help, and settled into bed, she knew that if for no other reason than her father would need her tomorrow, she should seek sleep immediately.

Juliana curled onto her side and stared at the shadowed wall of her room. She shut her eyes, but again they popped open, refusing sleep.

Her mind whirled with the day's events and all the overwhelming emotions they brought—the terror of her father's heart episode, the joy of making love with Ian, the bitterness of his betrayal, the sorrow of their long friendship and short romance, both now shattered.

Her father's health worried her indeed. While he had behaved awfully in offering Ian ten thousand pounds to marry her, that did not color the fact he was her sire and would always hold some measure of her heart. Any recovery he might make was in the hands of Dr. Haney and God.

Clasping her hands tightly to her chest, she gazed at the darkened ceiling and whispered, "Please do not take Papa from me. Not on Christmas." Her eyes stung with hot, insistent tears. Angrily, she swiped them from her cheeks.

Hoping God had heard her, Juliana closed her eyes once more and rolled to her side. Ian's pained, imploring face thrust itself into her memory.

Even in sleep the man would not leave her in peace. Why did he haunt her restless thoughts? Live in some stubborn corner of her heart, despite all he had done to her in the past five years? The sentiment was nothing short of foolish, for if she allowed him back into her life at all, he would barge his way into her days, cajoling friend, encouraging confidant . . . seductive lover.

No!

Grasping her blankets in desperate fists for comfort, Juliana huddled back into a ball. While she had managed to hold her pain at bay for some hours, now her parting with Ian seized her deep inside, shredded her composure. The rift seemed to be tearing down the life of independent bliss she had tried so hard to build. And why? Ian was not necessary for her contentment.

Was he?

Impossible. Today—in fact now—she would close her heart and her life to him. Though Ian had been a good childhood friend, recent events had proven him too treacherous a lover to trust. Let him wed mousy Mary from Yorkshire and spend the rest of his life learning her name. Juliana resolved to move on, do her best to build an understanding with her father until she could wed a man she truly cared for *and* could trust. Perhaps she would never love a man as she loved Ian, but certainly one could be happy without possessing simply everything they wanted, couldn't they?

She could. Starting tomorrow, she would.

As Juliana burrowed deeper in her bed, determined to find sleep, a blast of frigid air cascaded across her right shoulder, then hovered directly before her, chilling her cheeks and nose as surely as if she stood outside during a snowstorm. The scent of roses blanketed her next, heavy, pervasive . . . ominous.

The specter of Caroline Linford had returned, and from the tumult in the air, Juliana knew the spirit was much displeased.

She flung the covers aside and dashed from her bed. The odorous chill followed. And before Juliana could think to run out the door, the ghost materialized before her eyes—a shimmering, transparent vision of anguish.

Transfixed, her heart thumping painfully, Juliana stared as the ghost wrote furiously in her little red diary, on the last few pages. Luminous tears glistened down her cheeks and into the book, spattering the fresh ink. Juliana understood now why those last poignant lines were so smeared. But Caroline seemed not to notice. Her quill moved furiously as she sobbed.

"He is lost to me forever," the air seemed to whisper, the sound so faint, Juliana wondered if it was real.

Caroline's pain made Juliana want to reach out and comfort the ghost. A foolish impulse, to be sure.

Still, Juliana could not resist, not only to put the ghost at ease but to save herself from any further haunting.

"He loves you," Juliana said to the spirit.

The specter's head popped up from her journal. Blond ringlets brushed her shimmering cheek as she cast a furious glare at Juliana.

"What does it matter, when he will never be mine?"

Again, Juliana heard the words like the whisper of the wind. The spirit's mouth never moved.

"I face eternity alone," Caroline's haunting voice sighed.

Before Juliana could respond, the ghost closed her book and set aside her quill, then she lay down. With some shock, Juliana realized that Caroline had occupied this very room during her life, for the view from the spirit's window of the well-tended gardens looked to be her own. Did that explain why Caroline dwelt here so frequently?

At first, Caroline did little more than lay still, body shuddering with an occasional sob. Her delicate, translucent body stilled. Slumber overtook her.

Then her face and body turned brittle. Wrinkles lined her soft countenance, turning her pearly skin colorless and dull. Then deep ridges and grooves formed around her eyes, her mouth, cutting into her cheeks, hacking the beauty from her face. Caroline's mouth opened on a silent scream as her skin suddenly sagged from the shrinking flesh around her frail bones. Blood ran in rivulets down the white sheets. Juliana gasped in horror as the spirit clutched her heart and writhed against her fate, to no avail. She melted away in gray stages of anguish until nothing remained of the vibrant, independent woman Caroline Linford had been.

Death had taken her sad soul in a most terrible way.

Juliana gasped, trembling. With quaking legs, she sank back to the bed and tried to back away from the vision. Finally, a sparkling white mist covered it. She exhaled in relief that the apparition was quickly fading.

Drawing in a quivering breath, she inched back into her bed. A damp sheen covered her body beneath her twisted gown. Her breath came in shallow gasps as she tried to calm her racing heart.

She was tired, overwrought. Sleep would help her, heal her. Forcing her eyes shut, Juliana willed herself to sleep.

The air held quiet—almost too much silence. It felt like a grave suddenly, enclosed, cold, frighteningly lonely. Yet fear held her so that she could scarcely move.

What had killed Caroline Linford? Had she truly died of a broken heart, as her journal implied? As the vision suggested? Certainly not. Was such a thing even possible?

Not certain she wanted the answer to her own question, Juliana clutched her covers, squeezing her eyes tightly closed. She modulated her breathing, closed her mind to any more alarming thoughts. The clock in the hall chimed again. The remainder of the house slept without a whisper. Her mind drifted. . . .

Juliana sat alone on her bed, huddled in the dark. An impossibly bright flash startled her. She whirled around as the apparition appeared again, the same as before—yet different. This spirit wore this season's latest fashion, from the fluttering ruffle forming a V from shoulder to waist, to the lace-edged flounces at the hem, to the satiny sheen of the vivid fabric between, modestly covering her from bosom to heels.

This spirit possessed golden hair of a paler shade than before, proud shoulders, and hazel eyes . . . Juliana's own eyes.

Horror washed over her in an icy wave, chilling her both

inside and out. Fear followed, hard, pumping, unrelenting. She tried to rise, to run. But the vision held her in immobile, mute thrall.

The new apparition, the one that looked so hauntingly like her, began to cry, delicately at first. The weeping deepened, until the shimmering body shuddered.

Pain caused those tears. She could feel the thick despair emanating from the spirit—or was that her own anguish?

The vision began to age quickly, horrifically, skin decomposing, bones disintegrating. Juliana opened her mouth on a silent scream, feeling each excruciating moment of pain.

But not in the normal way. Yes, the vision bled tears, yet Juliana did not hurt physically. The ache burrowed deep in her soul, burning, throbbing, seeking any form of ease. And her heart . . . it drove the pain, as if it had been sliced in half, irreparably damaged.

Juliana turned away from the vision's final moments, unwilling to witness her own terrible death. The pain did not end but intensified. With her gaze diverted from the sights around her and her ears free from the ghost's agonized countenance, her senses turned inward, magnifying the anguish in her soul.

Nothing had ever hurt so terribly. She felt certain the strength of it could outlast eternity.

Suddenly, the vision of her corpse vanished, replaced by one of Byron Radford's mousy cousin Mary, red hair tucked in prim curls upon her head, her smile tremulous with anticipation and hope as she clutched a few white flowers. Ian blended into the image, and looked down at the girl. He smiled back but with more resignation than joy.

Then he slowly took the pins from Mary's hair, letting the mass flow around her shoulders. The girl's flowers vanished as she raised her hands to Ian's shoulders, and Juliana saw the unmistakable glint of a wedding band. Shock— followed by denial—hit her hard, like a typhoon. She could scarcely breathe.

Then Ian leaned down to place a gentle kiss on Mary's pink mouth.

Juliana's pain doubled, then doubled again when Ian took possession of Mary's mouth again, more fully.

When he reached for the buttons of Mary's dress, Juliana heart banged against her chest with another awful pang, resonating like a death knell. . . .

As if pried open by some force, Juliana's eyes flashed open. Panting, she gazed around the frigid room. It cooled her perspiring skin instantly. Her breath made a pouf of a white cloud with every breath. The scent of roses hovered.

She trembled and tried to slow her breathing. What a bloody awful nightmare! Thank God it had not been real.

But Juliana was not immune to the dream's message. She still loved Ian—unbelievably, unavoidably, undeniably.

She buried her face in her hands. What of all his ploys to manipulate her? Her pride raged against her heart's wish to surrender. How could she love him, wed him, knowing he had plotted endlessly to ensnare her so he could acquire the stud horse and breeding stables he had always dreamed of?

Yet how could she let him go and live with this terrible pain, to live life without him?

Heaving a shaky sigh, Juliana tried to sort through her racing thoughts. Had starting the stable been Ian's only reason for the deception? Had he ever cared for her?

Somehow, some way, she must learn the truth and decide upon her future—before Ian wed mousy Mary . . . and left her to suffer Caroline Linford's fate—an eternally broken heart.

Juliana rose late, her head fuzzy, eyes heavy. Lifting her lids only fractionally infused her vision with sunlight. Sweet heaven, what time was it? As if on cue, a clock in the hall chimed nine times.

"In here, please," she heard her mother's faint, teary instruction and frowned. "Yes, in Lord Brown-leigh's chamber."

She gasped. Her father. Had he lived through the night?

Bolting up in bed, Juliana threw aside the covers and tossed on her wrapper as she made for the door. Moments later, the chill of the hall greeted her as she sprinted toward her father's door.

God, please let him live.

Her heart cold with fear, Juliana made her way down the hall, not certain what she might find. Had Dr. Haney returned? Had someone fetched the minister to bless Papa's soul as he departed this earth?

Running now, her wrapper flapping behind her, Juliana darted to her father's room, completely unprepared for the vision before her.

Papa slumped in bed, propped up against a mountain of white pillows, his thin nightgown rumpled. Eyes closed, hands slack, he looked tired and weak. And he looked terribly old, with the deep lines around his eyes that dug toward his blue-veined lids and the wide grooves that engraved the rest of his long, nearly gray face.

But his shallow breaths told her that he lived—at least for now.

Shaking with relief, Juliana exhaled. Death had nearly taken him from this earth, from their family, from her life.

The thought of life without him dismayed her. The realization that his last memories of this earth could easily have been of their discord and harsh words filled her with something close to shame.

Perhaps her father had not behaved in the best manner where she was concerned, but his motives had been pure. He wanted her happy and cared for.

Most fathers wanted such security for their daughters. And she, afraid of losing her independence, her identity, had listened little and argued much.

And why had she been afraid? She was no longer a child, no longer in his legal control. Becoming a widow had made Juliana a woman free to make her own choices. Yet she had argued with Papa like a rebellious child, railing against the parental influence he tried to exert. Looking at his limp, sleeping form now, she felt her behavior made little sense. Certainly he would always tell her what he wished her to do with her life; that was simply Papa's way. He was not likely to change. However, his saying and her listening in no way meant she could not—and should not—make her own decision.

Why had it taken her so long to realize that?

They had lost so many years fighting, wasted so much time in their battle of wills. Realizing how easily she might have lost him forever frightened her. Their argument now seemed somehow . . . unimportant. Almost foolish.

For in the end, he was just a man, no more invincible than any other, no more implacable than she. Juliana saw clearly now that he was not the Godlike man she had painted in her mind. He was merely a mortal, imperfect and vulnerable. And life was too short for such constant strife.

"Juliana, there you are," her mother whispered, grasping her hands. "Your father is doing quite well."

"That is splendid news."

She glanced back to her sleeping father, the soft, warm center in her chest slowly coating the cold panic that had been eating at her. Suddenly, Juliana knew she could repair her rapport with Papa. She was a grown woman capable of listening to considerations where she must and making the right choices for herself in the end.

A splash of color caught her attention then, and

she looked about the room. Every Christmas decoration with which they had previously festooned the drawing room now adorned her father's chamber. From the garlands of holly to the stockings, even the Christmas tree, which several servants were settling into place, it all uplifted the spirit of Papa's somber gray and blue chamber with a festive glow.

"In fact," her mother continued on, "I daresay he improves with each hour."

When Mama squeezed her fingers, Juliana returned her gesture of assurance. "Wonderful, indeed. I must confess, I'd feared the worst."

"Underestimating me again, girl?" her father rasped in a broken voice from the bed.

Juliana zipped her gaze to Papa, who now peered at the world through half-open eyes. But the clarity in them was unmistakable.

"Apparently, a mistake on my part," she whispered finally, smiling. "Glad to see you awake and speaking."

He held out his hand to her, entreating. Papa had never been a demonstrative man, and Juliana tried to keep the shock from her face. She had no delusions of success, but her father said nothing, only extended his palm to her with a hint of a tired smile curving his mouth.

Juliana did not hesitate. On brisk feet, she crossed the room to his side and clasped his hand in her own. His grip was warm and encompassing and surprisingly strong. The touch jolted her clear to her heart. The fact he was still with her reassured her in a way she scarcely believed.

"Merry Christmas, little girl," he whispered.

Sinking to the bed beside him, she grabbed his other hand and squeezed tight. "Merry Christmas, Papa."

He stroked her hair momentarily, then glanced up at her mother. "Doesn't the room look wonderful?"

Juliana glanced around, taking in all the holiday decor at once. "Indeed."

"This morning when James woke," Mama began, "he said he wanted to spend Christmas with his family. Since Dr. Haney wishes him to remain in bed for some days, I decided to have Christmas brought up to your father, and he agreed."

Juliana cast a surprised glance at him. He had never been one for holidays or sentiment. Why the sudden change?

"It was a wonderful idea," she whispered.

His laugh was tired and gruff but still as quick as ever. "I see you're surprised. Nothing like a little brush with death to make you appreciate each moment. I wanted to celebrate this holy day with my family, and I did not imagine you would mind if we did so here."

Juliana's heart expanded. Tears stung her eyes. "Oh, not at all. I'm so happy to have you still to spend this day with. You scared us all terribly."

Impulsively, Juliana leaned forward to embrace her father. Slowly, with much effort, Papa raised his soft arms and wrapped them about her. How long had it been since he had embraced her? Had he ever? Feeling this kind of kinship and welcome from her father made the tears pressing the back of her throat more urgent.

Moments later, Mama joined them, tears swimming in her big brown eyes. She put her arms around them both. "Shall we open gifts? Juliana, I know how you've always loved Christmas, and having you home with us makes the holiday special indeed." She kissed her father's weathered cheek. "Having you here and alive, James, is the best present I could ever ask for."

Papa smiled at Mama. "Ah, but not the only present you will receive today. Juliana," he directed, "bring the gifts from beneath the tree over to the bed.

Together we'll celebrate each and every moment of this day."

Juliana did as her father bid. Slowly, they each opened their gifts. Papa sincerely appreciated the new pocket watch Mama gave him. Mama shrieked with delight at the sapphire earbobs and bracelet Papa had purchased for her. Juliana had given them each books, made them both mittens and scarves, as well as gifted her mother with a cameo pin. She had made a handsome robe from some silk she had brought with her from India for her father. Her parents gave her a lovely painting of a pastel field and a set of pearls for her throat. Smiles of appreciation and words of thanks filled the room, along with a peace the house had likely not seen in generations.

Juliana moved to hug her parents. Mama clung to her tightly, and she felt her mother's thankfulness to have her family together in the embrace. Juliana felt her eyes mist with happy tears.

After several silent moments, her mother released her, and Juliana turned to her father. Sitting once more on the edge of the bed, Juliana regarded her father with both joy and surprise.

Never had she seen such softness upon his face—and pride even. Juliana gazed back, certain her expression mirrored his.

"Your mother tells me we are too much alike, both stubborn to the end."

Before she could reply, Juliana felt a resurgence of tears at the corners of her eyes. "Mama tells me the same thing. I suppose we must give her credit for knowing us both well."

"Indeed." Her father reached for her hand. "What of your future, girl?"

Juliana took a deep breath. Here lay her opportunity to keep things right with Papa but maintain power over her life. These words she must choose carefully.

"I cannot say. I have made no choices, nor have I ruled any out. I know you wish me wed and secure. I very much appreciate your concern for me and my well-being. I am aware, however, that I must make this choice alone, for I must live with its consequences. Please know this is very much at the forefront of my mind, and I have no intent to neglect—"

"Juliana, my girl." His small smile was part wistful, part regretful. He squeezed her hand again. "I do wish for your happiness, but this episode with my heart has taught me that life is indeed too short to spend in a way that does not facilitate your happiness. If Ian does not content you, then do not wed him. Stay here with us until you find the future that pleases you. I'll put no more demands upon you to wed."

Juliana did not speak for fully thirty seconds. She merely gaped at her father in stunned silence.

Papa would no longer do his best to coerce her to wed Ian? He finally understood her happiness? Had enough trust in her to make her own decisions?

"Your father and I talked about this before you joined us, dearest." Her mother smiled at Juliana's shock. "We both agree that our joy in watching you wed would come only if we knew it brought you equal joy."

She looked from one parent to the other, now smiling like indulgent conspirators. The tears pressing the back of Juliana's eyes suddenly fell to her cheeks in a rush. Her heart felt as if it had grown wings and would fly right out of her chest, even as peace enveloped her like a favorite blanket, warming her within and protecting her from harshness without.

"Thank you," she said finally, tremulously. "That means everything to me."

"Your happiness means everything to us," Mama declared.

"Yes," Papa agreed. "We love you, both of us."

Tears of joy returned in earnest as Juliana enveloped them in a fierce hug. Never had she imagined matters would sit so well between her and her father. Her bliss with this outcome could not be more complete. And whatever Ian had done, he had made this moment possible by traveling to India and persuading her to come home. How else would she have learned to see Papa in this new light?

Yet she felt as if something were missing.

Disengaging from their embrace, she turned away and found herself peering up at the Christmas tree, tall, draped in gingerbread and candles, wrapped in pine scent. Rather than settling her unease, it brought to mind another tree—Ian's tree—the one they had decorated the night they had made love.

He represented what was missing from her life.

Never had she stopped to consider whether she, deep in her heart, wished to marry Ian, or if she truly loved him. Rather, she had focused on his intent and his actions. Examining the contents of her heart had seemed irrelevant. So she had lashed out with anger about his manipulations and his plotting. Stupid not to have realized his pressure did not limit her choices! Damned foolish not to have recognized the fact she loved him before she had run him off.

Juliana shook her head. Neither mattered, not really. The question was, what would she do about Ian now?

CHAPTER EIGHTEEN

That afternoon, Juliana and her parents ate a quiet dinner at a makeshift table in Papa's chamber. Her father imbibed a thin broth without complaint. The cook had prepared the rest of the meal to perfection. But Juliana barely tasted the juicy duck. She no longer had to entertain the notion of marrying Ian or suffer her father's schemes to that end, yet Ian haunted her thoughts.

Had he not withdrawn his suit, by the terms of her promise to Ian, she would have been bound to answer his proposal of marriage today.

What would she have said?

Yes! Her heart was so loud in its answer. Upon further reflection, she realized her mind concurred. *Yes!*

Ian, like her father, might be prone to schemes and management to win his way. But he had never forced her into anything. He had respected her when she'd said no. Still, her life choices were her own. Marrying Ian would not change that.

But if she did not speak up soon—today—he would

go to Byron's cousin Mary tomorrow to present his addresses and perhaps even make her an offer of marriage.

"Dearest," said her mother across the table. "Do you not like your pudding?"

Juliana emerged from deep thought, only to realize she had been holding a spoon full of plum pudding near her mouth for some moments. Quickly, she set the spoon down.

"I fear pudding is not on my mind." Then she turned to her father, uncertain how to admit his choice of a husband was the one she also sought. "Papa, I realize today is Christmas, but I must . . . that is to say, I think I have decided what course to follow in life and I should like to see to it today."

"Does it please you?" he asked mildly.

"Yes, very much." She nodded, smiling her happiness.

"Then you must go."

Juliana hesitated. "You understand I would go even if you did not wish it."

"Yes," he said, his expression one of acceptance. "The choice is yours. I merely want you to go with my blessing."

"Even though you cannot be certain of my intent?"

"You will do what you feel is right; I trust you in that."

"Thank you." Her voice trembled as joy blossomed inside her. A new smile broke wide across her face, and she leaned down to kiss her father. He touched a tentative hand to her shoulder.

Into her ear, Papa whispered, "Be happy."

"I will. I know I will." She touched the side of his pale face with love, then turned to her mother. "Good-bye, Mama. I may not return before nightfall."

Her mother, despite the soft wrinkles lining her eyes and the thirty years of marriage she and Papa had shared, laughed like a girl still in the nursery. "Give Ian our love."

She could never fool Mama. A sense of light and air filled Juliana with something so sublime, it defied definition. She laughed in return. "Right after I give him mine."

Mama moved to embrace her, a sharing of kinship between mother and daughter, something so simple and without doubt, Juliana felt her heart shift, expand, fill with joy.

"Go, dearest," she whispered. "Go with our blessing."

Juliana turned to leave and found their butler directly in her path.

"My lady, I have been holding a missive for his lordship. Is he well enough to receive it?"

With concern glowing from her blue eyes, Mama looked to Papa's lively though somewhat wan face. "James?"

"Bring it here, Smythe," her father said.

The elderly butler crossed the room, all arms and legs, something of a spider in a starched white shirt, then handed the note to Papa.

Juliana stood by, curious. Certainly something terrible had not happened on Christmas Day. But why else would someone send such an unexpected missive on a holiday?

Frowning, she watched as her father broke the seal and unfolded the note. Papa peered at the stiff white paper, squinting. Then he sighed.

He handed it to her with a shake of his graying head. "Girl, you'll have to read this. Can't see a thing without my spectacles anymore."

Another time she might have smiled as his annoyance with the aging process. Today, she merely grabbed the note.

The seal told her it was from Ian. Quickly, she fixed

her eyes onto the bold slant of his writing and read aloud:

My dear Lord Brownleigh,

I write to remind you that I have withdrawn my proposal of marriage to your daughter. To see us wed has long been your goal, and in keeping with that, you offered me the sum of ten thousand pounds to do so by today. With all respect, my lord, I refuse your offer. I will have no part in forcing a woman to my side.

I have decided to remain a bachelor and retire to my land near Salisbury, which I have explained to my esteemed father. There, I will begin my breeding program and hope to achieve eventual success.

It has been a privilege to have you as my neighbor and I wish you and your family all the best in the future.

Ian Pierce, Viscount Axton

Juliana lowered the note. She blinked, confusion whirling in a tangle of thoughts. But several realizations grabbed her: Ian had refused her father's offer. He had no intent to wed mousy Mary. He had decided to leave Lynton.

Her heart—the one that loved Ian so—felt certain he planned this because he wanted no part of scheming to bring her to the altar. He also wanted no part of wedding Lady Mary simply for his inheritance. And his leaving . . . perhaps he did so to avoid the inevitable painful gatherings they would face in this small corner of Devonshire.

He had given up everything—his inheritance, ties with his surly father, his hope for children, the money with which to begin his breeding program. And why?

Clearly, he did love her after all. She felt equally certain he had been worthy of her trust all along. He was managing, yes, but not mean-spirited.

A joy so pure she had never felt its like lifted her spirits far above the ground, so they nearly sang with the heavens.

"When was this message delivered?" she barked to the butler.

"Shortly after breakfast, my lady."

Juliana rushed out into the hall and stared at the clock quietly ticking away the seconds of her life. It neared three in the afternoon. Close to six hours ago.

Certainly, Ian had not left Lynton—left her—on Christmas Day? Then again, she had given him no hope. His father may even have tossed him out of the house. What did he have to wait for?

Dashing toward the door, Juliana could not leave the house quickly enough. She scrambled down the stairs, happiness and apprehension tripping inside her, her heart skipping in her chest. Ian loved her, enough to cast aside everything that had separated them. She must hurry!

As she rushed, regret shadowed her thoughts. Ian truly loved her—and she had not believed him. Juliana had not trusted her feelings, relying instead on the past, on assumptions, condemning him on principle. Pride, fear, and anger had ruled her for too long. The time had come for her to learn to trust the illogic of her heart.

Grabbing her cloak and mittens, she only hoped she was not too late in declaring her love.

Racing past Smythe, who held the door open for her, Juliana bounded out into the cold December sunlight. Wind whipped through the blue muslin dress she'd donned earlier. She threw her cloak over her shoulders and thrust her mittens over her hands.

Despite her delicate slippers, Juliana trudged through the snow toward the stables. She didn't care in the least about her freezing feet. For the first time in years, her heart was warm with Christmas spirit, with love, with hope. She smiled, ignoring her chilled toes as she bounded into the stables, breathless and eager.

There Ian stood, a few feet from his own winded mount. He looked disheveled and solemn, with a gaze so fixed upon her, Juliana felt her heart in her stomach. The scents of hay, horseflesh, and snow sharpened the silence between them.

As soon as the stable boy gave Ian's horse a pail of oats, she motioned for him to leave. With a bob of his limp brown hair, he was gone. She turned to Ian once more.

"I know you despise me," he began, "and I do not mean to interrupt your holiday, but my messenger said your father has taken quite ill." Ian took her arms in his grip. "How is he?"

The old Juliana might have been piqued that Ian had come only because of her father—after making a gross assumption about her feelings. Today, she smiled with soft understanding.

"He is weak, but recovering. Dr. Haney came by late this morning and pronounced his progress promising. We are all well pleased."

Some of the tension seemed to drain from Ian as he sighed and released her.

Juliana grabbed his hand, refusing to let him go. Her pulse raced so hard, she could scarcely hear her own words. "You are not interrupting my Christmas at all. You ... you add to my happiness by being here."

Now she had his complete attention. No longer was he concerned solely about her father. Juliana smiled and laced her fingers inside Ian's. His face was a sharp question even as she squeezed his hand.

"I do not despise you," she whispered, taking a step closer, then another. Their chests touched, their bellies. All the while, Ian watched her with a guarded, hungry blue-eyed stare. "And that is because I love you."

Ian said nothing, merely flinched, as if she had struck him rather than confessed her feelings. Before she realized his intent, he backed away from her, turned away, and stroked the tight square of his jaw with tense fingers.

"What brought about this sudden change?" he asked quietly.

Juliana heard the disbelief in his tone. She did not blame him for it. He could not know how much the past two days had changed her.

"You . . . and me." She sighed, trying to put it all into words. When she had envisioned their reunion, she'd imagined he would intuitively understand. Foolish of her, for sure. She was going to have to explain it.

Ian waited, his face as still and angled as a hawk's. Juliana resisted the urge to run to him, put her arms around him, kiss him. Words would have to come first.

"I was with Papa when he received your note. That you were willing to give up everything dear to you, although I had refused your proposal, told me without reservation that you cared for me."

"I told you from our earliest days aboard the *Houghton* that I did."

"That is so," she conceded. "I was too afraid of trusting you to actually believe you. And I was wrong."

With a muttered curse, Ian cast his blue gaze to the hay-ridden floor of the stable. "I never gave you any reason to trust me, Juliana. I know that. I thought I knew best what would make you happy. I assumed my devotion would see you content." He grunted, something between a self-deprecating laugh and a curse. "You are a strong woman with strong opinions and a very keen mind. I should have realized long ago you would know far better than I what would bring about your happiness."

"But you were right," she protested as she crossed the room. Grabbing his face, Juliana forced his gaze back to hers. His expression was one of pain.

"No—"

"Yes, blast you! You were, and I refused to listen." Smoothing her thumbs across the hollows of his cold cheeks, she thrilled to the feel of his skin, the beginnings of dark stubble beneath her hands.

He closed his eyes against her caress. "Juliana, I should never have forced you to make that promise to spend time with me, to answer my marriage proposal by today."

"Perhaps that is so, but I do not regret making the promise. I learned far more about you than I would have if I had not been . . . persuaded to make such a vow.

"And that leads me to the other thing I've realized," she went on. "I made the choice to accept that promise, just as I made the choice to find you today. You may have done your unorthodox best to coax me into marrying you, but in the end, the decision was and is mine. Every decision about my life is mine. Somewhere in my thoughts I assigned you too much responsibility for my future, and, thus, the blame for my anger. I resisted your attempts because I feared you were right, not because I knew you to be wrong. I should have had more faith in you. Can you forgive me for being stubborn?"

"Forgive you?" Ian sounded stunned. He shook his head, then regarded her with sincere apology in his eyes. "I should never have made that dastardly bargain with your father. Somewhere in my gut, I regretted it from the instant we sealed the deal. I'm sorry. I simply wanted you so much. Hillfield Park and Bruce, the wonderful Thoroughbred stud I've wished to acquire, incited my unfortunate greed. I behaved terribly.''

"Well, you weren't always the gentleman in your courtship, but I forgive you." She smiled. "In fact, I am a trifle flattered that you acted the swain to win me. Friends?''

"Yes, always." But he stared at her with an expression that bespoke an abiding desire.

"More than friends?" she dared to ask.

His eyes darkened like midnight, shimmering, transfixing. "That is up to you, but I suggest you move away now or I will kiss you."

Juliana laughed from somewhere deep in her chest. And felt good. Happiness shimmered in her veins like gold.

With more urgency than caution, Juliana raised her mouth to his. She soaked in his warmth and need immediately. The spice of his mouth, coffee and cider and something so essentially Ian filled her senses. She sank into the kiss, sighing when he accepted her mouth again.

In mutual silent consent, each opened their lips to taste the other. Tongues met, breaths swirled. The future glittered before them with the promise of golden tomorrows, of the bond that would never be broken.

Juliana clasped Ian to her, sublimely pleased to be alive, to be in England with him, to know she had the utter joy of today and every Christmas for years to come . . . to know her heart had found its other half at last.

Ian ended the kiss, and with a disappointed catch of her breath, Juliana released him.

He rested his forehead against hers, his breathing fast and shallow. "I love the taste of you." He groaned. "I love *you.*"

The breathy endearment raced through her body,

sparkling with awareness and love. "Good. Marry me, Ian."

Ian gaped at her. "M-marry you?" Then he laughed and lifted her tight against him. "You are asking me to marry you?"

"Indeed. What shall it be? I'm not certain I shall accept anything but a yes," she admitted with mock severity as she put her arms around him. "Will you?"

His expression became teasingly serious. "I think I may be persuaded to do that. Yes."

Juliana laughed, elation swirling inside her to mix with her spirit of the season. "When? Soon? This week? Now?"

A big grin broke across Ian's face, something perfect, like a shining rare gem. Then he planted a firm, passionate kiss upon her waiting mouth. The joy on his face mirrored the feeling deep within her, and Juliana knew they were finally, truly of one heart.

"As soon as we can, love. A few of the marriage laws have changed while you were in India, but I will do everything I can to call you wife by the new year."

"And what about your horse, Bruce? Can you begin the breeding operations without him?"

He hesitated. "I'll find some way to raise the money to buy him. It will work out."

Indeed, it would. Juliana vowed to speak to her father at the earliest opportunity. If no couple in Lynton had ever been given a prized horse as a wedding gift, well, they would be the first. Bruce would make an excellent present, one Juliana planned to surprise Ian with later.

For now, she stroked a soft hand across his smiling cheek. "I don't know when I've been so happy. Merry Christmas, darling."

His blue eyes twinkled no less than the candles upon her tree. She loved the sight of them. She loved him.

"Merry Christmas," he whispered.

Ian embraced her in a tender clasp. As Juliana wrapped her arms around him, she saw a flash of color to her right. At the gate between the stables and the gardens, the ghost of Caroline Linford watched them with a beauteous smile. Then she turned away, toward another figure shimmering beside her, that of a man, presumably her love, Thomas, dressed in somber blue. But his smile was radiant as he held out his arms to the girlishly happy Caroline.

"Good-bye," Juliana mouthed as she watched Caroline accept her lover's embrace for eternity.

Holding Ian to her, Juliana did the same.